Kenneth A. Studstill

iUniverse®

TREACHEROUS OBSESSION

iUniverse books may be ordered through booksellers or by contacting:

iUniverse
1663 Liberty Drive
Bloomington, IN 47403
www.iuniverse.com
1-800-Authors (1-800-288-4677)

ISBN: 978-1-4917-6054-3 (sc)
ISBN: 978-1-4917-6055-0 (e)

Library of Congress Control Number: 2015902066

Print information available on the last page.

iUniverse rev. date: 10/02/2015

PREFACE

This is a work of fiction. Central to the story, however, is the Florida legislature's amendment of a statute to allow the state to sue tobacco companies for reimbursement of Medicaid expenses paid on behalf of Medicaid recipients if their illness or disease was the result of using tobacco. To implement this statute, the state retained the services of a few private attorneys to represent the state's interest on a contingency basis. The story also essentially parallels the facts regarding how the attorneys' fees became an issue after the case settled. The characters in the story and their suggested motivations are pure fiction; names, characters, places, and incidents are the products of the author's imagination or are used fictitiously. Any resemblance to actual events, locales, or persons, living or dead, is entirely coincidental.

CHAPTER 1

On an auspicious morning in January 1993, Kevin, marveling at his good fortune, smiled as he reclined in his high-backed chair in his law office. A millionaire several times over and barely into his midthirties, he had just settled another case for over one million dollars, and 40 percent went into his pocket. But was he successful? Certainly he knew he should be. But something was missing, or was something just bothersome? Maybe it was the pedestrian, ordinary look of his office, but he didn't really believe that.

He was maybe satisfied, but he felt no real exultation. The word *earned* echoed in his mind. *I've got it, but did I earn it?* he wondered.

Suddenly, the intercom crackled with his secretary Jo Ann's voice. "Line one, Mr. Charles. It's Hugh Benson."

Kevin picked up the phone. "Hey, Hugh, what's up?"

"I'm coming down your way and would like to have lunch with you."

"Is this important?" Kevin asked. "I sort of had other plans—nothing that can't be changed though."

"I'd say it could be a very rewarding lunch. This is not just a social visit."

"Okay, you want to meet somewhere or just come by the office?"

"I'll be in your office around twelve."

Hugh was an impressive man with slicked-back black hair. Always decked out in a dark expensive suit, vest, cuff links, and an adequate amount of gold hanging here and there, along with an ostentatious Rolex, he wore his success on his sleeve, so to speak. Nevertheless, he wasn't a phony.

This has to have something to do with a case, Kevin thought. He smiled to himself, looking around his office, as that old saw about contingency contracts being the poor man's key to the courthouse crossed his mind. It was not entirely without some truth, but contingency personal injury cases had most assuredly been the key to his good life. It made him feel good to freely indulge his wife, Sherrie. And his one child, an eight-year-old daughter, Kathy, had great expectations. She was not as pretty as her mom, but she was smart.

Most of his practice was referrals from other attorneys. He grimaced when he thought about just how much his reputation exceeded his real ability. Sometimes he felt like a charlatan, particularly on the easy ones. He worked within the rules. He was always ethical and basically honest, and it could not be said he hadn't invested a lot of time and money in some chancy cases that were lost.

What was missing? The innocence of yesteryear maybe? He shook his head, got up from his chair, and walked to the large window perennially covered with a closed curtain. Still daydreaming of this and that, he drew the curtain back slightly to look out on the main street of East Bay, the county seat of East Bay County, below his second-floor office. The sun's glaring light somehow brought in the outside world. Kevin quickly closed the curtain and stepped back into his own little world. He did not really consider the world as "them" and "us," but there was an aspect of separateness to his perception of life. He slightly frowned, thinking of the bar's never-ending concern over the extent nonlawyers hated lawyers. He knew the bar's efforts were then and would always be futile. *We are envied and hated by the very people we serve*, he thought. *But what the hell—get used to being a member of a hated minority.*

Safely back in his own little world, he smiled as he thought of his wife in the wifely sense. *Maybe I'll just have to go home after lunch with Hugh*, he thought. His eyebrows came together as an unpleasant realization dawned on him. Recently his urges for a midday tryst with his wife had not been fulfilled. And that was not all. Sherrie's attitude toward him, even aside from any midday adventure, had been "well, if you just have to, okay." True affection had actually disappeared from their marriage. The divorce lawyers claimed every marriage was dysfunctional; the only issue was the degree. *So*, he wondered, *why am I now entertaining lustful thoughts for a woman who no longer reciprocates? Maybe that's what I'm missing.*

Later, at Jim's Smoke House, Kevin was still waiting for Hugh to let him in on the details.

"Just one glass of wine," Hugh said to the waiter before quickly turning back to Kevin and asking, "You sure you don't want to share a bottle? I'm buying."

"No, not today, but thanks anyway."

The waiter left the table.

"Have you ever considered how much money we could make if the legislature made it possible to successfully sue tobacco companies?"

"Can't say that I have," Kevin answered, and he put down the menu.

"Well, a group of us are trying to work with the governor and the legislature to get such a bill enacted. We intend to put the cost of the state's Medicaid expenses right where it belongs, if the Medicaid expenses are significantly related to the patient's use of tobacco."

"Sounds, well, pretty far-fetched. But you have my attention. Tobacco is by far the most deleterious product on the market. How do we get around the fact it's legal?"

"The legislature has already emasculated due process with reimbursement to Medicaid from any lawsuit, and it's passed muster with the Supreme Court ... Doesn't it chap your ass to have to pay the Medicaid expenses in full when you get some money for your client and the state hasn't done a damn thing to recover a cent? Hell, we're collecting money for the state. Doesn't that chap your ass?"

"Indeed it does!"

"The key, Kevin, is to get the attorney general to agree that his staff is not capable of such litigation."

"Yeah, and ...?"

"And he needs to hire some experienced litigators. You know, they're good at what they do, but they don't have the experience we have in handling tort cases."

"Like you do?"

"And you, Kevin. This will be big, man, I tell you. Big ..."

"Me? How do I play a role?"

"Think, Kevin. We'll have to negotiate a contract with the state, and the way we see it, we'll handle it just like any other contingency contract."

"Meaning?"

"Meaning, we will have to front the cost. Of course, that can be recouped at the end. But the cost …" He paused. "The cost will be pretty big."

"How big?"

"Not sure yet. A lot depends on how the Medicaid Reimbursement Act is amended, but if it's what we want, the cost will be four or five hundred thousand for each attorney who participates—insignificant compared to a combined fee in excess of a couple of billion dollars."

"Which means what?" Kevin questioned as he picked up a roll from his bread plate.

"We envision a consortium of trial attorneys, a dozen or so, who are willing to pay in at least five hundred thousand to participate."

Kevin, reflecting on the notion that what sounds too good to be true is usually not true, could manage only a quizzical expression. If the state wanted money from the tobacco industry, he thought, it could simply impose a tax.

"You look skeptical."

"No, I'm not skeptical," Kevin said, hedging. He didn't want to be rude and tell Hugh what he was really thinking. He also knew Hugh Benson did not engage in fantasy, or at least he had never done so before. Now Kevin wasn't so sure. "I just guess I can't think in such astronomical terms."

"That's the beauty of it. We limit the participation, and none of us ever have to work again."

The waiter served Hugh his wine and took their order. They both ordered baked grouper.

"You've got to win, you know?" said Kevin.

"The way the statute will read, we can't lose."

"Can't lose?"

"That's right. The traditional defense, the reason jurors won't return verdicts for the dying and dead from cigarette smoking, is that they feel the plaintiff is responsible for his problems. Hell, he didn't have to smoke, did he? That defense and all the others are going to be wiped out by statute. The only issue will be whether or not the person suffered from a tobacco-caused disease and whether Medicaid paid the bill. It'll be like shooting ducks in a barrel."

"The preparation will be a logistical nightmare, crunching all those numbers. I guess that's where the cost comes in, right?"

"Right. It's not going to take any real ability, not really. The real beauty of this thing is that we will, by statute, be able to use statistical analysis to prove the Medicaid funds were paid to treat a disease caused by the use of tobacco. Once that's done and the medical expense is introduced, the case will be won. Remember, the tobacco companies have no defense."

"Sounds almost too good to be true, Hugh."

"Well, anyway," Hugh said, right after the grouper was served, "that's the plan, and we wanted to know if you might want to be a part of this thing."

"I'm just a very fortunate PI lawyer from the insignificant enclave of East Bay. I don't have any real influence, Hugh."

"Sure you do—you're in the right political party and can lean on your legislators to pass the bill the governor and attorney general are going to sponsor."

"Well, I don't believe I'd be interested in parting with a half million dollars ..."

"No need to right now. Just tell me you will later, if we get the legislation passed. No need for money until that's done."

Kevin hesitated. He wasn't sure about the constitutionality of the whole planned scenario and didn't want to commit himself.

"We'd sure like to have you on board, Kevin, and we'll be talking to others." Hugh lifted his eyebrows as if to say, "Don't miss this chance of a lifetime, but if you do, don't complain later."

After a moment's contemplation, Kevin spoke slowly, choosing his words carefully. "If you get the legislation passed, I'd be interested in your offer to participate."

"Good enough. You'll be hearing from me because it's going to get passed."

They finished lunch, after which they shook hands, and Hugh said he'd stay in touch.

Kevin went back to his office wondering whether anything would come of the big plan—or perhaps it could be more accurately described as the big hope. He quickly dismissed any idea of going home. The rest of the day was routine until about five o'clock, when he got a phone call from Phil Griffin, who asked, "Didn't Hugh Benson speak to you earlier today?"

"Yes."

"What do you think?"

"Why does anybody care what I think?"

"Maybe we shouldn't, but you underestimate yourself. Always have. Somebody might call you or something, you know, and we've got to keep everything on a positive note." The image of Phil materialized in Kevin's mind—handsome, debonair, smart, and no doubt on his first cocktail before going to a fancy restaurant with a girl half his age. He was probably the best-looking bald-headed man in the world, with a smile no one could resist. To say he was persuasive would be a gross understatement. He was in his early fifties but seemed younger, and he and Kevin were semi-friends.

"Phil, it sure sounds interesting. I don't really know right now, but I've been thinking ..."

"About what?" Phil uttered.

"Well ..." Kevin paused and then continued with a slight note of sarcasm. "The plan here is not to really help the poor man get his key to the courthouse. Hell, Phil, we're talking about representing the state. I ..."

Phil interrupted. "You and I have both helped the downtrodden without reservation, and it has cost us plenty sometimes. This time we're going to help ourselves. Don't you think it's about time to do that, so we can continue our bread-and-butter good works?"

Kevin walked around his office as he answered. "Phil, I don't have to be sold. I told Hugh that if the bill gets passed, I would be interested."

"It's gonna pass. We've been talking to the right people already. It will be a House bill, and if they pass it, we have the Senate sewed up for sure."

"You sure as hell sound certain," Kevin said as he took a seat on his couch.

"I won't tell you all the details now, but Hugh wasn't with me the last time I spoke with the governor and his attorney general. Hell, they even came here to big Jax to see me. I got them eating out of my hands."

Kevin wondered why or how much Phil must have promised that pair from Tallahassee, but he said nothing. He knew Phil prided himself on his image of integrity—with a history of holding this and that bar office and making public statements about how lawyers devoted their valuable time to pro bono work. He was most enthusiastic about the bar dealing with wayward attorneys with a firmer hand.

"I don't want to overstate it, Kevin, but this thing is going to happen, and then ..." He paused.

"What will happen?" Kevin walked over to his window.

"Well, let's just say we will have done a fair day's work for ..." He paused again. "I was going to say for a fair wage, but I'm not going to bullshit you—the fee will be enormous."

"Yeah, I know, and you can keep me in mind, okay?"

"Good enough, Kevin. Don't want to leave an old buddy out. So we'll stay in touch."

"One thing: why is it I haven't heard anything about this before?" Kevin asked as he closed the window curtain.

"Good question. The last thing we want is publicity, and the tobacco people getting wind of it isn't the half of it. We'll have a meeting before long and lay out a game plan, okay?"

"Okay."

"Nice talking to you. And it might be best if you didn't say anything right now about this thing."

"Sure. Mum's the word."

Kevin relaxed back in his chair. He knew Phil, but he also knew that no one *really* knew him. There was talk he had actually been born in Hell's Kitchen in New York and had migrated to Florida in his teen years. Regardless of whatever his past was, he now exhibited all the attributes of someone raised in a privileged and moneyed life.

He had been a big noise at the University of Florida and then Harvard Law School. Out of law school, he initially landed a job in Palm Beach with a firm that had several Florida offices. Once he was there, his ability was quickly realized, and within two years, the firm asked if he would accept a promotion to run the Jacksonville office. He did well in Jacksonville and soon left to open his own firm. By then, he was married to a well-connected local girl, and the decision to stay in Jacksonville was more or less made with their wedding. But that was only the first of his marriages.

Even as a transplant from Dade County, he'd had no trouble becoming a stalwart member of Jacksonville society. Phil Griffin could have made it anywhere. He was his own man and was where he chose to be. Kevin admired his self-assurance, which seldom slipped over to arrogance. Yet Phil never suffered fools lightly, and a person couldn't always be sure of where he stood with Phil. Some strange indefinable quality about the man left you uncertain. Nevertheless, Kevin knew that if anyone could pull this thing off, it was Phil Griffin. After all, he had been friends with the governor and attorney general since their college days.

* * * * *

Was his ship finally coming in? No, it had already come in. Perhaps, he thought as he started turning off the lights and walking out, this thing was just some more of his good fortune.

"Yeah, some of us are born under a lucky star, and I'm one of them," he uttered to himself as he walked out and locked the door. *Not really*, he thought. *Life just isn't that one-sided.*

Kevin and his wife lived in an expensive but modest home on the beach. A few days a week, they employed help. After the drive home, he parked his four-year-old Volvo in the garage and entered directly into the kitchen, where his wife Sherrie was preparing a light dinner, boiled shrimp in a bed of lettuce. She was also sipping a glass of white wine.

"You look … oh, I can't quite make it out … amused? Or perhaps bemused?" she said just before pouring him a glass of a chardonnay. "You bothered by something or what?" she added when he didn't immediately reply.

"I'm not sure, at least not yet, but I think our future is golden."

"In that case, let's toast." She smiled as their glasses clinked. "So what's the good news?"

"Promise to keep it to yourself?" Kevin figured that since it was going to cost a lot of money, she should know about it.

"Cross my heart and hope to die."

Kevin thought about what he should say for a moment and then merely stated, "Phil Griffin and some of the other really important personal injury lawyers are going to be in line to get a contract from the state to sue the tobacco companies for Medicaid expenses paid out for the poor, if their disease has been caused by using tobacco."

"What's so secret about that?"

"I thought the same thing at first. If it actually materializes, lawyers are going to be retained on contingency contracts."

"You mean they won't be using state lawyers?"

"The attorney general will no doubt be involved, but the real lawyers will be us, or at least that's the plan."

"Well?"

"Well, they want a commitment from me that I will participate."

"Why not? Sounds pretty decent to—"

He stopped her before she could finish. "Yeah, I guess so, but to be one of the chosen, you have to pony up at least a half million dollars."

"Good god, what kind of deal is that?"

"The contribution will go toward the cost. The lawyers will agree to front the cost."

"Sounds kind of hokey. Why not let the state pay the cost?"

"The fee will be a sizable percentage as a contingency, and we'll front the cost like we do in any personal injury case." He paused and then said, "Let's forget about that right now. Let's just drink the wine, have dinner, and then, well, who knows …" Kevin let a knowing, lascivious smile spread across his face.

"Well, we'll see," Sherrie said with an unmistakable note of reluctance. She then turned her back to Kevin and started looking for something in the refrigerator. Her shoulder-length black hair sparkled here and there, and Kevin thought she had never been more seductive. Even after years of marriage, sparks of lust remained. But he did not suggest, or further insinuate, a romantic interlude. No, he had now decided she would have to come to him. She had for some time acted as if she did not understand the subtle, and not-so-subtle, invitations he sent out from time to time. The knowing smiles, arched eyebrows, and slight touching were no longer acknowledged. *What the hell?* he thought. *When I try to flirt with my own wife, she lets it fall flat, and that is no kind of life.*

Yet he continued to tell himself it was just a passing phase, even though deep down he really did not believe that. He would have to let whatever was going on play itself out. Indeed, he had wondered whether she was having an affair. But he just couldn't believe that. And he knew that divorce lawyers said most women who were running around with another man, or even more than one, increased their sex drive at home. No, he wouldn't confront her with what would be a false accusation; it would just make things worse. He would bide his time, and if things did not improve, he might suggest marriage counseling.

CHAPTER 2

The meeting was in a private dining room at the Ponte Vedra Inn and Club, often referred to as simply the Ponte Vedra Club, in late February 1993, a week or so before the legislature would convene in March. "Gentleman," Phil Griffin said after tapping his glass for attention, "we, as men of the world, know that things like what we want to take place in Tallahassee don't just happen; they have to be made to happen. Now, with that said, we are going to give you the breakdown of what we will get out of this thing, if we can make it happen. And we can. Believe me ..."

Someone called out, trying to ask a question.

"Before we get to any questions, let me turn this meeting over to Frank Dunn. In other words, please hold your questions until he's completed his presentation." Dunn was a young associate in Phil's firm. Energetic and healthy-looking, he dressed much like his mentor, tastefully and expensively. With his dark hair swept back with just the right amount of wave, he was clean-cut, if not an exactly handsome man, about Kevin's age. He presented several charts and diagrams to show just how much such a lawsuit against the tobacco industry would bring to the state's coffers, and he emphasized that the tobacco companies would have to capitulate. Kevin noticed he never once mentioned what the lawyers' fees would be. Frank Dunn's calculations envisioned a verdict somewhere between one and several million dollars in the first trial.

"Thank you for that fine presentation," Phil said.

A hand was raised, but before Phil had a chance to recognize the person, one of the attorneys asked, "You sure such a law will be constitutional?"

"Constitutional? I could tell you, like anyone in this room could, that any statute starts off with the presumption it is constitutional. Now let's get serious. This thing will be such a threat to the tobacco industry, they won't take a chance on it. After all, all they have to do is pass the costs on to the customer. Anyway, aren't we in the chance-taking business? Sure, we are! And if we handle this right, the chancy aspects can be considerably reduced." Phil paused, with a serious expression, as if reflecting on what he had just said. "Gentleman, if this thing goes the way we've planned, the risk factor will be zero. But we're going to need some operating expenses, so if you're on board, let me know later tonight. Now, let's adjourn to the bar, the one inside."

* * * * *

"Sort of reminds me of Bhopal," Kevin said with a distinct note of cynicism just before taking a sip of his scotch and soda.

"Bhopal?" echoed Hugh.

"Yeah, you know, that tasteless display of greed and avarice a few years back in India when a Union Carbide plant leaked some kind of poisonous gas."

"Uh-huh!"

"Made me ashamed to be a lawyer," Kevin said as he put his drink on the table.

"Bull, those people needed compensation." Hugh took a swig of his scotch and water.

"Sure, they needed whatever the remedies are in India. The world didn't need that shameless behavior by a lot of American ambulance chasers. Hell, I don't know ... I guess the smell of money, big money, trumps what's left of behavior that once would have been most embarrassing, not to mention highly unethical."

"For Christ's sake, don't be so cynical. Some of those *ambulance chasers*, as you say, might have sincerely wanted to help those unfortunate people. Admit it—you would have liked to have been in on that."

Kevin did not immediately respond.

"You're just pissed because you weren't in on it, Kevin." Hugh picked up his drink, looked in it, and then took a small sip.

"I'll admit, at the time, I would have liked to have a piece of that action, but you didn't see me in India. Nope, if a client, any client, wants to see me, he can come to my office."

"Well, this ain't Bhopal."

"I know it isn't. I just said it reminds me of it. The smell of greed was in that room—in here too." Kevin looked over the room while sweeping his hand around in an all-encompassing gesture. "Oh, what the hell! And it doesn't matter whether greed has a smell or not, does it? How much do we need to pony up?"

"I believe it'll be ten thousand for now. The rest will be due later when we know a complaint is going to be filed. You're going to be with us, aren't you?"

"Yes, I am," Kevin stated as he sipped the last of his scotch and soda. The conversations between Kevin and the others, on matters mostly unrelated to the purpose of the meeting, lasted another half hour or so, just the kind of give-and-take one would expect among professional men with a lot in common. Kevin watched Phil carefully for an opportunity to speak privately with him. Finally, he saw one of the lawyers shake Phil's hand and leave him in the vicinity of the bar momentarily alone.

Kevin got up and approached Phil Griffin. "Phil, when you get a chance ..."

"Kevin, my boy, when I get a chance? How about right now? Come on over here where we can talk." Phil led Kevin to an out-of-the-way spot at the end of the bar. "I like to stand sometimes when I'm drinking. It reminds me of something." He hesitated and smiled while looking about to be certain they had a measure of privacy. "You don't mind, do you?"

"No. This is fine."

"Well?"

"I'm just not too sure about this thing."

After a moment, Phil said, "Kevin, nothing in this world is sure. Pays to be cautious. Frankly, four of us are already committed to this thing, and we are going to do it. But it will no doubt make the whole thing easier if there are more of us with a stake in it. You know, the legislators from our respective districts need to be reminded of what an evil thing cigarettes are. Hmm, they are evil ... wish I had one right now. About time for a little sin." Phil chortled. "Crap, every time

I have a drink, I want a cigarette. Still haven't gotten over the habit. Hell, probably never will. Still smoke a pipe every now and then in the office. How about you?"

"Not bothered too much now. It's been over five years, you know."

"You never smoked that long?"

"I quit two or three years after law school," Kevin said as he reached for a bowl of peanuts.

"I wish I had. You think the longer you smoke, maybe it's that much harder to quit?" Phil began nibbling one peanut at a time.

"Don't know. But no one's having any real success suing the tobacco companies ..."

"Because they haven't framed a righteous picture of indignation, and they don't have the state behind them. Hell, Kevin, we'll be representing the state, the people."

Kevin reflected that they would be representing themselves too but said only, "And the statute will do what?"

"It will allow statistical analysis, and there will be a caveat to liberalize the evidence code. If Medicaid paid for the treatment, we'll be able to use an expert's opinion, based on statistical analysis, to show that smoking caused the cancer, heart attack, or whatever. Without that relaxation in evidence, the court would rightfully never let such an opinion in. The jury can decide whether the greater weight of the evidence shows the illness was caused by smoking or not. Other than that, we'll be using the standard stock-in-trade counts, but none of the traditional defenses will be admissible to counter the statistical analysis evidence to show that smoking caused the cancer or other disease and Medicaid paid for the treatment."

"Okay, I'm in for now. How much from me do you need now?"

"Send me a check for ten thousand. That ought to do it for now."

"Okay."

"Excuse me, Kevin. I see Tom Roth is hovering about to talk to me. If I don't see you again before you leave, drive safely." The two routinely shook hands to confirm the bargain.

Kevin wandered back to a table where Hugh Benson was sitting with a couple of other lawyers. "Mind if I join you?" Kevin asked as he took a seat at their table.

"You want another drink?" Hugh asked.

"No."

"I'm buying!"

"No, I'm driving back home tonight."

"You ought to stick around. Call the wife and tell her you're spending the night. There's going to be some activity in here a little later."

"I might hate myself in the morning if I did that, Hugh," Kevin said as he indicated to an approaching waiter not to bring him another drink.

"So what do you think?" asked Hugh.

"I think we're in for some surprises. Nothing could be so, so …"

"Clear-cut?"

"Yeah … and easy."

"It won't really be easy. But it won't be that hard either."

"Why not?"

"Well, you know all the common legal defenses—assumption of risk, comparative negligence, et cetera—will be abrogated. Add to that a statute which allows statistical analysis to proof causation, and for god's sake, we can't lose."

"Sure seems that way."

"You're on board, aren't you?"

"Sure, but when a person gets cancer and lives over a contaminated landfill that *could* be the cause of the cancer, but other folks living in the same area don't get the disease, that leaves a very big gap in the issue of causation. No matter what a statistician might say about the percentage of folks who get cancer based on a hypothetical set of facts, the statistics do not prove causation in an individual case. Smoking, of course, is the same. Some people who smoke never suffer any ill effects from it."

"Aha, Kevin, you are so right, but in this case, we will be able to use statistics and let the trier of fact, the jury, draw a conclusion. A vast step forward in common sense, I say." Hugh paused, looked at his drink, and quickly dispatched about half of it. Then he turned back to Kevin. "Hell, Kevin, if you've got reservations, it's no big deal—just don't be a part of this thing. It ain't like you just have to, you know …"

"No, I want to be in on this," Kevin quickly blurted out. "I'm just trying to get information. Just trying to get both sides. Playing the devil's advocate …"

"That's what makes you such a damn good attorney: you cover all the bases. I've heard defense lawyers say they just can't get one up on you. You always cut them off, and that's why we want you with us."

"I think it can be done, but it's not going to be as easy as it sounds, Hugh, and I don't want you to misread me—this whole approach seems a convoluted way of taxing the tobacco industry. That's what it amounts to, doesn't it?" Kevin paused, but no one at the table said anything. He continued, "This is the government extracting money from tobacco, claiming some kind of high moral ground, but the industry will have to pay to the state if we get a verdict. We've always taxed tobacco and booze to offset the cost to society of the undesirable consequences of their products ... and ..."

"And what?" Hugh said, sounding bored.

"And every pack dating back before Medicaid has the warnings printed right on the side of the package. The state allows tobacco to be sold. Seems to me, to be morally correct, the state should sue itself." He sat back, sipped his drink, and smiled.

"I don't know what you're selling, Kevin, but I don't want any of it. We don't need that kind of negative attitude. Hell, we'll be doing some good, I think," Hugh concluded, but the authority and certainty in his tone had slipped away. "Everything you said is, of course, correct, but ..."

"But?"

"But it doesn't matter. Like I said, the defenses are all out the window."

"Here's something else: why not pass a law now to abolish Medicaid payments for anybody with a tobacco-related disease?"

"Well, it couldn't be retroactive for one thing. Damn, I'm getting a little tight and should be on top of the world. You're ruining my night, Kevin. Hell, I can't figure out if you are with us or against us. Which?" Hugh hesitated as he looked at his empty glass and then motioned to get the waiter's attention. "Another round, but I'm not standing for yours this time," he said, nodding toward Kevin.

"No, thank you anyway," Kevin quipped. "In answer to your question, I'm with you for now. And now I've got to go. Got a long drive back tonight."

"Go on and leave, you pussy," laughed Hugh. "I know you want this thing, so why can't you say thank you?"

"Thank you, Hugh. Honestly, I thought I had already expressed my gratitude to have been invited to the greatest legal legerdemain event ever."

"Legal legerdemain ... Shit, haven't heard that ..."

"Since law school. Don't worry, I'll stay in touch. Good night, gentlemen." Kevin slid his chair back, stood up, and walked out of the bar. He stopped just outside to listen to the breaking ocean waves and inhale the salty air. Somehow it made him feel better. He'd had a fun time with Hugh, but he knew deep in the recesses of his being that something didn't smell right. He should be elated and in there with the others, celebrating the forthcoming riches. But he was not inside, and he was not elated. *Why?* he wondered all the way home.

* * * * *

He had, in an abbreviated fashion and with what he'd hoped was a lack of passion, been conversing with Sherrie about his comments to Phil and Hugh. He put his first cup of morning coffee down, hesitated, and then got up and prepared another cup. He really didn't like coffee that much, so he added a generous amount of cream.

Finally, Sherrie said, "You mean you don't believe you should get into this thing?"

"Not exactly. I just have some reservations. Five hundred thousand dollars is a lot of money."

"Yeah, but we have it."

"True. But ... well, I'm going to go ahead and send Phil the ten thousand on Monday."

"For god's sake, Kevin, don't pass up a chance to be really rich. From what you say, the fees alone will exceed a hundred million dollars. Now that's a lot of money. Phil and Hugh and the others know what they're doing."

"Oh, no one's doing anything out-and-out illegal, as far as I can tell ..."

"As far as you can tell?"

"Sherrie, I guess even the best sometimes compromise. Even Peter denied Christ, not once, but thrice. Money, on promises, is probably being exchanged. You know, every man has his price."

"Are you trying to tell me you don't?"

That stung a little. Kevin knew she didn't mean it, and he hoped he didn't have a price, but he couldn't be completely certain; maybe he did. That uncertainty rankled his conscience in a mild yet strangely significant way.

16

"I'm not privy to everything. Most of us won't be. But I wasn't born yesterday. When the stakes are this high, men sin."

"And women too," Sherrie said with an amused smile. "I guess you have to let your conscience be your guide. So far, you have been pretty lucky, I think."

"No question about it. I've been lucky. I had the right cases to establish a good reputation with and have never had to compromise to make ends meet. If I had to ... I just don't know ..." His voice trailed off as he fell into concentrated but brief thought. He shook his head and announced he was ready to go for his morning walk on the beach. "Sure you don't want to join me?" he said. Then, without thinking, he put his arms around her waist and pulled her closer.

"Hmm, do I see a little gleam in your eye?" Kevin asked, smiling.

"Go for a walk," she sighed as she took his arms from around her. "I need a bath. Maybe when you get back, if I've finished what I've got to do."

"Okay, I'll take my time so you can be sure to finish what you've got to do." And out the door he went. Once, he would have had visions of sugar plums dancing in his head. But now he was filled with dark reservations, fearing that for Sherrie the old sparks just weren't there anymore. For him, however, the rapture was not over, and he felt this too would pass.

CHAPTER 3

While the legislature was in session in March 1993, a few days after the meeting at Ponte Vedra, Hugh Benson and Phil Griffin met for lunch at the Florida Yacht Club. Located on the St. Johns River, it was the oldest yacht club in Jacksonville, having been built in the 1870s. The well-kept grounds and tennis courts confirmed that the membership had well cared for it over the years. The same was true for the inside. It was lushly carpeted throughout, and the stucco walls were lavishly trimmed or paneled in dark oak. The dining room itself was handsomely paneled in dark oak. And the tables and chairs matched the room's decor. The impeccably uniformed servers were efficient and helpful, with just the right amount of professional familiarity.

"You think that Kevin is going to cause trouble?" asked Phil. "You know he can be sanctimonious sometimes."

"Don't really think so, but I thought you ought to know what he was saying."

"Yeah, we do need to be cautious. Same thing I told him—always be cautious. I've always kind of liked him. Damn good legal mind and very persuasive with a jury or a judge. Even thought maybe, if we get that far, he could be lead counsel for the trial. But there's something prissy … or maybe not prissy, but …"

"No, not prissy. He ain't no sissy. Maybe it's just that we sense …" Hugh was going to say, "He's better than us," but Phil interrupted.

"Hell, does he run around on his wife?" Phil asked as he looked around the room.

"Like we do?" said Hugh. "No, not that I know of."

"He ever been drunk?"

"I've seen him a little tight a time or two." He held up two fingers.

"But always a gentleman?"

"Always." He flashed Phil the zero signal.

"I don't know," Phil slowly said, obviously thinking. "I've always had a little trouble trusting a man who doesn't enjoy the masculine—you know, the manly pursuits in life."

"Like chasing pussy?" Hugh said with raised eyebrows.

"Well, yeah, that's one of them. And keeping a bookie in business," Phil laughed. "I'll bet he doesn't even gamble?"

Hugh shook his head. "Maybe," he said, returning to his earlier thoughts, "we sense he might be made of better stuff, and we resent it, Phil. Think that's it?"

"Could be, but there's something about that man. I want him on our side."

"Well, like the rest of us, he's a winner, but he loses too, you know, just like the rest of us," Hugh said as he sat back.

"What does he value most?"

"Damned if I know. Why?"

"I'm thinking we don't need a man of his caliber ..."

"Quality," interjected Hugh. "But hell, you just said we want him on our side. You getting Alzheimer's or something?" He grinned.

"I was going to say a man of his quality against us. He might start some kind of campaign to throw this thing off-track. Maybe we ought to start thinking about how to diminish that sterling reputation he enjoys."

"Phil, I don't really believe we have a problem," Hugh said as he glanced through the menu.

"Yes, you do, Hugh, and that's the reason you told me how he was questioning this thing so fervently."

"Even so, all we got to do is simply count him out, if you really feel it's necessary."

"No, that would be the worst thing we could do right now. If he thinks we're shitting on him, god knows what he might do. He could write an article for the newspaper or get some paper like the *St. Petersburg Times* to investigate. Not only that, but some of those politicians wouldn't mind seeing our heads handed to them, particularly if it was handed to them by one of our own. I can see the headlines:

'Lawyer considered beyond reproach repudiates the governor and attorney general and reveals a web of chicanery that hasn't been seen in Tallahassee since Flagler bribed the entire legislature.' It would make that scandalous bit of business in Bhopal look like a tea party for the benefit of the needy. No, we can't cross him. Let's just wait and see. Hell, he's already paid his ten thousand dollars!"

"Phil, I don't think he has a mean bone in his body."

"Not mean, sanctimonious. You know, you don't have to believe in some kind of deity to be a sanctimonious son of a bitch," Phil said with a tight smile.

"Maybe we're jumping the gun here?" Hugh said with a wave of his hand.

"Let's hope so. But he is equivocating. I just know it. I could feel it when we spoke at Ponte Vedra. Call it intuition."

"No such thing as intuition," Hugh said.

"Yeah, I'm familiar with that psychological crap. No such thing as intuition? The hell there isn't. I've been guided by it far too many times."

"When's the attorney general supposed to get here?"

"*Brother* Sean Goodnight will get here when he gets here," said Phil.

"Just like in our fraternity days, huh? When was he supposed to get here?" asked Hugh.

"Sometime between the hours of twelve and one thirty," Phil said as he looked at his watch.

"I'm getting hungry," Hugh said.

"So am I, but we'll wait. How about one of those two martinis we're supposed to enjoy every day?"

"I prefer a manhattan," Hugh said, gesturing to get the waiter's attention.

* * * * *

"No one's with you, Sean," Phil said as they stood up and shook hands with the attorney general.

Sean was a tall, slender gentleman with a square head of gray hair. Though not really an attractive man, he did have a smooth way about him. "Just my driver, who will wait outside after getting a bite to eat at the snack bar on the wharf." While Sean's eyes flashed between the martini and the manhattan, he took his seat. "Well, shall we order, or do you just want to drink your lunch?"

"Don't you want a martini?" Phil asked in a skeptical tone.

"If you insist."

By this time, the maître d' had secured their waiter. "Another martini," Phil announced, nodding toward the attorney general. "We'll order in a moment." Then the three men fell silent, as if they were afraid of the consequences if they spoke. The silence grew palpable. A nefarious aura was descending on them in sharp contrast to the ornate but sedate oak-paneled dining room that exuded old-school charm, very old and very posh. Nevertheless, they looked like and postured themselves as polished gentleman, very much at ease.

Finally, the attorney general broke the oppressive, telling silence. "What I like about dining here"—he looked around, obviously admiring the quiet decor—"is the noise level is zero. That's the difference between this place and a downtown hotel restaurant. Excellent suggestion for our meeting, gentlemen." Sean paused and continued to let his eyes wander while he waited for Phil or Hugh to respond. But before either could utter a word, he continued. "Oh," he said in a low voice, "everything is on track. The President of the Senate and Speaker of the House had a meeting with the governor and me yesterday ..." Then he paused again and looked at Phil, as if he expected Phil to say something.

"Everything is being arranged on our end," Phil said.

"Don't give me the details," Sean cautioned as he waved his hand.

"Sorry!" Phil said. "I just wanted y'all to know ..."

Sean interrupted. "I'm not interested in how you do it, just that it's done. Y'all getting some trial lawyers lined up?" Sean asked as he buttered a yeast roll.

"Had a meeting last Friday. Looks good," Phil answered as he picked up the roll basket.

"Good. You all have got a hell of a lot to do. My office can provide you with a lot of statistical studies and such. You'll need those for your compliant."

"We already have a lot of it. A lot of information is available through ATLA and other sources. But we'll take anything you have too."

The waiter returned with the martini, and the men ordered lunch. "I think it's time for a toast," said Sean. Each solemnly raised his glass while Sean solemnly intoned, "All for one and one for all."

"Hark to the Grand Worthy," Phil and Hugh responded ritualistically. While they nursed their drinks, Sean acknowledged a few courteous nods and hellos from a few men who recognized him. The conversation was mostly small talk. When lunch was served, all three men stopped talking. Innocuous or not, their conversation was for them only.

"Ah, broiled Spanish mackerel," Sean said with obvious anticipation. "You know, Jacksonville has always had first-class seafood." The conversation during the meal continued to focus mostly on subjects other than the real purpose of their meeting.

Finally, as he finished his lunch of pan-fried red snapper, Hugh asked, "Sean, exactly who are the people, other than you and the governor, who have the full picture of what we're doing?"

"I don't know anything about a big picture in Tallahassee," Sean said with a shrug.

"Nothing at all?" asked Phil.

"All I can say is we'll stay in touch." He then pushed back his chair and announced, "That was first-class. As I said before, Jacksonville has always had great seafood."

"That's true, Sean. Do you want to stay, and we can give you a more thorough rundown?"

"No, can't do it; I have to go. Don't get up, gentlemen," he said as he stood to leave. But he could not hide a puzzling, cryptic expression, which must have been meant as a signal that the meeting had been most satisfying. Hugh and Phil eyed each other.

"Have you ever seen such a candy ass?" quipped Phil as he shook his head, more or less disdainfully. "He acts like if he doesn't talk about what we and they are doing, then he's not involved. Typical politician. Hmm, one might think he believes what we're doing is illegal, not just smart." Phil flashed Hugh a smirk laced with contempt. "How about that corny toast? That was just too much," he said, affecting a shiver. "But now that he's gone, let's get back to what we need to do about Mr. Charles."

"Phil, we don't need to do a damn thing as far as I'm concerned. But if all goes well, how are we going to take care of the boys in Tallahassee?"

"We'll do something as promised, but it doesn't really matter if we don't do anything."

Hugh looked puzzled.

"What can they do if we don't come through? Nothing." Phil turned his palms up and arched his eyebrows to emphasize "nothing." "With respect to Mr. Charles, well, I just don't know. You know, it seems like in so many situations, we make a big plan, and something or someone comes along and screws it up. But what the hell, I guess that's just life!" Phil hesitated and then with resolve quietly murmured, "But this time that isn't going to happen." Then more to himself than to Hugh, he quietly murmured, "The flesh is weak. Yes, sir, the flesh is weak ..."

"What the hell are you mumbling about?"

"Oh, nothing. Let's get out of here."

As Hugh reached for the check, Phil picked it up.

"This is on me today," Phil said. "I feel good."

CHAPTER 4

In June 1994, over a year after the Ponte Vedra meeting, Kevin was waiting for a new client to show up for her appointment. It was after five, but he didn't mind waiting; he had been more tolerant of everything since the legislature enacted Phil's proposed legislation in its March 1994 session. He heard the front door bell jingle and let her in. She was pretty and well groomed, dressed in a light blue button-down shirt, a straight, dark-gray, knee-length worsted skirt, and black pumps. She was a little taller than average, and her short swept-back dark hair complimented an unblemished complexion, exquisite dark brown eyes, and a friendly manner. "Mr. Charles?" she questioned with a warm, disarming smile as they shook hands. Kevin was impressed.

"How do you do, Mrs. Roberts? Everyone has left, but come on into my office."

"Thank you for seeing me this late, but it's a long drive to get here, and I didn't want to leave work for any more time than was absolutely necessary."

"Mrs. Roberts, we try to accommodate," he said as they both took a seat in his office. *She's a nice girl, probably not that well educated, but a nice girl*, he thought, *and if I were not married, I'd sure like to accommodate her.* But he quickly dismissed lustful thoughts. "Your full name is Victoria Roberts, correct?" he said. He continued in his usual professional manner to get the basic information: social security numbers, home address, general conversation about the facts of her husband's death nearly a year before.

Her husband, Cornell Roberts, had been a high school dropout but had been gainfully employed with Florida Power and Light for a number of years before his untimely death at the age of thirty-five. She believed he had been well liked by the company and the union and had a bright future before him; he earned over fifty thousand dollars a year. Considerably younger than her husband, she was a receptionist in a doctor's office. They had waited to start a family, and she could document that she'd gone off the pill just before his death. Damages for wrongful death would far exceed the monetary loss of his income for what should have been his working lifetime.

"Mr. Charles, my husband was a really sweet man. Smart too. I know he dropped out of high school, but that was because he had to go to work, and he did get his GED, you know."

"That's good. Why do you say he was a sweet man?"

"Because, well … he always helped me around the house …"

"You own your home?"

"Yes, sir."

"Good."

"And he was so good with his little nephew and niece. Children loved that man."

Damn, Kevin thought, *this could really be a good case. She's a first-class plaintiff, and it sounds like even dead, he could be too. I'll enjoy resurrecting him in the courtroom.* But he kept his thoughts to himself. "Sounds like you married a really good man."

"I did." Then she stopped talking. "Oh, I'm so sorry, but sometimes thinking of him causes me to get all choked up, and I go to pieces," she whimpered as she searched her pocketbook for a tissue.

"Would you like a glass of water or …"

"Yes, I would, if it's not too much trouble," she managed to say as she dabbed away the tears. Kevin quickly left and brought back the water. As she took it from him and began to sip, Kevin could not suppress the perception that she exuded vulnerability. Damn, he wanted to help this woman.

"You told me a grinding disk flew apart, a piece went through your husband's eye, into his brain, and as a result of that, he died?"

"Yes." She paused with a faraway look in her eyes. "You know, it was just another Saturday, and he went out the back door to just do a little work around the place. Nothing big. Nothing important really and …

25

and he just never came back in. I'll never hear him again coming in the back door, scraping his shoes off before crossing the kitchen floor and calling out for me. God, I loved that man!" Then she fell pensively silent, with her head slightly bowed but her eyes looking about.

Kevin waited for the poignant moment to pass. Then he asked, "Is there anything else?"

"I know he was using a sander because he made a comment about whether or not he should use a grinding wheel on a sander ..."

"Because it spins a lot faster," commented Kevin, completing her sentence.

"Well, I don't know."

"But I do know. That could be a problem. He didn't say he knew it was dangerous to use the grinding wheel, did he?"

"No, he was just sort of talking to himself."

Kevin speculated silently. "Okay. And you say it was just some parts to a tractor he was working on at home?"

"Yes."

"Not related at all to his business."

"No. I'm sure of that. We have a few acres, and he used that tractor about the place to cut grass and everything else."

"You still have the grinder disk or the pieces?"

"Yes, I figured something had gone wrong, so I saved the pieces, including the one that came out of his ... ah, him."

"How did you find me from way over there around Palatka? Must be a lot of lawyers between there and here."

"Gary LaBlanc referred me to you. I saw him a month or so ago. He first had me sign a contract, but when he found out ... I don't know why it took so long, but I think he made some inquiries and found out it wasn't going to settle—he said mainly because Cornell had put the grinder thing on a sander. Anyway, he said I needed a real expert." She stopped talking and raised her eyebrows beseechingly.

"Like me. Hmm, I think I've met LaBlanc somewhere." Kevin paused, searching his memory and trying to place the man, before he shook his head and uttered a resigned sigh. "Well, we've handled similar cases, that's true. And I'd be delighted to have you as a client. I'll get a contract. You've already signed one, so you know what I'm talking about, right?"

"Yes, sir."

"And ..."

"I have a letter releasing me from his contract. Here it is."

Kevin briefly perused the letter. He put the letter aside, looked at her approvingly, and said, "That certainly allows me to represent you, to take over the case." He paused and then continued. "Okay. I'll explain it all again." Kevin went through the details of the written contract. He would front the cost, and there would be no fee if he didn't win in trial or settle the case to her satisfaction.

After they'd spent about forty-five minutes discussing one aspect of her case after another, Kevin asked, "Do you have any questions?"

Victoria Roberts shook her head and then mumbled, "Not right now, I don't think," as if she wasn't sure. It seemed that perhaps she did have questions but for whatever reason felt she shouldn't ask, at least not right then.

"If there are no questions, then I guess that about does it for now. You'll be hearing from me, and if you have something on your mind about this case, don't hesitate to call me. I don't want you wondering about something that I can answer for you in a minute or two, okay?"

Kevin was anxious to leave, but she looked a little distraught, so he hesitated before suggesting it was time to go. "Mrs. Roberts is there something else?" he reluctantly asked.

"No, not really," Mrs. Roberts answered shyly. "But I don't like to drive after dark, Mr. Charles. Could you recommend a decent motel that won't charge me an arm and a leg?"

Kevin thought for a fleeting moment about suggesting she stay at his home, but he rejected the idea quickly. It would not be the professional thing to do. He thought for a moment and then said, "Your best bet would be one of the motels by I-95, right where you turned off to get here."

"No other place you could recommend?"

He thought he detected in her voice a shift from shyness to a seductive tone. Kevin didn't want that, but he didn't want to lose the client by offending her before the case even got started. This was not the first time a female client had wanted to take their relationship to another level. *On the other hand, maybe I'm reading something that's not there,* he thought. *She's probably just friendly. And she does seem a little bashful. I'm sure that's all.* He shrugged off any notion that she might have an ulterior motive.

"Well, you could try the country club, but their suites are expensive. If I were you, I'd try one of the motels at the interstate."

"Okay. And I'll hear from you?"

"When I've got a complaint prepared. We'll get the estate papers from the clerk's office. This case won't settle without a lawsuit. We'll get what we need and prepare the necessary papers for us to take over the probate. You will definitely be hearing from us."

Without further ado, and to avoid any further delay in leaving his office, Kevin stood up as a cue to Mrs. Roberts that the meeting was over. She rose from her chair as he came around the desk for what he believed would be a brief professional handshake. However, she held his hand with a soft touch a little longer than he felt was necessary, while her eyes searched his face—seductively, he thought. Was she flirting or what? Kevin quickly decided it made no difference. No matter what she intended, he was not getting involved. He pretended to be totally oblivious to what she was doing as he walked with her to the front door of his office, making pleasant but minimal chitchat. As always, he hoped his client was leaving convinced that she and her case were in good hands.

* * * * *

"She sounds like a really nice person. Why didn't you at least invite her for dinner?" Sherrie casually remarked that night as she took the dinner dishes off the counter.

"You know why. I never like to get close to my clients. Of course, there are some exceptions. The few commercial cases I have are for my friends, but—"

"The others are just clients, huh?"

"You know better than that. Familiarity can cause a problem. Much better to keep the relationship on a professional level. But she did leave her sunglasses in the office; she probably would like to have them back."

"Sure she would, and you make her sound so sympathetic. Maybe you ought to call her just to make sure she's settled in okay."

Kevin couldn't tell Sherrie that he felt Victoria Roberts might have been sending him seductive signals. As a matter of fact, he wondered why he had said as much to her as he had. It was not like him to discuss business at home. But he'd gone this far, so what the hell? He could placate Sherrie and then forget about it. Maybe she even had a point.

"Okay, I'll try to call her." He called all the motels at the I-95 intersection. There was no Victoria Roberts registered. *Hmm, that's strange*, he thought. But she had probably just decided to drive on back home. "No Victoria Roberts at any of the motels. I guess she decided to drive on home tonight."

"Well, you did the right thing anyway," Sherrie said before disappearing up the steps.

Kevin turned on the TV, but he wasn't quite satisfied with the conclusion that she had just driven home. That Victoria wasn't at one of the motels bothered him. But why should it bother him? Was there something here he couldn't put his finger on? Was it malevolent or benevolent? He shook his head to clear his mind. Something just did not feel right. Kevin, ordinarily not a suspicious type, chastised himself for indulging in what he knew was only speculation, unnecessary speculation at that. He couldn't, however, stop his mind from bouncing from one negative thought to another. Something about this case was leading to an uncertain apprehension. But apprehension about what? Losing the client? No. Losing the case? Hardly. He really didn't believe in intuition, but he couldn't control the uneasiness that kept creeping into his mind.

Eventually, Sherrie reappeared, and they tuned in to a program neither really cared for. He sat with his eyes on the set, but his mind continued on overdrive. He briefly wondered why Gary LaBlanc had not called about the referral to assure a split on the fee. But, he mused, maybe the guy had just gotten past that sort of crass, unethical behavior. For the time being, he wouldn't worry about it. Then he smiled—he had been wondering where his next big case would come from, and now he knew. Funny, but life in the legal business was like that, probably always had been, and would be the same after Kevin was dead and gone. The right cases just kept coming in the door. He knew that wasn't true for all lawyers, and it usually had nothing to do with any attorney's given ability. Some who bordered on downright incompetent were financially successful beyond his or anybody else's comprehension.

"What are you thinking about, Kevin?" Sherrie asked.

"Oh, you know, business."

"Your new client and her case?"

How did you know? he thought, but he quickly decided it would be in his best interest to be less than honest. "No, not really. I guess I was thinking about how lucky we are. You and I have a damn good life." He followed that misdirection with an engaging smile that said "all is well, and I love you."

"You know, you haven't mentioned that business with the tobacco industry in a long time. Is that still in the works?" Sherrie said as she adjusted the chair's pillows.

"The legislation was passed in the March session."

"Good," she said while gesturing for the remote.

"We ought to know something before long," he said, handing her the remote.

"It's about time." She started changing channels.

"Anyway, I've got my name in the pot. So when the time's right, somebody will get a hold of me."

"You sure you shouldn't call Hugh or Phil?" she asked as she sat up and turned toward him.

"You're sounding mighty mercenary. But no, I don't need to call anyone. They know where I am, and I've contributed my ten thousand dollars. They'll let me know."

"I hope you're right. I just don't want them to forget you."

"Sherrie, they are not going to forget me. If they do, so what?" Then he turned back to the television. "TV just ain't what it used to be when all we had was four channels."

"Here's the remote; you find something." She stood up to hand it to him. "Or maybe you just want to turn it off?"

"Good idea, so I can read my book," Kevin said as he took the remote.

"You're not ready for bed?"

"Not yet. You go on up. I'll be there in a little while."

"Try not to wake me up," she said as she got up and left the room.

Kevin sat for a minute and then turned off the TV and picked up a Tom Clancy novel. But before he got into it, he muddled over a recent thought of his: that maybe they should sleep in separate bedrooms. That way he could read in bed every night without disturbing her. But he didn't know how to broach the subject. *Problems, problems,* he thought as he opened the book to the marked page.

CHAPTER 5

In July 1994, Kevin's office received the requested information from the probate court, and after Kevin was substituted as the attorney in Victoria Roberts's deceased husband's probate, the legal papers for Mrs. Roberts to sign were prepared. One of Kevin's secretaries, Jo Ann, called the client to see whether she wanted to sign the papers in his office or have them sent to her.

"She wants to talk to you, Mr. Charles," Jo Ann said over the intercom.

"Okay." Kevin picked up the phone. "Yes, Mrs. Roberts?"

"What do you think I should do?"

"You mean whether we should send the substitution papers to you or you should come in?" Kevin reminded himself that clients sometimes seemed to become totally helpless, but he kept the thought to himself.

"Yes."

"Well, it's a lot easier for you and for us to send them to you."

"But things get lost in the mail."

"True, but we could just do the papers over again or maybe send them certified to begin with, and you could call me about any problems."

"I just don't know. I feel like I need to come to your office."

"Maybe that would be best," Kevin said. He might as well help her feel like it was necessary to do what he suspected she was going to do anyway. "Sometimes it's necessary to make a few changes before you sign, and if you're here, it can, of course, be expedited."

"Then I think I'd better come to see you."

"That will be fine, Mrs. Roberts."

"Again, though, it'll have to be late. I don't want to miss too much work. Is that okay?"

"Of course, I'll be here past five until you show up."

"Can I come today? I mean, this afternoon?"

"Sure. I'll see you when you get here." Why did clients so often put themselves out unnecessarily? Maybe, though, it wouldn't be so bad to see her again anyway. He smiled to himself as he leaned back in his chair; life could sometimes be interesting.

About a quarter after five, the phone rang. It was Victoria Roberts. "Oh, Mr. Charles, I'm really bushed."

"Where are you?"

"At the Ramada on I-95, the same one I stayed in before. I'm just so tired. Traffic was terrible, and it's been raining. Do you think maybe you could bring the papers here?"

Kevin paused, thinking. He really didn't want to meet her at a motel. "If we need to make some changes, we won't be able to do that at the Ramada."

"Well, maybe that won't be necessary. I bet it won't."

"But …"

"But if we do need to make changes, I can drop by in the morning and sign them in your office. How's that?" Her request didn't make any sense unless she had an ulterior motive, and Kevin suspected he knew what it was. Still, he did not want to be rude, and more importantly, he didn't want to risk losing her as a client. "Okay, Mrs. Roberts, I'll meet you in the lobby in ten or fifteen minutes."

"Make it thirty minutes, okay?" she said.

"Okay, see you then. Bye." He hung up the phone and smiled. He couldn't help feeling flattered. Yep, at first he hadn't wanted to admit it, but he was indeed flattered. Here was a younger, very attractive woman who found him attractive. He mumbled to himself, "I bet she won't be in the lobby. I'll have to go to her room on some pretext or other." He shook his head at the human comedy. Then he dictated a few notes for a letter in another case.

She was in the lobby when he arrived. He slightly grinned—*wrong on this lobby thing, but we'll see.* She stood up, and once again Kevin couldn't help acknowledging her good looks. She was dressed in a red short-sleeved blouse, very casual brown slacks, and tennis shoes. She smiled and walked toward him. "I feel a lot better now. Took a quick shower. You know, that just does wonders for you sometimes."

"It can, I guess," Kevin responded, hoping he sounded interested and indifferent at the same time.

"So the papers are in your briefcase?" she asked.

"Right here, Mrs. Roberts," he said as he lifted the attaché case slightly.

"Is there a lot to do?"

"No, shouldn't take any time at all, so ..." *God, I wish I hadn't said that*, he thought immediately. *Should have told her we need to get right on it. Now she has a reason to delay.*

"In that case, let's go to the bar and have a drink, and you should start calling me Vickie."

"Okay, and you call me Kevin," he said. But the last thing he wanted right then was a drink.

"You've got time, haven't you?"

"I guess so," he said as she began strolling toward the bar. They sat at a table for two and Kevin ordered a gin rickey for her and a scotch and water for himself. After finishing his drink, Kevin felt more relaxed and inquired, "Vickie, didn't you say you stayed here last time?"

"Yes, I did, and after I registered, I went to my room and watched the tube until I fell asleep."

"I called here to invite you to dinner at my house and was told you were not registered."

"I can't explain that, unless you called while I was still having dinner. I ate before I checked in."

"And, of course, you didn't drop by this bar later," he said with a smile.

"You're getting to know me. I never go into a bar alone. It's not ladylike. I've never been in this one," she softly whispered while glancing around. She flashed a dancing smile, followed by a shake of her head. "I can't imagine me in a bar alone. How about you?"

"How about me? Can't say I've never been in a bar alone. You know, I was a sailor for a while," he said with innuendo in his voice. *Damn! Now I'm flirting, the last thing in the world I ought to be doing.* Indulging in self-recrimination, he slightly shook his head and blinked his eyes in an effort to dispel any carnal thoughts he was having toward Vickie.

"A sailor—and a girl in every port, I bet."

"No."

"You wouldn't admit it anyway, would you?"

Smiling wryly, Kevin scratched his head lightly before answering, "Probably not." He wondered how he was going to get out of this adverse situation. "Mrs. Roberts, I've got to get home; my wife and I are expecting some guests tonight," he lied.

"Well, I wouldn't want you to miss that. You wouldn't want to miss it either, would you? And please call me Vickie."

"Okay, Vickie, it's not a question of wanting to miss it," he chuckled. "I can't miss it, so ..."

"So let's go to my room, where we can have some privacy to sign those papers."

"Okay, let me get the check." Kevin got up and walked to the bar to pay. He didn't motion for the waiter; he wanted to communicate that time was important while not giving the impression he was rushing her.

Seated at the standard motel room table, Kevin opened the briefcase and pulled out several documents while making small talk. With a copy in his hand, he went through the petition and other papers while she read them for any substantive changes. Finally, they were through. She signed the papers; no changes were necessary. "Now what?" She smiled with a twinkle in her eye.

"Oh, we'll send these to Palatka for filing tomorrow, and as soon as the judge issues the letters of administration, we'll file the lawsuit," he said while putting the documents back into his briefcase.

"No, I don't mean that," she said.

Kevin could no longer pretend he wasn't aware of her intentions. "Vickie, I'm a married man," he nearly whispered. Then he added, "And I love my wife." Then he stopped talking and for a moment entertained the notion of taking her up on what she was offering.

"For god's sake, I feel like such a fool," she muttered while looking away from Kevin. "I hope this won't interfere with you representing me."

"Of course not. If you want me to continue as your attorney, I'm more than willing."

"I'm so ashamed," she murmured with her hand over her mouth. "But I do want you to continue and ..." She paused and dropped her eyes. "And you can forget about this?"

"Did something happen here?" Kevin said with indifference as he got up. "Vickie, don't get up; I can see my way out. And we'll stay in touch. We'll definitely have to see you again when we receive interrogatories and such."

Once out the door, Kevin had second thoughts about Victoria Roberts. After all, nearly every man he knew strayed from time to time and still had what he considered a happy marriage.

Kevin was not cynical about the institution of marriage. But he thought of Jimmy Carter, who couldn't deny he sometimes had lust for other women. He couldn't help the way he felt, but he could control his behavior, and so far, he had been true to Sherrie.

Kevin came through the front door and went straight to the kitchen, where he found his wife. Before he could say anything, she said, "You're late. I know you weren't in the office, or if you were, you didn't answer the phone. Where—"

"I had to meet a client at the Ramada."

"The Ramada?"

"Sherrie, it's not that important, and it's not that late."

"Why didn't you call, though?"

"I should have, but I kept thinking I'd break loose. Next time I'll call, I promise." He moved closer to her, but she pulled away without a word when he tried to put his arm around her waist. "Kathy—where is she?"

"In her room," Sherrie said with a slight edge to her voice.

Kevin's nine-year-old daughter Kathy, had heard him in the house and met him in the hall, dressed in jeans and a summer-weight white sweater, as he approached her room. "Daddy, you're late!"

"Hi, sweetie," he said as he picked her up for a hug.

"You two, come on. Dinner's ready," Sherrie called out from the kitchen. "It's a little late; we had to wait for Daddy." Throughout dinner, Kevin sensed a tension. Something wasn't right, and he knew it was more than his being moderately late getting home. Sherrie didn't show a spark of good humor. She was truly out of sorts about something. Kevin shrugged it off, deciding to just let it go, at least for the time being.

Later, after Kathy had gone to bed, Kevin and Sherrie were indifferently watching something of little interest on television. Kevin resented the coldness of his wife and felt a little levity might bring her around. "What's wrong with you, Sherrie? You act like you swallowed a frog or something."

"Nothing's wrong with me."

"You sure you didn't swallow a bug or something?" he asked with a laugh.

"No, nothing's wrong with me. I guess I'm in a quandary about going back to work."

"Back to work? Why?"

"I miss it, Kevin. I'm not really the type to just cook and clean and do mom things," she snapped. "Kathy's old enough now to be trusted," she concluded with an unfamiliar flatness. "Anyway, why did I become a CPA if I wasn't going to use it?"

"Well, gee whiz," Kevin said with irony, "I never knew how much you valued crunching those numbers." He was fed up with trying to placate his wife over an unknown problem. "But since we are talking about changes, Sherrie, I think we would both be happier and sleep better if I moved into one of the guest rooms to sleep, don't you?"

"You want to move out of the bedroom?"

"Only to sleep. I like to read at night, and it bothers you. And I snore, and you wake me up all through the night, and I have trouble going back to sleep."

"Suit yourself." After a pause she added, "You're right. You can start tonight. You'll have to make up the guest bed. No sheets on it, just a bedcover." She didn't offer to help him.

Kevin felt relieved. He didn't think she had taken the decision to sleep in separate rooms the wrong way, yet he still sensed she was hiding something. *Most people have secrets*, he thought. He tried to interrupt his own troubling thoughts with some inane comment about the television program. But his mind kept wandering here and there, trying to grasp the essence of something, but the something eluded him. Instead, the image of Vickie Roberts emerged over and over in his mind's eye, like a recently heard musical tune that keeps playing over and over in a person's head.

Sherrie had met Kevin while she was getting a master's degree in business administration and while he was in law school. From the very first time they laid eyes on each other in the university cafeteria, they both knew their relationship would be more than just a passing fancy.

He had been standing with his tray, looking about for a table. She saw him and without thinking flashed a welcoming smile across the room. He smiled back. It might not have been that enchanted evening Rogers and Hammerstein had written about, but it was an epiphany, and neither his nor her life had been the same since.

"You don't mind if I join you, do you?" he had said with the unexpected courtesy of a real gentleman.

"No." While he was taking his seat, she wondered whether she could encourage him without being too forward. She felt giddy, like a middle-school girl. "I'm Sherrie Brinson," she said.

"Sherrie, I'm Kevin Charles." He sat back with that easy smile of his, and they shook hands. "I'm in law school, second year. You?"

"Working on my master's over in the business school," she said, and before she finished those few words, she knew he'd ask her for a date. She had never felt more comfortable with anyone, and in short order, she knew he was the man she would marry, or at least that's what she later told people.

After a few laughs and easy conversation, Kevin arched his eyebrows, paused a second or two, and asked, "Would you like to take a little time off from studying and go to the movies with me?"

There was no way she could refuse. "That would be nice, but what movie and when?"

"How about tonight? Downtown at the Roxy? I don't know what's playing, but we'll find something to do if we decide not to go." She loved the little touch of mischief in his tone.

"What time?"

"Say about six thirty, and we'll get a bite to eat downtown, on me."

She told him where she lived. The date was made, and it wasn't long before they moved in together, but they waited until he finished law school to get married.

The physical attraction was overwhelming in the beginning and had more or less remained strong over the years, or had it? She reluctantly acknowledged to herself that she was not so interested anymore, especially since Kathy had become a little older. She was now wondering whether it had begun to wane for him like it had for her. *No, he is still amorous enough, perhaps too much*, she thought. As for Sherrie, no other man was of any real interest to her.

Sherrie drifted in her mind from one bad scene to another. Was he having an affair or not? She couldn't really believe he was.

Sherrie had received a phone call earlier that week from a man who claimed to know that Kevin was having an affair. She hadn't said anything to Kevin about it. She had told herself it wasn't true and had decided not to tell Kevin, not right away anyhow. She'd thought about that phone call more and more when he hadn't come home at the usual time this evening.

So now he wants to sleep alone! Of course, she had also thought about possibly having an affair, but she knew her so-called thoughts were not serious. His suggestion about sleeping separately seemed to support the message of that recent phone call, though. Still, she didn't want to falsely accuse him. She slightly bit her lip, resolving to not confront him then and there with the phone call. If it was true, something else would be forthcoming. In a way she felt she should be angry, but it wasn't so much anger she felt; no, it was more like despair. She was overcome by a bewildering depression. Despite her longing to let it all out and solve what had become a nagging problem, she gritted her teeth and vowed to keep her emotions in check.

"Sherrie, I'm going to go to bed," Kevin said. Then he added, "After I've made it up."

She didn't laugh.

"Should I turn off the TV?" he sighed, acknowledging the failure of his effort to be humorous.

"Yeah, I'm going on up too, so turn it off."

That night they slept in separate rooms.

CHAPTER 6

Frank Dunn was busy dictating in his office when the intercom interrupted him. "Mrs. Roberts is here early. Can you see her now?"

"Yes, send her *right* in." This was a high-priority matter, one that had to succeed. The day before, Vickie Roberts had gone to her second appointment with Kevin Charles. Phil had told Dunn in no uncertain terms that the consequences of failure would not be pleasant. He definitely would not put Mrs. Roberts off, not even for one minute.

"Mrs. Roberts, please have a seat," he said as she entered. "Would you like a cup of coffee or a Coke or …?"

"No, thank you, Mr. Dunn," she answered impatiently. "You know why I'm here. I need some guidance on this thing."

"Yes, we've been discussing your call. Tell me again?" Dunn said in the most soothing way he could muster. His so-called discussion with Phil had really been a histrionic diatribe from Phil. Dunn knew that if she decided to throw in the towel, his prospects with the Phil Griffin Law Firm would be over. Phil's parting words had been "do not fail."

"Well, I've been trying to seduce the man, and by the way, he doesn't seem like such a bad egg to me—just the opposite. Anyway, what is it he's supposed to be interfering with?" Her voice was escalating, becoming slightly shrill. And her eyes shifted excitedly. "I know that you and Phil have not told me everything. And now that I've met him, I'm more frustrated than ever. Do you understand what I mean?"

"Now, Mrs. Roberts, the less you know, the better."

"Yeah, I've heard all about that," she said in a more moderated tone. Then she paused, uncrossed her legs, and sat forward in her chair. "If I hadn't been so strapped for money," she said slowly, "I never would have agreed … but you don't give a damn about how this affects me, do you?"

"Please, Mrs. Roberts, don't get upset. Look at it this way," he said in an effort to quiet things down. "You are going to profit handsomely from simply seducing him and then reporting it to the bar association."

"I'm not sure I can get it done," she answered with slightly less edge in her voice.

"Not even if it means he might lose you as a client if he doesn't have a little romance with you? For Christ's sake, you're a gorgeous woman, and I might say a damn smart one too." Dunn hoped flattery would go a long way. He knew it never hurt. Besides, she was indeed gorgeous and smart.

"I'm not going to have a lot of other chances, you know."

"I know." He paused, stroking his chin, thinking. "It must seem unplanned, casual …"

"That's impossible now."

"No, it's not impossible. You and he just have to be together, and it just happens. Nothing else, of course, will work. I agree with you wholeheartedly on that point."

"How are we going to manage that? I don't think he'll want to meet me again in a motel," she said with a distinct note of capitulation.

"There's going to be a lot of interrogatories—you know, questions for you to answer on paper—and a lot of documents for you to produce. You'll get a call, or you might just receive the stuff in the mail with directions to do the best you can and then contact them for an appointment to go over the questions and the demand to produce and so on."

"Yeah, he explained all that is part of getting into a lawsuit."

"Well, what you do is mess around with it and then call them for an appointment. Let me know when that is. Now, it's important you let me know, okay?"

"Sure, I'll let you know, but what then?"

"When you are in his office, look into your briefcase for something and make out like you left some documents in your room at the motel."

"He won't see through that?"

"No, clients are always leaving things at home. And anyway, he will not want to see anything untoward. He'll go to the motel and finish up going over that stuff with you. There is no way he's going to make you drive back to your room and then back to his office. Believe me."

"Okay, I understand. Do you have … you know?"

"Yes, right here." Frank reached into a drawer, and as he handed her the envelope of cash, he said, "This is only ten thousand, but rest assured, you will be paid a hell of a lot more when you finish the job."

"That's all I get now?"

"As I said, for right now."

"Okay, I guess. I hope you guys know what you're doing," she concluded while looking around Frank's plush office.

* * * * *

Phil entered Frank's office about an hour after Vickie left. "Okay, Frank, how did it go this time with Mrs. Roberts?"

"Okay, I think."

"You think?"

"Hell, Phil, she's not exactly a dyed-in-the-wool criminal type. How you got her to go along with this is mystifying."

"Nothing mystifying about money. Of course, it helped that she agreed when we were lounging around in my beach cottage." His face glowed as he contemplated an obviously fond memory.

"No doubt naked," Frank chuckled. "How is she anyway?"

"How is she? Hell, you just spoke to her today. You ought to know more about how she is than I do."

Phil was clearly ignoring the true question, and Frank was not about to bring it up again.

"But anyway, that's unimportant," Phil continued. "What's important is getting this jerk down there in hot water with the bar. That new Supreme Court ruling to disbar lawyers who screw their clients with or without consent is really a godsend for us." He paused. "Frank, you think that would apply to queers?" After a moment, he chuckled and answered his own question. "Probably not. Then again, probably would—we can't discriminate, you know." Then he stood up, smiling, clearly enjoying his own wit, and walked to Frank's liquor cabinet. "I think we're on a roll with this thing," he cavalierly remarked as he prepared a scotch on the rocks. "You want a drink too?"

"Sure!" Frank answered. He rarely if ever refused an offer to drink with Phil.

"Then you can come over here and fix it like you like it." Phil returned to his chair, where he hesitated, thinking, and then sat down heavily, stirring his drink.

"Phil, what are we going to do, though, if Vickie can't deliver?"

"We'll go to plan B."

"What is plan B?"

"We'll get her to lie about sex with him."

"Jesus Christ, Phil, it's been hard enough holding this thing together as it is. She'll never consent to that."

"Wrong, Frank. She'll consent, if the money's right."

"Because everybody consents if the money's right, right, Phil?" Frank sarcastically remarked. "But Phil, everybody doesn't have a price. There is such a thing in this world as principle, you know."

"Sure there is, and principles are compromised on a daily basis. Anyway, we've ventured into this rather unsavory aspect of our business, and we've got to finish it up. None of us are proud of what we're doing."

"But if it ends up making us a pile of money, then …"

"Then it's acceptable—in fact, desirable." Phil took a big sip of his drink.

Frank quietly prepared a scotch and water with his back to Phil. At that moment, he had nothing to say. He knew that not only did Phil thrive by living on the edge but that this also was one of his greatest assets in his profession—and with the opposite sex. Life to Phil was a sport with minimal rules; all that mattered was winning. Frank admired that drive to succeed, yet he knew he personally was not constitutionally capable of really living on the edge. He would not thrive; he would die. The ensuing silence was giving him time to think, and the word "qualms" kept popping up in his mind. He couldn't help but be disturbed by the ever-emerging memory of calling Kevin's wife and telling her that he was a friend and Kevin was having an affair. Worse, he couldn't really tell whether she'd believed it. There had been a stony silence at first, and then Sherrie had asked who he was. He had repeated the lie—just a friend—before hanging up.

* * * * *

Within a few weeks, Victoria called Frank Dunn and let him know she had made a late-afternoon appointment to see Kevin about the interrogatories the defense had propounded.

Frank went down the street to a pay phone and called Sherrie Charles. "This is your friend again, Mrs. Charles. I must be brief, so forgive me. But if you're at the Ramada hotel between five thirty and eight o'clock this Friday, you will get a confirmation of what I told you before."

"Who are you?"

"Just a friend," he responded and then quickly hung up the phone.

Sherrie hung up the phone nonplussed. She still didn't believe the so-called friend. It definitely wasn't a friend, she mused. A friend would never tell her such a thing. Then again, she thought about Kevin moving out of the bedroom, and he had come home later than normal several times. In reality, she was seeing something old as new. Kevin had always been late from work from time to time, and she had paid no attention to it. She knew he was a good man. Still, it might be worth investing in a private investigator to watch the motel a few hours. She picked up the phone, and within minutes she had an appointment.

The investigator's office was located on the end of an older strip mall. As soon as she opened the old-fashioned door, opaque glass in its upper half, Angel Bigger rose from his chair at the far end of the room to her left and motioned for her to sit on the other side of his desk. She declined his offer of coffee as she took a seat in front of a cheap metal desk. He resumed his position on the other side.

The gray-colored desk, and for that matter Bigger himself, fit right in with the rest of this small, drab office. The whole office was no bigger than ten by fifteen feet, with the cheapest kind of wood paneling tacked to the walls. A single dusty globe light fixture, suspended about a foot from the Celotex ceiling, provided barely adequate illumination. Mr. Bigger sat in a well-worn, low-back, brown leather easy desk chair in front of the only window in the room. A cream-colored curtain covered the window. Sherrie was sitting in one of two straight-backed wooden chairs for clients. A gooseneck desk lamp sat to Bigger's right on the desk, and further to his right, in the left corner of the room, was a small table with a coffee pot, packs of powdered creamer and sugar, and paper cups. The only other furniture was a very small desk set at the other end of the room. It had a solitary secretary's chair, but no secretary. That desk looked like it had become the receptacle for miscellaneous items. The office was shabby but, except for the dusty light fixture, clean.

Sherrie couldn't shake the nagging notion that she should have simply talked to Kevin. How many times had she heard him say people find out things they really don't want to know? But she swallowed her objections. "Mr. Bigger, there …"

"You sure you would not like a cup of coffee?" he interjected.

She shook her head.

"Please, call me Angel, and I shall call you …" He paused and arched his eyebrows. "Sherrie?" With facial features like a boxer, he was a burly, older, bald-headed man, dressed in a cheap maroon polyester sport coat and awful tie. He definitely didn't come across as formal in any way.

For god's sake, she thought, *he's already on the make, wanting to be familiar right off.* So she didn't smile or try to sound friendly when she said, "If that's customary in your trade, then I will call you Angel."

He picked up on her tone and quickly replied, "Good, good, Mrs. Charles; hopefully, I haven't offended you by my suggestion. Most people these days … they prefer to use first names, you know. It goes along with the way they dress. But so much for the current fashions. What can I do for you?"

"This Friday, the day after tomorrow, I want you to set up a surveillance, or whatever you do, at the Ramada on I-95."

"You brought a picture of your husband?"

"Here it is."

"Oh, for god's sake, I know Mr. Charles. Everyone does. I just didn't connect the two when you called."

"You've never worked for him, though?"

"No, no. There's no reason I can't do what you've asked. But why hire me? You could do it yourself."

"No, he might see me."

"Yeah, I guess that's a possibility."

"So what do we do now?"

"I charge forty dollars per hour for this type of thing. You'll want photographs. Tell you what: pay me two hundred fifty now, I'll do the job, and if you owe me any after that, I'll bill you."

Sherrie nodded in agreement.

"Now give me as many details about Friday night as you can and anything else you know."

Sherrie told him what she knew and paid the two hundred fifty dollars. As she left Angel's office, she felt a strange sense of emptiness and then a weakening nausea in the pit of her stomach; her mind spiraled into conflicting, ambiguous scenarios of things to come. On the one hand, she truly hoped she had spent the two fifty for nothing. On the other hand, she felt it could be the best investment she'd ever made. She was still young and attractive; worse things could happen than her marriage ending, and maybe it was already ending. Either way, she knew a good segment of her life was coming to an end.

Her steps slowed as she nearly turned back to tell Mr. Bigger to forget it. She approached her car with mixed emotions; she hesitated, looked back at Bigger's place, shook her head, opened the car door, and slid into the driver's seat, convinced of absolutely nothing.

* * * * *

After some small talk about her job, how she was coping with her home, and how bad the traffic was, Vickie opened a briefcase and began laying papers on Kevin's desk, allowing him to push a few things aside to accommodate her. Vickie was casually dressed in a khaki skirt, white blouse, and ladies' tennis shoes. "For heaven's sake, Mr. Charles, I can't find some of the stuff," she remarked as if truly astonished.

"Such as …"

"My tax returns—I mean, our tax returns—some of his work commendations, some photographs. God, I must have left a whole bundle of things."

"Well, I guess you could send that stuff later."

"No, no, I know I brought it. It must be in the motel. Mr. Charles, I'll just drive out there real quick and get it. It won't take that long."

"Not the first time that's ever happened," Kevin said as he sat back in his chair. "Leave what you do have, and I can go over that while you're gone. Shouldn't take you more than thirty minutes to drive out there and back."

Crap, she thought. *This isn't the way it was supposed to go. I've just got to deal with it.* "Oh, that should be about right," Vickie answered, but she didn't get up. She was in a quandary. Then she added, "If I don't get lost or something."

"You won't get lost. Surely you know the way by now," Kevin said.

Vickie hesitated. How was she going to get Kevin into the motel room? This part of the plan wasn't working, and it crossed her mind that the whole plan could fail too. *Damn, why didn't I prepare for this?* She had to improvise, but improvise how? As she argued with herself, she reluctantly rose to her feet to walk out. Kevin stood and walked to the door, apparently suspicious of nothing. At least she hadn't given the show away; she consoled herself with that thought as she cavalierly said, "I'll be back in thirty or forty minutes. Sure you don't mind waiting?"

"No, we'll be right here. Or at least I'll be if it's later than five."

"It will be later than five. It's about that time now."

"I often work late," Kevin responded. "Drive carefully now." Vickie walked on out and down the stairs to her car, wondering what she should do. Maybe just give up, mission a failure. No, she wanted the money that came with success. All of this was on her mind as she sat in her car. She hoped the car wouldn't crank as she turned the ignition key. She sighed in relief when the engine leaped to life, purring like a kitten.

At the motel she racked her brain and even thought about calling Frank Dunn or Phil for a solution to this unexpected problem. "No, I won't call anymore," she mumbled as she let herself into her room. She had to be more resourceful than that. She doused her face with water, took a good look at herself in the mirror, and then, exasperated, sat on the bed and called Phil's office. Neither Phil nor Frank was there. She hung up. *I'm on my own, and I've got to take the bull by the horns.* She smiled as the phrase "bull by the horns" reverberated in her head. Kevin Charles was the only man who failed to look lasciviously at her. She had to hit him straight on; there was no other way, she finally concluded.

She rang Kevin's office. He answered.

"Mr. Charles, I'm at the motel in room 118. Would you be so kind as to meet me here? I'm just bushed and a little bit unnerved …"

"Unnerved?"

"Yes, unnerved. I damn near had a real bad wreck a while ago. A big truck ran a red light just as I was pulling away … you know, just starting to step on the gas. I saw him coming from the right just in time to stop. I don't think he missed me by more than inches."

"Well, I'm glad to hear it was only a near wreck. Okay, I'll come on out there."

"You're sure you don't mind?"

"No, I'll just come to your room, and we can finish our business there."

"Oh, I'm such a pest."

"No, don't think that. No reason for you to have to drive back here. It's really no trouble."

"But if we need to make corrections?"

"We can do it later. I'll come directly to your room, okay?"

"Okay," she said. *What's a little lie to convince a man to do what he really wants to do anyway?* she thought.

Driving to the Ramada, Kevin kept thinking of all the little inconveniences he went through for his clients. Sometimes he felt like asking how in the hell they had gotten this far in life being so damned disorganized. Vickie came out to meet Kevin, and he walked across the parking lot toward her.

She was smiling, certainly not acting like she was stressed out from almost having an accident. *What the hell,* he thought, *I guess some people get over that kind of thing pretty fast.* So not thinking much about it, he greeted her with a smile and followed her back into her room. They sat at the standard motel room table and went through some of the paperwork. She had everything, and nothing had to be extensively changed. That took about fifteen minutes. During that time she was in exceptionally good spirits, and when he asked her about the truck almost running into her, she indicated it had shaken her up, but she was now over it and appreciated him coming to her room.

Of course, even though her dark hair was somewhat disheveled, Kevin could not help thinking, *There stands a really fetching woman— innocent, a tad saucy, and above all else, loaded with sex appeal.* It couldn't be explained; she did nothing obviously provocative. Now she was in a motel room right next to him, and her scent was unbelievably fresh yet intoxicating, with just a hint of Chanel No. 5, a perfume he recognized. As they completed the paperwork and he replaced the documents in his briefcase, she moved closer to him and, looking into the briefcase, commented, "Are we sure everything is there?" As he turned to say something, her breast brushed his arm.

He closed the briefcase, picked it up, and hesitated for a moment before saying, "I need to go home."

She looked up, and their eyes met in a meaningful way. She arched her eyebrows, silently delivering the sweet message "do you really want to go?"

He took in a deep breath, buried his better instincts, and quietly murmured, "But I don't want to go," as he laid the briefcase back on the table. Without saying a word, he took her face in his hands and kissed her. Her lips were soft, and her tongue slipped into his mouth and intertwined with his for a brief moment. He pulled back for a second or two, long enough to ask, "Are you sure?" She responded by putting her arms around his neck and pressing up against his body as he embraced her for a truly sweltering kiss. He had never desired a woman more than he did at that moment. The kiss broke, and they fell across the bed.

"Kevin, I'll never cause you a problem," she said. They began to slowly kiss each other on the neck and cheeks and nibbled on each other's ears. There was no rushing. They were taking their time, getting to know each other. There was no real conversation, just short endearing comments to let the other know they cared. And of course, they were engaging in long, sensuous kisses, passionate but not hungry. She was on her back, and he was halfway on her when her legs parted, and he inserted his leg between hers. She was so soft yet firm. He couldn't think of anything except her; nothing else mattered. Not his wife, not his child, not his business, nothing.

He rolled off of her, and they sat up long enough for her to remove his shirt and her blouse. She pulled slightly away, and he could feel her removing her skirt. It was easy for him to slip out of his trousers and shorts. When she reached over to fondle his erection, he slipped his hand into her panties and began to fondle her. She lifted up for him to slide her panties off. They continued to kiss each other, not only on the mouth but also on the neck, cheeks, and ears, and from time to time he would nibble at and suck on her breast. She became wetter and hotter and began to thrust with a slow, erotic rhythm. He told her to let him know when she was ready.

Soon she whispered, "I'm ready."

"Are you sure?"

She whispered back, "Yes," as she began to pull him over on her. As he entered her, she wrapped her legs around him, and they began to thrust in a mutual rhythm. Moving slow and easy at first, they gradually picked up the pace, and their lips met for a long, passionate kiss as they finished. Her legs were still wrapped around him, and she said, "Kevin, I believe I love you," as she gave him a little extra squeeze with her legs. "That was wonderful; you are a really good lover. I want to do that again." Then she gave him a final hug before easing her legs down on the bed.

He rolled off of her and lay on his back for a moment before raising himself on his elbow to look at her. He lightly brushed his fingers over her breast. After a moment, appreciating what a lucky man he was, he tried to warn her. "Vicki, you shouldn't fall in love with me. You know I'm a married man. I would be lying, however, if I told you you're not really special to me. Right now all I want is you."

"I wish you were married to me."

"But I'm not, and I hope my marriage stays together, although there might be some doubt about it right now. You need to understand that. I have no intention of leaving my wife."

"I didn't think you would, but remember, if you do and you want me, I'm available. And I'm not going to cause you any trouble; don't worry about that." She paused a moment before she asked, with some hesitation and almost shyly, "Kevin, can you stay long enough for us to do it again?"

"I'm going to stay whether I have the time or not." He kissed her and massaged her breast. She was more excited about doing it again than he was, but he took it slowly. He needed a little time, but nothing could have stopped him from making love to her again.

"Can I get on top this time?" she asked as she moved over and onto him. So as golfers would say, he got a mulligan that was just as good as his first shot, except she was on top. After finishing the second time, tired but not exhausted, they rolled over. She once again wrapped her legs around him as they hugged and kissed and as she whispered little sweet things. He hadn't had sweet sex like this for years. Sex like this with Sherrie was just a fond memory.

Lying there in bed with Vickie, dreading having to get up and leave her, he said, "I don't want to go, but this time I have to."

"I know, and I wish you didn't have to either." Eventually, they crawled out of bed, washed up, and put their clothes back on. He actually felt good all over. *Maybe*, he thought, *I've lost my mind, but so what!*

Angel Bigger knew Kevin Charles's car and spotted it immediately when the attorney arrived at the motel. Bigger immediately went to work photographing. Kevin was inside the motel about an hour.

CHAPTER 7

S everal days after Kevin and Vickie met at the Ramada, she was in Frank Dunn's office, seated in a big red leather chair in front of his ornate walnut desk. She was dressed in faded jeans and a light blue pullover sweater that innocently accentuated her well-rounded, firm breasts. Her hair was somewhat windblown, and the sandals on her feet complemented her blood-red painted toenails. Looking at her, Frank knew Phil had been telling the truth when he once said (while probably drunk) that she was the most sensuous woman he had ever known. But Frank knew she was out of bounds for him and quickly proceeded with the business at hand. Nevertheless, he felt that special tingling up his leg.

"You just couldn't get that man to tumble, huh?" Frank asked as he adjusted his blue striped tie. *The man must be made out of stone or maybe queer*, he thought. Frank couldn't control the tumescence between his own thighs. But he had to stick to business, so he clenched his teeth and assumed a serious but friendly expression.

"No, and I guess that's about all I can say about it, but I did try."

"Well, Phil will want to see you."

"Why?"

"He's got something to tell you." As she moved to stand, Frank added, "No, don't get up; I'll call him in here."

Frank pushed the intercom button. "Phil, she's here. Yes, sir, I'll tell her." He re-cradled the phone. "Mrs. Roberts, he said he'll be here momentarily. Would you like a cup of coffee or something?"

"No, thank you."

Phil came to the door. "Well, well, Vickie, you look great," Phil said with a warm smile, just before giving her a light peck on the cheek. "Smell good too." He then took a seat in the chair next to her. "Frank tells me we have been partially unsuccessful. Is that true?" he questioned in his peculiarly unctuous way.

Frank marveled at how Phil could be condescending yet somehow not offensive. He was now at his best with Vickie as he smoothly retrieved his tobacco pouch and began to fill his pipe bowl. For most men, that would have been an affectation, but not for Phil. Somehow, for him, the pipe thing seemed natural and appropriate, anything but an ostentatious prop.

"Only partially unsuccessful—what does that mean?" Vickie asked.

"That means we'll simply have to resort to plan B. Mind if I smoke?" Phil asked as he packed the tobacco.

"I would prefer that you didn't." She paused. "And plan B?"

"Yes, my dear, we'll simply switch to plan B. Is it true that you blew the guy a kiss?" Phil paused, with arched eyebrows, as he extinguished a match and put his pipe away.

"Not really." She took a deep breath.

"But it looked like you did. Couldn't have been better planned. And Mrs. Charles had a private investigator taking pictures …"

Vickie looked puzzled.

"You want to know how we know? It was easy. Our investigator just checked with the local private investigators—only three or four in that county, and money talks."

"But nothing happened!"

Frank interjected, "That was a real stroke of genius, Phil, having me call Mrs. Charles. Now we have that photograph."

"True, and I won't deny my intelligence," Phil said as he put his pipe in his pocket.

"Photograph?" Vickie questioned.

"Yes, the guy got several, but the one with you standing in the doorway blowing him a kiss is all we need—in fact, more than we need," Phil said as he held out his hand to Frank, who opened a desk drawer, retrieved a photograph and handed it to him. Phil held up the photograph for Vickie to see. "And you, Vickie, are in error saying nothing happened. The law says what should have happened did happen. Here's a married man and an unmarried pretty woman going into a motel and staying about an hour, and low and behold, when he leaves, she blows him a kiss from the doorway. No one will believe what ought to have happened didn't happen. The truth from him would sound like the lamest kind of fabrication. And that thing at the end, the kiss, that cinched it." Phil looked again at the photo.

"I don't believe he even saw me do it ..."

"No matter. Angel, the PI, did."

"But I was really just physically expressing my relief that it was all over; it was more like a sigh of relief. And I might have waved my hands, so it could have ... no, must have looked like something it wasn't. But so what? It's all over."

"Now, that's where you're wrong. It is not over, not by a long shot."

"What could possibly be next?"

"Frank, you need to pick up here. I've got something in my office that just won't wait. I'll be back in a few minutes."

Vickie began to protest, "What the ...?"

"Now, now, dear, don't get exasperated. I'll be back," Phil said in his most reassuring voice. Frank and Phil left the office for a few minutes, and only Frank returned.

"Nothing has changed. Plan B is the same plan we had before," Frank calmly said as he retook his seat in the big chair behind his desk.

"What do you mean, nothing's changed?"

"Just that."

Vickie rolled her eyes to the ceiling and sat back in her chair. "Does that mean ...?"

"What you think it means? Probably. All you have to do is drop Kevin as your lawyer and file a grievance stating that you and he had carnal intercourse—you know, you knew him in the biblical sense. And I suggest you spice it up by saying it was somewhat kinky. You know, he wanted to be beaten, and in turn he spanked you really too hard, et cetera, and you had never before done anything like that. You state that you are a good girl who felt any deviation from simple intercourse in the missionary position was somewhat abusive ..."

"Mr. Dunn," she blurted out, "can you hear yourself? I believe you're getting some kind of cheap thrill just telling me all this."

"Please don't interrupt, Mrs. Roberts. I'm only making suggestions. Details, however, make truth sound truthful, and more importantly, in this case, details make a lie sound truthful."

"You're a wicked man."

"Now, now, as Phil would say, could be birds of a feather flock together," said Frank in an effort to calm her down. "Here, let me fix you a drink. Gin and tonic, isn't it?"

"Yes, but I don't want a drink."

"Sure you do. It's late in the afternoon, almost closing time, so let's have one to shake away the troubles of the day," Frank urged as he mixed them both a drink. "Just bear with us a little longer. I know you must understand it will be worth your while."

"Worth my while? I'm beginning to wonder, Mr. Dunn, if anything is worth … you know, being so deceitful."

"Here," Frank said as he handed her the gin and tonic. "This should help you see more clearly."

She took the drink with a faraway look in her eyes. Then she looked at the gin and tonic as if in a momentary trance. Suddenly she gushed, just before taking the first sip, "Where's Phil? What does he have to do that's so important?"

The door opened, and Phil strolled back in. "Ah, I see you two are getting along splendidly," Phil observed in his usual suave manner. "And I'll join you for the first drink of the evening." He stepped over to the bar to fix himself a single-malt scotch on the rocks. "Anything transpire between you two I should know about?" he asked as he took his seat in the big chair next to Victoria.

"No, but tell me again now just what I am to do, and …"

"There will be another hundred thousand in cash. Half now and half after the grievance is finished, after the bar finds Kevin Charles to be an unethical lawyer and disbars him, or whatever they are going to do," said Frank.

"I get the money today?" She looked toward Phil.

"Yes, indeed, today. And not only that; you get to have dinner tonight with yours truly. That is, if you don't have another engagement."

"No, not really. I'm just here to see you all."

"Okay."

"Are we through now?"

"Not quite. Frank has a few things you need to know about, but I'm afraid I need to get back to my own office, and I apologize again for that. I'll be back in a few minutes, and you and I can leave the office at the same time. Any questions you might have after talking to Frank …"

well, we can go through all that tonight. He leaned over, gave her a slight peck on the cheek, finished his drink in one swallow, and left.

"Why does he leave this to you?" she asked as Frank handed her an envelope filled with cash.

"I work for him, that's why. And I do it because everything I have, I owe to him. Okay, what you do is …" Frank proceeded to outline how she should terminate Kevin as her attorney and then file a grievance with the Florida bar. Of course, they would pick up and continue with her lawsuit, and there would be no fee for their services.

* * * * *

Phil was delayed in his office, and it was nearly six before he and Vickie left and walked several blocks to the bar in the Omni Hotel. The hotel was one of Jacksonville's best, and the bar was located apart from the hotel's first-class restaurant. Black leather stools surrounded the black circular bar. A few small black tables rested on the dark red carpet between the bar and the wall. The walls were covered by attractive, but somehow lascivious, ornate red wallpaper. The ambience was that of an upscale saloon. The place was not crowded, and Phil chose a table next to the wall, where they sat on well-cushioned chairs opposite each other. "I like this little bar, don't you?" Phil said with a slight nod of his head, wrinkling his brow.

She nodded.

"Good. I'll be right back in a minute." Phil got up and stepped over to the bar. He returned with a single-malt scotch on the rocks for himself and a glass of chardonnay for her.

"Let's have a toast to a sweet evening. It's been a while, you know," Vickie said with a smile as she extended her glass for a toast. Their drinks touched, and then Phil sat back and polished off about half of his scotch. Vickie started to say something about him not drinking too much, but she kept quiet; she knew he could hold his liquor, and she didn't want to have any conflict with him that night. She took only a slight sip of her wine before saying, "Phil, I want to talk to you about what went on in the office this afternoon."

He looked at her, smiled, and waved his hands, with the palms toward her. "Vickie, I'd rather not discuss business right now." Then he took a big swig of his drink to signify that was the end of the matter.

She didn't want to argue. "I guess it doesn't matter right now anyway. Let's just have a nice night, okay?"

Phil polished off the rest of his drink. "I think I'll have another. You?"

"No, not just yet."

Phil looked at his glass, shook the ice, and took one last sip before getting up and going to the bar for another scotch on the rocks. "I'm beginning to relax now," he said as he returned, taking a small sip of his second drink. He sat back down. "I hope you're feeling relaxed and comfortable," he quietly said as he reached over and put his hand over hers.

She gave him a slight squeeze and a knowing smile. "Yes, I'm relaxed and comfortable. But what are we going to do tonight?"

He gave her a mischievous smile.

"Oh, I know what we'll eventually do, and I'll tell you *when*, but between now and then … are we just going to stay here and drink until suppertime, then eat, and then you-know-what, or what?" She took a small sip, brushed her hair back with one hand, and looked around the bar. "Hmm, so this is a cocktail lounge. *Cocktail.* Now that's an interesting word, isn't it?"

"I've never thought about it being interesting. But it is made up of two very interesting words …"

"That's what I mean—*cock* and *tail* to signify a place where people drink and think about cocks and tail to get horny. I think about little things like that once in a while, don't you?"

"Not really. I guess I've been so busy trying to make a living and make something out of myself that I haven't had time to be, for lack of a better expression, philosophically inclined. Have you checked in anywhere?"

"No, I haven't. I just assumed you would want to put me up for the night. But I didn't want to call and ask you for a date—because if you want me, *you* have to ask." She smiled and let her foot brush by his leg, which immediately caused him to shuffle around in his chair. Their eyes locked.

"I thought we would go out to dinner at the beach, then go to my cottage."

"Will I have to change my clothes?"

"No, I think we will have at least one more round of drinks here, and then we can go to the Oyster House out at the beach. We've been there before, and you said you liked it. Is that okay?"

"Sure, sounds good to me, and you know it's after Labor Day; there will hardly be a soul out there ..." She let her sentence trail off.

"So, well, you and I might have the beach to ourselves, and ..." He paused to take a sip of his scotch.

"And maybe we can go swimming in our birthday suits. Of course, I've brought my bikini, just in case." She then sat back, crossed her legs, and smiled at Phil.

They sat there and chatted mostly about nothing really important to Vickie. Phil had only one more drink, which he drank slowly as he talked, maybe too much, about how difficult some of his cases and clients were and how unfairly his ex-wives treated him. But he said more than once how happy he was to see her. After about an hour and a half, Vickie said, "Aren't you getting hungry, Phil? I am."

"Yeah, I think I am." They got up and went over to the bar, where Phil paid the bill. They went to the parking garage where both Phil and Vickie were parked and picked up Vickie's small suitcase she had brought for the night.

They left the garage in Phil's car and went over the Main Street Bridge to get on the main road to the beach. Once on the highway, Phil reached over to feel her leg. She moved his hand and in a playful, friendly tone said, "Don't get too frisky, Phil, not now. I'm not going to play with your thing or do anything on the way to the beach, so don't ask." She hesitated for a few seconds, looked at him with a thin smile, and added, "That will just have to wait. I don't want to be hard to get along with, but I prefer to eat supper and all first. I'll tell you when."

"Did I say I wanted you to do anything?" He furrowed his brow a bit grumpily. Phil then put both hands on the wheel and whistled a few bars of "Dixie."

She thought for a moment before answering. "You didn't say it, but you were thinking it, right?"

"Well, yeah, probably I was," he said with a grin. "You blow—I mean *know*—me pretty well, don't you?" He was still grinning.

"You think you're so funny, don't you?" she chuckled. She paused like she was thinking. "Hmm, maybe later, after supper. We'll just have to wait and see." She giggled and reached over to touch Phil on his leg. "Don't worry, we're going to have a really good night." She then sat back and looked out the window, making comments about what she saw. That was the extent of their conversation until they drove into the shell-covered parking lot at the Oyster House, a freestanding old beach restaurant.

After a bottle of Cakebread cabernet sauvignon, a seafood dinner for her, and two dozen chilled oysters on the half shell for Phil, he asked, "You think it's warm enough tonight for a swim?"

"Sure, it'll be fun. The sooner the better."

"Then no dessert right now." He wickedly smiled.

"No, not right now." She coyly smiled back as her eyes caught his.

They were soon undressing each other in Phil's beach house. Located in the old section of Neptune Beach, it was a twelve-hundred-square-foot cypress board-on-board cottage. Vickie was again impressed with Phil's physical attributes. His chiseled—perhaps even patrician—facial features, generally piercing gray-green eyes, and full heavy beard, which always showed a five o'clock shadow despite a clean shave every morning, complemented a firm, athletic body. He was well over six feet tall, and she particularly liked to let her fingers wander about his broad, hairy chest. She wondered how, living the kind of life he lived, he stayed in such good physical shape. He had told her before that it was his genes, that he came from a tough down-and-out family.

They laughed and giggled as they undressed each other and slipped into their bathing suits, but he bowed to her preference, and they refrained from passionate caressing of each other; there was only some incidental slight touching. It was part of a ritualistic foreplay. Without much delay, however, they were heading out the back door to the beach for a late-night swim. It was a clear, moonless evening, and the sky was filled with twinkling stars.

Their mutual interest was unquestionably carnal, but above all else, it was money. They were soon bobbing up and down in the waves. She said, "I'm ready," as a wave lifted their feet off of the sandy bottom, and Phil slid his hand underneath her thong and gently stroked between her thighs. "Oh, that's good," she murmured as her hands fumbled under his bathing suit to reach his erection.

"Jesus, Vickie, it's a good thing the beach is deserted. If you keep this up," he managed to say through shallow breaths, "we've got to move to the shallow surf ..."

"So we can fuck," she whispered. With their feet touching the bottom most of the time, they began walking and floating toward the beach. As they lay side by side, facing each other on the wet sand, her hand was busy removing his bathing suit; he rolled over on his back and drew up his legs as her hand pushed off his trunks. As his bathing suit slipped from his lifted feet, he entered her mouth. After a few moments, she pulled her head up and said, "Are you ready for me to lie down?"

"Yes," he said while removing the skimpy little bottom of her bathing suit. Once it was off, she spread her legs, and Phil went on his knees between them. He began stroking her pubic area and sliding his fingers in and out. Then he lowered his head between her legs. She held her hands on the back of his head as her pelvis hunched upward in a rhythmic motion.

"Uh-uh, I'm about to come. Put it in," she said as the muscles in her stomach and thighs tightened. Phil raised his head and entered her. After a minute or so, she made one final thrust. Then she fell back, euphorically relaxed. "Oh, that was quick but good," she said.

He slightly shivered and then made two slow final thrusts. They just lay there for a minute, catching their breath. She moved her legs from around his and let them drop restfully on the watery sand.

"Was it good, though?" Phil asked. He hadn't yet made any moves to get off of her. He just lay there, completely relaxed.

"Was it good? Didn't you hear me say it was? I love it when we come at the same time. But you're going to have to get off of me or hold yourself up on your elbows or something. You know you're heavy," she said as she gently pushed on his chest. He rolled off of her and lay on his back. She sat up for a minute and slid her thong back on. "Phil, put your bathing suit back on. You know somebody might just walk by."

"Huh, you didn't seem to care much about where the bathing suits were a while ago." He paused for a moment. "And I just might want to do that again. Give me a little time here. Let me recuperate. Then ..."

"Then nothing," she said as she handed him his bathing suit. She was looking up and down the beach. "Well, I don't really see anybody, but you're not ready again anyway, not now," she said as she looked at him.

"I guess you're right. I'm not quite ready, at least not yet. But I'm going to be."

She smiled.

"Vickie, you are a beautiful woman, and I mean beautiful all over. Sex with you is out of this world, but there's something else, something about you that makes me feel wonderful. Do you have any special feelings about me?"

"Phil, I obviously like you a lot. And tonight you'll get whatever you want. So put on your bathing suit, and let's take a walk down the beach, okay?"

"Oh, I don't know. I guess we can do that, but why do you want to take a walk?" he asked. Then he leaned over and kissed her. She kissed him back.

"Oh, Phil, that was nice."

"Now, Vickie, why did you say you wanted to take a walk?"

"I didn't say … Come on. We don't have to walk a long way, just a little walking to get reinvigorated, okay?" She put her arm around his waist, and they started strolling down the deserted beach. Neither one said anything for a while.

Leaning close to her, Phil murmured, "I can't help it, Vickie, I believe you are the most beautiful woman I have ever known." Hugging her for a moment, he then added, "You know what you said a while ago?"

"About?"

"Being reinvigorated. Well, I think I'm getting ready for something." He raised her chin up and kissed her. She pressed against his body.

"I think I am getting ready too. Let's walk back up to the house." She hugged his waist as they started angling across the beach toward Phil's cottage.

The outdoor shower was just an open area over a cement slab on the north side of the cottage, but it was well shielded from observation by a fence. As they stepped onto the slab, Phil said, "This will be a little cold—that okay?"

"Sure, turn it on. We'll get used to it in a minute." The cold water was refreshing, and it didn't take long to feel comfortable. She picked up the shampoo and began to shampoo what hair he still had and her own. They both slipped out of their bathing suits and hung them up to dry. She picked up the soap and lathered her front, while Phil soaped her back. Completely covered in suds, she began lathering the front of his body; then he turned around at her request, and she lathered up his back, below his waist, and down and up his hairy legs. He was covered in soap. She moved around and pressed her body up against his chest.

He drew back a little and said, "I think a little blow job would be nice, don't you?"

"Well, we'll just have to see, won't we?"

"You're teasing me, aren't you?"

"Like I said, we'll see," she said as she slid her soapy fingers up and down his back. She then backed away and wrapped her fingers around his nearly flaccid phallus. "Hmm," she said, giving it a slight squeeze. Then she giggled, let go of it, and stepped fully under the shower. "It's time for us to rinse off and go inside."

Vickie again wondered about Phil, about how different he was when he was out of his office and with her, either here in the cottage or anywhere. She felt he actually might have a soft side.

CHAPTER 8

Once inside the cottage, Vickie went to brush her hair while Phil prepared himself a scotch on the rocks. When she returned to the living room, she found him seated on the couch with his drink. She fixed herself a mild gin and soda and joined him on the couch. Wearing only a terrycloth bathrobe, she pulled her legs up under her, like women do, and faced him.

"I think I'd like some munchies. Do you have anything in the fridge?"

"I think there might be some nuts or something."

"Okay, I'll be back in a minute."

Vickie walked to the kitchen and searched the refrigerator for a snack. She found some kind of breakfast rolls and a can of unopened cashews. She sauntered back into the living room holding the can of nuts. Phil was still there, wearing only his bathrobe, taking a sip of his scotch on the rocks—but only a sip. When he saw her come into the room, he put his drink back on the table. She took a seat on the couch beside him, opened the can of nuts, and then placed them on the coffee table.

"Well, Vickie, I see you found something."

She lightly laughed.

"What's so funny?"

"Oh, I don't know. I guess I thought it was ironic that all I could find to eat was this can of nuts." She picked up the can of cashews, took some for herself, and offered the can to Phil. He picked up a few and gave her a quizzical look.

She smiled innocently as their eyes met and lightly pushed him on the shoulder. She picked up her glass for a small sip. Phil did the same. *Good*, she thought. Phil began running his fingers through her slightly wet hair. Then he put a barely touched drink back on the table and reached under her robe for her breast. She pushed aside his robe and began to fondle his hairy chest.

"Vickie, you smell so good. Hmm, I don't think I'm going to be able to resist you, not much longer anyway." He slid his hand down from her breast to her pubic area. "I'm ready," he whispered while searching her mouth for another tongue-filled kiss.

Finishing the kiss, she said, "What do you want, a blow job right here and right now?"

"It'll be fun; let's do it right here." He then took a final sip of his drink and leaned back on the couch.

"And you're all ready?"

"All you have to do is lift up my bathrobe to find out."

She pushed his robe open. "Well, it's obvious that you're ready." She took it in her mouth. A couple of minutes later, she moved onto her knees between his legs.

Phil moaned, "Oh, that's wonderful. But I want to do you, okay?"

"Okay."

"Sit here on the couch," and while she was moving, he got between her legs, with his face in her groin.

"I thought you wanted me to suck you off."

"I did," he said. "Just wait a minute; then I'll stick it in."

"Hmm." She placed her hands on the back of his head.

In a minute or so, Phil looked up at her and said, "You ready to fuck?"

"Okay. Let's go get in the bed?"

"No, let's do it right here on the floor."

"All right, if you say so."

"It'll be kind of fun doing it here in the living room. Just lie down."

She positioned herself on the rug. Phil got a couch pillow, and she lifted up so he could slide it under her ass. "Thanks," she said. "Better for you too, you know."

"Yeah, I know." Then he entered her, and she wrapped her legs around him. They fell silent. Five minutes later, after they both had finished, Phil leaned over her and kissed her on the neck and shoulders and then rolled off onto his back, exhausted, with his right hand under his head as a pillow. With his left hand, he slowly caressed her arm, which was loosely resting on his chest as she lay on her side next to him, with her leg slung over his. The only sound now was their ebbing heavy breaths. Then he said, after a couple of sniffs, "Damn, Vickie, can you smell that great sex?"

"Uh-huh, and speaking of smelling, neither this cottage nor your place in town smells like anybody has been smoking."

"That's because nobody has been smoking here, or anyplace else where I live."

"But you smoke your pipe in your office."

"Years ago, I quit smoking cigarettes, but I promised myself a pipe smoke every now and then in the office. I intended to eventually quit smoking it also—you know, taper off."

"How many years ago did you quit smoking cigarettes?"

"Probably about twenty," Phil chuckled. "It's taking me a long time to taper off the pipe, but soon ..." He let the sentence trail off with a smile. "You and I have got something going here, girl, that can't be beat. Thank you for the best sex—no, loving—I have ever had."

"You're welcome."

"I think I'm about ready to go to bed to go to sleep. How about you?"

"I think I'm ready too," Vickie said. She patted his chest and started to get up. "I'm going to the bathroom to brush my teeth, wash up, and get ready for bed."

"So am I," Phil said as he began to stand up.

She was already naked in bed when Phil came in. He opened a window, saying, "I like to hear the ocean at night, don't you?" He then sat down on the side of the bed before rolling over to her; he was naked too.

Was this the time to tell him she really did not want to go through with this plan to ruin Kevin? She needed the money, but ... "Phil, I can't really figure out how to say this. You really have been so good to me. But I just don't feel right about out-and-out lying."

"Vickie, none of us feel right about it. It's been bothering me too," he sighed. "Tell you what," he continued as he rolled over on his side. "We'll talk some more about it in the morning, okay?" He then turned off the light and patted his pillow. "I'm sleepy. Let's go to sleep."

"Okay." But she wasn't happy that he wasn't ready to talk about it, and what would his attitude be in the morning? Was he telling the truth tonight? Phil would lie, and she knew it. But she didn't feel like she could deal with it, not right then. He was beginning to breathe like he was sleeping. The night was quiet except for the soothing sounds of breaking waves. She kept cogitating on different solutions if Phil didn't agree to do the right thing, until she was mentally exhausted and slipped into a deep sleep.

During the night they had shifted around, and Phil was now snuggled up next to her back when she awoke to the sounds of breaking waves. It was barely daybreak. Phil was not awake yet, but she could feel him next to her. She felt him stir a little and slightly move away from her. He smacked his lips and started hunching. *Is he awake, or is he having a dream?* she wondered. She was getting aroused. *But if I'm to succeed*, she thought, *I'd better hold off till later.*

"Phil, you awake?" she asked as she rolled off the bed.

"Yes. Don't you want to get back in the bed?"

"No, I'm going to get dressed."

"Well, not okay, but I need to get dressed too and get on into the office. I've got things to do. Let's take a shower, have a cup of instant coffee and a sweet roll—which is all I have here for breakfast—and head back to Jacksonville. Will you forgive me for not buying breakfast this time?"

"Oh, I don't need a big breakfast. Anyway, who knows, I might have a little something on the way back to Jacksonville," she said with a closed-lip smile and arched eyebrows.

CHAPTER 9

Later, when she came into the kitchen fully dressed in jeans and a pullover white blouse, she found Phil in the kitchen sipping a cup of instant coffee. He had on last night's suit. She fixed herself a cup of coffee and began munching on a roll as she sat down at the table. "Phil, are you ready now to talk to me about what went on in the office yesterday? You said last night that you would talk about it with me today."

"And I will. I've been thinking about it myself. I think we can abandon this whole damn thing," he said. "I'm trying to figure out something ..."

"What the hell do you mean, you *think*? All you have to do is *just not do it*," she said with an edge to her voice. She knew he was lying. He wasn't going to change anything. He was lying to her because he wanted something from her, probably a blow job.

"No, Vickie, it's not really that easy. I just used the word 'think' rhetorically. I'll explain it to you on the way into town, okay? Finish up your coffee so we can go. I want to try to beat most of the early morning traffic."

He finished his coffee. Vickie sat at the table and speculated on what she might do. She knew he loved sex, was greedy, and was a liar. She also knew that she herself loved sex and had recently become greedy, but she really didn't think she was much of a liar, even though she had been lying a hell of a lot more lately. She flashed him a doubting smirk as they got up to leave the cottage.

As they merged onto the main four-lane highway back to Jacksonville, the traffic was beginning to build up. Phil was engaging her in some chitchat about a hearing scheduled that morning. She was barely listening. How could she get Phil to do the right thing? While she was thinking and Phil was rambling, he began spreading his legs. She watched him start stroking his groin.

"I'm not in the mood for that, and it's your fault."

"Really?"

"Yes, *really*, and you know what I'm talking about." She sat back in her seat.

"Come on, Vickie, just touch it. You said earlier you would probably have something on the way into town. I thought that meant you wanted …?"

"No, Phil, that was just an offhand remark. But knowing you …" She let the sentence trail off as she looked out the window with a disgusted expression. "And even if you really believe I meant it, you can now believe I've changed my mind. I'm not going to do it, not here. I just don't want to."

"If I say please?"

"If you say please, maybe I'll *think* about it," she said sarcastically.

"Please, Vickie, you know it might be a while before we see each other again." He then unzipped his pants and pulled it out. "Just touch it; you don't have to do anything else. Just touch it."

"Maybe when we get to Jacksonville. Let's talk about something else. And put that back in your pants."

"Well, we can talk about anything, but my mind will be on you-know-what," he said as he put it back in his pants.

"Phil, I like you a lot better when you don't insist on me doing something I really don't want to do."

"I'm actually a considerate sort of guy. Maybe when we get to the garage, okay? We'll be there in just a little while anyway. Probably be best to wait, particularly since the traffic has picked up so much."

There wasn't much conversation between them for the rest of the drive, except for a few comments with respect to the early morning news Phil had turned on after realizing there would be no sex on the highway. Finally, they reached the Main Street Bridge, and Phil had to contend with the early morning traffic coming into Jacksonville.

Soon Phil was guiding his tinted-windowed Mercedes into a secluded parking space three floors up in the parking garage. "Well, we're here," he said as he cut the engine and slid his seat all the way back.

"Don't unbuckle your seatbelt. Leave it on. Just let me do it."

"Can I touch you while you're doing it?" he asked, but he left his seat belt strapped over his waist.

"It will be okay to touch me, if I do this. Just don't touch my head. You know I really don't want to do this anyway." She took off her seatbelt and moved around in the seat to face him.

"For Christ's sake, what do you mean, *if you do this*?"

She pointed her finger at him. "I'm pissed, and you know why. I do and do for you. But when I ask you to just talk to me about something, you think you can just shrug it off."

"You can't say I didn't do some really nice things for you last night."

"I have to admit that's true, but—"

"But what? Why the hell are we arguing? Don't you really want to do this?"

"Not right now."

"Well, I'm ready. Are you?" He pulled it out.

"No, not yet. I need to know what you have come up with about Charles."

"Well," he said, hesitating, "I haven't come up with any real answers that would allow us to change the plan."

"What the hell are you talking about?"

"It didn't occur to me last night, but I've got to control my secretary."

"Control your secretary?" *Where is this coming from?* she thought, more mystified than anxious.

"Yes, you know, the prim and proper woman who sits outside my office. You should also know she is really great sex, and I pay her very, very well."

"So what does she have to do with us?"

"She heard you, when you first came to my office, say you didn't believe you had a decent case because your husband had clearly stated that morning that he knew it was dangerous to use the grinding wheel on his sander, but he was going to take a chance. And even if it flew apart, he would just have to buy another wheel."

"I never said that—not to you, not to anybody!" she protested. She knew what he was saying: he would destroy her case if she didn't go along with the plan, or at least he was threatening to destroy it. "You son of a bitch."

"Yes, my dear, you did say it, and it's not privileged. My secretary heard you commenting about it, in my presence, as she was taking notes. And I might say, she has given me some sharp glances when you come to the office. Oh yes, she knows," Phil lied.

Vickie was speechless for a moment. "How could you sink so low? There's nothing you haven't thought of, is there?"

"I certainly hope not. But I think I might have just talked myself out of you-know-what."

"You can repeat that in spades." She was stunned by this new revelation, and the last thing she wanted to do was have sex with this bastard. She now felt the biggest mistake of her life had been getting personal with Phil. This new twist left her more and more nauseated as she slowly opened the door to get out. She felt people were basically rotten, but she had expected better out of him. She certainly was not in love with him, but she did like him, or she had until now.

"So let me walk you to your car, okay?"

"You stay in the car. I don't need you to walk me anywhere."

"Sure?"

"Goddamn sure," she snapped. She got her suitcase out of the backseat, closed the door, and walked away. *Phil doesn't know it yet*, she thought, *but he has met his match this time.* She was calming down, but not forgetting or forgiving, and a thin smile suffused her face. Her plan to extract money from Phil by lying to him about whether she'd slept with Kevin (she had expected him to simply offer her more money to try again) had gone as far as it would go—indeed, had already gone better than expected. But when she reflected on her follow-up plan, the smile disappeared. She could have gotten even more money but was now thwarted by Phil's exhortation about his secretary. *I will have to work on that*, she thought. *But why am I working on anything like this plan to do Kevin Charles in?* She blanched and shook her head in the darkness of the garage; she couldn't help but have second thoughts. The only thing sure was that nothing was sure. No sir, not in this world. No one really knew anything.

Her early life and impoverished circumstances had left her skeptical and cynical. Although she had managed to hide it well, it was always with her. When Cornell came into her life, all that had changed. He had made her happy, and with his death, her nearly forgotten old feelings, that the world and the people in it were basically rotten, regained a foothold in her view of life. Trying to understand, she concluded the unfairness of Cornell's death had made her bitter. Maybe that was it. That simple thought wafted through her mind as she cranked her old Honda and started for Palatka.

* * * * *

Phil sat quietly in his Mercedes and watched her walk away. *Should I get out and go after her? Jesus, what am I thinking? What is wrong with me? She's made her choice, and so have I. I can't waste my time thinking about her.* Try as he might, however, he couldn't stifle the temptation to go after her and promise her anything if she would agree to see him again. He rubbed his brow and shook his head. *But I will not grovel—she would love that.* Still in the car, trying to make up his mind, he saw her Honda leaving. With a "who gives a damn" shrug, he started the car and slowly maneuvered out of the garage. As he proceeded to his downtown condominium, he tried to bury any and all thoughts of Victoria under the myriad other concerns wafting through his mind.

But as he drove to the condo, entered, and changed clothes, the image of Victoria continued to slip into his mind over and over. No matter how hard he tried, Phil could not convince himself that he could stick with his decision. The idea of never seeing her again, in the personal sense, left him with a strange emptiness. *Why did I act so rashly? Why couldn't I have just stuck with my decision last night, to work out any possible problems with Mr. Charles some other way? Why did I change my mind when we parked and have to dream up that crap about my secretary?* His mind began to flash back to other disturbing events in his life, and a feeling of worthlessness washed over him like a bad omen.

Perplexed by his inability to shake her out of his mind, he gritted his teeth and mumbled, "I'm not that weak. No, nothing will happen to me if I never see her again. I've still got it. I can keep my eye on the ball. Right now she is a necessary evil, and I've just got to put up with the bitch." Yet when he left the condo, contradictory thoughts about her raced through his mind until he walked into his office. Upon arriving, he was his usual affable but serious self, throwing out the customary morning greetings.

Once seated behind his desk, however, he found images of Vicki continuing to cross his mind. *God, I don't think I can stay away from her. If I can't patch up this riff, what am I supposed to do? Am I going to do what she wants me to do and hope for the best as far as Mr. Charles is concerned?*

Then he heard a knock. "Yes?"

"Phil," Frank said as he opened the door and stepped over the threshold.

"Not now," Phil said, stopping him before he could say more. "Please don't bother me unless it's something that you *must* bother me about."

"Okay. I'll get back in touch with you only if I have to."

"Good," Phil said.

Later, toward noon, Phil knocked on Frank's door and quietly asked, "May I come in?"

"Sure. You seem like you have the weight of the world on your shoulders," Frank said.

"Sometimes I feel like I do, Frank. But I've got to make sure about that case you're working on. Why do I feel like I have to do everything around here myself? Can you tell me why? I know the people around here—at least I hope the people around here—are trying to help me. But I just never know … I haven't been able to really focus this morning. We must all stay vigilant … You understand I'm depending on you. I've got a lot to think about, but I need to really get with it for the rest of the day."

Frank said nothing but just patiently waited.

Phil felt like he couldn't stop the urge to call Vickie, but he barely entertained the thought before dismissing it; he had to wait a day or several days. *I simply can't let my passion for her distract me from the central task,* he decided. *I have to do what my intuition tells me I must do to ensure success; Mr. Charles must be struck from participating.*

"Vicki is a sweet woman," he said aloud, "but can be intractable if she wants something. I don't believe she will ever change her mind. Because of that, I should stay away from her." Again he stopped talking and rubbed his chin, thinking. *If I'm around her, I'll give in to whatever she wants. The truth is, I don't think I have control anymore. If I keep her out of sight, then I can keep her from getting what she wants.* "I think it would be better if Victoria and I were never alone together. It would probably be best if we never saw each other under any circumstances."

"Okay, Phil, we'll try to work it that way."

"Fine," Phil snapped.

CHAPTER 10

I n September 1994, Kevin got a call from Vickie. "You can't meet me at the Ramada Friday afternoon?" she asked.

"No, Vickie, I can't," he replied.

"Well, when can we get together again? It's been nearly three weeks now, and I want to see you."

"I don't know."

"You haven't even returned some of my phone calls until a day later."

"That's not unusual."

"But I thought we had something special, that's all. I'm getting the feeling you don't want to really see me again," Vickie said with a note of distress in her voice.

Damn, Kevin thought, *I knew better than to let this kind of thing get started. She's vulnerable, and I took advantage of her; that she wanted it too is beside the point.* But he knew she had to be placated. "Tell you what I can do; I can see you in my office Friday at three o'clock in the afternoon."

"But that's your office," she softly replied.

"I know, but that's the best I can do." Kevin was feeling like a cad and a fool. No doubt, he had misled her. He had, however, also misled himself. *I don't want to hurt her*, he thought, *but ...*

"Okay, I'll see you then."

Kevin waited for her to hang up before murmuring, "Damn," to himself. He then turned to busy himself with matters piled up in his intake tray.

Vickie hung up the phone and looked wistfully from the back porch out on the small farm she and Cornell had called home. Tears welled up as her eyes focused on the red barn where Cornell had died. She had come a long way from the wrong side of the tracks in Jennings.

Her mind drifted back to her childhood. She tried to forget, but sometimes, when she felt alone, the bad memories emerged. She could once again smell the alcoholic stench of her father as he placed his big rough hands under her pajamas and slid his sweaty nude body into the bed next to her, drunkenly slurring how much he loved her and how he had to have her. She was only ten years old when it began and thirteen when it ended. She had wanted to tell her mother, but he said if she did, he'd kill her and her mother. Her two older brothers were always trying to see her naked too. Her mother beat them for that sometimes. Her mom worked all night as a waitress in a diner and didn't seem to be around that much. Dad, a supposed mason, engaged in only an occasional day-labor job.

She shivered at the memory, cleared her eyes, and rubbed her forehead. Had she really killed her dad? She had lied to him that wintry night that seemed both like yesterday and like long ago; it could have been another lifetime. He had stood in her doorway, naked from the waist down, with a bottle of whiskey, acting like he wasn't sure whether he wanted to come in or not. He had just stood there, slurring words she couldn't understand.

She had jumped out of bed and retreated to the corner of the room, holding a three-foot metal pipe tightly in both hands. When he crossed her threshold, she warned him that she had told her teacher at school what he had done, and the police were going to arrest him. It wasn't true, but it stopped him in his tracks. She knew she would kill him if he came any closer. By a glimmer of light from the hallway, she could discern his tormented face, particularly his eyes, wild and on fire with rage. He let out a wild, eerie scream and started to chugalug the whiskey as he turned away from her. Throwing the empty bottle down, he drunkenly slurred, "All is lost," and then staggered into the hall, where she heard him fall. No one else was in the house. Her mother was working, and her brothers, both older, were hanging out somewhere in town. She quickly picked up the bottle and placed it in the kitchen. Then she dragged his body into the kitchen, so that her brothers wouldn't see him in the hall when they came home. She was thirteen years old, and she hoped he would die, either from the fall or from the whiskey. She didn't care which.

The next morning, her mother's loud howl from the kitchen shocked Vickie awake. She had found his dead body.

Vickie jumped out of bed and walked to the kitchen, where her mother angrily accused her. "You did this, didn't you? I don't know how you did it, but you did it …" Vickie knew her mom had seen her father cast incestuous glances at her. Her mother had even accused her, falsely, of trying to manipulate him for favors. Reflecting on the whole sordid mess, Vickie also knew that her father was her mom's man, and her mother wanted to keep him, no matter how worthless he was.

"No, Mom," she'd guiltily responded, with a slight bit of self-recrimination, because she actually did feel some guilt. But damn it, she couldn't help but be glad the son of a bitch was dead.

By then her mom was insanely trying to revive the dead by slapping him in the face and demanding in an ever-escalating tone of anguish, "Live, you rotten bastard! Live, goddamn it! I said live! You can't leave me like this!" She went on and on for at least five minutes.

Suddenly, she stopped and told Vickie to call 911. She then collapsed into a kitchen chair with a bewildered, lost look on her face. The boys were up by then. The emergency medical people came and took his body. Eventually, the autopsy revealed the cause of death to be acute alcohol poisoning.

Her mother refrained from accusing Vickie again for a couple of years. Then one night, she again alluded to the death of "the love of her life" being somehow due to her ungrateful daughter. The next morning, Vickie was gone, and she never returned.

She got a job as a waitress in a truck stop. It was there she had met Cornell, the best thing that had ever happened to her. The truck stop, south of Jacksonville, was called South of the Border, just over the Duval County line on US Route 1. It was well known as a house of ill repute. But the proprietor had let Vickie work only as a waitress. Pretty and alluring, she was expected to get the men she waited on anxious for sex, so that they would then go upstairs, where it could be bought. Cornell was different. He wasn't concerned about buying sex. He'd told her soon after they met that she was the one and only for him.

Vickie's melancholy reminiscing slowly faded as she walked into the kitchen to dab away the tears with water from the sink. She had to keep focused on the matter at hand, she told herself as she splashed water on her face. She knew it wasn't true, but her mom's accusation lingered the longest when she thought about those dark days, almost like the accusation made it so. *And now,* she thought, *I have to deal with this Kevin Charles thing.* Should she just tell him what was going on and let him help her resolve it? She knew she would if they started having sex regularly—what nice people called an affair. She might anyway; she felt she might already be in love with him, but if not, she definitely could fall in love with him. But if they didn't continue, well, she didn't know; she would simply have to wait and see.

* * * * *

"You think we could slip away for just a while? I have really missed you," Vickie said immediately after Kevin closed the door to his office. She put her arms around his neck and pressed up against him.

"No," he said as he took her arms down and backed away. "Have a seat." He held the office chair for her and then sat beside her in the other chair. "Vickie, that one afternoon was a mistake. You were, well, for lack of a better word, vulnerable, and I took advantage of you. But it can't happen again. I am … well, let's say, very fond of you, and if I were not married, well, maybe something could come of it …" His voice trailed off. After a short pause, he continued. "But I am married, happily, I think." In truth, he was beginning to have second thoughts about his marriage. "Please try to understand. The last thing in this world I want to do is hurt you." He paused again. "And, of course, my wife."

"Oh, Kevin, I just want to love you." she said with disappointment in her voice.

"I hope this doesn't affect our professional relationship …" Kevin's concern about losing a client with a big-money case was escalating. He hoped his tone would not betray him. Somehow he had to turn the situation around without giving in to her. He was about to suggest that she needed to put this relationship back on a professional level, but before he could, she spoke with what seemed calculated anger.

"You hope not. Listen to yourself. You're no different from any other man who wanted to get in my pants. How could I have been so stupid?" She shook her head and pointed her finger at him. "Kevin, I thought you were really a sweet man. I came here to tell you something, something important, but not now."

"Please, please!" Kevin pleaded while quickly considering that her behavior in this moment was not consistent with what he knew about her. But then he didn't really know anything about her. He knew he would make no more overtures; what was going to happen was just going to have to happen. With that realization, his regret melted. In fact, he felt relieved. What she had told him about Cornell and the other facts she'd supplied for her wrongful death case may or may not have been truthful or maybe she was delusional. "Vickie, let me get you a drink."

"No, Kevin, If we can't have a personal relationship. . ." she said, burying her face in her hands. Then she looked up and with wet eyes firmly stated, "Kevin, I want to change lawyers."

"Vickie, if that's what you want to do, I'll definitely not try to stop you, and for the work I've done, well, I'll contact whoever you go to ..."

"You're not going to get a goddamn thing out of this. You've had your pound of flesh, and that's all you get. Don't you try ..." She spoke with force and conviction even while dabbing the tears away. Kevin stood up, went behind his desk, called a secretary on the intercom, and held his hand up for Vickie to quiet down.

"Yes, Mr. Charles?" Carol asked.

"Mrs. Roberts has decided to change attorneys. Get the file prepared so we can expeditiously deliver it to her new lawyer with the information we have so far. And make sure her new lawyer knows we are not asking for an attorney's fee lien."

"Is that all, Mr. Charles?"

"For right now, yes." He hung up the phone and turned back to Vickie. "Vickie, if there was anything to say that would help rectify this situation, I would say it, but I don't think there's anything I—"

"Correct, Mr. Charles," she said, cutting him off. "There's nothing you can say. And you'll be hearing from my new attorney in a few days," she said as she got up.

Sometimes we succeed, and sometimes we fail, thought Kevin as he watched a million-dollar case saunter out of his office and probably out of his life. He wasn't sure he liked either loss, but he would survive. Somehow, however, a strong foreboding that this would not be the end of it lingered. His wife had been acting cold and unhappy but wouldn't really tell him anything, and now Vickie had done this. Surely she was aware that a tryst had been her idea. And he had never said anything to make her believe it was anything more than a casual episode. On the other hand, he knew that people, particularly women, could read into a person's words things that simply weren't there. He tried not to let a perplexing thought emerge, but he couldn't suppress it. The state bar frowned on an attorney having sex with his client, and it could actually lead to disbarment. Would she go that far? Hell has no fury like a woman scorned, or something like that, Shakespeare had said. On the other hand, she wasn't scorned. He also knew it ultimately didn't matter if she wasn't. What mattered was her perception.

He shook his head as he walked over to the window. There was something here that wasn't right, but he couldn't zero in on it. There had to be more to all of this than what she'd said, but what? A lot of scenarios were floating around in his brain and one came to the surface. Had she really been at the Ramada that first night?

He called the Ramada again and checked to see whether she had registered at any time that given night and was told she hadn't. So on that first night, she definitely was not registered at the Ramada. Why would she claim she was? Kevin massaged his chin and blinked his eyes in puzzlement. The refrain "something evil this way comes" kept emerging in the recesses of his mind. Why couldn't he squelch that ominous foreboding that something truly evil was afoot? Why hadn't Gary LaBlanc called him for a referral fee? "Goddamn it, I can't just sit back and let things happen," he mumbled. He would make things happen. He always had. A sense of satisfaction surged through his being as he resolved to take action. But his resolve had to be tempered with thought and caution. He buzzed Carol. "Get me Gary LaBlanc on the phone. He's a lawyer in Palatka."

A minute later, Carol buzzed him back. "He's on the line," she said.

Kevin picked up the phone. "Gary, we met once at a continuing legal education thing in Orlando. I was one of the lecturers, Kevin Charles. I also recently took over a probate case you were handling."

"Sure, I remember you."

"The lady we are doing the probate for came to see me a few weeks ago. Her name is Vickie Roberts. Her husband was killed when a grinding wheel flew apart. Someone referred her to me."

"Why are you calling me?"

"She told me it was you."

"Kevin, a lady with that kind of case did come to see me. That's all I feel comfortable saying. You know how sensitive certain folks are with confidentiality."

"I sure do. Thanks anyway." An inordinate silence followed. "You sure you don't have something else to say about this matter?" Kevin asked with caution. At least for the moment, he would not argue if LaBlanc said no. He wouldn't challenge the man if he chose not to tell him anything.

There was a short pause before LaBlanc said, "Kevin, as far as I'm concerned, we never had this conversation, okay?"

"Not quite okay, but I guess it will have to do … and, well, thanks." Kevin hung up the phone, more puzzled now than ever. Something smelled, and he had to find out what it was. LaBlanc knew something, and his reticence to discuss it went far beyond the normal lawyer-client confidentiality. *I've got to figure out some way to resolve this thing*, he thought, *but where do I go from here?*

* * * * *

"You're terribly silent tonight, or are you just sour?" Sherrie said while standing by the microwave across the breakfast bar from where Kevin was sitting, waiting for some kind of frozen-food concoction for dinner.

"Let's just get a bottle of wine, okay?" he said with a certain surliness.

"You get it if you want it."

"Okay," he calmly said as he got up to go to the bar. He reflected on the fact that lately, meals had been mostly of the same low quality as tonight's dinner. He returned with a bottle of white wine.

"Why did you get white wine when we're having meatloaf?"

"Because I like white wine, that's why, and any kind of ripple will do with the kind of meals we've been having lately …" He stopped himself from saying more, with an exasperated expression, but hoped she would take it as a joke.

"Oh my, my, I do believe we're sour," Sherrie said, stringing out the words sarcastically, all the while smiling.

"What's happening to us? And where is Kathy?" He was serious, trying his best not to take the bait.

"She's at her friend Betty's house, and maybe that's good," she said while handing him the corkscrew.

"Good?" *Crap! What is she up to?*

"Yes, good. We need to talk."

"You can say that again. We don't talk; we've been snapping at each other. And ... and what the hell, I might as well say it—we don't kiss anymore. I've tried, Sherrie, but it seems like everything I do or say doesn't sit well with you."

"Kevin, I'd say you're *really* sour tonight," she said, serving the frozen dinner. "But this ought to cheer you up."

"And why shouldn't I be, with this for dinner?" he said, grimacing at the distinctly less than appetizing dinner in a foil plate. "Oh well, maybe the Kendall-Jackson will be good," he mumbled more to himself than to her as he poured from the chilled bottle.

"Something must have really happened today."

"Huh, nothing, really. Nothing really important ... I just watched a million-dollar case walk right out of the door, that's all."

"Oh yeah, what did you do to cause that?"

"Not a damn thing." He hesitated before continuing. "Maybe it was something I didn't do. I don't want to talk about it."

"I think I know who it was; it was that girl from up around Palatka, right?"

"Yeah, but how did you know?"

"Because I know you've been screwing her."

Kevin was struck dumb. His stomach dropped into his feet. He knew the blood was draining from his face, but he tried to hold himself together.

"And by screwing her, you screwed up." Sherrie left and came back with an envelope. She opened it and shook out pictures of him and Vickie going into the motel room. "I've been wondering whether I should confront you with these," she said, laying them on the breakfast bar. "Sort of been thinking, maybe it's just a passing fancy, and nothing would come of it ..."

"It was not even a passing fancy."

"Now, now, let's not be rash and start lying."

"I'm not lying, Sherrie," he said, trying to soften his voice while shaking his head. *Damn, why doesn't she really get emotional and go into a rage? I could handle that better than this sterile, analytical show of control.* In a flash of insight, he answered his own question: she wasn't really torn up emotionally; she didn't really care. Could that be? He felt even sicker, and his stomach began to churn.

"Uh-huh, and I'm not looking at these," she said, pointing to the pictures.

"How long have—"

"Have I had them? Since the day after the event. But I knew before that day."

"What did you do, hire a private investigator, or did you take them yourself?"

"Hired somebody. You can't deny it anymore, Kevin. Anyway, it was her case, right?"

"Yes, but aren't you interested in what happened?" he pleaded, hoping for understanding.

"No, I know what happened."

"Well, please, let me explain. It's not what you think."

"Okay, lover boy, explain."

Kevin told her nearly everything, even that he felt there was more going on than met the eye. But he denied any sex with Vickie.

"Is that all you have to say?"

"Well, I—"

Sherrie cut him off. "For an hour you were in that motel room."

"Like I said, she went over every document word for word. She was killing time so it would look like what you think happened actually did happen. It was all part of some kind of nefarious plan. Can't you see I was set up? It couldn't be any clearer. Can't you understand something foul is afoot?"

"You through now?" Sherrie flatly asked.

"I guess so." He felt better. At least she had listened, and he thought he really sounded sincere.

"Okay, when?"

"When?"

"When are you moving out of the house? I would like to have you out of here tonight, and you can probably talk to my lawyer tomorrow."

"You can't mean that, Sherrie. I don't want a divorce. You must know I still love you."

"I wish I could believe that. But if you were me, and I'd done what you've done ..."

"But I haven't done anything, Sherrie," he lied, hoping his tone was persuasive.

"All the evidence says otherwise. Are you going to get out, or do I have to have you thrown out by the judge?"

"Come on, Sherrie," Kevin pleaded as he got up and tried to hug her.

"No, don't hug me," she quickly said, pulling away.

"You sure this is what you want?" he clearly asked as he stepped back. *I've got to give her time,* he decided. *I've got to go along with whatever she wants. The worse thing I could do is let this sink into a confrontation of loud shouts.*

"Kevin, I want you to get out. Then we'll see."

"Can't wait till tomorrow?"

"Okay, but I don't want to talk about it anymore tonight. Now I mean that."

"Okay, I'll leave tomorrow," he said quietly. Kevin sat in front of his thawed dinner and wondered what was going to happen next. He could reconcile his marriage, he thought, but it might take some time. The best thing he could do now was abide by her wishes and get out. He'd have to rent an apartment or something. After about thirty minutes, the initial shock had almost melted away. Once he accepted the reality of what she was doing, he felt that, well, this was life. *I'm just coming to terms with where I am; it doesn't have to end in divorce.*

I'll rent a place down on the beach, he thought, *and just maybe, an opportunity will come knocking. After all, when tossed a lemon, make lemonade.* He smiled a little at the thought. Then his mind filled with self-condemnation. He wanted to save his marriage, not play the field. Yet he couldn't quite get away from the notion that living alone might have its advantages. A myriad of things wafted through his mind while he sat before the TV set that evening and refrained from broaching the forbidden subject. They sat in silence; not a word was exchanged. She left the room and went up the stairs to bed during the last newscast before eleven. She said nothing—just got up and walked out. After she left, he waited a few minutes before he turned off the TV and then the lights and also went slowly up the stairs to bed. His mind worked overtime, and his last thought, before falling into a restless sleep, was that he should—not had to, but should—make the best of it.

* * * * *

Sherrie turned out the light, but sleep would not come. She wondered whether she'd done the right thing, whether she'd handled it right. After all, spouses stray sometimes, but the marriage endures. But there was more to it than that. What about that bit he'd pulled a few weeks ago about sleeping in a separate bedroom? True, he had a reason, maybe, but for years they'd been happy as two bugs in a rug. Surely there was something else.

God, she just wished she knew for sure. She had to admit the passion, at least for her, had slowly yet ineluctably drifted out of the marriage. Even so, she believed she still loved Kevin. Or maybe he was just a habit. But she'd be damned if she'd let him humiliate her. Of course, no one really knew. But she knew, and it hurt. She wanted to hurt him back. Deep down, however, she knew she didn't want to hurt him too much. Kevin had been a good and generous husband and father, and she didn't know whether she was ready for—or really wanted—all that to change. Maybe she ought to get up and get in the bed with him, let bygones be bygones. But the image of that woman blowing a kiss from the motel doorway kept getting in the way, and she rolled over and buried her face in the pillow to stifle an uncontrollable burst of tears.

CHAPTER 11

Three or four weeks after moving out of the house and renting a cottage, Kevin had more or less reconciled himself to bachelorhood. His wife's attorney was a pleasant man who knew what he was doing. Their property was being split fifty-fifty, Sherrie would receive lump-sum alimony, and he would pay child support, in excess of the amount actually needed. Sherrie would have primary custody of Kathy and would get the house as part of the lump-sum alimony. Kevin agreed to most everything. That simplified the end of their marriage. Nevertheless, in the hope she would change her mind later, he asked Sherrie to delay actually dissolving the marriage. She would let it linger for a year.

It was just another morning in November 1994 when he picked up his mail before his secretary had opened it and found a letter from the state bar. He opened the envelope in his office while still standing, knowing such a letter could be bad news. As he read it, it felt like the bottom of his stomach dropped out. His legs became weak, and he collapsed into a chair before he fell. There it was in black-and-white, a complaint to the bar that he had raped his client, Victoria Roberts. The details were the most surprising of all. She alleged that he had forced her to have sex—had actually held her down and ripped her clothing—and the complaint included allegations of sodomy and oral sex. She claimed it was the reason she had terminated his legal services, even though he had told her she was irrevocably bound by the contract. She further claimed she had some memory of signing something called "A Client's Legal Rights," but through trickery, Kevin had kept her copy.

Kevin put the paper on his desk and reflected on how he had acted contrary to his intuition in that motel room on that fateful occasion. *Damn*, he cursed himself, *always, always, follow your gut instincts.* The shrinks were just wrong; there was such a thing as intuition. But why had she complained of things that had never happened? Hell, this thing could have been—and therefore would have been—filed even if he'd never had carnal knowledge of Vickie. He shook his head in puzzlement. No time for self-recrimination. Somebody was trying to ruin him. First, his wife had thrown him out, and now a serious grievance needed to be addressed. He knew nothing good would come from parsing the allegations, and he quickly rejected a reply essentially stating the allegations were not true. He had done nothing to Victoria without her consent—or indeed, without her encouragement. She was a very passionate, uninhibited woman. No, he wouldn't pull his punches.

Recovering from the shock took a while. He got up, went to get a cup of coffee, walked around, and looked out the window. Then he was ready. He called Jo Ann into his office and dictated a reply that was a general denial, emphasizing that whatever had happened had occurred with her unqualified consent. But he strongly denied her claim about the clients' rights document—that he had kept her copy from her—and her claim that he had tried to stop her from breaking their contract. "Jo Ann let me see a finished letter as soon as you have it ready," he said as she left his office.

Having finished his response, he somehow felt better about it all. He also noted that it was a man, Sam Wilks, who would be handling his case for the bar, and that was encouraging. Very few grievances had ever been filed against Kevin; none had resulted in a probable-cause finding, much less sanctions; and Sam had been involved with the last meritless complaint. He felt like he knew Sam, and Sam knew him. Did he need a lawyer at this stage? No, he didn't think so, and if he got one now, it might send the wrong message to Sam. No, he'd handle the matter for the time being.

Another matter was bothering him. He was not getting referrals from his usual feeders. The change was not drastic enough for him to inquire into whether something was up, but he wondered. No, it must be just a coincidence. There had been other dry spells; he shouldn't let his imagination invent problems that weren't really there.

A few minutes later, he emerged from his office. "Have you got that letter to the bar finished?" he demanded of Jo Ann. The letter was actually to Vickie Roberts, with a copy to the bar.

"All done," Jo Ann quickly answered. "I can't believe something like this. Don't people have any shame?"

Kevin ignored the comment, briefly looked at the letter, and signed it. "Get it out of here today," he said as he walked out of the office for a hearing in the courthouse. As he walked along the sidewalk, he thought of revenge. But revenge on whom? Vickie Roberts wasn't doing all this. It wasn't that simple. No one had called to say they were taking over her case either. Why? This failure to communicate had to have some significance. What had he done to anybody, other than his wife that would provoke such a course of action? Sherrie definitely wouldn't be up to this type of cheap behavior. She had way too much class. A few times he had flickers of something in his mind, but nothing would clearly emerge. At the courthouse he called Jo Ann and told her to call the clerk where Cornell Roberts's probate had started and check to see whether any attorney had now filed an appearance to replace Kevin. However, because a substitution of counsel ordinarily was done by stipulation of both attorneys and the client, in a written document, he didn't expect to find anything.

After his hearing was over, Kevin's mind continued to play tag, with one idea leading to another, while he walked back to his office. "Find out anything?" he asked Jo Ann as he entered.

"Yes, sir. Apparently, a Mr. James Ross, attorney from Jacksonville, with Phil Griffin's firm, has filed an appearance as a successor attorney for the personal representative, Vickie Roberts, and she signed the appearance notice. There was certification that you had been furnished a copy, but I never saw it if it came."

"Phil Griffin, huh? Well, I guess that's who now has her case." *Far worse*, he thought, *I believe this means I will be kicked out of the group suing big tobacco. I'll get back to that later.*

"But shouldn't he have notified us?"

"Of course, but ..." Kevin let the thought trail off as he disappeared down the hall. *I need to appease my anxiety. Sharing a problem sometimes helps.* The only person who came to mind was his wife. Kevin had never made any really close friends except his wife. He thought about it briefly, and still convinced he should share this with her, he dialed her number.

"Sherrie, is that you?" Kevin said into the phone.

"Kevin, why are you calling? You are supposed to communicate with me through my attorney."

"For Christ's sake, can it, Sherrie!"

He heard the click of her hanging up.

"Damn, should I call her back?" he mumbled to himself. He redialed the number.

"Hello."

"Sherrie, don't hang up. Please, bear with me for a minute. I need to talk, and you're the only person I know I can talk to."

"So talk."

He proceeded to tell her about the grievance filed by Vickie Roberts and about Phil Griffin taking over her case.

"Well, what do you want me to do?" Sherrie asked.

"I want you to let me come back home. I need you. That's the only way I can put it."

"Why, Kevin, I'm surprised you need somebody!"

"Sherrie, don't make light of it, please."

"Well, you know you shouldn't have screwed Mrs. Roberts."

Should he admit the truth or continue to lie? He had to lie if there was any hope of getting her back. He had no choice but to lie.

"I didn't. I can't prove a negative, and I guess you'll just continue to believe what you want to believe. But it never happened." Instantly, he wished he hadn't said that. It sounded shrill, the opposite of what he wanted.

"You through?"

"I guess so," sighed Kevin. He knew it was no use pleading, yet he heard himself saying, "I just hope you don't believe now, since apparently you once did, that I did anything with that woman." He felt totally helpless. He'd be in the same situation even if he was telling the truth. He crossed his fingers and sent up a prayer to the god he was ambivalent about.

"You through now?"

"Yes." He was through begging. He had some pride left, but he hoped his "yes" was soft and endearing.

"Then there's nothing else to say. By the way, I think I'm going to be seeing somebody. Bye." And she hung up the phone.

How could this woman, the mother of their child and his confidant for years, be so cold and uncaring? He really needed her, but no, she was kicking him in the shins. He replaced the receiver in the cradle, swiveled his chair, and sat back, trying to relax and think. But nothing positive developed. He had to think about his cases and other people's problems.

Over the next few days, every case was reviewed, and even matters that could wait were taken care of anyway. For once, he was truly dedicated to getting ahead of the game.

Before he knew it, more than a month had passed and Christmas was only a few days away. He would pick up his daughter's Christmas presents in the next day or so. He had heard nothing more about the grievance. He also had refrained from calling Phil Griffin or his lackey James Ross. He would not give them the pleasure of believing the loss of Vickie's case was particularly important to him.

But the case against big tobacco was important to him, and he hadn't heard a word from Phil or anyone else. Why?

Not having a family anymore, Kevin began to take more afternoons now and then for a game of golf. He liked golf because it was not really a competitive game; it was not like the way he made his living. All he cared about was hitting the ball well and improving his game. No one ever heard any profanity from him on the golf course. Until his recent problems, Kevin had been, without a doubt, a laid-back man who didn't take himself or his work too seriously. He did his best, and that was it. Golf relaxed him, and concentrating on the game was not a total distraction from thinking about more important matters.

He had begun to believe—no, wanted to believe—that the grievance matter would simply disappear, but then between Christmas 1994 and New Year's, he received the formal complaint alleging what amounted to a rape charge against him, filed by the bar. It wasn't even a shock. He almost welcomed it and proceeded to reread the accusations, looking for what could be a flaw in the pleadings. The longer he pored over these false—in fact, defamatory—allegations, the more his initial concern dramatically diminished because of his sure knowledge, fortified by an adrenaline rush, that he would now take control. He would make things happen. He dictated a thoughtful response, again denying the allegations of forced sex with Victoria Roberts. But what about the consensual sex with a client? That too was frowned on by the bar; it could cost him his license to practice. But since the complaint contained no allegations of consensual sex, he did not have to address that issue.

He did not have to admit sex with Vickie. Yet he knew, regardless of the folks who prosecuted complaints to the bar, that he had done nothing wrong. But if that were true, why did he keep repeating to himself that he'd had the encounter on only one occasion? If he had to testify, well, he'd cross that bridge when he came to it. It would serve no one's interest for him to lose his license; far too many people depended on him. Anyway, Vickie was lying. He just had to find out why. It would be only her word against his. The photographs were a problem, but he could handle that. He even included in his response that the allegations not only were untrue but also had been instigated by someone with a plan to ruin him.

Now what? he thought. *I've done my response. It will be in the mail to the bar soon. But what can I do at this point?* He mulled over the possibility of hiring an investigator. But to investigate what? The only answer that came to mind was "nothing." No, it couldn't be simply nothing. But only the other lawyers who were suing the tobacco companies would benefit if he was excluded. Surely, none of those men could be out to ruin him. But something was truly amiss, and he just had to wait and watch for it. The answer would come. He would hire a lawyer later.

He thought about what had turned out to be a very fateful day, the day he'd gone to Vickie's room at the Ramada on I-95. He had been in a good mood in his office, and when she called requesting that he come to her room, it had not seemed out of the ordinary. When he left his office, he really wasn't thinking about anything other than going to her room, getting the paperwork completed, and going home. He knew she was available, but that was not particularly on his mind, although he did appreciate that she was a really good-looking woman. Then she had surprised him by meeting him in the parking lot. However, he had attached no significance to that. Now he was thinking, like he had told Sherrie, that this—being visible together in public, outside the hotel— was part of a plan. He was trying to remember every detail of what had happened. Maybe he would come up with some answers to the problem if he went back over that fateful day. After he thought of every aspect of meeting Vickie, he shook his head; the only thing he knew was he had felt like Jimmy Stewart in *Bell, Book and Candle*. But she had said she wished they were married. But what the hell, that didn't mean anything.

CHAPTER 12

E ven after the bar filed a formal complaint, Kevin still expected a fortuitous revelation. A patient man, he took the absence of any positive information in stride. He knew it would come, or at least that's what he told himself, and he was not yet openly desperate about his situation. Still, every time his mind was on something else, and he was enjoying himself, this terrible turn of events would inevitably emerge to haunt him. He was not having many good days, and he needed to call Hugh.

"Hello, Hugh. I'm sorry to have to let you know a serious grievance is pending against me."

"And I'm sorry to hear it. But damn, you know what we have to do. When do you expect the complaint to be filed?"

"It's already filed and I've answered. If things change, I'll let you know. And tell Phil he need not pay me the ten thousand dollars until you all have won the case."

"God, Kevin, I don't know what to say, but I'll pass the word along."

"Thanks."

Over a year later, in February 1996, Kevin was having a drink at the club after an afternoon of golf, thinking of nothing in particular, when an assistant state attorney, Larry Singer, took a seat next to him and ordered a bottle of beer.

East Bay's country club, a rustic-orange, rough stucco building, was quintessentially old Florida Spanish architecture, with appropriate arches, spiraling columns, and a brick-red barrel roof. The horseshoe bar of polished blond oak, with its well-cushioned tan leather chairs, was comfortable, perhaps even posh.

"Been a good day on the links?" Larry casually said to Kevin. Larry was a little old to still be an active trial attorney in the prosecutor's office. Square-jawed, with a full head of brown hair, now turning gray, and piercing brown eyes, he looked more like an older athlete, who still did not look his age. Kevin guessed he enjoyed his job and had probably refused more lucrative prospects.

"Yeah, pretty good. I had some really good shots on the back nine. Score wasn't so hot, though. What brings you out this late in the afternoon? It's almost night."

"You do. I heard you had been seen here fairly often since your wife kicked you out. At least, that's the way I got it. She kicked you out, and ..."

"That's about right," Kevin said without a trace of rancor. "But it's not over yet, you know."

"You all aren't seriously squabbling over something, are you?"

"No, not really, but who knows what can happen?"

"Anyway, I'm glad to see you with a good attitude because I've got some good and bad news for you."

"For god's sake, what is it?" Kevin said, worried something had happened to Sherrie or Kathy, or both.

"Some inexperienced nitwit in the sex intake department has filed a sexual battery case against you. That's the bad news."

Larry said more, but Kevin heard nothing. He'd never dreamed such a thing would happen. A grievance was one thing, but being charged with a crime left him with a sick feeling and a mind so blank, he couldn't even feel anger.

"God almighty, I guess I had better get a lawyer and turn myself in ..." He paused. "What's the good news?"

"The good news is it was assigned to me for trial. You don't need to turn yourself in or get a lawyer at the present time."

"Why?"

"First off, I've already canceled the warrant, and for the time being, I'll be your lawyer."

"Damn, Larry, thanks. But what's next?"

"Oh, you'll have to appear and plead not guilty—do that by mail, you know—and I'm going to investigate this thing, starting with Victoria Roberts."

"I should have known, I guess, but after all this time ..."

"That's who filed the grievance against you—yeah, we have all that stuff. You have obviously done a damn good job keeping that thing from coming to a final hearing. The irony is unbelievable. The bar has dragged their feet because you have kept arguing if there was anything to the charges, you would have been charged with a crime."

"And your investigation will show there's no truth in the charges, and that should cause them to dismiss the grievance?"

"Should, but you never know. After all, you did have sex with her, *I think.*"

Kevin started to say something, but Singer cut him off.

"You don't have to say a thing, so don't, capisce? As you well know, the grievance stuff is privileged. We can't use it, although from a criminal standpoint it's most assuredly not incriminating. This thing was buried in the intake division for months. Nobody would say yea or nay down there. Finally, some fool did it. My boss won't let me just drop it. I've already asked. Thought you'd like to know that also. I went by your office earlier this afternoon to tell you what was coming down, and they told me you were out golfing. This thing will be picked up by the papers, and you wouldn't want to find out about it in the morning paper, would you?" Larry paused and took a big drink of his Miller High Life."

"Damn, you're right. This will be in the papers for sure," Kevin said. Considering that he and Larry were merely speaking acquaintances and definitely not close, professionally or otherwise, he felt grateful. "Thanks, Larry."

"You don't need to thank me. I'm a public servant. Just doing my job ... But you're probably wondering how I could pull the warrant."

"Yeah, that's one thing."

"Just takes a little imagination—the same way I got the bar grievance case that, you know, is supposed to be confidential. I didn't think you'd care. You don't, do you?"

"No."

"You just go on and file a not-guilty plea to this information." Larry handed him the one-page charging document. "The one thing you are not going to have to do is be booked into the jail, capisce?"

"But Larry, where do we go from here?" Kevin asked while looking at the charges, not really seeing or comprehending the specifics. He knew it was two counts of rape. Either charge was a felony, with up to thirty years in prison and/or a fifteen-thousand-dollar fine.

"I'm not sure exactly what I'll do tomorrow." Larry paused, drumming his fingers on the bar. "Do you think it would be a good idea to request that this Victoria Roberts do a polygraph?"

"I assume the police haven't done that then?"

"No, they didn't."

"Damn right, I think it's a good idea."

"I'm glad to hear you say that. The police investigators just took her word for it. No physical evidence at all. No inquiries where there ought to have been some inquiries. At least that's the way I see it. Drop by the office tomorrow, and I'll let you copy my file, or whatever you want out of it ..." Larry hesitated, took a drink, and continued. "Kevin, obviously, you don't need to talk to me. In fact, maybe you shouldn't. You know anything you say can be used against you."

"Is this a cryptic way of saying ..."

"No, no, not at all. But if it turns out I believe the evidence supports the charges, I have to prosecute vigorously, so the rules say. Of course, so far, you have told me nothing incriminating. Let's just leave it that way for the time being. I don't know what it is yet, but something about this case stinks, and I want to find out where the bad smell's coming from, capisce?"

"For now then, I'll just enter my plea pro se, so to speak." Kevin couldn't even smile at his own dark humor. "Let me buy you a beer, Larry?"

"Just one. Can't let the prosecutor get pulled over for DUI."

"Heck, I might have a few more things I'd like to ask you about. Why not stay, and dinner will be on me?"

"Like to, Kevin, but the wife's waiting on me, so I need to go home."

About that time, the bartender approached them. "Two more for us on my tab," Kevin said.

"Kevin, give me a chance to get my feet into this thing."

"Do I have a choice? ... Damn, Larry, that didn't come out right."

"You're upset and justifiably so. You don't owe me any apologies. I've seen very few innocent people falsely charged with criminal behavior. It has happened, but you ... hell, I guess you like any other man, or even some women, could rape somebody—you know the law now allows a woman to be prosecuted for rape. But the way this case has been handled leaves a lot of questions in my mind. None of it makes any sense. I'm skeptical in every case as to the defense. Here, it's just the opposite. Of course, East Bay County has more crime than most people realize, and in 99 percent of the cases I see, the defendants are guilty. Here, even the cops had some real problem with the case—they submitted it to our office rather than just arrest you on probable cause. Now that tells me something."

Larry Singer's words and attitude made Kevin grateful that this prosecutor had the case. Kevin felt a little better as Larry continued to tell him how he had analyzed the case to reduce Mrs. Roberts's credibility to zero. Kevin certainly fit no known profile of a rapist, yet he was sure she would really lay it on when she was interviewed. Larry was certain she would refuse a polygraph after being told how accurate they really were.

In Kevin's befuddled mind, he kept repeating, *You never know who your friends really are, or for that matter, in this case, who your enemies are.* "Larry, I don't know if it'll help or not, but this thing is far more sinister than just a woman's false accusation."

"I have already come to the same conclusion. None of it rings true. I might have a question or two later. Right now, you just rest assured I will do what's right. And what's right means this goddamn thing will be buried."

"Thanks again. You sure you won't stay for dinner?"

"Not this time. Maybe some other time. Got to get home to the little lady. You know how that is." Larry stood up and pushed the bar chair back as he delivered his parting remark: "I'll keep you advised."

Kevin was left with one scenario after another tumbling around in his head. Things could certainly be worse, but the fact that his life had deteriorated so much so fast kept surfacing in his mind. He ordered another drink, the one he'd promised himself he wouldn't have. The scotch and soda sat like a monument to despair before him. He looked at it, shook his head, signed a check, and left the full drink sitting on the bar. *You have enough problems*, he thought. "Getting drunk would solve nothing," he mumbled as he walked to the dining room and sat at a table.

Tomorrow he had work to do. No, this was no time for hangovers, he decided, silently rejecting the waiter's offer of the wine list. Something he had been waiting and watching for had arrived, he thought. Who would have ever predicted it would be none other than the state attorney's office in the guise of Larry Singer? Whoever was behind all this had stepped into a snake pit by pushing the criminal case. Like all those up to no good, they would eventually do themselves in; they had gone too far. *The very thing they think will do me in, the criminal prosecution, is going to be the very thing that does them in. I just know it.* He smiled to himself, fully relaxing for the first time in weeks.

When Kevin arrived home that night, he found an envelope in his mail box without a return address that contained a short note. Printed from a computer, not handwritten, it read, "Stop worrying; you have nothing to worry about." What the hell was this? He read it several times. *Should I tell Singer about this?* he wondered. *Not right away,* he decided. *But it has to be from Vickie, doesn't it? Well, no. It could be something from ... from ... whom? I'll keep it to myself for the time being.* The note, and what it really meant, remained in Kevin's mind until he finally drifted off into another night of fitful sleep.

CHAPTER 13

About three weeks after she filed the original complaint against Kevin with the Florida bar, a man arrived at Vickie's home in Palatka, Florida, and identified himself as an investigator for the Florida bar. He had a billfold full of credentials that proved who and what he was. Well dressed in a three-piece suit, this gentleman told her she had to file a criminal complaint against Kevin, or the bar would not proceed with the grievance matter; he claimed it was a matter of credibility. He explained that if the events had happened as she claimed, it was reasonable, indeed expected, that she would report the crime to the police. He did not suggest she was not telling the truth; he only reminded her that the bar did not want to file something against a lawyer if they did not feel the case was strong enough for the bar to prevail.

She told him she did not want to file any more charges against Kevin Charles because she felt like it would be tremendously burdensome personally. He told her it didn't matter whether the state actually proceeded with criminal charges against Mr. Charles. What mattered, he said, was that she simply report a crime to the authorities. He also assured her that, in all likelihood, the state attorney would not bother to prosecute Kevin Charles because she had not reported it immediately after it had happened (for which she had a reasonably decent explanation as far as the bar was concerned) and had not gone to the hospital to be checked out for bruises and such.

She called Phil, and since he wasn't in, she was advised—in fact, admonished—by Frank Dunn that she had to proceed with filing some kind of criminal charges so that the grievance would be filed in accordance with their plan to exclude Kevin from participating as one of the chosen. He reminded her that the content of the police report had to be the same as the grievance and essentially assured her that no criminal case would ever really be brought against Kevin. Of course, she knew that if no grievance was filed, and there was no adverse ruling against Kevin, she would never see the rest of the money promised her, and her wrongful death suit would no doubt be turned into shambles.

Against every better instinct in her body, in October 1994 she went to the local police and made the complaint, explaining that she really was not concerned with Kevin being prosecuted criminally, but she did feel that he should be disbarred for what he had done to her. She explained that she was filing the criminal charges so that the grievance would be successful.

She did not hear anything else about it until February 1996, when a subpoena was served on her to appear before one Lawrence Singer at a specified time in the state attorney's office to testify in the case of *Florida v. Kevin Charles*. She automatically asked the deputy serving the subpoena, "Do I have to go?"

"Yes, ma'am."

"And if I don't?"

"The court could issue a pick-up order and jail you until Mr. Singer can talk to you."

"Nothing else I can do?"

"You might want to call your own lawyer—I really can't advise you, you know, except to tell you to show up. So I'll leave you with it."

After the deputy left, Vickie made a call to Phil Griffin's office.

"Yes, Vickie," Phil said in a clipped way, like her problems were not his problems.

"You don't sound like you want to hear from me."

"Now, now, let's not be rash. I always want to hear from you. I am delighted you called. It's just that I'm awfully busy at the moment. Maybe, if you have time, you could, shall we say, make an unexpected trip to Jacksonville to see me, or perhaps a planned trip?"

"No, that's not why I called."

"No?"

"No. I called because I've been subpoenaed to go to the prosecutor's office."

"Oh, that's not unusual; you filed a criminal complaint, you know."

"Don't tell me what I already know. That's not helpful. Will you go with me?"

"For what?" he asked.

"You know for what. I have to give a statement under oath, you know."

"Why are you so apprehensive? All you have to do is tell the truth. There's nothing to worry about, and I've got a client that I excused myself from in order to speak to you. So I've got to cut it short now."

"That's it?" Vickie asked, frustrated.

"Oh, now let's not be so ... so like that. Maybe we can get together soon. Now I have to say *au revoir.*" Vickie heard him hang up.

So I'm on my own. But what else could I have expected at this point? Despite her outward appearance of calm control, she was afraid of the upcoming interview with Mr. Singer. She was going to lie, and it scared her—not the lying, but the possibility of being caught.

In March 1996, Vickie arrived at the state attorney's office on time, well dressed in a conservative blue pants suit and pumps. She took a deep breath and told the receptionist who she was. She was immediately ushered to the entrance to Mr. Singer's office. She couldn't completely suppress some lingering trepidation, and she bit her lower lip as she got her first glimpse of the public servant who represented the state's interest in the case against Kevin Charles. He rose from his chair as she entered his office.

Walking around his cheap metal desk, Larry Singer welcomed her with a firm handshake and introduced himself. She then took a seat in an equally cheap metal chair.

After taking his seat, he said in a professional tone, "Mrs. Roberts, this case has been assigned to me for trial. I'm not the person responsible for filing these charges. I have read the file and have all the preliminary information about you. You know, how old you are, your husband's death, and so on. You have earned a GED and are attending a junior college. Can you think of anything you want to add?"

"No, I'm sure you have what you need. But if you have anything specific to ask, I'll be happy to tell you," she replied in a most accommodating tone, but she could feel a slight flutter in her heart.

"Good. Then we'll get right to the necessary aspects, okay?"

"Sure, Mr. Singer."

He sat back before he spoke. "You sure you want to do this today? It can wait, you know."

"No, let's not put it off. I'm not happy about talking about it, but I know I have to, so ..." She dropped her eyes and looked at her hands, as if they did not belong to her.

He cleared his throat. "Okay, Mrs. Roberts, how did you first meet Kevin Charles?"

Through several questions and answers, they established that she had retained Kevin for the wrongful death of her husband.

"Now, Mrs. Roberts, you say this Gary LaBlanc referred you to Mr. Charles?"

"Yes, but what's all this got to do with what this man did to me?" she protested.

"Just bear with me, Mrs. Roberts," he said. "Now, Mrs. Roberts, did you consult any other attorneys about the case LaBlanc referred you on?"

This question caught her off-guard, and she gave him a puzzled expression.

Singer quickly continued. "What I mean is, did you go to an attorney other than LaBlanc about the unfortunate death of your husband either before or after seeing Mr. LaBlanc?"

Again Vickie said nothing. She looked around nervously. She was frantically trying to calculate whether this man already knew everything. But how could he? Then again, secrets did slip out now and then. Or was he fishing? And if so, why? *If he knows, then he knows, and I'm sunk anyway*, she decided.

She answered, "No one else before I saw Mr. LaBlanc, and since I fired Mr. Charles, I've retained Phil Griffin." Was she seeing things, or did Singer's expression say he was having trouble believing her? *No, I'm just overreacting. I've got to regain my confidence*, she thought, and she managed to dredge up a weak but, she hoped, innocent-looking smile.

"So that there won't be any misunderstanding, and you know this is all being recorded, you're telling me you went to LaBlanc on Cornell's death case, he referred you to Mr. Charles, and after you fired Mr. Charles, you retained Phil Griffin, who you still have as your attorney."

"That's right, but what's all this got—"

"To do with the case against Mr. Charles," Singer quickly said, finishing her question. "You might be surprised what it has to do with it, or maybe you wouldn't. But no matter. I make the rules here about what's relevant, capisce? And I don't intend to be rude, but we've got to finish, unless you just want to drop the case. Now that *would* be another matter." Singer paused, wrinkled his brow, and squinted his eyes as he made direct eye contact with her.

She slowly shook her head. "No, I don't want that. Please continue."

"Now once you got to Kevin Charles's office, exactly what happened at the first meeting?"

"I thought we'd already covered that," she said hesitantly.

Singer remained silent for a moment, furrowed his brow again, and squinted his eyes. "I'm waiting for an answer. Cat got your tongue?" he snapped.

"Oh, well, he just took down all the information about Cornell and …"

Mr. Singer cut her off again. "Did he ever recommend that you stay at a motel that night?"

"Well, yes, he did."

"The motel was one located out on I-95?"

"Yes, but what's that got to do with all of this? I'm sorry. I didn't mean to question …"

"Mrs. Roberts, I need the full story, all the facts. It's absolutely necessary as a protocol in this office. You have been the victim of a serious crime, or at least that's what you say …" He observed her closely, poker-faced.

"Well, it was late when I saw him, and I didn't want to drive all the way back home at night. So, yes, he did recommend that I stay in a motel." She suddenly felt better; speaking the truth was somehow liberating, even for Vickie.

"Did you stay in one?"

After some fidgeting, and again feeling constrained, she slowly said, "Yes, I did."

"Which one?" he asked quietly.

"Oh, I've forgotten."

"There's only three motels there at that intersection, and you don't remember which one?" He asked the question like he was mystified, but in a soft voice.

"Oh, this whole thing is so stressful, I can hardly remember my name."

"But you're certain you stayed that night in one of those motels out there, the date you gave me as your first meeting with him—I believe it was a Friday?"

"Yes, in early August of '94. I'm sure of that, I think," she said, biting her lip slightly.

"You think? Mrs. Roberts, in a criminal prosecution you have to be sure," he admonished her, but in a quiet, controlled voice.

"I'm sure ... yes, I'm sure."

"Okay." He casually stroked his chin for a moment, as if in deep thought. "Now there was a second meeting, and on that occasion, tell me exactly—"

"Is this really necessary?" she asked abruptly.

"Again ... yes, Mrs. Roberts, it is. And if you think my little interview is bothersome, or even offensive, just wait till a defense lawyer gets wound up. First, he'll go over your life history in absurd detail in a deposition that will no doubt take hours. Now, a lot of that, he'll not be able to use or ask about in the trial—but he doesn't give a damn. He'll want you to get so flustered and frustrated that all you'll want is out. Of course, the deposition is just in the presence of the lawyers and a court reporter.

"Now, assuming you put up with all of that and take the stand in a trial, then you're testifying to salacious details before a jury and all the other people who serve the court—indeed, anyone else who might be in the audience. It is not a happy thing to do. In fact, it is a real ordeal. You up to it?"

"I have to be. That's all I can say. I have to be." After a moment, she continued to answer his earlier question. "I had to sign a bunch of papers for probate, and when I got to the motel, I was just so tired that I called Mr. Charles and asked if he could drive by, and we could do the paperwork at the motel. It was definitely the Ramada. I was just too tired to drive on into town to his office that late in the afternoon."

"And?"

"And he agreed. So once we were there, I thought we'd just do our business in the lobby, but it was sort of noisy, so we had a drink at the bar, and he suggested we go to my room."

"Yes, go on," Singer said as he made a steeple with his fingers on his desk.

"So once we got into the room, we did discuss matters related to the case, and then he began making suggestions ..." She rubbed her forehead.

"Suggestions?" he said as he intertwined his fingers.

"Yes, sir, like 'Well, here we are in the motel, just the two of us,' and sort of smiling ... you know, like he had something on his mind," Vickie explained while shifting her eyes toward her lap.

"You could tell?"

"Yes, sir. I could tell. He wanted me."

"But did he touch you or anything?" Singer took a drink of water.

"Not that time. I was able to maneuver him out the door. I don't know why I let him into my room again. I guess I thought he was a real gentleman. I mean, there's no harm in trying in a nice way. Matter of fact, it's sort of flattering, but taking sure isn't."

"So how did you maneuver him out the door?"

"I just kept my distance and started talking about being tired and walked to the door and opened it."

"And he left?" Singer said, putting out his hands, palms up.

"Yes, but he still had a little smile ... not really a smile, more like a grin, and he lingered too long before he left." She touched her fingers to the desk and sat up straight as she spoke.

"After that, you still felt safe with him, even though you had a hunch, or let's say, a lady's intuition, that he might be up to no good. Is that true?" He sat back.

"At that time, yes. Yes, you could say that."

"Then we come to the time you were raped ..."

"Mr. Singer, I don't know if I can be as detailed as you want me to be."

"You have to be. Not only here but most important of all, before a jury in a court of law. So tell me about that time." He leaned forward and added, "Just relax; take your time."

"Okay. I had to take him some papers; some questions had to be answered and documents produced."

"Interrogatories?" Singer asked.

"Yes, that's it, and some documents had to be produced. Anyway, I went to his office but left some of the stuff at the motel by accident, so he offered to simply go by the motel to, well, finish our meeting there, where I'd left it. I tried to get him to let me drive back and get it and then, you know, go back to his office."

"But he wanted to go to the motel?"

"Yes, sir. It was late in the afternoon. We did do some review of the questions and other stuff right after we got in my room."

"Go on. I'm listening." He intertwined his fingers over his chest.

"But then, as we stood up for him to leave, he started saying things like 'You know you want it, and I want it too. Let's stop kidding around.' And he grabbed me and pushed me onto the bed and began trying to kiss me. I struggled, but he was really strong. I guess I let him kiss me, but I was also trying to tell him I didn't want to do anything, you know …"

"But he continued despite your pleas not to?"

"Yes, sir, so I just pleaded with him not to do what he was doing …"

"Which was?"

"He had his hand under my dress and was pulling my panties off, and then he sat back a little and looked at my panties. Then he sort of smelled them," she said, holding up her hand like she was holding the panties.

"He smelled your panties?"

"He sure did."

"Then what?"

"He threw them at the TV set," she answered, mimicking a throwing gesture.

"Any reason you know of for him to aim at the TV?"

"No. But I had heard him say he didn't care much for TV. Then he said, 'Your panties are off, so I might as well take off my pants,' and he quickly, somehow, you know, pushed out of his pants and shorts and pushed up my skirt while squeezing in between my legs."

"And you resisted?" Singer asked, fiddling with his pen.

"I sure tried, but I couldn't get my legs back together. Still, I squirmed and told him I didn't want to do it—to get off of me."

"What did he do or say then?"

"He said, 'Sure you do, and you know it, so just relax and enjoy it.' Then he forced himself into me."

"He put his penis into your vagina?"

She nodded while mumbling, "Yes, that is exactly what he did. Anyway, I couldn't protect myself anymore."

"Did he ejaculate?"

"I'm pretty sure he did, but I really don't have a specific memory of everything that was going on. You know, I was really scared of what he might do."

"Well, what did he do?"

"He got me naked and ripped his own shirt getting it off, so he would be naked too. Then he laid down next to me like we were making love. I was shaking the whole time but kept my mouth shut. Then, after a while, he reached over and put his fingers in, you know, my vagina and around down there."

"You never screamed or anything?"

"No, I didn't."

"Why not?" he asked, raising his arms in the air.

"I was scared, I guess, but mostly I was embarrassed. I've thought about why I didn't yell for help, and I believe it was because I was just so ashamed something like that was happening to me."

"Well, I only know what you tell me ... Anyway, he put his fingers into you after he had already ejaculated in you?"

"Yes, he did."

"Mrs. Roberts, you said he put his fingers, plural, into your vagina. Just how many fingers did he ... I'm afraid there's no other way to say it: how many fingers did he stick up your vagina?"

"Mr. Singer, this is really embarrassing, and I was in such a state, I don't think I can actually say. But do I have to be so detailed?"

Singer cut her short. "Again, Mrs. Roberts, I know this is embarrassing and unpleasant, but if you think I'm being detailed and disgusting, just wait till the defense lawyer has his turn." He paused for a moment. "You'll think our little tête-à-tête is a Sunday afternoon garden party, with the ladies of the First United Methodist Church, compared to what the defense will hammer you with."

I have to do this, she thought. *I can't back down, no matter how unpleasant this is.* "I might be a weak little woman, but understand, I'm tough, Mr. Singer. I can take it—anything they can dish out, I can take. You don't have to worry about me." She sat back in her chair then. "I'd say he stuck at least one, maybe two fingers up me. I can't do any better than that."

He cleared his throat, sat back in his chair, affected a relaxed pose, and asked, "How long did that last?"

"Seemed like forever. He kept doing that and pulled me over on top of him. Then we had intercourse."

"Again?"

"Yes, sir."

"And?"

"Finally, he finished."

"Ejaculated?"

"Yes. Then he pushed me off and said, 'Now that wasn't so bad, was it?' Then he started toward the bathroom. He knew he had done something I didn't want him to do. I was still afraid of him, and boy, was I relieved when he said he had to go. He said that while he was in the bathroom washing up. I got halfway dressed—really all the way, I guess, just not made up—and tried to be friendly. I didn't want him to hurt me, and I felt partially responsible for what had happened."

"Is that why you stood in the door to blow him a kiss?" Singer asked.

Vickie looked over at his desk and saw that he had pulled out several photographs, the same ones Phil had shown her, taken by the investigator Kevin's wife hired.

"I didn't do that. That photograph doesn't really show that. I felt so humiliated and ashamed; you just can't imagine how dirty I felt. I wanted him to go so I could take a shower. I would have already been bathing, but I didn't want to be naked again with him in the room."

"Anyway, is that all he did to you—nothing else in the way of sexual assault?"

"Yes, sir, that's all he did. Isn't it enough?" she quietly said while dabbing her moist eyes.

"He did not force you to have oral sex … you know, fellatio?"

She shook her head while slowly saying, "I don't think so."

"Well, did you have oral sex with him?" Singer turned his swivel chair sideways and rocked a little.

"No, I don't think so, and I thought I had already told you that."

"Well, I guess I understand what you're saying." He continued to rock.

"Please, Mr. Singer, I just don't remember everything in detail."

"Okay, was there any anal sex?"

"What?"

"Anal sex—did he penetrate your anus with his fingers or anything else?"

"I sure don't remember anything like that."

"So you didn't report this right away?"

"No, I didn't think anyone would believe me."

"When did you decide to get rid of him as your lawyer? Maybe that's a stupid question, but when did you?"

"I didn't want him as my lawyer anymore, but Mr. Singer, he had told me there was no way I could get rid of him; he said that our contract was binding. But to be honest, I questioned that. I'm not that dumb."

"But sometime after that, you filed a rather detailed grievance against Mr. Charles, and if I read this thing right," Singer said while patting the file, "it was *after* this that you filed this criminal complaint ..."

"I got a call and then a visit from someone with the bar grievance people. That person told me to file the criminal charge, or the grievance would be dropped."

Singer stopped rocking and looked straight at Vickie. "Who told you that?"

"Gosh, I don't know."

"You don't know? Didn't you ask what—"

She aggressively interrupted. "Sure, the man said his name, but I just can't remember."

"Was it Sam Wilks?"

After some hesitation, Vickie said, "Could be the man. I'm just not sure."

"The reason I suggested Sam Wilks is he's the bar's attorney who is handling your grievance against Mr. Charles, and he'd probably be the only person talking to you."

"That name does sound familiar."

"Oh well, if you don't remember, then you don't remember," Singer said, arching his eyebrows.

"I just can't say for sure, that's all," she said. "Don't you believe me?"

"Believe you? I don't have to believe you. That is really irrelevant. The big question is, will a jury believe you? Not knowing details always has an adverse effect on a witness's credibility. So no one else had anything to do with you going to the police with this claim?"

"Mr. Singer, what's that got to do with this complaint? I know you have to do what you have to do and all, but I don't see the reason for that question."

"Do you have some reason, Mrs. Roberts, not to want to answer it?"

"No, not really."

"Then answer it please."

"No. No one else had any influence on me. I wrestled with this thing myself, spent sleepless nights just crying over how I'd been violated. And so when whoever it was suggested a criminal prosecution, I was ready to do it. That's all. Your questions and the police's questions aren't a hell of a lot of fun, you know."

"Not any fun for me either, lady." He dropped his pen on the desk.

"So are we through?"

"Mrs. Roberts, you have implied, or at least I think you implied, I might have some question about your credibility. I'm not going into any real detail, but what you have told me is not exactly what you told the police … in fact, it's far from what you told them. And I can understand a true lapse of memory in a case like this. But we don't have to get into that right now. We can remove all doubt, however, if you take a polygraph. You know what that is, don't you?"

Vickie let out an audible sigh but without emotion said, "Those things aren't accurate, so why do it?"

"They aren't admissible in court, unless everybody agrees to it. But a polygraph only errs on the side of the liar. Some people lie with such aplomb, their blood pressure isn't altered one iota. So?"

"So what?"

"You want me to set up a polygraph?"

Vickie sat in silence. She looked up and then down. She did not know for sure, but she suspected Singer was trying to corner her. "It would probably be okay, but let me sleep on it?"

"Hmm." Singer's finger barely tapped his desk.

"What good could it do? I don't have to do it, do I?"

"No, you don't have to, but what if some defense counsel fires a question to you like 'did the state give you a polygraph?' It's an objectionable question but still would or could create a problem—but not if you have taken it. I would not object, and you could quickly answer by saying, 'Sure did, and I passed with flying colors.' Could be a little trial trap for the overly exuberant defense lawyer. They don't always abide by the code of conduct, you know." Singer again drummed his fingers on the desk as he waited for her to answer.

"I'll just have to let you know, okay?"

"Okay. Unless you have some questions or want to tell me something else, I think that does it for now."

* * * * *

Later that day, Vickie phoned Phil. "Phil, I've got to talk to you."

"Okay, talk."

"Over the phone?" she said. She needed to convince him that she was in trouble and it could lead to him.

"Sure beats the hell out of driving to Jacksonville … unless you'd really like to see me."

"Not now and probably never. I just left the prosecutor's office, and frankly, I told him some things that were not true and did it under oath."

"He went further with questions than the bar grievance people did?" Phil questioned.

"Quite a bit further."

"Well, don't let that bother you. On any material issue, the only person who will refute what you've said is Mr. Charles, and that's to be expected and means little to nothing. The other matters were …?"

"Well, about Mr. LaBlanc referring me to Mr. Charles, where I spent the night the first time I met him, who encouraged me to bring a criminal charge, and who now represents me in my wrongful death case, and I told him it was you. He even suggested a lie detector test for me, Phil."

"All those matters are immaterial, and you can never be charged with perjury if that's what's bothering you."

"I can't be charged?"

"No indeed. Perjury has to be lying under oath on a material matter. You don't have anything to worry about, my dear."

"That's sort of a relief," she said, while cursing herself; she could still be in a lot of trouble.

"Anything else?"

"No."

"Okay, I've got someone waiting to see me, so I'm going to have to cut this short. We'll get together soon, okay?"

"Don't be too sure about that. Bye."

"I hear you. Bye." She heard him click off.

As she hung up the receiver, she caustically reflected on Phil's penchant for cutting her off. There was no one there who couldn't simply wait. Mr. big shit—she grinned at her own wit—was hiding something. No way was that man giving it to her straight. Yet if it all worked out in the end, it would be worth it. *At least, I think it will be,* she thought. *No, it will be, if all goes as I've planned. Mr. big shot doesn't know it, but it doesn't matter what kind of sleazy sideshow he might put on for me. I'll come out on top.*

* * * * *

Phil Griffin was standing by a large office window looking out over the St. Johns River and the Jacksonville skyline. "Come in, Frank, my boy," Phil said.

"What's up, Phil?" Frank questioned as he sat down in the big plush chair before Phil's desk.

"We might have overreached in our little business about Mr. Kevin Charles."

"Such as?"

"Such as having Victoria file criminal charges." Phil was still standing by the window, and he offhandedly pushed a curtain to the side. "You know, Jacksonville is a damn busy port. That St. Johns River down there dwarfs all the great rivers of Europe … But to the matter at hand: do you have any suggestions about what to do?" He flopped into his large comfortable chair, leaned back, and swiveled to the side.

"For Christ's sake, Phil, I don't even know what you're talking about," Frank responded.

"Oh, don't you remember getting that private dick we use sometimes to visit Vickie, masquerading as a bar investigator? We fixed him up with his phony credentials, made right here in the office on your computer and everything. Don't you remember? Of course you do. I need a smoke." He started messing with his pipe. Finally, he lit it. "Now, Frank, it appears the state attorney's office isn't just rolling over for Victoria's claim of rape. Some bastard in there is really questioning her, and I believe he will finally conclude she has brought a false charge."

"How do we know?"

"She called me."

"Is she about to cave in?"

"Not yet. I mollified her, I think. But that is just for now. Who knows what's going to happen later?" Phil said.

"By later, you mean if she caves in and tells all?"

"No, I mean *when* she tells all. There is no *if* here. If what I suspect and feel is going on, she'll be confronted with the lies and offered a way out if she tells the rest of the story, as Paul Harvey would say." He again shifted his gaze to the large office window.

"So what do we do, Phil?"

"I don't know, Frank. I suppose we don't do a goddamn thing."

"There's nothing to do but hope for the best," said Frank. "I can't count the times I've anguished over some perceived problem that eventually was resolved, without any dire consequences, just by my doing nothing. Hmm, I just don't know … Maybe we could send her out of the country and just let the whole thing wither on the vine and go away."

"Lucky for us, we've already excluded Mr. Charles in the biggest lawsuit ever brought in the state. She was a hell of an asset to us at the right time and place. I couldn't believe his attitude—his good attitude—when Hugh reminded him why we had to cut him out as one of the state's lawyers. Even said we could keep his ten thousand dollars if it would help, just to pay him back if we were successful. Damn man's just too much. I just can't help but like him."

"I do too, and I hate to admit it, but maybe we misjudged him. Do you think so?"

"Could be we did, and it's probably too late now to do anything about it. The criminal case will most assuredly be dropped."

"The grievance will go out the window too, won't it?"

"I'm not sure, but it probably will. But it doesn't matter really. It has never come to a final hearing, and when it does, and Vickie recants, well …" Phil let the comment die.

"God, Phil, I can't even say it —disbarment, ruin, and maybe even prison. But what's really going to happen?"

"The only thing I can say, my boy … is what will happen will happen."

"We have got to somehow stop Vickie," said Frank.

"Tell me the obvious, Frank," Phil said with a note of sarcasm and finality.

"You think if we went to Kevin …?"

"He's a nice guy, but no one is that nice. We screwed him all up with the bar, got criminal charges lodged against him, and cut him out of about two hundred million dollars in fees. And if …" Phil stopped for a moment, thinking. "Well, no one could expect him to forgive. No, Frank, it ain't a good idea."

"Maybe we're being overly concerned here?"

"You mean don't worry about it until it drips, as they used to say in the army."

"Yeah, something like that."

"Well, Frank, it's about to drip. Let's get the hell out of here and have a drink. Not at the club. No, let's find some sleazy bar that fits my mood." Phil put his pipe away and got up, and he and Frank departed for the tenderloin of the city.

CHAPTER 14

In the three weeks since his interview with Vickie Roberts, Singer had done some checking on her version of her case.

"Welcome back to East Bay Mrs. Roberts, and have a seat. Sorry to bother you again." *Why in hell did I say that?* he wondered. *I'm not one bit sorry. In fact, I'm conducting this little meeting with the utmost pleasure.* "Not really sorry, I guess. It's absolutely necessary. Luckily Palatka is not on the other side of the world." Then, more to himself than to her, he mumbled, "Now let me get my tape recorder ... yeah, this is the same one we recorded on before. This will just be a continuation of the same tape. Yep, it's working."

He looked at Vickie. "I know it's a long drive, but some things have to be dealt with in person ... you know, face-to-face," he said in a professional but definitely not friendly tone. He paused to gauge Vickie's expression. Her face communicated nothing. He wondered what she was thinking. She was too smart not to know, by now, what this meeting was all about. Her facial features, however, revealed nothing, absolutely nothing. "Hmm, now let's see ... it's been about three weeks since we last spoke." He perused papers in the file. "Mrs. Roberts, it looks like, from what I'm looking at"—he patted the file—"you haven't been entirely forthright with us. Is that possible?" He looked her right in the eyes with a cold, piercing glare he reserved for special occasions.

"I don't see how that's possible," she said.

For Christ's sake, she's still lying, he thought, but he did not let her see his shock or exasperation. "Well, it says right here in the investigator's report that you did not register or stay in one of the motels out on I-95

110

at the time you said you did. Did you use an assumed name?" he asked tersely.

"No, no, I'd never do that."

"Also, it says here, and I found this out myself, that Gary LaBlanc never referred you to Kevin Charles—that he really referred you to Phil Griffin up in Jacksonville." He paused, waiting for her to say something. She remained silent and actually appeared contrite.

"Not ready to answer that, huh?" He stopped again, stroked his chin, and then added, "This issue would have been so easy for you to avoid. All you had to do was tell Mr. Charles you'd heard of him from some nebulous friend." He paused again. She remained silent, with downcast eyes, as if the tears were about to flow. "Still can't talk? Okay, I'll talk. I have learned that when people are up to some kind of bad activity, they make just these kinds of dumb mistakes, the kind that can be easily traced, capisce?"

She quietly murmured, "You know all that?"

"And more, little lady. I know Gary LaBlanc referred you to Phil Griffin. I know you went to his office on June the first, three weeks before you first had an appointment with Kevin Charles. I know that you made in excess of ten phone calls to Phil Griffin's office after you retained Mr. Charles to be your attorney. I know you lied to me when you told me you were ready and willing to prosecute Mr. Charles; the police report states otherwise and reveals your inconsistent attitude. The way you portrayed Kevin Charles to me versus your obvious reluctance to prosecute the case when you filed the charge with the police tells me something, but I don't know what—*yet*. Would you like to enlighten me?"

She shook her head.

"No, I guess you wouldn't, or perhaps you can't. I don't know yet exactly how Phil Griffin plays into all this, but he showed you the motel photos, right? Would you like to tell me about that?"

She again shook her head and then held up both hands in a gesture for silence. She sat back in her chair and calmly said, "Please, Mr. Singer, please, don't say anything else. Am I free to go?"

"Free to go? Sure, you're free to go, but—"

"But nothing," she said. "I know you can't prosecute me for perjury, even if I wasn't quite honest on some points; those were immaterial matters. And the essential offense—that is, what he did to me—has been the truth. Maybe some of the details are not exactly the same ... but all this has so upset me that I hardly know my name ... and you said yourself, in cases like this memory lapses are common, or at least you understand ..."

Singer interrupted her. "Now you just hold on, little lady. Somebody forgot to tell you there is a statute in this state making it a felony to lie under oath. Materiality has nothing to do with it." He gave her a look he hoped would chill her. As he spoke, her face grew more pallid.

She finally mumbled, "You mean ...?" She could not finish the sentence. She wilted in her chair and dropped her head, seemingly seeking a hiding place as the truth of her situation washed over her like a tidal wave.

"I mean, what you have done, on at least three occasions in this office, to the police, and to the state bar: these are all felonies. Woman, we could bury you. How in the world did you ever expect to get away with it?"

"But the bar—they filed a complaint."

"The bar. You mean that bunch that police the profession? My god, woman, they have to give lip service to the type of claim you made. We don't. Right now I'm glad that nitwit in intake did, though. It's given me a chance to see the truth here ... Damn, I just can't see what you were to gain from ruining a perfectly innocent man. Don't tell me he's not innocent. I know better, and I know you weren't scorned. No, there's something else here, and it's tied in with Phil Griffin." Then he hesitated. "I don't believe we can go forward without you passing a polygraph. Do you now think that would be a good idea?"

"No, I don't think that would be a good idea."

Singer didn't give her time to reflect much before he continued. "What made me think you wouldn't think a lie detector was a good idea?"

The silence that followed left Vickie casting her eyes anxiously about the room. Finally, she looked down at her hands and began fidgeting with her rings. Obviously humiliated, she managed to squeak out, "Mr. Singer, can I do anything to help myself?"

"You haven't even been charged with anything. Hell, I don't know yet how far this thing is going to go. We'll cross that bridge if we come to it," he concluded with a slight tone of conciliation. Singer was not really interested in prosecuting Vickie. He suspected she had been duped. Of course, he also knew she wasn't without guile. "Was it money, Mrs. Roberts?"

She sat very still, looking down at her lap.

"I know you have nothing in your past remotely resembling this kind of behavior. In fact, just the opposite. But sometimes temptation just can't be resisted." He stopped, sat back in his chair, rubbed his eyes, and waited. Finally, he interrupted the silence. "Mrs. Roberts, you don't want to dig the hole you're in deeper, do you?"

Tears welled up in her eyes.

"Now, try to be calm and compose yourself so we can go on with this," he softly said.

"Mr. Singer, just give me a minute," she said with pleading wet eyes. "Could you get me a tissue?" she asked as she looked around in her pocketbook. "I don't seem to have anything in here."

"Be back in a minute." Singer stood and left the office. On his secretary's desk he found a box of tissues. When he returned, he handed Vickie a handful of tissues.

"Thank you, Mr. Singer," she said while dabbing away the tears. "This may sound really strange, but would you let me go over to Kevin's office and talk to him?"

"Yes, but first I would like for you to execute this drop-charge document." He slid a form in front of her. "It is not an admission you lied under oath. Sign that, and you can go anywhere. Of course, you can go anywhere even if you don't sign it." Singer thought he knew human nature, and given a choice at this point, he thought she'd do the right thing.

"While I'm doing this," she said, looking over the document before signing, "would you call Mr. Charles and see if he's there ... and if I can come by to see him?"

"Sure." He dialed the phone. Kevin wasn't there, but his secretary said Vickie could see him the next morning at nine. Singer repeated to Vickie that she could meet with Kevin the next morning, and she nodded her head. "Thank you. She'll be there," Singer said, ending the call. She was still looking at the drop-charge statement.

"Now I can't guarantee you this is the end of it for you, but I believe it is. Of course, I can't speak for the Florida bar." He glanced at his watch just as his intercom buzzed. He picked up the phone. "Yeah, I know about it ... They called? Oh crap! I better get over there." He hung up the phone and looked across the desk at Vickie. "Mrs. Roberts, please sign that."

She did and handed it to him.

"I've got to leave," he said as he slid it into the file while at the same time getting up to leave. They walked out together, and he put the file on his secretary's desk.

As soon as Larry Singer stepped out of the room to find her a tissue, Vickie had bit her lip, quickly picked up a stray tape on Singer's desk, and traded it for the one in his recorder. *Damn*, she thought, *where does this kind of nerve come from? It has to be the strongest instinct we all have: survival.* She slipped the tape he had been using into her purse just before he reentered the office.

* * * * *

"Thought I might find you here," Larry Singer said as he took a seat next to Kevin at the club's bar. "Figured you'd be here when your girl told me you were out for the afternoon. She said you needed some time off, but you would be back in the morning and had no appointments."

"How you doing, Larry? No appointments, huh? Should I take it I now do have one?"

"You do."

"With?"

"With one Victoria Roberts," Singer said with a satisfied tone in his voice.

"What the hell?"

"What the hell, my ass—she signed the drop charge this afternoon."

"Damn, that's the best news I've had … I started to say in a long time, but maybe ever. How did it come about?"

Larry explained what had happened, how he'd closed the case down with her lies on immaterial matters. "What I want to know is, what does Phil Griffin have against you? Did you steal his wife? Or in his case, I guess it would be more like his girlfriend."

"I don't think he has anything against me. Hmm …" Kevin rubbed his chin, obviously thinking. "At least I can't think of any reason why … am I just naive or what?"

"I'm not sure yet, but what dealings have you had with him lately?" Larry looked at the bartender, who was talking to another patron.

"Well, he gave me an opportunity to be one of the *chosen* representing the state's interest in the tobacco case. You know the state is suing for Medicaid expenses related to the use of a legal commodity," Kevin commented sarcastically. He stopped at the approach of the bartender and looked at Singer. "Miller?"

Larry nodded. "That'll do."

"A Miller for him on my tab," said Kevin, pointing his thumb to himself.

"I've never quite understood all that," Larry said. "But if he did that, you had to be on the inside of what was going on. It's my understanding the legal fees will be in the billions."

"Well, I guess I was. But after I advised Hugh about the grievance, the group abided by our contract, which excluded any of us who had that kind of trouble, and let me know I had to be terminated as one of the chosen. I understood their apprehensions, so ..."

"So you bowed out gracefully."

"How did you know?"

"I know you. Tell me this: a while ago, you didn't say it explicitly, but I think you were, or are, critical of that plan to sue the tobacco industry. Is that right?"

"Damn, Larry, I'm not following you, at least not exactly."

Larry's beer was served. "Thanks," he said. He took a sip before asking, "How did Phil put that thing together? What was the procedure?"

Kevin quickly recounted the first calls he'd gotten from Hugh and Phil about it, the meeting in Ponte Vedra, and his investment of ten thousand dollars to be one of the chosen.

"So you were one of them?"

"I guess you could say that."

"And now you aren't?"

Kevin rubbed his hands together and then opened them, palms up. "I guess you could say that too."

"Doesn't all that strike you as bizarre?"

"Not really. I had these problems, and what they are doing is questionable, at least according to some of us."

"Tell me what you mean," Larry urged as he sat forward on the bar stool.

"The whole thing is contrived. The governor and attorney general got the legislature to pass an amendment to the Medicaid Reimbursement

Act to reimburse Medicaid for payouts on diseases caused by the use of tobacco, a legal product. The statute emasculated all the traditional defenses—you know, like the plaintiff chose to use the product, et cetera. It truly left the tobacco companies without any ability to defend themselves. But what really smelled about it was the decision by the governor and attorney general to contract with the tort lawyers … you know, just a garden-variety contingency contract with the state to sue the industry. Their fee would be costs plus 25 percent of any recovery. To take some of the smell off of it, the lawyers would front the cost like we do in all personal injury cases." He sipped his scotch and soda.

"I agree there is something smelly about it."

"Not only that, but what struck me as unreasonable or maybe just odd was the schizophrenic aspect of the whole plan. The state, if it gets a verdict—no, there is no issue on that; the only question is when it gets a verdict or settles—the state will have to keep the tobacco companies in business so they can pay the judgment. Otherwise, it will truly be a Pyrrhic victory because a judgment of that size will bankrupt the companies. Anyway, a multibillion-dollar judgment might be hard to collect. The whole thing struck me as nonsense. If the state wants money from tobacco, the traditional and accepted way is to impose a tax. I saw it all as basically a relief act for those few—the chosen, you might say—who could afford to invest the cost money."

"And you made your feelings known at Ponte Vedra … or someplace?"

"Probably did. Everybody was commenting on it. But hell, if there's a chance to make that kind of money, who's going to get in the way?" Kevin said with raised eyebrows.

"I think you just told me something."

"I did?"

"Yep. Phil Griffin—I think he perceived you as possibly getting in the way. I can almost piece it together now. Did you speak directly to Phil or someone else?"

"Heck, I can hardly remember."

"Try. Give me the sequence of events, so to speak, and what you said when and to whom."

"It started with a general meeting. Maybe there were about twenty of us."

"You hadn't told anyone before that meeting your concern about it?"

"No. Anyway, the meeting was short. Frank Dunn made it look like we'd all be billionaires, without really ever saying it. But no one missed the real message."

"He cloaked it all in do-goodness, huh?"

"You bet. Then we adjourned to the bar, and those of us who were really interested had private chats with Phil ..." Kevin let the thought trail off as he blinked his eyes and stroked his chin.

"And you did too?" Larry asked as he pointed his finger at Kevin.

"Sure did. I wasn't the first. But I spoke with him briefly at the bar and agreed to deposit ten thousand with him and come up with what might be necessary later."

"How much, if you don't mind my asking?"

"It wouldn't be less than four hundred thousand."

"Wow, but you did not then tell Phil any reservations you had about the plan?"

"No." He shook his head.

"Then who did you tell?"

"After I spoke with Phil, I joined a table and talked pretty openly about what I thought. Hugh Benson, the first lawyer to apprise me of what Phil was planning, was at that table."

"So you let those guys field your concerns?"

"Yeah, I suppose you could say that."

"So if Hugh, or one of the others, told Phil, Phil could have drawn the conclusion you might be a liability, right?"

"Damn, Larry, I never thought of anything like that, and I really don't believe such a thing happened. For Christ's sake, I could still cause a ruckus."

"Not a credible one. You have had both a grievance and a criminal charge brought against you. The people, and I mean the ones who count, would want you disbarred at a minimum. You'd be painted blacker than the prince of darkness for attacking momism and apple pie. Anything you said now would simply be seen as sour grapes over your being cut out of the opportunity of a lifetime."

"You really think so?"

"I think Phil Griffin thinks so. Let me tell you what I know." Larry proceeded to fill Kevin in on the specifics, including the phone calls from Victoria to Phil's office after she hired Kevin.

"Jesus, Larry, I'm numb. What you're saying makes far too much sense. How did you get LaBlanc to tell you anything? Frankly, I felt something was up. You see, I knew she didn't stay in that motel after our first appointment, and LaBlanc never called me for a referral fee. After I received noticed of the grievance, I called him, but he was very circumspect. Wouldn't tell me anything. Pretended to feel like it might be in violation of the privilege."

"Hell, I got him on the phone, and he started that horseshit with me too. I told him that I'd have his ass before a grand jury within a week, that all I wanted was a simple fact, and that would be the end of it—no big deal. So he told me he had been asked by Phil Griffin, in person, to not reveal who he'd referred her to." Larry finished his beer.

"How could Phil Griffin have been so stupid?" Kevin mumbled before taking a big swig of his drink. Then he got the bartender's attention and said, "Two more for us?"

"Thanks," Larry said. "I think I need another beer. Kevin, it's been my observation that smart people make dumb mistakes when they are up to no good. It doesn't take a rocket scientist to show how they could have done what they wanted to do, and no one but you would have known the truth; only you and the perpetrators would know. But what the hell, that's life. We catch 'em every day—nothing new. I'll tell you something else: you check with Sam Wilks over there at the bar grievance place, and you'll find neither he nor anyone else with the bar ever told that woman to file those criminal charges."

"She said that happened?"

"Sure did, and it's just another lie as far as I'm concerned."

"God almighty. But what's this about Vickie coming to see me in the morning?"

"She wanted to see you, she said, so I went along with it like it was important. Hell, I don't care if you talk to her or not. But some of this story is not that clean. I got what I wanted and quit, at least for the time being. She might very well tell you some things we both need to know."

"Like?" Kevin said, gesturing with his palms up.

"Oh, I don't really know, but maybe like what kind of deal she had with Phil Griffin. Did he have something on her? You don't have anything to lose, but at a minimum, I'd record anything you two say. But remember, she has to be told that the conversation is being taped."

Kevin's mind was already focusing on what a conversation with Vickie would be like and exactly what he needed to do to prepare for it. Or maybe he should refuse to talk to her. Sam Wilks would no doubt take care of the grievance once he knew the state had dumped the criminal case. But if responsibility for it switched to someone else over there, then what? On the other hand, Kevin thought, in the deep recesses of his brain, more than just something could be salvaged from this mess. A big ruckus now would get Phil into trouble, but that's all. He needed to concentrate on real revenge and some way to be readmitted to the group suing big tobacco. He couldn't quite define it yet, but he knew a way was there. Just maybe, Victoria Roberts could shed the light he needed to see where he should go.

CHAPTER 15

K
evin arrived in his office early, with a smile on his face. For the first time in months, his sleep had not been plagued by frequent interruptions in which he dwelled on his image in prison gray. Some might equate "the good news" with the Gospels, but for him the good news had been delivered by Larry Singer the night before. He was elated with the turn of events. Not only was this thing going to be resolved, but he would even capitalize on it. He didn't know how, but he'd always been resourceful, and he felt he could turn this mess to his advantage. He prepared a cup of coffee, sat back in his big chair, sipped the steaming beverage, and then got up to look out the window to see if Victoria was on her way. When he heard Carol and Jo Ann arriving and cluttering about at their desks, he turned away from the window. Then it happened. Over the intercom, Carol announced the arrival of Victoria Roberts.

Victoria Roberts, he thought, should have known him under different circumstances. He couldn't help but recall the most exquisitely seductive dark brown eyes he'd ever had the pleasure of seeing. "Tell her to come on in," he announced over the intercom. He stood when she strolled through his office door. She was obviously familiar with the place and without hesitation took a seat in one of the two leather chairs for clients. He thought again to himself that she was one of the most disarming women he had ever met. *What's more*, he thought, *she might very well be the most sensuous woman I've ever seen, much less known.* He smiled; maybe she was worth all these trials and tribulations. Yet he reminded himself, in no uncertain terms, that the flesh was weak; he was convinced he had to resist temptation if he hoped to capitalize on this recent development. Still, he knew he could not completely suppress his salacious passion for this woman. In any event, he was encouraged as he retook his seat and watched her sweep back her dark hair as she sat and crossed her legs. The sound of her stockings rippling together sent a tingle up his spine. Was he a fool or what? "Now, Vickie," he began in an easy tone, "Larry Singer told me what went on yesterday."

"He did?"

"Yes. I frankly don't know whether to be grateful—that is, whether I should thank you for dropping those charges … after all I've been through … but I'll survive, I think."

"I haven't dropped any charges," she said.

Kevin was startled out of his easy manner. All carnal thoughts of Vickie evaporated. After a short pause to regain his composure, he couldn't help but caustically ask, "Then what the hell was Singer telling me?"

"Don't know," Vickie said in a distinctly condescending tone.

"For god's sake, Vickie, get with it and quit playing games. Singer and I both know you lied about where you stayed that night you had your first appointment with me," he said, obviously frustrated, yet with a note of confidence.

"I didn't lie about that," she coolly said. Then she smiled.

He choked on the insulting smile, took a deep breath, and in a calmer voice responded, "What the hell are you trying to pull?"

She just sat in silence with that knowing smile.

He waited a few seconds before continuing. "Didn't you sign a drop-charge document before Larry Singer?"

"Not my signature. By the way, this is not being recorded, is it?"

"No, would you prefer that we record it?" Kevin quickly said, knowing full well she'd say no.

"No, sir, I won't agree to that. You think you're so funny, don't you?" she said with a distinct note of coyness. "If you do record it, it's a major crime, you know."

"I know all that. But what did you do with the drop-charge thing?"

"I wrote, 'Who Knows.' I knew he wouldn't read it."

"You did what?" Kevin asked, shaking his head in disbelief.

"You heard me."

He blinked desperately, trying to fathom what was taking place. "Yes, I heard you," he sighed, still slowly shaking his head. "I just can't believe I'm hearing any of it. What goes on in the state attorney's office is always recorded, you know, and ..."

"Kevin," she quietly interjected, "you're without a doubt the nearest thing to an honest man I have ever met."

With those flattering words, Kevin immediately relaxed but continued to wonder what the hell she was up to. "Didn't you sign it right in front of Singer?"

"He got a call and was rushing out when I signed it."

"Yeah, but—"

"I just wrote on it and gave it back to him, and he slipped it into his file as he left. So ..."

"So what are you here for, Vickie?" he said in what he hoped was a calm voice as he leaned forward and wrinkled his brow. Time to get serious.

"Don't you want to know what all this is about—I mean, the grievance, the criminal charge, you getting cut out of the biggest fee any lawyer will ever have? Do you mind if I get a cup of coffee?" she asked as she stood and started toward the alcove where Kevin's coffee and liquor were kept.

"I guess I should have offered you one, but since you're up, I'll let you fix it yourself," he said somewhat flatly as she walked across the room.

"You ought to switch to Kopi Luwak, or at least Starbucks, Kevin," she said as she prepared her coffee. "But this is surprisingly good for a cheap brand."

"It's all in how you make it, Vickie, and it isn't cheap," he said as she retook her seat. He couldn't help but compare this visit with the last time she had been in his office, and he shook his head, criticizing himself for now thinking of that incident as a lost opportunity. "If you don't like the coffee, goddamn it, you don't have to drink it, you know!"

"No, it's good," she said with a smile.

And you're good, Vickie—damn good, Kevin thought. *Nothing shakes you.*

"Kevin, what if I should tell you Phil Griffin is behind all your troubles?" she said with unbelievable equanimity.

"You'd be synchronized with Larry Singer. That's what. Speaking of Larry Singer, you know he's got you on tape, don't you?"

"No, I don't think his recorder was on. Have you heard the tape?"

"No, I haven't, but—"

"But this time, I don't think his machine was on. You can check that out later. Right now, I want to see if there's a way out of all this for both of us."

"What's this about his machine not being on?"

"Trust me on this one. There is no tape."

"Uh-huh, no tape."

"No." She smiled and fluttered her eyes, signaling the end of that matter.

"But how am I supposed to trust—"

"Me?"

"Yeah." He was being far more civil than he wanted to be. She could seduce in more ways than one.

"I'm going to tell you something, something I didn't tell Mr. Singer. After that first appointment with you, I did stay at the Ramada."

"Uh-huh. I checked—you weren't there."

"If you check for the name Rosie Poe, you'll see she was there."

"Rosie Poe?"

"Stupid name, isn't it? Rosie Poe, from Panama City. Even got a credit card. You can do anything with a computer these days. I'm a bereaved widow, fighting to get justice from those who took my husband's life. If there was a record of me staying there and some man could say I had a really good time that night, wouldn't that be counterproductive to my suit?"

"I suppose so," Kevin muttered. It was like a light bulb had suddenly been turned on in his brain.

"There wasn't any man, though. And I used my real name after that first night because I knew after I met you, there would be no other men." She felt *the last time with Phil didn't count*. Then she relaxed and picked up her coffee.

"I guess I'm following you. But Vickie, Singer is going to hit the roof when he finds out about the drop-charge paper," he said as he got up and walked over to refill his coffee cup.

"You know, I almost wrote 'kiss my ass' on that thing, but I was afraid if he did read it, he might actually do it," she laughed. "No, he won't hit the roof, if you run interference for me."

"Just why would I want to do that?" Kevin said as he stirred his coffee.

"That's what I'm here today for. Don't forget, it hasn't been dropped yet."

Kevin caught the threat and shot back, "Well, Vickie, I'm waiting with bated breath." He wanted to be accommodating, but he couldn't control the sarcasm.

"That's one thing I like about you. You never lose your sense of humor," she said facetiously.

"Don't count on it." Kevin couldn't help but let a slight smile slip out.

"Let me start at the beginning." She explained that she had first gone to Gary LaBlanc, who opened the probate but who then referred her to Phil Griffin for the wrongful death case.

"Why did you get it all bawled up?"

"You would know Gary LaBlanc had opened the probate, so what else could I tell you? It was dumb, but we just felt like it was such a big case, if Gary didn't say anything, you'd conveniently forget a referral fee. Phil talked to him and told him not to let you know anything and, if you called, to just brush it off without demanding a referral fee."

"What difference did it make whether I gave him something or not?"

"Phil didn't want LaBlanc tangled up in what he'd planned for you. That's the only answer I can give."

"You all were really taking a chance."

"Not really, Kevin. You didn't contact LaBlanc until you received the grievance."

"Touché. Anyway, go on." He sat up, resting his elbows on the desk.

"Phil and I got too cozy. He actually—"

"Yeah, I was going to ask you why he didn't keep your case. He could have gotten top dollar."

"That's what I'm trying to tell you. We were, you know, seeing each other at his beach cottage frequently after the second time I went to his office. You know he can be downright charming when he wants something."

"And he wanted something from you?" Kevin chortled as he sat back.

"True and how," she laughed.

Kevin's eyes rolled back, and he sighed. "Christ, what's happening here? Are we being friendly or what?"

"Oh, let's be friendly," she said as she crossed her legs.

"For the time being. Go on."

"He was always telling me stuff, legal stuff. Anyway, he got to talking about a bar case where some lawyer had been suspended for a couple of years for having consensual sex with a client, and some of the justices favored a complete disbarment. But then he just laughed and poured himself another shot of that single-malt scotch he drinks. Anyway, one day he got real serious, and I was needing money, Kevin. I was about to lose my house and had bills, bills, bills ..."

"So?" The ensuing silence left Kevin wondering how he could have a scintilla of civility about what she had done. But he was actually beginning to listen with a certain amount of compassion—or was it passion? *Damn*, he reflected, *how can I possibly be empathetic with this woman after what she did?* He despised himself for the way he felt. Indulging in self-recrimination was not, however, cathartic. *I'm probably just a goddamn fool, but really, I have no choice but to hear her out.*

"So he promised me a lot of money, in cash, to seduce you and then file a grievance. Of course, I had to be your client. He explained to me that after you had been hit with the grievance, I could return to him, and he'd handle my case for a reduced fee. That meant I'd at least get a couple of million tax-free, plus a hundred thousand or so in cash."

"But why was he so bent on—"

"Hurting you? Because he thought you were going to hurt him."

"Hurt him?"

"Yes. He was really wrapped up in getting that legislation through, so the select group of lawyers would be hired to sue the tobacco companies."

"You know, under that legislation, the dairy industry and damn near any other food processor could be sued. All anybody would have to do is show the use of the product led to someone getting a disease that resulted in a payment by Medicaid."

"I know, I know."

"I always had some apprehension about the thing ever being successful. But as you know, the legislation was passed, and they got their contract, and a suit has been filed. But what did he have against me? I never did anything to Phil Griffin."

"I don't think he had anything right then. I think it was more of a hunch. He wanted it so bad, he perceived all kinds of reasons it would fall apart and fail. Somebody told him you were really questioning the whole thing's legality, even suggesting that it might be an unconstitutional law. He just let his imagination run wild, I think. Intuition, he'd say— his intuition told him to get you out of the plan. But of course, that wouldn't be enough. He had to destroy your credibility. He even talked about killing you. Of course, I didn't think he was serious, but you never know, and I sure didn't want that to happen."

"Oh, he wouldn't have …"

"Killed you? No, I don't think so now. At the time I really didn't know. But I did think, if I did what he wanted me to do, you'd only be put through the grievance and maybe get suspended or something."

"But you even filed the criminal charges."

"That, Kevin—and please believe me, although I don't know how you can—I did the grievance thing and that only after he threatened to ruin my wrongful death case."

"How?"

"He said I blew it by saying in front of his secretary that Cornell knew the danger because he'd told me that morning it was probably dangerous, or the wrong thing to do—that is, to put the grinding wheel on a sander. Honestly, I really didn't want to, but I felt I had no other choice, so I filed the grievance."

"But your husband never said that, did he?" Kevin said, while reflecting on the fact that she'd certainly had other choices. But he quickly decided nothing could be gained by arguing. He would let it go, at least for the time being.

"No."

"And you never said that to his secretary or to him?"

"Of course not. It never happened."

"God almighty! I knew he was really aggressive. But I never dreamed he was downright evil." He paused for a moment. "Why did you file the criminal charge?"

"A man from the bar came to my house and told me I had to file the criminal charges or the grievance would be dropped. Everything I had, including my wrongful death case, would go down the drain, and I really had some fear Phil might do something more drastic to you if the grievance was dropped. So because the grievance depended on me reporting the matter to the police, I did. I really didn't want to do that, and honestly, I don't believe I would have if Frank Dunn and Phil hadn't told me there was little likelihood you would ever even be arrested." She shook her head. "Now I don't believe the so-called bar investigator was even actually with the bar. He worked for Phil; I just know he did."

"Hmm, I wonder what city is actually graced with the sewer he crawled out of," Kevin quietly mumbled, more to himself than to Vickie.

"Kevin, when I came to see you and told you I was changing attorneys, my original plan was to tell you everything that was going on, but that was only if I could start seeing you on a personal basis. I wanted to love you. You just don't know how much. But—and I'm not blaming you—you turned me down. I was hurt, so I did what I did: I fired you, so I could file a grievance against you. Honestly, I never thought it would all go this far."

Kevin sat back with a recognition of reality. This was a stinking world, and he would just have to put up with it. After a moment, he once again cast a peaceful eye toward Vickie. "So the disciple of the prince of darkness is trying to do both of us in?"

She nodded.

How absurd life gets, he thought. Here he was, contemplating conspiring with the enemy, someone who had been perfectly willing to do him in for money. "Curiosity," he mumbled to himself, "could kill more than a cat."

"What's that?" Vickie asked.

"Oh, nothing, just talking to myself. Frankly, I don't know what to do. But I guess there's nothing to lose by listening. You have my curiosity in overdrive, yet I ought …"

"Ought to show me the door?"

"Maybe."

"But you won't," she said, smiling. "You know I wrote that note to you not to worry, don't you? I was called by the prosecutor's office and told the charges had been filed and you would be arrested. So I just had to let you know I would never let anything really bad happen to you."

"I suspected you wrote it but certainly wasn't sure."

"I just needed a little more time to make sure Phil didn't sabotage my case and leave me with nothing."

"Well, I don't know … is that supposed to make me feel better and forget all the sleepless nights?"

"At the time, I hoped the note would do just that."

"Well, we can talk about all that later. Right now, you haven't told me anything yet about why my wife kicked me out and how she got those compromising pictures. You must know something about all that."

"Well, not really …"

"Don't lie now. If you do, I'll know it, and we won't go on with this little tête-à-tête."

"No, no, I did know about it, but only after the fact. I didn't know there were going to be any photographs. I was just supposed to have sex with you and then do the grievance thing. I even lied and told them I'd failed. However, Phil, instead of paying me more money to try again, which was *my* plan, said since we had the photos, I would just lie about seducing you. It was Phil's idea to try to screw up your marriage.

"That was *really* personal. But he said it would help in the grievance thing to have some pictures, but they would have to be compromising, and the best way to do that was to have your wife unknowingly assist us in doing you in. I think it was Frank Dunn who made the anonymous calls to your wife, as a supposed friend, to let her know that you were having an affair with me. Frank and Phil had told me your marriage was about over, so when I heard about her hiring the investigator who took the pictures, I figured she was getting evidence for the divorce. But Kevin, I know it's hard to believe I didn't know anything about interfering with your marriage and taking pictures. But I didn't, and even though you told me you were in love with your wife when we finally got together, you were so tender and loving, I thought you loved me—confirming that your marriage was about over. Just the fact of having sex with me indicated you didn't really love your wife and your marriage wasn't going to survive whether you were grieved or not."

"You made the complaint to the bar like it was rape, rather than consensual sex to support the criminal charge later, I guess."

"Frank Dunn told me to do that and add the part about the contracts and stuff. So I just did what they wanted me to do. But, Kevin, I didn't know there was a plan to criminally charge you until well after I filed the grievance as I've already told you."

"Good god, did this just all of a sudden occur to Phil, or what?"

"It came more or less in stages," she said with an expression of relief.

"I ought to just go to the police."

"With what, Kevin?"

"With the truth. You have falsely accused me of a crime, and Phil Griffin is just as culpable as you are. That's for starters," Kevin said.

"Oh, you're so handsome when you're serious. But seriously, if you don't want to hear me out, I'll go."

"God almighty, Vickie, can't you turn it off?"

"No, it's just the way I am." She then stood up and walked to the coffee area and set the cup there.

"I feel like the vicar in that old Somerset Maugham play *Rain*. He knew that Sadie was the personification of the devil but simply couldn't resist temptation."

"I told you, you are an honest man."

"Yeah, yeah, now I want you to listen to me, okay?" She was a victim too, he concluded, and she knew Phil had used her. *I know she likes me. But can she be trusted? We'll see.*

"Okay, what do you suggest? That's really why I'm here. I'm not a complete fool. What I've done could catch up with me ... well, anyway, what do you think we can do?"

"First off, we know something Phil doesn't know."

"True."

"And that always gives one the advantage in bargaining. We also know—no, I don't know: what have you told him? Anything?"

"Yes, I called him after my first meeting with Mr. Singer. I knew what Singer was up to, and frankly, I think he knew I knew. Anyway, I called up Phil and told him I thought matters were falling apart. That's when he lied to me about the law on perjury. He told me not to worry because I was lying on immaterial matters, but he failed to tell me about a statute ..."

"That makes it a felony to lie under oath," Kevin said, finishing her sentence.

"Bingo. And I haven't seen him since, though I've tried to call him. He is definitely avoiding me."

"Out of sight, out of mind, I guess. What you're telling me is he now knows you probably will turn against him, and he doesn't know exactly how far you will go. He's just hoping now that he won't hear anything else about it, that it will all just go away." Kevin mused on all this as if it were simply an academic matter. Then he just sat with a pensive expression and rubbed his chin.

"So?"

"If we now plant information to really make him scared, maybe we can capitalize on his chicanery."

"What's this *we* business? What's in it for me?" Vickie said as she uncrossed her legs and sat forward.

"Vickie, I just don't know. Do I have any options?"

"Options for what?" she questioned.

"Getting you to drop the criminal case and the grievance thing."

"Oh, I think you do, but ..."

"But," he interjected, "you want to benefit in some way for doing what you ought to do, right?" He casually gestured toward her with his open hand.

"Well, yeah, I thought we could work something out. You know, you get what you want, or maybe ought to have, and I, well, I ought to get something."

"Vickie, there's no *maybe* to it, and you know that, but ..." He arched his eyebrows and made firm eye contact with her. Before she could respond, he continued. "If I do nothing, Singer will take care of the criminal case, don't you think?"

She nodded but said, "Maybe."

"No, he will. I know he will. He doesn't need for you to sign a drop-charge document. The prosecutors just want something in the file in case the victim objects later. When he does drop it, that will most assuredly affect the bar matter. They should drop the grievance ... but those folks don't always do what they should do! I'm just thinking out loud here, but pay attention. Since that is really an unknown, somebody other than Wilks over there in Orlando could perceive—probably would perceive—the lies you've told as irrelevant to whether we had sex. This is particularly true since consensual sex with a client is now considered to be such an ethical no-no." Kevin paused, stroked his chin, stood up and walked to the window, and looked out as if the answer could be outside—outside the box, so to speak. He slowly turned back and looked at Vickie across the room.

"What are you thinking?" she said.

"We, or at least I, have a moral dilemma." He had decided he must do what was necessary to get her to drop the grievance complaint and the criminal case too. He wasn't Socrates and had no intention of drinking the hemlock. "You and I both know you should do what's right, drop the grievance matter, and file a drop-charge document with Singer. The latter, you might already have done."

She looked puzzled. "But I haven't …"

"Maybe you have. 'Who Knows' could be your signature."

"You really think so?"

"No, not really, but it's something to think about, and it doesn't affect the grievance."

"So?"

"So am I, or are we, morally and ethically compromised if …" Kevin stopped.

"If you pay me to do the right thing?" she uttered as she looked away.

Kevin said nothing. He wanted her to mull it over in her mind. If she didn't go along, he would probably pay her anyway.

Finally, she said, "Okay, I'll drop all the charges. No strings attached." She then sat back, as if all the life in her had been sucked out, as if she had a defeated soul, or perhaps more accurately, a defeated ego.

"Vickie, you have just made my day … and hopefully yours too."

She swept back her hair and raised her eyebrows. She was listening.

"Now I feel we—that is, you and I—can work something out."

"Something out?"

"Yes. I think I can come up with something, a plan to get even …" He stopped.

She still looked slightly perplexed.

With a soft smile, he continued. "A plan of some kind that will benefit both of us." This woman was not only pretty and no doubt corrupt but also smart, he thought. "You're not altruistic, are you?" he inadvertently blurted out.

"Altruistic? Maybe. Who knows?" She heard her own words and chuckled.

He grinned.

"I really didn't mean to say that."

"I know … but you'll do what we need to do, if there's something in it for you, right?" He gave her another comforting smile.

Kenneth A. Studstill

The doom and gloom she had so recently exhibited faded as she leaned forward and nodded. "You said the plan would benefit both of us …" She let the sentence trail off.

He did not promptly respond.

She then cautiously asked, "What's in it for me?"

"A large portion of anything we can siphon out of the big noise in Jacksonville." He furrowed his brow and paused in anticipation, looking at her. She was beginning to look positively ecstatic. "But not to exceed ten million."

"Whew, that's more than I expected. And …"

"And once you really sign the drop charge, I'll forget you've agreed to do it with no strings attached and give you fifty thousand dollars, plus another fifty thousand when the grievance is dropped."

"That's all?"

"That's all for now. But keep in mind, I'll get several hundred million at the end, if all plays well and you'll get at least ten million of that."

"I don't really know … no, no, I mean I'd rather throw in my lot with you. Okay?"

"It's okay, Vickie. I know you're not an ingrate."

"Oh shit, Kevin, sometimes things just get so screwed up."

"I'll endorse that," he said, and he stood up, signaling the meeting was over.

As he watched her walk out, she turned partway around and hesitated, like she was thinking of saying something more. Should he ask if she'd like to have dinner or something? If she were to suggest it, he knew he wouldn't be able to say no. He also knew that combining sex and business was usually a bad idea, so he buried an overwhelming urge to ask her out. His relief was palpable when she only momentarily lingered without turning completely toward him. She turned her head to face the door and briefly paused again, before strolling ever so gracefully out of his office. Five minutes later, he dialed her cell phone.

"How are you, Kevin?"

"I just wanted to tell you bye again and to have a nice weekend."

"You know, Kevin, we could really have a nice weekend if you wanted to."

"I think of you a lot, and I'll stay in touch. Drive carefully; I don't want anything to happen to you. But I've got to say good-bye now."

"Okay. If you decide you want to see me, you know where I am. Bye-bye."

* * * * *

A week or so later, Kevin called Singer's office, but he was not in. Singer's secretary believed he was in the courthouse for a late-afternoon hearing, so Kevin went to the courthouse to find him. But he wanted it to appear like the meeting was just by chance. He found Larry at the short-order counter. With a nonchalant air and a friendly smile, he approached him.

"Hey, Larry. Fancy seeing you here in the courthouse."

"Here or over at my office, it's damn easy to find me on any given day. Can't say the same for everybody in the office. Want to have a cup with me?"

"Sure, and I'll buy. Two medium coffees," Kevin said to the lady behind the counter. "Let's get a table." Once they were seated, Kevin asked, "Anything new on what we discussed at the club?"

"No, unless you have something to tell me about your meeting with Mrs. Roberts."

"She did confirm what you have already figured out. And she knows she's in trouble and is looking for a friend. She believes she's a victim, and I think she might be. We'll just have to wait and see."

"Hmm, we can get back to that later. I just don't know how far I want to go. You're important to me. The rest ... hell, I just don't know. Can't clean up all the sin in the world." His voice trailed off as he stirred his coffee.

"Larry, you seem to be in deep thought," Kevin said, wrinkling his brow in concern.

"Oh, forgive me, Kevin. I'm just thinking about this ridiculous motion some overpaid defense lawyer has scheduled for the last hour of the day. But what the hell! Anything new with you?"

"No, nothing really new," Kevin answered, hedging. "But I've been wondering about a few things."

"Only got a few minutes, but shoot," Larry said as he reached for his cup of coffee.

"Larry, once you contact the grievance people about this, do you think we'll get any repercussions?"

"Never can tell. Who knows what Sam Wilks will do?"

"But once they know, do you believe they might expect your office to do more?"

"You mean pursue Victoria and Phil Griffin?"

"Yeah, not that I really care. It just struck me they might have some concern—the bar, that is."

"Hmm, you might have a point. Never really thought what we did was any of their business." Singer paused, sipped his coffee, and looked at Kevin. "Kevin, you just might have stumbled onto something. That bunch makes any attorney activity their business. Yeah, we'll probably have to pursue it, at least as far as Phil Griffin. Beyond that, I just don't know. But what the hell, that's my job." He continued to expound on the trials and tribulations of being a prosecutor, with some emphasis on how politics intervened from time to time.

Kevin heard but didn't really listen. He was smiling to himself, yet in some inexplicable way, he felt guilty for manipulating the system to prosecute a man who should not only be prosecuted but should also be convicted and sent to prison. This tiny victory, if it could be called that, was bittersweet at best.

"Oh, by the way," Singer said, "let me ask you something: if a person scribbled out something nearly illegible that is supposed to be a signature, is it a signature, though it is not the person's real name?"

"Why would you ask me that?"

"Oh, just lawyer-to-lawyer talk … or could be just lawyer-to-lawyer talk. But"—Singer affected a bemused expression and stroked his chin—"that woman's signature on the drop-charge form does not look like 'Victoria Roberts.' So my question to you is has she actually done what she stated she would do?"

"I don't know, Larry. What do you think?"

"I don't know what to think, at least not yet. But what the hell, I've got to go. Been nice talking to you. You've given me some things to think about."

Singer walked off, leaving Kevin to scratch his head, wondering just how much Singer knew and how far he intended to go in his investigation.

CHAPTER 16

I n April 1996, with the tobacco suit well underway, Phil Griffin was beginning another day's march to that pot of gold at the end of the rainbow. He was up, up, up, aggressively pleasant as he focused on the pursuit of riches.

"Never nurse your hangover like it's a badge of honor, Frank."

Squinting his eyes and rubbing his forehead, Frank was pouring himself a cup of coffee.

"Get your coffee and come on into my office. We've got tons of work to do."

"I don't know how you do it. You must have a constitution of steel. You put away your share, but you never seem to suffer the next day from last night's good time."

"Not always. There have been—"

"Yeah, I remember, and how."

"Don't remind me. That was months ago, and I haven't spoken a word to Victoria since that last phone call, when she checked in for guidance because she believed the prosecutor knew she'd lied to him about the case against Mr. Charles," Phil said. He couldn't show his true pusillanimousness by admitting he wouldn't accept her calls. Then more to himself than to Frank, he mumbled, "And I won't, not until we settle her case and maybe not even then. We don't get a thing out of it." He paused again. "Hopefully, I never will speak to her again. But if we have to, we'll just deal with it, just not quite like the last time. No, Frank, I don't ever need to be that drunk again. I'm just grateful we survived. The day after that night left me actually swearing off booze and wondering whether or not I had the clap, or worse. The hairs on my head felt like they would split in two. I took so many aspirins, I threw up. Nothing could make me feel better, not even the ice bags I piled up around my head, and if I moved … well, you know, but I was really at low ebb. It still worries me sometimes. But we can't let that kind of sideshow distract us from the main event, can we?"

"No, sir, and I'll be along in a minute, okay?"

"Okay," Phil said. He sipped on his cup of coffee while walking to his office, shook his head, and smiled to himself. Sure, he had always been able to pretend no aftereffects. But he felt it all right. He just didn't brag about it. He viewed himself as a superior being, and he smiled while indulging himself with such self-flattery; the notion that he was better than others was still lurking in his mind when he pulled out a file and recorder and began to dictate directions and comments to all the other attorneys working on the biggest case in the state's history. Did he really believe he was making history, not just plodding through life until he died? He shook his head and kept on smiling to himself.

"Mr. Griffin," said his secretary over the intercom.

"Yes."

"There is a man here with some papers to serve on you."

"Tell him I'll be right out," he hastily replied, thinking it was some service of process on a corporation he was resident agent for. He jumped up and rushed out to his secretary's desk, resenting the momentary interruption.

"Are you Mr. Phillip Griffin, attorney at law?" the man said.

"Yes, I am."

"Then this is for you," he said, handing the papers to Phil.

Phil looked at them but failed to grasp their significance for a moment. Then the blood drained from his face so quickly that he must have looked like he was dead standing up. "For god's sake, this is a subpoena to appear before a grand jury," he mumbled as he started back into his office. Encountering Frank at the threshold of his office, Phil urgently commanded, "Get in here, Frank, now!"

Once inside Phil's office, with the door shut, Frank asked, "Did I hear right? That's a subpoena?"

"You heard right. Goddamn it. They are subpoenaing me to appear in East Bay for a grand jury. That's down there where you-know-who is …"

"Kevin Charles?"

"The one and the same."

"What are you going to do?"

"I'm going to go. I have no other choice. That son of a bitch."

"Maybe I should call Kevin and see if he knows anything—you know, like we are totally in the dark, and since he lives down there, maybe he can shed some light on this thing, or ..."

"Or what?" Phil asked.

"Or we might call the state attorney's office and try to speak to someone."

"No, no, I don't want to do that. Those guys are always reading something between the lines. Plus we don't know them. Let me think. We've got three weeks, but we can't procrastinate. If we can contain it now, we need to do it."

"Phil, we don't really know—"

"Yes, we do. This is directly related to Victoria's phone call. God, I can't get over the irony. We were just talking about that little matter, and now that little matter has morphed into big trouble, almost as we were speaking."

"It is uncanny."

"Jesus, I don't know what it is in my life that's always leaving me with all kind of apprehensions."

"It's the profession, Phil, that's all."

"For god's sake, Frank, I just meant that rhetorically. What we're facing now hasn't really got anything to do with our profession."

"Well, what are we going to do?" Frank asked as he plopped into one of the big leather chairs. "My head aches, my stomach's queasy, and now this."

"I think we have to go on the assumption they know everything, right?"

"Believe so."

"All of this relates directly to Kevin Charles, right?"

"Right again."

"And maybe Victoria?"

"Right again."

"The only reason they want me for a grand jury is to see if I will lie. Can't be for information, right? In fact, I could be arrested right now, but they want to see if I'll lie under oath before the grand jury, right?"

"Yes, but you can take the fifth."

"True, but I will be arrested anyway when I come out for conspiracy to fabricate a crime, obstruction of justice, and god knows what else, and you know what that would do."

"Nullify your interests in the tobacco suit, that's what it would do."

"Bingo, Frank, and no doubt get me disbarred. So ..." Phil tossed the subpoena onto his desk. "We need—no, have—to avoid appearing before the grand jury and get this thing stopped. Of course, we can't simply not go because it's scheduled at an inconvenient time."

Frank picked up the subpoena from Phil's desk. "How are you going to avoid the subpoena? I guess you could try to quash it. Actually, right now it's not enforceable," Frank said as he flipped through the papers, "since it looks like they forgot to include a check to pay you."

"No, that would never work in the long run. A judge would just tell them to pay. And if I just failed to show up, they would probably have me arrested, clean everything up, and properly subpoena me for another day. It would just get us a lot of unwanted publicity. It's not quashable anyway."

"Well?"

"Let me think." Phil reached for his pipe and began packing the bowl. He looked out the window as if the answer was out in the Jacksonville skyline. "Keep in mind that all of this goes back to Kevin Charles. He's doing this to us. So we have to get to him."

"You aren't talking about killing him?"

"No, although it wouldn't bother me if someone did. No, we don't need to kill him." Phil contemplated his persuasive powers. "I simply need a meeting with him. If possible, it should be here on the home court." He took a puff from his pipe, lost in thought for a moment. "But if necessary, any goddamn place he wants it!"

"You sure you don't want to inquire about whether you might be granted immunity from anything you say?"

"Before the grand jury? Frankly, I don't see what good it would do if I was granted immunity. That's only good for what I say, and either the truth or a lie would do me in. I will have stopped nothing. I feel like I'm on a railroad track with a locomotive bearing down on me. No, we have got to stop the train or somehow get off the track, and the only person who can stop the train or get us off the track is Kevin Charles."

"You don't think they'll subpoena me, do you?"

"Why would they want to do that?" Phil said, implying that Frank was far too insignificant to be subpoenaed before a grand jury. "Probably would have already done it if they were going to. It's me they're after, not you. But the fact they haven't is more proof they're not looking for more evidence. Victoria has turned, that's for sure. But ..." He hesitated. "Frank, you call Kevin Charles and see if there's anything to discuss. You know, be my attorney and find out as much as you can without admitting anything. I can't believe I said that. The cat's already out of the bag, but we'll pretend for the time being it isn't."

"And the case against the tobacco companies?"

"Oh that," Phil answered. "Frank, it's going as expected. It's just about time to settle it."

"Is there something I should do?"

"No, I'll take care of that. You go ahead and contact Mr. Charles for us."

* * * * *

"Phil, I've set a lunch engagement at the Omni for you and Kevin Charles," Frank dutifully reported over his intercom. "He said he had to be out of town next week, but he has some business up here Friday of the next week, so it will be convenient for both of you."

"What else did he say?"

"Not much."

"Surely he wanted to know why you were calling for me."

"Actually, you're right; he asked right off if he needed a lawyer too."

"And?"

"And I told him, as casually as I could, that I couldn't answer that. I tried to laugh the question off."

"And?"

"And he was not amused."

"What do you mean, not amused?"

"He quickly snapped, 'This isn't a laughing matter.'"

"Well, did he mention anything else about the grand jury and the subpoena?"

"Not really."

"What the hell does that mean?"

"I told him you'd been subpoenaed, and all he said was that was too bad—that he knew how distressing such a situation could be, even if the investigation was a big lie."

"You know what he meant by all that?"

"Not really."

"Quit saying 'not really'!" Phil tersely commanded.

"It's just an expression, Phil. I made it clear that what you wanted was a meeting, and he said okay but that no one can be there but you, and you have to bring the subpoena so he can actually see it."

"Get in here, Frank."

Frank dutifully obeyed orders. In a minute he stood before Phil's desk.

"Okay, now we are face-to-face. Did you agree to all that?"

"Only tentatively. I said I'd call back."

"And?"

"He said you should call back. He wants to talk only to you from here on out. He does not want any misunderstandings. So I guess it's up to you."

"It's always up to me."

"Hell, then just don't meet with him and ..."

"Abide by the subpoena? No, sir. I'll meet with Mr. Charles. I don't really see anything to lose and maybe a lot to gain."

"Meaning?"

"Meaning nothing." Phil was already debating in his own mind how much it would cost him to placate Kevin Charles. Phil, the polished gentleman from Jacksonville, had not always been even a gentleman, much less polished. Having been born and raised on the lower west side of Manhattan before moving to Miami in his teens, he had thought for a long time that the only way a person got anything done, legal or illegal, was through who he knew or a bribe. It was a way of life and involved no moral turpitude. You paid for what you wanted. It had actually come as a surprise, much later in his life, that the corruption found in too many of America's bigger cities was not even tolerated, much less embraced, by every community in the country.

Phil had never let his intellectual prowess—indeed, superiority—interfere with his early education on the streets of New York and Miami. He knew his street smarts had always given him an edge.

He was again running an old mental tape through his brain. *Howard Hughes was not wrong when he said every man has his price*, he thought. He smiled to himself when he thought about how easy it had been in his formative years to feign something was wrong with a meal to get out of paying the bill.

"Well, you've already done a 180-degree reversal from what you said just after being served."

"And that was?"

"That you would abide by the subpoena."

"Did I say that?"

"Yes, you did."

"Then I was talking like a buffoon. But talking like one and being one are two different things!"

"Sometimes," Frank said cynically.

* * * * *

"Hello, is this you, Kevin, answering your own phone?"

"You dialed my back line; it rings directly into my office. If you called, I didn't want one of the girls putting you off. Your time is valuable, and I respect that, Phil." Kevin smiled as he imagined Phil's discomfort.

"Kevin, I'm glad that you can make it up here in two weeks. If that Friday isn't convenient for you, we can reschedule, and if necessary, I'll drive down there."

"No, I'll be up there anyway, and the lunch hour should be no problem. If it is, I'll call, and maybe we can adjust it and still talk."

"That's fine. To be on the safe side, I'll keep the afternoon open, okay?"

"Sounds fine to me."

"Kevin?"

"Yes."

"Do you have any information, or insight, into this goddamn subpoena served on me to appear before the grand jury in a few weeks?"

"Not really. Tell you what, I'll make some discreet inquiries, and by the time I see you Friday, I ought to have something useful for both of us."

"Good. Then I'll say good-bye until Friday."

"Until Friday." Kevin hung up. He looked across his desk to Victoria and smiled wickedly. Kevin loved the game as much as anyone. Living on the edge had its rewards. "He's bitten the bait, Vickie. But we don't want to get too sure of ourselves yet. We presume nothing. You know if we get caught having issued a fake subpoena for a grand jury, some folks, in some quarters, might not see the humor."

"What if he just decides to appear before the grand jury?" Vickie questioned.

Kevin took a deep breath, furrowed his brow, and said, "If he does that, he will have accidentally done the smartest thing he could do, and our plan will be toast. But a man with *his* ego won't do that. No, he'll try to buy his way out."

"I agree, but what if?"

"What if anything, Vickie?"

"But you said serving a fake subpoena is a crime, a third-degree felony."

"It is, and that's the reason we didn't try to fabricate a check from the state to be served with it, you know. If it's not an enforceable subpoena, is it a subpoena? Maybe not. On the other hand, no problems if you're not caught committing the crime—any crime."

"You're sure the guy who served it won't rat us out?"

"I'm not sure the sun will come up in the morning, but that guy used to be our investigator, and in the past he was a bail bondsman. He's the one who told me the subpoena forms were kept in a big compartment thing sitting in the hall over there in the state attorney's office. Anyone could just pick one up. And frankly, I have a lot on him. Believe me, he won't talk."

"But you paid him to do it?"

"Yes, I did. He knows the game. Aside from him, it can never be traced to us. Vickie, if there's something to be gained, there's always a risk. Also, he would expose his own chicanery if he talked. Moreover, the same goes for Phil if he should find out the truth about the subpoena and try to do something about it. The risk is actually minimal."

"And we have so much to gain ..."

"That's why we're taking the risk."

"I can't help feeling apprehensive all the time. I've been that way pretty much ever since—"

"Ever since you threw in with Phil Griffin?"

"Please, don't throw that up in my face again."

"Sorry, but that is what you were going to say, isn't it?"

"Yes."

"Vickie, we are business partners now, that's all." Then he smiled as their eyes met. "Well, maybe a little more than that, but our business should be characterized as a joint venture. Once we've done him in, that's the end of our business."

Vickie nodded her head.

"Then I'll do what's necessary to get any charges dropped against you. Since you'll be the star witness against Phil Griffin, that will not be any problem at all."

"But?" She slightly bit her lip.

"You'll just have to trust me."

"I told you once you're the nearest thing to an honest man in my life, and I still believe it, Kevin."

"Well, it's costing me a hell of a lot of money to get justice—your expression."

"Maybe it will be worth it," she said with a twinkle in her eye, and Kevin did not misinterpret her erotic invitation.

"I don't want to talk about that. Whoever said justice can be bought was right," Kevin said with a grim expression.

"You sure you don't want to talk about *that*?" She smiled as she emphasized "that."

Looking at her at in that moment, casually dressed in khaki shorts, a blue striped blouse, and tennis shoes, he said, "I would love to, but we just can't do that right now."

"Well, I can't say you don't know what you're missing, can I?"

"No, you can't, but for better or worse, it's all in the past, over."

"Don't be so sure. Nothing's done and over till you're cold in the grave." She got up. "I guess I'm supposed to go over to the state attorney's office at four o'clock and this time really drop the charges."

"Sign a drop-charge document."

"Oh, you are so precise."

"Not precise enough sometimes," Kevin mumbled. Louder, he said, "That's our deal. You take care of that thing over there."

"That *thing*! My, we are being precise …"

"Vickie, I've got fifty thousand dollars for you when Singer calls me and says you've done the right thing—and a lot more than that down the road." Walking around his desk, he brushed her cheek with a light kiss. Even seeing her casually dressed in shorts, blouse, and tennis shoes and with her hair a little disheveled, he could not ignore the overwhelming lust he had for her as he caught a whiff of her scent, highlighted by Chanel No. 5, a very good perfume. "So … hasta la vista," he said. As he watched her stroll away, he wondered one more time how long he was going to deny himself.

* * * * *

The day after Phil was served the subpoena, Vickie went to see Singer. She was casually dressed in a straight khaki skirt and a light blue blouse.

"Well, Mrs. Roberts," said Larry Singer, "what brings you back to this den of bureaucratic rectitude?"

"Mr. Singer, I need to fix something."

"Fix something, huh? Mr. Charles—of course, you know who that is—seems, for whatever reason, willing to forgive and forget. Do you know why?" he concluded with a slight scowl.

Vickie shook her head. "Probably not, Mr. Singer," she softly replied.

"So you want to fix something. Hmm." Singer looked thoughtfully at her, meshing his fingers together as if to crack his knuckles.

"Yes. Do you have the file of my case against Mr. Charles?"

"Yep, got it right here." He laid a file before her.

"Why haven't you already dropped this case?"

"Oh, I think something was screwed up in here," he said, patting the file. "I decided not to do it, at least not yet. But I will get around to it, you can be sure of that." The inflection in his voice left no doubt he meant what he said. Yet he did not sound hostile or even agitated. He was simply making a fact crystal clear, that's all.

She took a deep breath and tried to look pleasant. "Let me see that affidavit I signed."

"It's not an affidavit. It's just a statement indicating you want to drop the charges. Let me see … do I still have it?" he said as he opened the file. "Yes, here it is." He handed it to her. "Mrs. Roberts, if you're going to do what I think you're going to do, well, let's just say you will have made my day."

"What do you think that might be?" she said with a cryptic smile. She simply could not suppress her flirtatious nature.

"Surprise me."

"What makes me think it's no surprise?" she said as she marked through her earlier supposed signature and wrote her true name. She handed the document back to him and tried to look apologetic as she said, "I now feel a lot better, Mr. Singer."

"So do I, Mrs. Roberts. By marking that out, you have just saved yourself and others a lot of grief—yourself because I'm not going to file a multitude of charges and others, including me, because we won't have the distinct displeasure of seeing you in prison. You have finally done the right thing and restored my faith in the human race."

"You knew?"

"Yes, I've known since you called and asked my secretary if the case had been dismissed. Then I took my time to see what you had written. Could have been downright embarrassing if I'd acted on it. But I just let it sit and hoped something right would happen. Don't get me wrong—this case was going to be dropped anyway, and you, little lady, would not have been happy, capisce?"

Vickie thought she was pretty much no good and wondered why she was blessed with such good luck. "That leaves only the grievance," she whispered.

"Yeah."

"I'm just going to not show up next month at the hearing. If I'm not there, there is no case, right?"

"So they tell me."

"Can I go now?"

"Yes, and try not to jeopardize yourself again. Money is only money."

"You're right," she said, getting up to leave. Oh, she thought, if Larry Singer only knew how much cash she had already been paid by Phil, and there was no way he could get it back without exposing his own dirty laundry. But that was her secret, and he would never know. Everything was falling into place, life was exciting, and her adrenaline was flowing. She already had more money than she had ever dreamed of having while she was married to Cornell, and there was more to come.

Before she was out of Mr. Singer's office, his phone rang. He picked it up, motioned for her not to leave, and then said, "Okay, I'll tell her. That was my secretary, Mrs. Roberts. The message was for you to call Mr. Charles when you're through here. You're welcome to use one of our phones if you don't have a cell phone with you."

"Thank you, Mr. Singer; I'll call him when I get outside." She left Mr. Singer's office and called Kevin once she was outside the building. "Hello, Kevin."

"Hello, Vickie. I'm glad you got my message. Everything go okay?"

"Yes, but you knew it would, didn't you, so why are you really calling?"

"I would love to have dinner with you tonight at one of the restaurants on the beach. Or if you prefer, we can go to the club here in town. You know we've never celebrated our business venture. Maybe we could have a bottle of champagne?"

"Of course I'll have dinner with you, but I need to change clothes, take a shower, et cetera, and I didn't bring anything else to wear and haven't yet rented a room anywhere, so ..."

"That's even better. This time you can stay with me. I'm leaving the office right now. I'll meet you in front of the courthouse in a few minutes."

"Okay, Kevin. I'll see you in a few."

"Hasta la vista, Vickie."

After Vickie slid into Kevin's Volvo, he closed the door, went around the car, and took his seat behind the steering wheel. "Oh, Kevin, I'm so glad you called. Give me a kiss?"

He leaned over and kissed her. "Mm, you taste good."

"You do too." She kissed him again before sitting back in her seat. They stopped by her Honda for her overnight bag and she quickly hopped out to retrieve it. "How far is your place?" she asked as she climbed back in the car, placing her bag in the backseat.

"About twelve miles down on the coast. It's just a two-bedroom, one-bath, stucco cabin. It's kind of secluded ... nothing fancy, but I like it." He started the car, and he put his hand on her leg. "You want to drop by the club for a drink?"

"Only if you do."

"I'm not really interested in a drink right now. We can just go to my place, freshen up and then go out to dinner. That okay with you?"

"Sounds fine. How long will it take to get there?"

"No more than about fifteen or twenty minutes. There's not much traffic on old US-1. Now tell me what you've been doing in school."

"Oh, nothing special. But last semester I got a 4.0."

"Great. You're a smart woman. And before long, you're going to be a well-educated one."

"God, I hope so. That's what it's all about."

They talked some more about her classes, her teachers, and books (they both had read Grisham's *The Rainmaker* recently). He talked about some cases he'd had in the past. And before long, they arrived at his cottage.

"This is nice," she said as they entered his home. She walked through the living room and looked into both bedrooms and the kitchen before stopping to gaze out over his back porch to the breaking waves.

She turned toward him and his arms went around her for a passionate kiss. He could feel her breasts pressing against him and the warmth of her body radiated through him, right down into his loins. "You have the softest sweetest lips . . ." He paused for a moment. Then he kissed her again. "Let's take a shower before going out for dinner."

"No swim or walk on the beach first?"

"Do you want to?"

"No, I want to get naked with you."

"So. . . let's get in the shower?"

"Okay.

"But I only brought a few things other than my underwear, so when we go out for dinner this skirt I'm wearing will have to do."

"You would be fine anywhere out here, but we'll go to the Surf. It's close by and very informal."

"Sounds fine to me." And she started toward his bedroom. "Come on, we can bathe each other."

"I'm right behind you." They helped each other undress. "Let me get another bar of soap."

They stepped into the shower. "I forgot my shower cap. Oh well, I'll do something with it." She began washing his back.

"Turn around so I can wash your back?" Instead of turning around, however, she reached around him and started washing his genitals, lightly laughing while rubbing up against his back. Then she turned around. He began soaping her back while she lathered her front.

"Oh, that feels good." Then he reached around and slipped his fingers into her vagina, over her vulva, and stroked her clit. She looked over her shoulder. "That feels good too."

"Think we'll finish this shower without fucking?"

"I don't know, but it would be a little difficult to do it here. Why, do you want to? Hmm, I guess I could just bend over, though." Then she turned to face him and began stroking his soapy member with both hands.

"We could try it like they do it in the movies. But this isn't a movie, so ..."

"So let's rinse off and get out." She moved directly under the nozzle for a moment and then stepped out of the way so he could get under the water. While pushing her hair back, she stepped out onto the bath mat and grabbed a towel. He rinsed off and followed.

"Even with your wet hair falling straight down to your shoulders, you're one good looking woman. Give me a kiss." And he cradled her face with his hands and kissed her passionately.

He then put his arm around her waist and they took a few steps to the bed where he laid on his back, with her partially on him. She started stroking his erection. "You're quite good looking yourself."

"Not really, but thanks."

"Yes you are. And do you exercise or something to stay in shape; a little thin, but nice."

"I work out a little, careful about sweets, and I often walk the golf course." Then he buried his face in her wet hair. "Hmm, you smell like you just took a bath."

"No kidding. You do too." Then they passionately kissed. When the kiss ended, she moved down and casually began blowing him. It wasn't long before she looked up. "Can I get on it?"

"Sure."

Then she straddled him. "Oh, this feels so good." They quickly found the same easy rhythm.

After a minute or so, he mumbled, "Oh, oh ... I'm coming."

"I am too." Her legs tightened up, and she gave him a kiss, sucking his tongue in and out of her mouth until the orgasm subsided. After one last soft suck, the kiss ended and they relaxed.

"God, we must have been hotter than a couple of firecrackers," he said as he pulled her close. Their lips met in short, easy kisses. Then she rolled off of him.

"Oh, Kevin, that was quick, but wonderful." She kissed him again. Then they laid back while he softly caressed her breast.

"Vickie, your tits are gorgeous." *Much more than a mouthful, but not too big.*

"Thank you, and I might say, you are well endowed." She kissed him again and let her fingers drift through his full head of dark hair, cut short, but long enough to comb if he wanted to. "You usually don't comb it do you?" she said as she roughed up his hair.

"I comb it, but sometimes I use just my fingers."

"Uh-huh, well I like it. Your hair is so you—laid back and easygoing." Then they just lay in the bed, talking about how life was beginning to look favorable for both of them, until Kevin sat up. "If we're going to eat, we need to go."

"Okay and I'll pull my hair back into a ponytail," she said as she headed toward the bathroom.

He washed up when she came back into the bedroom, and slipped on a pair of khaki pants with a maroon short sleeved sport shirt.

When they returned, after a dinner of pompano and a bottle of champagne, he suggested breaking out another bottle.

"Good idea. We can have it on the porch, okay?"

"Sure and I'll play some Ella Fitzgerald and some CDs I had put together of some of my favorites. The music will rotate randomly from one disc to another."

"Sounds fine to me. I love Ella."

Soon they were standing by the deck's railing, and Ella was singing, "They're writing songs of love, but not for me." He poured the wine and handed her a flute of Dom Pérignon. "I've been saving this for a special occasion."

"Thank you." And she took a sip. "This is really good. . . . Maybe it's a woman's intuition, but this night is going to be more special than you think—I can already feel it." She reached back to her ponytail, untied a piece of ribbon, and shook her head as her hair tumbled to her shoulders. "It's about time I let my hair down, don't you think?" And she pushed her soft silky-brown hair back a little.

"Why did you let your hair grow out?"

"Just wanted a change." And she fluffed it up a little.

"Well it's beautiful, so soft and lush with a nice subtle wave, very sexy. Let's toast. . . it's you that makes the evening special." Their glasses touched.

"What a sweet toast." Then she put her arms around his waist and they kissed on the mouth, cheeks, neck, and nibbled on each other's ears.

While nuzzling her hair and neck, he paused for a moment, deeply inhaling her scent. "Vickie, you smell so good. . ."

"Thank you, it's the Chanel."

"I don't know if it's just the perfume, but whatever . . ."

With the music drifting through the salty night air, they passionately kissed. He held her close as they started dancing in small steps, while sipping the wine in between whispering endearing nothings to each other. Upon stopping for a moment to refill their glasses, he became totally quiet, looking out on the sea.

"Something's on your mind—what is it?"

"It's you. I can't think of anything or anybody but you." He paused for a moment looking at her, then with half closed eyelids his gaze shifted again to the sea, and a strange serenity enveloped him. *I'm falling in love.* He then turned to her.

She placed her glass on the porch table, then embraced him for a long passionate kiss, softly caressing him from the base of his head down the nape of his neck. Ella's sweet rendition of "You Do Something to Me" floated through the star covered night.

"I've never had such a meaningful kiss," he whispered as their lips parted.

Then he picked her up. "I think it's time to go inside." At her suggestion, he sat on the couch in the living room with her on his lap.

"Kevin, this is really romantic—sitting on your lap. It's like I belong to you. Now kiss me again."

He pulled her to him, put his hand under her blouse—no brassiere—and massaged her well-rounded, firm tits; the nipples were already hard. He kissed her on the mouth and then on her neck and ears. She kissed him back.

She whispered, "Put your hand under my skirt as she opened her legs.

Pulling her skirt up, he slipped his hand between her thighs—she was not wearing panties—and slid his fingers into her and began massaging her clit. After a few minutes he quietly asked, "Vickie, are you ready to go to bed?"

"I'm ready." She kissed him in the mouth, got up, and headed for the bedroom. He followed, stepping out of his pants and taking off his shirt as she undressed.

He kissed her on the mouth, then kissed and sucked her breasts, before moving down to kiss her stomach. He then knelt between her spread legs. *Her pubis,* he thought, *is gorgeous.* "It's beautiful, Vickie, just simply beautiful."

"Do you want to—"

"Uh-huh." And he kissed the inside of her thighs before burying his face in her lush mound.

She quickly picked up a rhythm.

After a minute or so she indicated with her hands on his temples to lift his head. "Kevin, come up here and kiss me." He moved up and gave her a passionate kiss. When the kiss broke, she slipped down and began blowing him. Then she looked up. "Are you ready to put it in?"

"I think so."

"Then let's do it this way." She got on all fours, hiked up her ass, lowered her head to a pillow, and reached back between her legs to guide him in. "Oh, Kevin, it feels sooo good. Take your time, okay?"

"I'll take it slow and easy." He gently pulled back on her hips. "Do you want a reach-around?"

"No, not right now."

Then they were quiet except for his heavy breathing. Soon he could feel her pushing back harder. "Oh, Kevin … I'm coming," she said.

"So am I." With one last thrust from him, they finished and settled on the bed pleasantly exhausted, with him still on top. "Kevin, that was so good," she said, as he rolled off.

She snuggled up close to him and he hugged her. "Sweetie, there's no one in the world I'd rather be with than you."

"I feel the same way. I just love being with you. Let's just cuddle for a few minutes." After a while, with the velvety voice of Linda Ronstadt cooing, "I'm coming back some day, come what may, to Blue Bayou," Vickie said, "Honey?"

"Yes?"

"A while ago, if you had asked, I would have given you a blow job?"

"Sure about that?"

"All you had to do was ask."

"Vickie, you stopped and asked me if I was ready to put it in."

"So I did."

"Are we having an argument about whether you would rather fuck or give me a blowjob?" And he chuckled.

"No argument, just a discussion," she chortled. "Anyway, what I meant was did you want to do that as opposed to me blowing you. I guess I could have made that clearer. So. . ." She let her voice trail off.

"From here on out, we'll have to decide what we want—you know, talk about it. We don't know each other yet. But we will. You have to let me know what you want."

"Actually, it feels so good in me, I'm glad we did it the way we did."

"How about before we went out for dinner?"

"No. That was just something I knew I'd like and you would too. But I wanted you to fuck me. I was taking it slow and easy, strictly foreplay. Understand what I'm saying?"

"I think so. And while we're on the subject of oral sex, I love your sexual scent, it's intoxicating," He paused and looked at her with that easy smile of his. "Just listen to us—is this sex talk or what?"

"Yeah, it's sex talk." She kissed him, and he kissed her back. "Kevin, we can talk about sex forever. But changing the subject a little, I never had any intentions of having sex with you to help out Phil. I needed money, so I lied to him and said that I would."

"I knew that without you telling me, but I'm glad to hear you say it."

"But that's not to say I didn't feel like dropping my panties the first time I saw you in your office. Not for Phil, but for you and me. But I've told you that, haven't I?"

"Not in those words, but yes, you have. Now I wish I had followed my feelings and started seeing you on a personal basis. You knew I was attracted to you, didn't you?"

"I hoped you were, and yes, I thought you were. I had a hard time dealing with your refusal to have sex with me, particularly after we did it. But I figured you wanted to be a faithful husband. I understood that all right. Phil originally told me a lie that your marriage was on the rocks. But after you turned me down and I acted so awful, I still hoped we would somehow get together."

"My marriage was a little shaky. And I'm sorry we didn't start seeing each other, and believe me I wanted to; if we had, all this trouble we've both been through wouldn't have happened. But it's all whiskey under the bridge."

"Touché."

Then they just lay there, listening to the waves and the music and softly talking, mostly about what was going to happen to Phil.

"Vickie, I'll wash up after you do and then meet you on the porch. We'll finish the champagne. You can put on my robe, it's in the bathroom."

She slid out of bed and headed for the bathroom. As she came out a few minutes later, he went in. "I'll see you in a minute."

He slipped on his pants on his way to the porch. Vickie was standing next to the rail around the porch, with the salty breeze rustling her windswept hair. He approached her with two glasses, handed her one, and quietly said, as their glasses touched, "To the prettiest and most irresistible woman I've ever known."

"You make the sweetest toasts." She kissed him and then held her glass up for another toast. "Here's to you, a generous and giving man." She was smiling—the kind of smile that says 'I love you'—as their glasses lightly touched. Each took a small sip, and each was silent; they were searching the others face with caring eyes.

He spoke first. "Your toast was really gracious—thank you—but both of us are coming out of a truly trying time. And we've only been intimate on two occasions. But what the hell, I love kissing you." He kissed her again. When the kiss broke, he sat in one of the four chairs on the porch. She sat in a chair by him.

"Don't you love me? I love you." Her hand was on his thigh.

"I'm not sure, but you must know I love being with you. We don't know each other yet. Oh, I know you told me a lot about yourself in the preparation for your case, but there has to be more—and you don't know much about me."

"I feel like I've known you all my life. And I don't really like talking about my life way back."

"Why?" he asked. Ella was singing, "We'll have Manhattan, the Bronze and Staten Island too."

"My childhood from ten or eleven wasn't very pretty. Before that, well, I was just a little girl, doing what poor kids do."

"If you don't want to tell me, okay, but maybe I ought to know."

"Okay." She told him about living in the sticks in north Florida and how her father had abused her and her mother's wild accusations about his death. Kevin listened to the whole sordid tale without interruption.

"Vickie, I am so sorry. Your mother and your brothers—where are they now?"

"I don't know. I guess they're still there. And as far as I know, neither Mom nor anyone else has ever tried to find me. Of course, I have no interest in seeing them again. Kevin, I just can't help it; they can all die and rot in hell."

"I'm glad you told me. Your early life tells me something; I'm just not sure what." *She's a sweet woman who deserves a good life, and to the extent I can give it to her, I'm going to.*

"Don't dwell on it. I don't. Most of the time, it's like none of it ever happened." She took a sip. "But then it comes back to me and I know it did happen."

"I'm a little surprised you're so uninhibited."

"I'm sort of surprised too. I didn't have anything to do with sex after that bastard died, until I met my husband. As you know, I was working at a truck stop." She repeated a lot of what she'd told him in preparation of her wrongful death case. "You know sex, from the missionary position to whatever, actually comes naturally. You just feel that's what you want to do and you know it's going to be good for both of you. Think about it a little. Everybody kisses and kissing is just another form of oral sex, or a substitute for oral sex."

"Hmm, that's interesting. Maybe you're on to something."

"Anyway he was a good man, and I fell in love and found out how sweet life could be. He changed my view of things, and he left me with a healthy attitude about sex. But I'm talking about sex with just you. We just seem to go together, don't you think?"

"Yes I do—we really do." And he softly placed his hand on hers.

"Not much else to tell."

"You and he had a good sex life, I take it."

"Most of the time."

"What do you mean?"

"Well, if he hadn't died the way he did, he would've fucked himself to death and me with him." She lightly laughed, "If I was in the same room with him and bent over, he was ready for sex. He just loved me too much. Don't get me wrong, he was a good guy, but even a good thing can be overdone."

"Thanks for telling me that. Let me know if I'm ever overdoing. I think I might." He kissed her.

"Okay I'll tell you. But the way I feel about you, it would be impossible for you to want too much sex from me. It might be the other way around, and I think you know it."

"Can we talk about something else?"

"Fine with me."

"Well, since you're no longer married, why not live with me?" She took another sip from her glass.

"It's not a good time for that. I've got my business to tend to, you're in school, and I'm going to be leaving, though I'm not sure when, for Europe and maybe a few other places."

"Why are you leaving to go anywhere?"

"There are some places I've always wanted to see, and I'm interested in art, classical and modern. I have the money now to do it. It's just something I need to do, get it out of my system." *And*, he thought, *I might need to give us some time apart.* Then he finished his glass.

"Well, maybe later?"

"Maybe, Vickie, but no promises."

They finished the bottle of champagne over conversation about things she was doing in school, plus some movies and books, including *Tess of the d'Urbervilles*, which she had just read for her Victorian English class. As Kevin sat back in his chair, The Pied Pipers were singing, "Dream when you're feelin' blue."

"Vickie, I'm about ready to turn in. You?"

"I love this song." And she hummed a couple of bars. "I feel so strange like I'm in a dream," she softly whispered. The clear starry night, the music, the mild ocean breeze, and the sound of breaking waves were indeed dreamy, in an endearing way. "Do you feel sort of like that too?"

"Like none of this is real? Yes, yet it's the most real feeling I've ever had. Maybe the champagne's getting to us."

"No, it's not the wine."

"The wine is doing its thing, but it's something else, isn't it?"

"Yes, it's something else," she whispered as she got up and sat in his lap. She hesitated for a moment, then gave him a tongue filled kiss.

"I wish this night would never end. . . but it's well past midnight, so I guess we ought to go to bed, this time to sleep."

They got up, and went inside. She was first to use the bathroom to brush her teeth. When he got into the bed she cuddled her nude body next to him and laid her head on his arm.

"I can't remember ever having such a romantic evening." He pulled her close "Do you realize we've not once checked the tube to see if anything was on worth watching? We've literally spent the evening with only each other. Vickie, you're wonderful. You didn't know that did you?"

"No I didn't, but I'm glad you think so. And you're right this has really been a wonderful night."

She paused for a moment, thinking. "You had a good childhood didn't you?"

"I think you could say I did."

"Tell me about it, okay?" Linda Ronstadt was beginning to sing, "I've got a Crush on You". She propped herself up on an elbow and let her hand drift through the hair on his chest, delicately massaging his nipples. "I love this song."

"This song is really sweet just like you." And he gave her a light kiss.

"What a nice thing to say—thanks."

"You're welcome. Anyway, getting back to my child hood, there's not a whole lot to tell.

As you know I was born and raised in a two stoplight town, Pine Hill, about fifteen miles north of East Bay. Mom was a school teacher and dad was an accountant who worked from time to time, particularly during tax time. As a little boy I was just your average country kid, not outstanding at anything but not deficient either."

"I bet you made good grades in school."

"I did okay, but was never the top of the class. Read my share of comic books, played a lot of pick-up games, and liked to play cards and even gambled a little—you know, penny-ante stuff. Watched a little TV. Went to church and Sunday school. Helped out around the house, like cutting the grass, and after I was about fourteen worked at a filling station on Saturdays. Mom and dad were generous with me. And I knew they loved me."

"High school?"

"The usual trial and tribulations but I was able to get in the University of Florida. You know the rest."

"Didn't you tell me your dad died a few years ago?"

"Yes he passed on, but Mom still lives in Pine Hill. You'll meet her."

"Oh I hope so. I wish you were younger or I was older and we had grown up together. You would have been the only man in my life. God, I can't help dreaming."

"It's good to fantasize or dream sometimes. Gives your imagination free reign."

"I agree, but we can't let unreality take over. We have to live in and deal with the real world."

"You're right, sweetie, and reality has slipped up on me. I'm not as sleepy as I thought I was, so. . ." He pulled himself up a little on his pillow and turned to her.

"Neither am I. You're interested in you know what, aren't you?"

"I thought I was done for the night. "But I should have known better. As soon as we finish having sex, I want to do it again."

"Oh, Kevin, I feel the same way." Then he felt her hand on his erection. "Come on, get on top. That okay with you?"

"If it suits you, it suits me." She spread her legs and he entered her. "Oh, Kevin, I love it. I was more ready for this than I thought." With her legs wrapped around him, they fell into an easy rhythm for several minutes. "Honey ... I'm going to come." She hungrily kissed him, then pulled him close before her legs dropped to intertwine with his. "That sure didn't take as long as I thought it would. If you haven't finished, just keep on till you do."

"I did."

"It still feels hard."

"It'll go down in a minute." He hugged her. "You're wonderful. That's all there is to it," and he rolled off of her. After they had rested a moment, he said, "Couldn't you tell when I did?"

"I thought you did when we kissed. But since you've been telling me when you came, I just wasn't sure."

"I think we're again engaging in sex talk."

"And so we are." She kissed him.

After a few more minutes of relaxing and small talk, he said, "It's about time to call it a night again; you go first to the bathroom, okay?"

She agreed and slipped out of bed. A minute later, she was back. "We can go to sleep now. I'm a contented and happy woman. Now kiss me good-night?" He gave her a soft kiss on the mouth.

He then got out of bed, but was soon back under the covers. "Good night again, Vickie, and I turned off the music." He then gave her another easy good-night kiss.

"Good night," she said as she cuddled up close.

The next morning, Kevin opened his eyes and felt her arm over his chest. "Good morning." He hugged her. "Did you sleep okay?"

"Like a log."

"I did too."

"Kevin, I feel like we're on our honeymoon. I want to kiss you, so go brush your teeth. I've already brushed mine."

"I'll be right back," he said as he left the bed.

Back in bed, he rolled over to her and gave her a kiss. "Vickie, I'm really happy to see you this morning."

"And I'm really happy to see you." She cuddled up close to him. Then began fondling him. "Oh, that feels good. It's really hard."

"You ready."

"I'm good and ready, I've been thinking about it before you woke up." She laid back, spread her legs and he entered her. Then he gave her a passionate kiss.

Before long, she started thrusting harder. "Kevin, I'm coming." She squeezed him a little, then lowered her legs to intertwine with his for a better purchase. You?"

"Not yet."

"Well don't stop." She raised her legs around him. "Don't get anxious. Take your time."

"Okay." They continued another few minutes. He began thrusting harder. "I'm coming, Vickie."

"So am I." She lifted her hips, squeezed him with her legs, then dropped them to intertwine with his for a few final thrusts. "Oh that was so nice. That's the first time I've ever done that." Then they settled down in the bed, kissed each other and lay back to catch their breaths before he rolled off.

"Kevin you're a great lover, or maybe it's just because I love you. I never dreamed I could have multiple orgasms. And what a nice way to start the day."

"Thanks for the complement. And you're right—it's a great way to start the day. And if we had time, maybe—? But we need to get up and get dressed. Let me go to the bathroom for a minute. Then you go and while you're in there, I'll put the coffee on and fix some eggs and bacon, maybe a couple of biscuits, and shower after breakfast. Scrambled okay?"

"Sure, but I didn't know you could cook."

"See, you're learning new things about me," he chuckled as he put on his robe.

She came into the kitchen dressed in her khaki skirt, a blue oxford shirt and sandals. "As usual you look great. That ponytail kind of does something for you. Give me a kiss?" After a sweet kiss, he said, "You ready for me to start fixing the eggs?"

"Can hardly wait. I'm hungry."

"Then have a seat and I'll pour you a glass of chilled orange juice and a cup of hot coffee." She sat at a small breakfast table, one side of which was next to the wall. Kevin served the meal in about two minutes then took a seat directly across from her. Over breakfast their conversation was basically around her plans involving school and the morning's radio news he had tuned in while she was in the shower. He placed the dirty dishes in the dish washer and started to the bathroom. "It won't take me long to shower and shave."

Before long they were in his car, traveling on old US-1 toward East Bay. He was dressed in a grey suit and tie. *I probably shouldn't go see her tonight*, he thought. *But I want to ...* "Vickie, is it okay to come up to see you tonight?"

"Sure you can, and you don't have to ask. Just let me know when you're coming."

"No pun intended?" he quickly asked with a smile.

"No," she said with a chuckle while playfully slapping his leg. "No pun intended. Now let me kiss you? But are you okay with a little kissing while you drive."

"Sure."

She took off her seat belt and started kissing his neck, ears, and here and there on his face until she gave him a tongue-filled kiss on the mouth. "Oh, I love you, and I think you love me." Then she plopped herself back in the seat. "I won't have a lot of time tonight to fix us the kind of dinner you'll deserve." And she lightly squeezed his leg while looking at him with a cryptic smile. "I just can't get enough of you?" And she loosened the seat belt so she could kiss his cheek.

"Or me of you." He put his hand on hers.

"But I have some work to do, so wait till around six tonight," she said, patting his leg.

"In Jacksonville?"

"No, all I have there is a room. You come to my farm in Palatka." She told him how to get to it.

"Any decent places to eat in Palatka?"

"Several chains, but the LongHorn Steakhouse has good salmon and stays open late. Knowing us, it's going to be fairly late before we get around to dinner. You want anything special to drink or just a good bottle of wine?"

"Champagne suit you?"

"Sure."

"Then that's what we'll have and I'll bring it.

"Vickie." And he briefly paused. She could see he was thinking, but he only said, "I really wish you weren't going to school in Jacksonville."

"I've got to finish, you know, and get myself a degree."

"Yeah, I know, and I admire you for that. I didn't mean for you to quit school; I just wish you were closer."

"Kevin, we're going to see each other, aren't we?"

"Sure we will, starting tonight at six."

"I mean we'll see only each other, nobody else."

"That's what I mean too." He turned to her and put his hand on hers. "Vickie, you know I'm in love with you, don't you?"

"Oh, Kevin, I felt like you were, but it makes me happier than you can believe to hear you say it. I love you more than I thought I could ever love anybody. You do something to me that no one else has ever done. I need to give to you—to be with you—it's like I'm part of you and you are a part of me—know what I mean?"

"I think so. And I feel the same way. Now come on over here again so I can hold you." And he extended his arm to her as she undid her seat belt and leaned over to him. His arm went around her and he pulled her close while she ran her hand through his hair and down the nape of his neck while giving him a sweltering kiss. Finally the kiss ended.

"Kevin, let's do that again." And she passionately kissed him one more time. He returned the passion.

"I still say you have the sweetest kisses in the world, and he lightly kissed her again.

"Why do you say that?"

"Probably because I'm crazy about you, and your lips are so nice and soft and you taste good." He then broke into a broad grin before lightly kissing her again on the lips.

She drew back a little, hesitated, then her face lit up with an endearing smile and her eyes sparkled. "I'll love you till the day I die. But since we're coming into town, I should move over." She then slid back into her seat.

"I wish we could spend the day together, but we can't. I'm taking a doctor's deposition this morning, a new client is coming in this afternoon, and there's always routine office work. I don't see how we could possibly—" His voice trailed off as he drove into the courthouse parking lot. "Vickie, don't cry," he quietly said as he put his hand on her leg. Tears were welling up and a little slid down one cheek.

"Oh, I know you've got things to do today and so do I." She was dabbing the tears away with a tissue, and fluttering her eyes. "Oh, honey, I'm sorry, I'm just so happy." She hugged him when he stopped next to her Honda.

"I'm happy too." Then they hugged again and softly kissed.

She sniffed a little while dabbing away the tears. "Well, it's time to go. I need to get on the road, so. . ." He then got out and opened the door for her. She unlocked her car, and turned to him. He kissed her again. "I love you, Vickie."

"I love you too. And I've had such a sweet time. Can you believe that tonight you'll be in my house with me? I'm really a happy woman." He put her overnight bag in her back seat. She lightly kissed him, then slid behind the wheel, and he closed the door. She rolled the window down, and he kissed her passionately."

"Drive carefully, Vickie. I want to see you tonight. And I'll be there at six." She cranked up and he waived good-by as she drove away. He then started for his office. *God I'm already missing her. I must be losing my mind. This woman is taking over my life, and I can't do a damn thing about it. I can't control who I fall in love with. And whether I admit it or not, I'm in love with her.*

Later that day, Kevin went to Singer's office.

"Kevin Charles is here to see you," Mr. Singer's secretary said into the intercom as she directed Kevin to Singer's office.

"Hey, Larry. Good news or bad news?" Kevin affably said as he entered Larry's office and took a seat.

"Good news. Victoria Roberts came by and showed a lot of remorse for not being more precise in her report." He paused. "And I might add, she signed the drop charge with her real name. What in hell did she think 'Who Knows' would buy her?"

"What's that?"

"That woman signed the drop charge with 'Who Knows' instead of her signature. Of course, I caught it ... but why do it in the first place?"

"Damned if I know. She's a strange person," Kevin quibbled, as if the question were merely light conversation and not truly important, just something to say. Although he hoped his terse response would satisfy Singer, he could not squelch his apprehension that the inquiry was not just rhetorical. That Singer wanted to know something became unmistakable when he looked away and then down at his steepled fingers; he slowly intertwined his fingers while remaining stone-silent. Seconds passed. Kevin's resolve was about to break. He was a big believer in letting others know only what they needed to know, and Singer definitely didn't need to know that he and Vickie had a somewhat devious arrangement to obtain some kind of justice for both of them. Nevertheless, Kevin wondered whether he should just tell it all. No, he would not deviate from his original reticence. He still had time to change his mind. He had not lost his credibility with this man, at least not yet. He crossed his fingers and, though hardly a true believer, sent up a little prayer.

Finally, Singer looked up and around the room before directing a not-too-harsh glare directly at Kevin. He slightly puckered his lips and stroked his chin, as his eyebrows moved closer together in a frown that looked more puzzled than mean. Then he took in a deep breath and sat back in his chair. It appeared he had resolved something, or at least had satisfied himself even if it remained unresolved.

"Hmm, you really don't know," Singer said. "Anyway, I just don't know how she expected to get away with it, and now we might have to go back to using drop charge affidavits. I liked the simplicity of just having the victim sign a document." He stopped and looked at Kevin as if he expected a response.

Kevin merely arched his eyebrows and affected a quizzical pose.

"Oh, what the hell, I've quit asking myself these kinds of questions. Anyway, it's always the same answer. People look after their own interests. At least that's what I think, don't you, Kevin?"

"I can't disagree with you."

"You can't, or you won't disagree?" Singer responded with a tone of irony.

"I meant you are probably right, but ..."

"But nothing," Singer said softly. His expression was one of kindness and understanding.

Kevin relaxed. Singer might be somewhat unhappy, but he wasn't angry. He recognized the difference between what he needed to know and peripheral matters he would just like to know about.

"So what now?" Kevin quickly said, grateful for Larry's astute perception.

"Well, you said you felt Mrs. Roberts had been duped into doing what she did, and though I have some doubts about that, we're going to grant her full immunity to testify against Phil Griffin. You don't have a problem with that, do you?"

Kevin shook his head.

"No, I didn't think you would. What he did to you, and to some extent her, just plain stinks. And if I have anything to do with it, and I will, he'll do time. You'll be around to testify, right?"

"Larry, you don't need me," Kevin replied defensively.

"True, but just in case, you know. We never really know what we might need, so ..." He opened his hands as an invitation to Kevin to say something.

"I'll probably still be here. As a matter of fact, nothing would give me more pleasure."

CHAPTER 17

O ne early Tuesday morning in April 1996, about one week after Phil
was served the subpoena, his secretary appeared in his doorway.

"Mr. Griffin," she said, "Mrs. Victoria Roberts is here to see
you. She refuses to see Mr. Dunn. I know we are to send her to him,
or anybody other than you. But she is really upset because you haven't
returned any of her phone calls and is threatening to take her case
elsewhere."

Phil's stomach turned upside down as a strange numbness crawled
from his head to his toes. For a minute, he could hardly get his breath,
but after a moment, he was somewhat composed and told his secretary to
show Victoria in. He walked around his old, expensive, highly polished
mahogany desk—he had acquired it from England some years before—
to meet her as she came through the door.

"How are you, Vickie? Just dropping by, I suppose, since you were
in the neighborhood?" He feigned a light laugh. As he directed her to
sit in one of the two deep plush leather chairs in front of his desk, he
added in his best and most cordial way, "What a pleasant surprise. I've
been thinking about you a lot lately."

As she took her seat, she wryly said, "I bet."

Phil couldn't help but notice how sensuous she was as she eased back
in the chair and crossed her legs. Dressed in a straight gray skirt and
white summer sweater, she was obviously comfortable in the expensive,
elegant surroundings. Phil began to hope she would agree to have a
more familiar meeting than he had at first anticipated. Toward that end,
with more confidence than he should have had, he took a seat in the

other client's chair. He felt that if he was ever going to bring her in line, it had to be sooner than later. She was obviously hostile. Nevertheless, he had to try. He tried to touch her leg, but she pulled back and pushed his hand away. As he looked at her, the words "vulnerable" and "vixen" ran through his mind.

"You bet you know what I've been thinking?" he said, as if she was being serious.

"You bet I do. Don't forget, Phil, I know you."

"True, you do. But gee, I didn't know you could read my mind—thanks for telling me what I think."

"Cut it out, Phil! I'm here on business. You have used me and abused me. No more. I want my case transferred to a new lawyer."

"Now, now, Vickie, let's not be hasty." He knew it was essential that he keep the case. She had to believe that his concern was making sure she got the best representation possible. Even though he wasn't sure he could do it, he had to try to get her on his side. "You know, if you transfer it to a new lawyer, you'll have to pay him a fee. And we have just about got it ready to settle. Their offer now is substantial ..."

She quickly interjected, "Aren't you supposed to let me know of any offers?"

"We have. Copies of the letters are all in our file."

"You haven't sent me—oh, forget it. I'm through with you, and I'm not concerned about the attorney's fee. I'm through with you and all the nasty things you made me do. All of that is just about over, though, and they are going to get you. You're going to be disbarred and go to prison," she said.

"Now, now," Phil quickly admonished. Then he turned silent, breathing deeply to regain his composure. Her last remark about prison had indeed disconcerted him, but if he was to be in control of the situation, she couldn't know that. Calmly and coolly Phil, asked, "Has anyone actually told you that?"

"Well, yes and no."

"And what does that mean?"

"Just what I said. Sometimes one of them sort of acts like that's what is going to happen, but when I ask anybody specifically, the answers are always noncommittal. But they know everything, because I told them."

"And they believed you?"

"They believed Kevin Charles."

Phil's mind flipped back to how noncommittal Kevin Charles had been about what he knew and didn't know. No doubt, Kevin knew a hell of a lot, and maybe he had been pulling the strings, or maybe she was lying.

"So they believe Mr. Charles, huh? They might not continue to do that."

"Who are you trying to kid, Phil? For god's sake, you know what you did, unless you're totally delusional."

"What I did or didn't do is now irrelevant. It's what we do from here on out …"

"No, sir." She shook her head and immediately cut directly to the chase. "Either you are going to give me two million for my wrongful death case by next week, or I'll file a grievance against you so fast, you'll wonder what happened to all that polish I once thought you had."

"Damn, what the hell is this? Why are you doing this to me? You know I can't get that much money by next week."

"Then you have a big problem."

Phil knew any subsequent attorney on her case would eventually discover just what he'd been up to. He had to keep the case. "Vickie, I might be able to raise one million by next week, but—"

"No," she said, cutting him off. "I'll be back next Tuesday at 9:00 a.m. for a cashier's check or my file. If it's the money, then I'll wait for more from my case if you get more when it settles. Now that's a fair deal, Phillip."

Phil had nearly forgotten the lie about his secretary. He was now afraid to broach that lie, but he buried his fear and cautiously, even reluctantly murmured, "Aren't we forgetting something?"

"What?"

He cleared his throat before stating, in what he hoped was a convincing voice, "That my secretary could sink your case completely."

"Uh-huh. So you're pulling that little stunt again. You are just too much. You and I both know that's a lie. Call her in here and see if she'll say anything." She stopped talking and just glared. Phil said nothing. "Well, I don't see you ringing her. No, Phil, that's all bluff, and I'm calling it."

"You're forgetting something, aren't you?"

"What?"

"I can pay her, you know."

Vickie stood up and started for the door.

Phil jumped up to cut her off. "Just where are you going?"

"To get her and bring her in here and confront her with everything you've said. It's all recorded." She quickly flashed a handheld tape recorder. "Too bad for you the thing was accidentally turned on," she said with aplomb as she returned it to her purse.

"Give me that," he demanded as he attempted to grab her purse.

"If you touch me, I'll scream," she said, pulling away from the door.

"No, no, that's not necessary. Please calm down and retake your seat," he said as he backed away, showing her his open palms.

"And if I do?"

"You won't have to call her in here. Let's just let bygones be bygones." He tried to sincerely smile, again resorting to what he perceived to be his irresistible charm. He hoped it still worked. Before she could respond, he continued, "Now that we have that little matter settled, wouldn't you like to stay over tonight? We could go to the club and maybe a midnight walk on the beach. Frankly, I've missed you." Phil's last statement was indeed true. She had an extra dimension that set her apart from any woman he'd ever known. *One of a kind*, he thought.

"Damn, it's tempting," she lied. "You just get busy so we don't have to have a run-in next week."

"You're not staying over?"

"No, I'll see you Tuesday," she said as she rose from her chair. And without a glance his way, she walked out of his office. Her exit left him speechless.

Damn, he wanted that woman, and he needed to placate her to give himself more time. That he just maybe didn't have "it" anymore left him numb and depressed. He really had no idea where he was going to get the money as he sat back down. He rubbed his chin and looked out his window. He had already sunk over seven hundred thousand dollars of the firm's money into the case against the tobacco companies. He had some stocks in the market, but the market was down, and he didn't want to sell. He was divorced and paying over thirty thousand dollars a month in alimony to two ex-wives and substantial child support. He scowled when he thought of the child support for three under the age of fifteen and one in college. None of them ever displayed any desire to see him; he just went with the flow. *Damn it, I should have been causing all kinds of problems about visitation over the years*, he thought, but he decided it was too late now. He was paying two women money for children he hardly knew. Other than the market, he drew a blank and was still cogitating on the money matter when Frank Dunn knocked on his door. "Come in," Phil said in a soft tone. "Close the door, Frank."

As he entered the office, Frank said, "I need to talk to you about—"

Phil stopped him with a raised hand. "Whatever it is, it can wait, Frank. I need to get your idea about where I can raise two million by next week."

"Hell, Phil, you look like you've lost your last friend, and excuse me for saying so, you even sound like you're in shock."

"Do I?"

"Yes. You ought to be able to hypothecate a couple of cases, particularly Victoria Roberts's case, but crap," he said as he shook his head, "there's no fee in her case. But we have others, you know."

"That's the reason I need the money."

Frank looked puzzled.

Phil continued, "She just came by and demanded two million dollars by next week, or she'll take her case to someone else, and you know we can't let that happen."

"No, sir. Why don't you get busy and try to settle it?"

"Because that would be against the game plan. I'm trying to get top dollar. A mediation is set up a few months down the road. I think we can get it then. If I move now, they'll detect it and lowball us. Anything less than our best will lead to a malpractice suit. That woman would be delighted to do it."

"You really haven't got that much?" Frank asked.

"When you live like I do, there is never any ready cash and ..." Phil paused.

"And?"

"And I do not have as much as everybody thinks I have."

"So maybe I can help you, Phil. I've got a couple hundred thousand I've been holding onto to invest when I think the time is right, and probably some of the other guys in the office can help out too."

"You mean all four of you?"

"Yeah, I'll talk to them."

"No, I'll talk to each one myself."

The lawyers who worked in Phil Griffin's firm knew they were well positioned in life and in their profession because of him. Before the day was out, Phil had nearly half of the funds he needed, and if he had to, he could borrow again against his 401K. But he much preferred a no-interest loan from individuals.

* * * * *

Phil stood at the entrance to the Omni's crowded dining room, adjusting his eyes to the subdued indirect lighting. Phil was running late and was genuinely concerned that Kevin Charles might not have waited. His apprehension grew as he scanned the baroque room mostly full of businessmen in suits and didn't immediately see Kevin. The central area of the ornately tasteful dining room was a couple of feet lower than a narrow elevated portion on three surrounding sides. Large stone pillars, strategically placed where the elevation of the floor changed, prevented him from seeing some of the elevated tables. Still scanning, he began walking through the room, about the tables, acknowledging with a nod of his head or a quiet hello those he knew, which was nearly everyone. He was about to give up when he saw Kevin seated, alone, at a table for four behind one of the pillars. Phil felt confident as he strolled across the plush carpet toward Kevin's table, until he realized Kevin was giving no sign of recognition. What was this all about? After all, Kevin had waited. Yet Kevin remained seated as Phil approached his table. That was not the way it was supposed to be. They were colleagues in an old and noble profession! Cordiality and respect were a given between members of the bar.

Despite being disturbed by Kevin's strange behavior, Phil quickly resolved not to show his concern. Kevin continued to make eye contact only—no facial expressions, hand signals, or anything else to acknowledge they had arranged to meet for lunch. Phil refrained from any attempt to shake hands when Kevin didn't stand for the usual greeting. He was just sitting there, slowly and calmly drumming his fingers on the tablecloth. The mixed signals meant something, but what? Unable to admit to himself that things might not be going well, Phil mentally rationalized. After all, Kevin had waited for him to arrive.

"Have a seat. I haven't ordered yet. Only been here a few minutes," Kevin said.

Phil took the seat offered, sat back, blinked his eyes, looked around the room, and then leaned slightly forward before saying, "You know, I know most everybody in this room."

Kevin said nothing. He merely gave Phil a blank look.

"This place really does a good luncheon trade."

Kevin remained unresponsive.

"I'm sorry I was late. I tried to be right on time, Kevin. I was in a hearing. You know how that can be."

"As I said, I have been here only a few minutes. Somewhat late myself. Anyway, I had to eat lunch somewhere, you know," Kevin responded while looking at his watch, a good but moderately priced instrument, in sharp contrast to Phil's thirty-thousand-dollar Cartier.

"I'm glad we're having this meeting. I really mean that. It's always good to see one of my favorite people," Phil said with a slight tone of urgency.

Kevin continued to show no emotion. "Phil, now just why did you need to talk to me?"

"Oh, I didn't really need to," Phil chuckled. "I just wanted to know if you could shed some light on this subpoena I got from down your way to appear before a grand jury."

Kevin held out his hand. "Let's see the subpoena."

Phil handed it to Kevin, who perused it slowly.

"Okay, this is what I was told was going to happen by a gentleman in the state attorney's office. I got one too."

"You did?" Phil asked.

"Yep." Kevin dropped his head slightly but stared up into Phil's face without a trace of amusement and waited. "Cut the crap, Phil," Kevin finally snapped with authority. "You know what this is all about. Don't try to deny it."

"I do?"

"Hell yes, you do!" His tone was soft but intense.

"Well, well, thank you, Mr. Charles, for telling me what I know ..."

"I told you to cut the crap. If you don't, you're going to find yourself sitting here dining alone." Kevin stopped and glared with his cold, piercing blue eyes. They both remained silent as the waiter approached.

When the waiter left with their order, Phil said, "Well, if you're going to be that way."

Kevin pushed his chair back and began to rise.

"No, no, Kevin, I have to talk to you. Don't go. Lunch will be on me," he said, feigning an amused chuckle.

Kevin sat back in his chair. "Okay, Phil, you ready to really talk about what this is all about?" Kevin coolly said as he pointed a finger at him.

"Okay, don't get excited. I need to know if there is anything you can do to stop what I think is going on down there."

"And what do you think that is?"

"God, I don't know what to think, Kevin."

"Now you're being circumspect …" Kevin smiled for the first time. "No, Phil, what do you think is going on? Tell me, and then I'll let you know what I know."

"I think Victoria Roberts is a mental mess and is probably doing some things to harm us both."

"If that's what you really think, then we don't have anything else to discuss. So let's enjoy our lunch, and we can talk about the latest in the NFL or something."

"Are you serious?" Phil furrowed his brow.

"Deadly."

"Since you put it that way, maybe I haven't made myself clear. I think she has falsely charged you in a grievance—by the way, is that still pending?"

"Yes."

"Too bad. I thought you were cleared …"

"Phil, excuse me for interrupting, but we are supposed to be shooting straight," Kevin said. "Keep it up, and I'm leaving."

"I was just going to say, I think she also took the same charge to the state attorney's office or police and had you charged with a serious breach of sexual etiquette, to put it delicately."

"To put it delicately, you don't think she has implicated you in her nefarious activity? I shouldn't need to remind you, Phil, but I expect you to tell me the truth."

"The truth? I wish I knew the truth about anything."

"Phil, I'm not here for a philosophical discussion." Kevin's body language as he sat back in his chair said loud and clear that he was running out of patience.

"Okay, okay, Kevin," Phil said while holding up both hands, pleading for more time.

"Get to it then," Kevin stated in a flat tone.

"To get right to it"—Phil hesitated, took a deep breath, and blinked his eyes—"do you think that subpoena for me has anything to do with what she did to you?"

"Give the man a Kewpie doll," Kevin said. "Phil, I just never thought you'd get to the truth. But now I do believe you are onto something. You apparently know what they're investigating."

"Now what? Damn, Kevin, I can't go before a grand jury. I might ..." Phil stopped himself.

"You might what?"

Phil remained silent.

"You might lie and be indicted for perjury? Is that it, Phil?" Before Phil could respond, Kevin continued. "Or you might tell the truth and be indicted for substantive criminal activity." Kevin wrinkled his brow, lowered his head slightly, and glared with his penetrating blue eyes.

"I wouldn't put it that way. You never know what prosecutors might be up to, though."

"Cut it out, Phil. You know what these prosecutors are up to."

Phil could not look at Kevin. He shifted his gaze to the tablecloth.

"You're scared, aren't you?"

Dropping all pretenses, Phil lamely whispered, "Yes." He paused and looked away before saying, "Can you be of any help on this thing? You know those guys down there. Maybe you have a friend. I shouldn't have anything to fear since I've done nothing wrong, but I can't take any chances."

"You want me to help you?" Kevin questioned in a deeply cynical tone.

"Yes," Phil said as he sat back in his chair and pinched the bridge of his nose. They stopped talking while the waiter served them both broiled Channel sole over a bed of wild rice.

"So you knew all along the reason for that subpoena," Kevin said as he took a bite of fish. "Pretending not to know was a subterfuge to arrange lunch with me?"

"Yes, I suspected ..." Phil sighed and began to eat.

"Cut it out, Phil. You knew, didn't you?" Kevin pointed both fingers at Phil.

"Yes, I guess I did," he said and hung his head. He could not look at Kevin.

"You guess? You guess because you put her up to it. Quit lying to me. You wanted me knocked out of a chance of a lifetime. I want back in as a full partner, but I'll settle for one-half of your bloated portion. I've picked up some talk that the governor and attorney general are about ready to settle. Is that true?"

"Yes."

"So if you want me to help, sign this." Kevin slid an agreement, with the style of the case so that it could be recorded in the courthouse file, acknowledging Kevin's interest in Phil's attorney fee, and it was to be paid directly, by the state, to Kevin Charles, the same as the other attorneys were to be paid. They all knew any verdict or settlement would be so big, the tobacco industry would need years and years to pay it, so the settlement would provide for the fees to be paid over the next twenty-five years or so.

"Kevin, can you help me out of this thing?"

"You'll have to trust me." Phil capsulated his thoughts in a second. If Kevin didn't help him, Kevin would stay tossed out of the suit. So it was in his interest to stop the train before Phil was run down. Not only that, Kevin was proposing that Phil give him half and not his whole fee. A true gentleman of the old school like that could be trusted, and Phil started to sign the agreement.

"No," Kevin said, stopping him. "Let's go to the manager's office and get it witnessed and notarized."

As they were walking away from the manager's office, Kevin said, "Now that we have this taken care of"—he held up the properly executed document—"we need to talk about some additional incentive to get the state to cancel that subpoena." He then surreptitiously folded Phil's subpoena into his copy of the agreement and casually slid both into his inside coat pocket.

"Additional ..."

"Yeah, come on over here, and let's have a seat right here in the lobby, so we can talk. I'm going to have to really stick my neck out for you. But Phil, if I've learned nothing else, I've learned every man has his price. It shouldn't be much, probably in the neighborhood of a hundred thousand dollars. But it must be cash."

"I hadn't thought about that, but it makes sense to me."

Sure it does, Kevin thought. Kevin was finding it difficult to remain civil.

"But I'm a little short right now."

"Short! Phil Griffin, in short supply of money! What is this world coming to?"

"As strange as it might sound—and it's so ironic—I've got to come up with a big payment next week. In fact, I was actually contemplating asking you to help with that. After all, we are now partners." He arched his eyebrows and wrinkled his forehead in expectation.

"You're not kidding, are you, Phil?"

"No, I'm not, so …"

"So how much do you need, and when do you pay it back?"

Phil took a deep breath and said, "One million. I need it by Tuesday. I've already got one million. I need one million more."

"Just like that, you ask me for a million dollars?"

"I know of no other way as efficient."

"Phil, you're a real piece of work. Did you mention when I'd be paid back?"

"As soon as the state makes the first distribution of the tobacco money."

Kevin quickly balanced the pros and cons of loaning the money. If he loaned it, it would more or less legitimize his new partnership with Phil, removing any suggestion he'd had Phil served with a false subpoena. This was actually a fortuitous turn of events. The agreement they had just signed recited past work and the need not to have Kevin listed as a named attorney in this suit because of false claims against him, and it justified Phil's share being over twice that of any other attorney involved.

"I'll expect to be paid back with interest in three months."

"Okay, if you insist."

"I do insist. Now why did you say you need the money?" Kevin questioned.

"I didn't."

"You want to tell me?"

"Not really, but I will if you insist."

"Can't be any secrets between partners."

"Well, it's Victoria. I saw her Tuesday, and she wants that much money next week. Of course, I'm going to settle her case for more than that, but that's months away."

"What's the leverage? Why can't she wait?"

"That woman scares me, Kevin. I think she's just being a real bitch, but no telling what she might do. She also told me that right now it's you the prosecutors are relying on, but ..."

"But we can't be sure of that, can we? Listen, I'll loan you a million, but you're going to have to supply me with a hundred thousand dollars in cash, remember?"

"Yes, I recall something like that."

"I can have the million to you by Tuesday morning. But I can't do anything more for you until I get the cash. Do not ask why."

"No problem, partner. That detail, I do not need to know. Come by this afternoon after four, and I'll have the cash. That little matter has got to be taken care of. And I want you to know things always work out best between mature lawyers, you know what I mean?"

"Yes, and I think I have finally matured as a lawyer. Anyway, Phil, your fee is going to be really substantial when Victoria's case settles or there's a verdict," Kevin said, as if he wanted to reassure Phil he was still doing well.

Phil cleared his throat. "Kevin, there is no fee. She gets the whole enchilada."

Kevin looked away, annoyed. The "no fee" deal had to have been at least part of the payoff to Vickie. Even though he knew she had been paid somehow by Phil, he sat back, slowly shaking his head. Victoria had told him Phil's fee was reduced, not that it was zero. Damn, he thought, and he wondered about his own plan.

Since he was going to be in Jacksonville that night, Kevin had arranged to see Vickie. After her classes, she met him in the bar adjacent to the dining room of the Ponte Vedra Club. She looked right at home in a full beige skirt, an expensive blue blouse, and high heels.

"Oh, Kevin, it is so good to see you," she said as he stood to give her a light kiss.

"You look great. We can go on in; the table's waiting on us."

As they took their seats, she said, "Well, tell me about your day."

"Everything worked out fine, and I have us a suite here at the club." He didn't say more until after the waiter had taken their order. Then he gave her the details.

Soon a bottle of Dom Pérignon champagne was served, followed by a splendid dinner of pompano en papillote. "My meeting with Phil today confirmed what you told me over the phone—that everything went as planned when you met with him on Tuesday," Kevin said as he forked a piece of fish. "Tell me again what Phil tried to pull."

"It almost got out of hand when he started threatening that he could still ruin my case with that crap he claimed his secretary heard me say. He said he could still pay her. The implication was clear: she would lie for him." She looked around at the posh dining room and took a sip of wine. "I'm going to join this club someday and live here on the beach."

"Why not get an out-of-town membership right now?"

"That's what you have, isn't it?" She took another bite of the pompano.

"Yep, and it's only five hundred a year. Remind me, how did you handle that problem with Phil?"

"I started to walk out and said I was going for his secretary to bring her into the office to let her say whatever she had to say." Vickie brushed her hair back with her hand and told Kevin the whole story of showing Phil the tape recorder, threatening to scream, and so on.

"That was by far the smartest thing you could've done, Vickie. Good for you."

"I had my recorder because I carry it around with me so I can dictate things that occur to me about my schoolwork. Of course, it wasn't turned on."

"But Phil didn't think he could take a chance. Even if you had recorded what he said, without his okay, it wouldn't have mattered. Even in a criminal case, it's admissible to rebut the defendant's or any other witness's testimony. You wouldn't have been in any real trouble even if you'd had everything he said on that tape and he'd taken it away from you. How could he use it?"

"He couldn't; it would incriminate the hell out of him."

"Bingo. He knew that, so when you resisted and threatened to scream, he had no choice. If he had gotten it and started tearing it up while people were coming to the aid of a screaming woman, well, you can see how that wouldn't be in his favor."

"I was smarter than I thought I was," she said, just before taking another bite of fish.

"Changing the subject some, how much is Phil putting into his pocket from your case?"

"Nada, not a cent," she said, lightly laughing as she put her knife and fork on her plate. "Why?"

"Just curious. Something came up about him not getting a cent out of your case. It's not important. Forget I even mentioned it, okay?"

"Okay, why don't we have an Irish coffee and then get out of here, change clothes, and take a walk on the beach?" She paused for a minute, glanced around them, and as she lightly squeezed his hand, added, "I'm so glad you can stay the whole weekend."

"Vickie, I am too," he said as he motioned for the waiter.

Several days later, well into May 1996, Kevin went to see Singer again. "I need a favor, if I may be so bold as to ask?"

"A favor? Hmm, I don't know if I should be passing out any favors at this point," Singer said with a slight, friendly smile. "But what is it?"

"Can you delay actually filing the charges until the tobacco suit is settled?"

"You know it's going to settle?"

"Pretty sure it is."

"Hell, it'll be six months anyway before we'll get a case together and be ready to file against Griffin. I'll tell you what, we won't have him arrested without checking with you. That okay?"

"Sounds fine."

"But if it doesn't settle, and it looks like it's going into a long protracted trial, we'll just have to pick him up anyway."

"I understand."

Singer paused. "Oh, what the hell, you got some interest now in the tobacco suit?"

"You might say that."

"You don't want to talk about it?"

"Not really, but I guess I need to. My interest stems from Griffin's, Larry, and if he's criminally charged before the case is put to bed, he could possibly lose his fee …"

"That's enough, Kevin. Don't tell me anything else." He held up his hand, signaling the end of the conversation. "Now your grievance hearing is next Tuesday?"

"Tuesday of next week, that's right."

"Mrs. Roberts says she's not going to show up."

"But you will, right?"

"I'm going to call them after I fax some stuff and ask if it's necessary to even have the hearing. If so, I'll be there for you."

"Thanks, Larry."

"You can buy me dinner sometime."

"Is that all?" Kevin barely smiled, but his eyes flashed comfort and satisfaction.

"Yeah, that's all. At least for now."

"Okay, let me know if anything develops," Kevin said as he got up to leave.

"You'll be the first to know. You can see your way out?"

"Sure."

"Okay, I'll see you later."

CHAPTER 18

In late May 1996, Kevin mentally reviewed what had transpired over the last few weeks. He felt good and gave a closed-mouth smile of victory to his empty office. In effect, he had won another case. He got up and walked to a window on the far side of his office. Hardly discernible in his mind was the realization he was acting like, if not becoming, a charlatan. He could not articulate it, at least not yet. He knew Phil thought the hundred thousand dollars was bribe money, and Phil was a crook for so readily agreeing to it. He also knew, however, that Larry Singer would have been more than just offended by the offer of a bribe. No, Kevin couldn't take a chance of screwing everything up. Singer was not the kind of public servant who pretended to take umbrage at someone else's offer to pick up a dinner check. He was not such a phony. Of course, Kevin had never bribed anybody. Singer probably knew he'd paid Victoria, and he no doubt had a good idea of some kind of skullduggery with Phil Griffin. But what Singer didn't know wouldn't concern him, at least not in this case.

He knew Larry Singer hadn't been anxious to pursue Phil Griffin. He had been inclined to shut the book on the whole thing once Kevin was cleared. Phil would have gotten away with it if Kevin hadn't subtly recommended prosecution. Kevin still grimaced when he reminded himself that he had planted the notion with Singer that the grievance people would expect a criminal prosecution of Phil. Yet somehow, he derived a certain satisfaction from knowing it was his machinations that would result in Singer prosecuting Phil with all the powers of the state.

Satisfied and perhaps inwardly gloating, Kevin picked up the phone and dialed Phil Griffin. "Phil, this is Kevin."

"Hey, Kevin, you have the good word?"

Kevin said, "Oh, ye of little faith, you can deep-six that subpoena."

"Will I get anything in writing?"

"No, and Phil, it would not be wise to call down here about it. I'm guaranteeing you're never going to have a problem if you don't show up."

"You have really been a true friend, Kevin, and … just thanks again, partner."

Kevin could not control the rising self-denigration for his being so brazenly deceptive. He felt like a real lowlife. He could never understand how criminal defense attorneys could, with a straight face, publicly extol the innocence of their guilty clients. Kevin swallowed hard and continued. "Phil, we've got to work together from here on out. Bygones are bygones. All animosities must be buried; otherwise, none of us will get through this."

"I agree."

"How is our tobacco case shaping up?"

"It's going to settle at mediation. As you know, we're having a conference with the attorney general and his people next week."

"In Tallahassee?"

"Yes, then on to the mediation with the tobacco companies."

"Phil?"

"Yes."

"Am I invited to the conference?"

"Of course. That's where we are going to decide the parameters for settling."

For a fleeting second, Kevin wondered how Phil could be so self-assured about the case settling. But he shrugged it off. After all, the tobacco companies had no defense, if the law was constitutional.

* * * * *

In the living room of a suite in the Tallahassee Hilton Hotel in June 1996, Hugh Benson called the meeting to order. "This is an organized meeting, but as I said earlier, informal. We have dispensed with Robert's Rules of Order. And I'm happy to say, we now have with us a more than just welcome addition to the team, Kevin Charles. I'm sure he needs no introduction. Is there a motion from the floor?"

Phil Griffin immediately stood up and with unquestionable enthusiasm announced, "I move that Kevin Charles be included as one of the attorneys representing the state's interest in this case, and his remuneration will be one-half of my fee, which means one-half of 30 percent. My fee was set with the idea in mind to split it with Kevin. We did not want it known until some unwanted and unwarranted problems were cleared up. And it is, of course, with great pleasure I can say all of that is now behind us. So let's give a big hand to Kevin." Immediately, Phil began to clap and smile as if he were handing out an Academy Award.

With the courteous but light applause wafting through the room, Kevin wondered again how a man could so unabashedly lie. Was that the mark of a great man, or what? His thoughts trailed off as the clapping died down, and someone seconded the motion.

"All in favor say aye and raise your hand," said Benson. All hands went up. Kevin had previously thought of this group as good men being led by a skunk. The irony was he was now one of them. He shook his head in an effort to dispel the still undistinguished but definite feeling he'd crossed a moral Rubicon and could not go back. He was startled from his momentary moral assessment by another round of polite applause, their way of recognizing him as one of the chosen. Kevin stood, smiled, and mouthed "thank you" a couple of times before sitting back down in one of the straight-backed chairs moved into the room specifically for this meeting. The meeting continued with the discussion about what should go into the mediation process.

Finally, they all agreed that Phil Griffin and the attorney general would represent the state in the scheduled mediation. They would try to extract 15.5 billion to be paid out over twenty-five years but would settle for 13.5 billion. However, it was also agreed they could deviate from the amounts and time of payout if in their judgment the deal as posed would be substantially within the parameters discussed. Kevin wondered whether he was imagining things or the stench of greed and avarice was actually palpable. He'd never discussed it with anyone, but he had sensed the malodorousness of greed for years. It had a peculiarly painful scent. Like evil, it burned your lungs. He was sure an acrid, perhaps sulfurous essence had materialized to complement the unholy desires of this band of legal brigands.

He was again abruptly shocked from his cynical, disturbing thoughts when Hugh announced the meeting was adjourned, and one of the others nudged him, saying it was time to get out of there and get a drink.

"Hugh," Kevin said as they were leaving, "let's go some place for a cup of coffee."

"How about the hotel's coffee shop?" suggested Hugh.

They found a table for four and sat opposite each other. This was the hotel's only restaurant. It was late afternoon, and hardly anyone was patronizing the place. "This is perfect. Nice and quiet," Kevin uttered as they took their seats. Once comfortably seated, Kevin looked around, got the sole waitress's attention, signaled for two coffees, and then casually said, "Hugh, everybody seems pretty certain this thing is going to settle."

"Oh, I don't know, maybe we're just a group of positive thinkers."

Kevin started to reply by raising the same argument he'd made before but thought better of it. "I don't want to be misunderstood, Hugh, but what if it doesn't settle?" Kevin was concerned since his fee was intertwined with Phil's, although today's action made him a player in his own right.

Hugh paused before responding since the waitress had returned to serve their coffee. "Then we'll have one hell of a case to put on," he said as she walked away. "But Kevin, so will they, the tobacco companies. Their attorney fees will be astronomical. If they settle with us, they avoid all the later ifs and buts and the unknowns of a trial." He stopped for a moment, thinking and stirring his coffee. "And they avoid the appeals that would be sure to follow." Hugh sipped from his cup and arched his eyebrows in a consoling expression, as if to say, "Does that satisfy you?"

Phil Griffin was a smart and gifted man. And he was acting as if settlement was a slam dunk. He knew something. Kevin wondered just how far this corruption extended. But he quickly questioned his own conclusion: was it corruption?

"What the hell are you in such deep thought about?" Hugh asked as he finally put his cup down.

"Oh, I didn't realize it showed. I guess I was just wondering what in my life justified my having such good fortune," Kevin lied with a smile.

"We've all wondered that from time to time. Some of us are just blessed, I guess. Others … well, maybe they weren't born under a lucky star. Damn, Kevin, it's good to hear all that crap against you is over. I've always had some apprehension about what some unhappy client might do."

"So have I, and now I know. Just hope it never happens to you. But that's our system."

"If you don't mind me asking, did you actually have a grievance hearing?"

"No. The state attorney notified the bar of some facts that led to the bar summarily dismissing the proceedings. So I didn't have to put up with that humiliation."

"Why did you say you wanted to have this little coffee break?"

"I guess I didn't really say, did I?"

"No, I don't think so."

"I just wanted to know if you knew why Phil's so certain it's going to settle. And I wanted a cup of coffee. Usually have one about this time every afternoon. Nothing mysterious ..."

"Heck, I thought you might want to talk about that grievance thing or something. I don't want to cut our visit short, but I'm driving back to Daytona, and it will be dark before I get there."

"I'm driving back tonight too."

The two men finished their coffee over brief pleasantries and parted. Kevin could detect nothing untoward in Hugh Benson's conversation or demeanor. Still, he had not answered the question Kevin raised. He liked Hugh and he valued his friendship. Still, Kevin felt something was missing. *There's an aspect of this whole scenario that keeps eluding me*, he thought. *I'll have to cogitate on it driving home.*

* * * * *

About ten days later, Kevin picked up the morning paper and to his amazement read that the big lawsuit had been settled by the governor and the attorney general with the tobacco companies. Worse, the elected state officials were publicly claiming that the attorney fees were unconscionably exorbitant and excessive, and the state would not pay the lawyers the amount negotiated, 25 percent of 13.5 billion in settlement payable over twenty-five years, amortized at statutory interest.

"What the hell?" Kevin mumbled to himself. Disappointed but not upset, Kevin perfunctorily contemplated what this all meant before mumbling again to himself, "So what?" He felt he should be physically sick; he was sure most of the chosen would be. After all the clandestine manipulation and moral compromising had in a way paid off. He would still enjoy a well deserved victory over Phil Griffin who was going to be criminally prosecuted and no doubt disbarred, which was more important to him than the money, though he wanted that too; he didn't need it, but he wanted it. And Vickie expected a sizable amount. He wanted her to get it. And to lose the best game he'd ever played was in and of itself most disturbing on an intellectual level. He sat back in his chair, closed his eyes briefly, and tried to conjure up an answer but to no avail. *No*, he thought, *the only thing to do is call Phil*. With his jaw firmly fixed, he dialed the big man's number.

"Phil," Kevin said over the phone, "what the hell happened?"

"Now, now, let's not get excited. I was shocked too."

You don't sound shocked, Kevin thought.

"But no matter what those two in Tallahassee say, our contract is ironclad. We'll get the fee."

"Then why did they do this?" Kevin asked, although by now he had a suspicion as to why they'd done it.

"Obviously, I'm not privileged to their private thoughts, but for some reason they must feel it's smart politics. You know there has been a quiet but persistent groundswell from some quarters and from those who want to get into the media about the amount of our fee."

"You're not worried?"

"Can't say that exactly—and the trial judge might try to knock us down—but my people are preparing a complaint against the state for breach of contract as we speak."

"Well, that's good."

"After a month or so, things will settle down. Something else will pop up to entertain the public. A war with Mexico or something." Phil chuckled. "And I predict the state will quietly give in, and we will have arrived on Easy Street." He again followed with a light chuckle. "Yes, my boy, our ship has finally come in. Damn, Kevin, you know how much 15 percent of a 25 percent fee is on that kind of settlement? I have a hard time conceptualizing it, don't you?"

"Hell yeah! Are you going to ramrod the breach of contract?"

"Hugh Benson will be the point man, but we're all in it. Quit worrying. We'll get it all."

Kevin mentally speculated on just what was up. He had suspected that the governor and attorney general had been in on this thing from the beginning, and they hadn't gone along with it simply to do something beneficial for the state. But he refrained from inquiring further. No, first he had to assess in his own mind what was going on. "Okay, Phil, let me know if I can do anything. Bye."

His first reaction of indifference had strangely morphed into a quiet desperation. Even Phil's assurance could not calm an inner frustration. Also, Singer had told him the state would arrest Phil in December on perjury and conspiracy to commit perjury. That just might be a problem if the tobacco case wasn't settled by then. *But what the hell*, he thought, *I should get mine anyway now that I've been formally reinstated.*

He had compromised in all kinds of ways to defeat Phil Griffin's chicanery. It didn't matter that what he had done was in a real sense self-defense. It still wasn't right. "Goddamn it, I want that money," he mumbled, and at the same time he felt rotten for saying it. Kevin rose from his chair and slowly walked to the window overlooking a busy street, something he often did when he felt his mind must be given free rein. He knew he hadn't dwelled on it, but deep in the shadows of his soul had rested the possibility, perhaps the hope, that the tobacco fee would be his ticket out of this bucolic little town of East Bay. Now he just didn't know. Still contemplating various scenarios, he continued to survey the meaningless scene on Main Street from his office window.

After a moment, he cleared his throat, returned to his desk, buzzed his secretary, and told her to get Hugh Benson. *If he's as confident as Phil, then they know something, and that something is that this whole curious process was set up, but by whom?* And why in hell would the tobacco companies capitulate now to such a questionable claim? Up to now, they had fought claims with vigor unmatched since a handful of Spartans tried to hold off the entire Persian army at Thermopylae. Their first line of defense had been that nicotine was not addictive, and the image of nine or ten tobacco CEOs swearing nicotine was not addictive before Henry Waxman's congressional committee emerged in Kevin's mind. Then they had argued that tobacco wasn't unhealthy, and finally, they had successfully argued to juries that they should deny a plaintiff's claim because the plaintiff had freely chosen to smoke. The last argument Kevin wholeheartedly agreed with, having stopped smoking himself.

"I have Mr. Benson on line one," the secretary said over the intercom.

Kevin picked up the phone. "Hello, Hugh. You have no doubt read the papers?"

"Sure did, and you just caught me. I'm driving up to Jacksonville to see Phil. We're going to file suit today."

"I know. I've already talked to Phil. He's his usual assured self. How about you?"

"Kevin, we are like a client. No matter what we tell our clients sometimes, they remain agitated and unsure. I just don't see how the state can weasel out of their contractual obligation, do you?"

"Seems like way back I saw something about how it was unethical to charge an exorbitant or excessive fee."

"That may be true. But our fee was not exorbitant. In fact, 25 percent contingency is less than the usual 40 percent."

"That's true."

"No, I think we'll get some bad publicity in the short run, and then we'll get our money."

"Is there anything I can do?"

"No, just let Phil and me get the suit filed. Duck when the fallout covers the front of every newspaper. We'll weather this. Damn, at the very least, we're entitled to our costs and the value of our services aside from the contract."

"That's what they're aiming for, isn't it?"

"Probably, but I really don't know. Anyway, what will be will be."

"That's mighty philosophical of you, Hugh," Kevin said with a mild chuckle.

"You don't sound all that worried yourself, Kevin."

"I'm not worried; I'm just wondering what the hell is up."

"Politics, Kevin, just politics. I'll let you know. In fact, I'll let all the attorneys in this thing know what's going on."

"Okay. I guess that's it for now. Bye." Kevin hung up. He was sure now that all was well with the lawsuit, but somehow he still felt unsatisfied.

Two months later, in September 1996, Kevin got a call from Hugh.

"Hello, Hugh. Any news about our money?"

"Somebody in the governor's office or somewhere in Tallahassee realized they couldn't possibly get away with breaching their contract with us, and the state threw in the towel 100 percent. They also didn't want to be liable for additional attorney fees for wrongfully trying to breach our contract. Anyway, it's settled."

"Great."

"We get our money over twenty-five years, beginning January 1, 1997."

CHAPTER 19

In February 1997, Victoria purchased an ocean-front condominium in Ponte Vedra Beach, just south of Jacksonville Beach, Florida. Living alone, she obviously did not need it, but she fell in love with the three thousand square feet of marble-tiled elegance on the corner of the second floor of the Royal Palm Condominiums, the most expensive on the beach. She considered the purchase price of nearly a half million slightly excessive. Even so, she wanted it, so she bought it. She liked the idea of owning a three-bedroom condo. Whether she needed it or not was irrelevant. She reveled in walking through her expensively furnished living room onto the large balcony overlooking the Atlantic Ocean. She referred to it all as her "domain." The grand panoramic view, of the ocean and the beach, through the large living room windows confirmed how far she had come from truly humble, if not outright miserable, circumstances.

A lady now in her own right, she could be occasionally seen at the Ponte Vedra Inn and Club, an old, yet still imposing two-story white stucco grand hotel that spanned several hundred feet on the beach. It was old Florida, once a revered Mecca of the well-to-do from south Georgia and north Florida. Now known mostly as just the Ponte Vedra Club, the resort now entertained guests from anywhere. Without the breeding, she was convinced it would take more than money to acquire class, or at least the appearance of class. Toward that end, she continued her college education at Jacksonville University.

It was now December 1998, and Vickie hadn't seen Kevin Charles in nearly four months. She couldn't help but think of him while looking out from her second-story condominium on the wide beach, with wave after wave stirring the surf and the ocean breeze rustling her hair. He really liked the seashore, she mused. If Kevin hadn't left the area, she would have called him. Not really, though, because if he hadn't left, he would be with her. Yet for many sweet reasons, she experienced an endearing nostalgia from time to time, daydreaming that she and Kevin were walking arm in arm on the beach, bathed in a vermillion sunset. Her eyes wandered to some faraway place or time, and she lightly smiled as memories of what they had together drifted through her mind. She heard from him often by phone, letters, and e-mail. She passionately missed him. She knew, however, he would come back to her, and that gave her a measure of comfort, if not unbridled exultation. Her reverie was abruptly interrupted by the annoying ring of her telephone. She blinked her eyes and frowned as she picked up the receiver. A man's voice asked if she was Victoria Roberts. "Yes, this is she, Victoria Roberts."

"Mrs. Roberts, this is Larry Singer in East Bay. You remember me, right?"

"Sure, Mr. Singer. Funny you called right now. I was just thinking about something related to the case." She did not mention Kevin Charles by name. "You're prosecuting Phil Griffin for perjury and conspiracy of perjury down there in East Bay."

"Yep, and the case is scheduled for trial in three weeks. Do you have any problem appearing at that time?"

"No, sir."

"Then you should receive a subpoena tomorrow or the next day."

"Is everything okay?"

"I think so. We made him a good offer, no jail time—something I wouldn't have done except Kevin Charles actually recommended it—but Mr. Griffin's got either a hard head or a hardhead for a lawyer. I guess I shouldn't have said that. His lawyer is good at what he does, but … Listen, can you get here the Friday before the Monday it is scheduled to start?"

"Don't see why not."

"Good, try to get here at one o'clock. The dates often change, so I'll call you again with an exact date. The date we now have is the first day of a three-week trial period. If there's a problem for some reason, call us. I'll work with you."

"I'll be there." She wanted to say "with bells on" but refrained; she didn't think it would be in good taste to be too anxious. No, she would do only what she had to do. No more.

"Okay. If you don't have any questions, I'll sign off."

"No questions, not right now."

So the day has just about finally arrived, she thought after hanging up the phone. She would have to testify against Phil. She didn't really relish the idea, but she was glad it would soon be over. After all, she had to save her own hide. Her recent good mood, however, had slipped away like a fading sun dropping below the horizon.

* * * * *

Phil Griffin threw the file on an otherwise clean well-polished mahogany desk and shoved it across to Mike Jones, one of his associates. Mike was of average weight and height, but with a diminished chin, he was not very attractive. His head of dark hair always appeared a bit casual, roughly parted on the left and brushed back with a slight wave on the right.

The file on the desk was the only file Phil could think about. "I've reviewed this thing from one end to the other. It's a simple four-count charge. The first two are second-degree felony counts of perjury; count one is for perjury before the grievance folks where Vickie swore under oath, and count two is her lies to the police. Counts three and four are for conspiring with Victoria Roberts to commit those crimes. You're my lawyer. Tell me how you're going to defend me. How are you going to win this thing? The trial is in three weeks, and we can't get another continuance. For god's sake, the charges and the grievance have been plaguing me since December 1996."

"Phil, I don't think Kevin is around to testify."

"They don't need him," Phil said. His irritation with everything and everybody around him had grown by leaps and bounds as the trial date grew closer.

"If they don't put him on, I'll be able to at least argue that lack of evidence is a reasonable doubt, so the jury ought to find you not guilty."

He shot back, "I can take the stand, you know."

189

"Yeah, I know," said Mike, "but you ought to really think about that."

"What the hell are you talking about? You think I'm guilty as hell and can't take the stand? Well, I am guilty. There, I said it—so what?" With an exaggerated smirk, he rose from his chair and went to his bar for a quick shot of single-malt scotch. After a short pause, in a more subdued voice, he politely queried, "You want one too?"

"I'll pass for now." While Phil prepared his drink, Mike casually asked, "I know you must ... but do you ever get *really* drunk?"

"Hell yeah, why else would you drink?" Phil chuckled.

"Good answer, I guess. But hell, Phil, maybe there just isn't anything else we can do but take our chances at trial, and if that comes out bad, appeal."

"Hmm, that doesn't sound all that good. What you're telling me is to prepare for a conviction. Isn't that right, Mike?"

"Phil, you said it, you know. You're—"

"Guilty," said Phil, his tone escalating. "Listen, you nitwit, the guilty go free every day. The fact that I'm guilty is not even a material issue, but damn it ..." He paused before continuing in a calmer voice. "I have to agree with you, and I'm sorry I referred to you as a ... you know, a---"

"A nitwit?"

Phil did not say anything; he just nodded his head.

"That's okay. Sometimes I am a nitwit," Mike chuckled. "Phil, you've been under a lot of stress. Why not take the deal? After a few years you could get reinstated. You've got plenty of money."

"Not as much as I should have. I put a lot of work and money into that tobacco suit." He paused. "And preparing to sue the state for our fee wasn't so easy either," he said even though he knew all of it, including the governor's claim that the fee was exorbitant, had been a charade. "Mike, that thing gave a rush like nothing else. We hit the tobacco companies hard—including a fortune for that turncoat Charles. He's got his, and I've lost mine. Oh, what the hell, that's all water under the bridge ... Anyway, I can't take the deal. That would be admitting I'm a criminal, and that I will not do. There has to be another way. Do you agree there is no case without Vickie?"

"Yes, since Frank killed himself."

"Yeah, that was sad about Frank. I miss him, don't you? He was a good friend, a damn good guy. You know, he just wouldn't take the state's offer for less than a year in the county jail in exchange for testifying against me. Thank god he had no children, just a young wife."

"Nice-looking woman. He left her well fixed too. She ought to do okay."

"You know, he saw a doctor when he was trembling all over and couldn't sleep, but apparently he couldn't take the medication—I think it was Lexapro. So he medicated himself with booze. Too bad he didn't stay on his medicine."

"Yeah, I heard about that. I saw him when he looked like he was drinking, but I didn't think he was drunk."

"Yeah, he was left alone by his wife while she visited her folks for a weekend, and according to the autopsy, he was drunk as hell when he blew his brains out."

"Jesus, it must have been an unimaginable shock to his wife when she found him."

"Yeah, that would be hard to live with."

"You think that offer we have was probably triggered by his death?"

Phil paused, thinking, and then shook his head. "Let's get back to the business at hand. I think there is a way out of this!" His voice trailed off as he pulled the window curtain back and gazed out on the city skyline for a moment, still pondering the impossible. He stepped away from the window. "She still living out at the beach?"

"Vickie? As far as I know. It's easy to check."

"Then find out for me, okay? No one knows where Kevin Charles is at the moment?"

"He's out west, in California, I think, but he might be in Europe."

"He really doesn't matter. He's never coming back to testify against me ..." His voice trailed off again as he again looked out the window, lost in thought. "Hell, maybe I ought to just take the deal and go west myself. A lot of nice things out that way," Phil uttered, though he didn't mean it. "No, I will not go down. No, sir. Let me know about Vickie before noon if you can."

"You want to tell me what you have up your sleeve?"

"If I knew, I could tell you, but I don't really know myself."

"I'll get right on it," Mike said as he got up to leave.

As soon as Mike closed the oak-paneled door to what was perhaps the finest office in the city, Phil's face, stoic to the world, crumbled, and he slumped over his desk, shaking with fear. "Now I know how Nixon felt. If I just hadn't taken that extra step—a totally unnecessary one as it turned out," he mumbled to himself, cringing. "The irony is Kevin Charles was just as greedy as the rest of us and never would have queered the deal," he quietly ranted to his empty office.

The intercom buzzed. "Phil?"

He recognized Mike's voice. "Hold it for a minute." He delayed long enough to calmly but irrationally ask, "Mike, is that you?"

"Yes, and Phil, she is still at the beach." Mike proceeded to give the specific address. "She is a member of the Ponte Vedra Inn and Club and has been seen around the club out there once in a while."

"Thank you, Mike."

* * * * *

Phil left his office well after the usual lunch hour and instructed his secretary he would not be back that day. He still did not have a firm plan in mind. As he drove through the heavy downtown traffic, across the Main Street Bridge, and then onto the crowded highway to the beach, his mind raced through various scenarios of what he should do, including returning to his office and following the advice of his attorney. The term "my attorney" floating through his mind caused him to smile. Mike was a smart man, but no, if this matter was going to be favorably resolved, he would have to do it himself. And legal mumbo jumbo would not do it. This little task was going to take a lot of imagination and ability, and if anyone had that, Phil thought, he did. The image of a fool embarking on acts of desperation also kept emerging in his muddled brain. Still, some wise man had once claimed that desperate times call for desperate measures. He could be arrested for tampering with a witness a lot faster than he had been arrested for perjury. *But for me the situation is desperate,* he thought, *and now that I've made my decision, there's nothing to lose. It's meet her and work out a deal, or all is lost anyway. I know how much she loves money. Surely, I can buy my way out. Even so, she will never agree to see me. No, it must be a chance meeting.*

What his eyes perceived, his brain did not retain. The traffic and scenery along the highway were only fleeting phantom-like images. But he knew the road to the beach like he knew his name. He pushed on, oblivious to everything other than the possible scenarios bouncing around inside his head, until the city limits of Jacksonville Beach flashed by. He then slowed to below the speed limit, keeping his eyes open for State Road A1A. Upon reaching it, he turned right to head south. To his left, when his view was not obscured by a building, he caught glimpses of the blue Atlantic Ocean and white-capped waves crashing upon the bright Florida beach. Soon he was in the boardwalk and carnival area that was the heart of this small beach town. It was December, months after Labor Day, so most of the rides and shops were closed, and the usual busy streets were deserted. Nothing odd about that. Yet for a fleeting moment, Phil sensed a deep, inexplicable, strange foreboding, just before a run-down beach bar caught his eye.

A red neon sign announcing to the world that the establishment was a bar blinked above a weathered wooden door, and a small parking lot across the street was nearly empty. "Well, well, here's a bar that is actually open this time of year. Good fortune is already shining on me," Phil reflected as he smoothly drove into the parking lot. He got out of his car and took note of the sparse traffic before crossing the narrow two-lane street and opening the weather-beaten door. Momentarily blinded as he crossed the threshold from the bright day to the dark, dimly lit bar, he was then immediately hit by the strong smell of beer and booze intermixed with some other malodorous scent that no doubt included sweat and the moldy stench of smoked tobacco. *This place stinks*, he thought, *just the kind of place I'm looking for.* After a moment, his eyes adjusted, so he could see well enough to walk over the concrete floor and take a seat on a plain wooden stool. The bar itself had seen better days. The padded plastic bar rail was still there, but it was split and coming apart in some places. He wasn't sure he wanted to stay after all. But what the hell! The sole bartender was shuffling toward him, having just served a beer to one of the other two "gentlemen" at the bar. They both looked as if they could use a bath and a good meal. Before the bartender could address him, Phil asked, "Do you have a single-malt scotch?"

"I believe so," the bartender grunted in a gravelly voice as he turned around and looked at the selection behind the bar. "We've got a bottle of Glenlivet. Will that do?"

"Yeah, that will do. Fix me a scotch on the rocks."

The bartender was considerably overweight, with long, dark, greasy hair, large tattoos on both arms, and what looked like a two- or three-day beard. While the bartender prepared the drink, Phil thought about what a shithole he had just dropped into. Three or four unpainted wooden booths lined the opposing wall. The booths and the bar were separated by a well-worn pool table and a couple of tables for four with cheap, cushionless wooden chairs. Phil and the two other men at the bar were the only customers. Phil's drink was served. As he took a sip from one of his favorites, he rejected any and all self-criticism that might be lingering in his psyche about drinking so early in the day. *This is what I want to do*, he thought, *and now is the time for me to indulge myself. To hell with everybody else and what they might think.* Even so, he consciously nursed the scotch on the rocks, trying to relax. Instead of relaxing, however, he grew more agitated as a solution to his problem failed to crystallize. What seemed to be the right answers consistently slipped just beyond his grasp; his brain just would not focus.

He slid off the stool and stood to stretch. His drink was still on the bar. He picked it up, looked around, and this time could not help but chastise himself, not for drinking, but for drinking in such a dump. *What in the hell am I doing in this shithole?* The thought engendered a grimace, and he put his drink back on the bar as he contemplated leaving for more suitable surroundings. He thought about just how far he had come from places just like the one he was in. Scenes from the old sleazy watering holes in and around New York and Miami played out in his mind's eye. *Oh, what the hell, the past is the past. Let it go and forget it,* he told himself. But his mind raced on, reliving old grudges and triumphs, like the immeasurable satisfaction of winning a case against a major automobile manufacturer being represented by an ex–Miami judge in a multimillion-dollar products liability case. Time slipped away as he sipped and his mind raced on.

With respect to his problem with Victoria, one fragile solution swirled around in his head for a minute or so to be replaced by another weak, inadequate idea, just one thing on top of another. Would he be successful in affecting a chance meeting with Vickie? And if so, would she succumb to his pleas for understanding? Pleas reinforced, of course, with money, or perhaps personal affection, or both money and affection. *Should I hope for sexual affection?* he wondered. Hope never really hurt anybody. On the other hand, hope could lead to serious disappointment. Still, a tryst with Victoria would be most satisfying. Scenarios overlapped, intermingled with, and followed one another. Suddenly realizing it was way past lunchtime, he caught the bartender's attention and, more or less just to have something to say, asked, "Is the Oyster House right down the road open?" Phil was pretty sure it was.

"Yes, sir, it's open." The bartender looked at the nearly empty glass and asked in a most suggestive way, "You want another?" while hesitantly reaching for the glass.

Phil thought about it for a short moment before answering. "Yeah, I think I'll have one more," he said as he held up his index finger and nodded to the bartender.

His second scotch on the rocks was placed on the bar. Phil slid a twenty-dollar bill toward the bartender. "Will this take care of it?"

"Yes, sir, and then some."

"Good, you keep the change." Phil sat back down to take a sip of his scotch and to again ruminate on what he needed to do—or what he would do. But he only decided that if nothing developed to change his mind, he would finish the drink and leave for the oyster bar.

Sometime after the second or third sip of his drink, he was startled when the door opened and let the bright light of day pierce the unholy darkness of the bar. Phil guessed that the slim woman walking in like she had been there many times was anywhere from thirty-five to forty-five years old; it wasn't always easy to tell a lady's age in a dark bar. Dressed in white clam diggers and a pink halter top, she noisily shuffled across the concrete floor in flip-flops, slightly jiggling a set of car keys. Phil watched her from the corner of his eye with his head slightly turned in her direction. When she stopped nearly behind him, Phil turned to face her. As expected, her calling card was the obnoxious but slight scent of cheap perfume. Everything about her said "here's another bleached blonde with too much lipstick and makeup." Unfortunately for her, even in this dim light, the crow's-feet at the corner of her eyes and the lines around her mouth were more than just vaguely visible; the cosmetics were not enough to cover the tracks of time. Phil decided she was closer to forty-five. With absolutely no expression, only a blank face, he turned away. Then he heard, "Well, hello. You don't look like the kind of guy a lady would find in this place." He did not immediately respond. She proceeded to sit next to him and continued, "You don't mind having some company, do you?"

"No. And if you hadn't already perched yourself on that stool, I would have offered you a seat." *Why did I say that? No doubt because I'm a well-mannered member of an old and noble profession.* He smiled at his own facetiousness. Reflecting that she too was no doubt a member of an old and perhaps even more noble profession caused a friendly grin to spread across his face.

"My name is Sally," she said as she placed her keys and a small cloth handbag on the bar. "I don't believe I have ever seen a real gentleman in here before. But I guess there's a first time for everything."

"Oh, I don't know. It could be you still haven't seen a real gentleman in here for the first time," Phil indifferently said, just before picking up his drink for another sip.

"You sound sort of tired, or fed up or something. You're in some kind of state, aren't you?"

Phil looked away but said nothing.

She continued with expectation in her voice, while lightly touching his right arm, "But you know what a real gentleman would do now, don't you?"

Phil looked at her, blinked his eyes, and smirked. He was tired of being friendly and casually uttered, "Probably walk out." He wanted to say that a real lady would not ask such a question, but he restrained himself.

"Damn, fella, you sound like a real asshole. Won't even buy a thirsty girl a drink?" As she spoke, she exaggeratedly wiggled to settle herself on the stool.

Phil couldn't help but smile. It always amused him when a person, particularly a woman of her ilk, tried to act indignant about anything. "Not today. This is my day to be ..." He paused, opened his hands with palms up, and furrowed his brow as if thinking about what to say next. He then threw her a mischievous smile. "What was that you said about me? Oh yes, it's my day to be a, a ..."

"Asshole."

"That's it! I just can't help it sometimes." This type of verbal jousting always entertained him. That it might be at the expense of others was irrelevant.

She sulked. "What are you doing in here anyway?"

"I'm in here to have a drink."

"So ..." She didn't finish what she started to say. By then, the bartender was waiting for Phil to decide whether or not to buy Sally a drink.

Phil looked first at Sally and then nodded to the bartender. "Oh, what the hell, bring her whatever she wants."

"Well, la-da-da," she said. "I'll have a White Russian." The bartender acknowledged her order and turned away to prepare it. "Maybe you ain't so bad after all."

They talked for a few minutes about nothing in particular—whether the city was going to allow cars on the beach again; how much nicer it was on the beach without the crowds; how dead the town was, but not as dead as it used to be after Labor Day. She eventually asked the inevitable question. "Where're you from?"

"Why in the world would you want to know where I'm from?" Phil said while casually shaking what ice was left in his drink. He was no longer looking at her. His mental gaze had shifted to somewhere completely out of the bar. He could not keep his mind off of his desperate situation. What could he do about Vickie, short of killing her?

The bartender served Sally her drink. "And here, my dear, is your White Russian," Phil said, "compliments of, let's say, your new friend, the man you have described as a true gentleman and—well, being a gentleman, I won't say the other descriptive term you used to define me."

"Why do you have to act like that?" she said as if he had hurt her feelings. "I'm just trying to have a conversation."

"Act like what?"

"Like you have an attitude."

Phil wanted to maintain his demonstrated "attitude" by saying something like "everybody has an attitude." But he decided not to say anything, to just look interested. He raised his eyebrows, wrinkled his forehead, and pretended to listen.

"You know," she continued, "if we are going to sit here and drink together, don't you think a girl ought to know who she is drinking with?"

"So?"

"So what's your name?"

Again he did not respond; he only sat and smiled.

"Don't I need to call you something—you know, a name?"

After a moment's hesitation, as if he were truly contemplating something, he let a smile wash over his face. "Not necessarily. You could refer to me as 'you.' Anyway, you have already had the pleasure of calling me some kind of name, remember?"

"Oh, I didn't really mean anything by that, and thanks," she said as she picked up her drink. "How about a toast—a sweet one, okay?"

Phil looked at his scotch on the rocks. He hesitated, thinking he might order another, but there was a little left in his glass, certainly enough for a meaningless toast. He raised his glass as a concession to her unabashed effort.

She raised her glass up next to his and said, "Strangers when we meet but not when we part." Their glasses clinked upon touching. And just before each took a sip to celebrate the toast, she quietly said, "Now that wasn't so bad, was it?"

"I have to admit that was a nice toast."

"How about a couple of bucks for the jukebox?"

Phil handed her a five-dollar bill, and the bartender reduced it to appropriate change. A minute later, Phil was pleasantly surprised to hear Frank Sinatra softly singing, "I've Got You Under My Skin." Sally took another minute or so picking out something else on the jukebox. As she returned, she lightly hummed and then mouthed the song's words: "*I've got you deep in the heart of me…*"

"That's a good song," Phil remarked as Sally took her seat.

"I really like ol' blue eyes," she said.

After a few minutes of truly idle chitchat and another White Russian for Sally, Phil, not without some reluctance—the booze and the music had mellowed him to some extent, and he was actually enjoying himself—sighed, "I have got to go now, but let me say it has been a real pleasure meeting you. I think you are probably a truly honest woman."

"You really going? I believe I could really get to like you. You know, we could really have a good time this afternoon. You don't even have to give me your name if you don't want to. Wouldn't that be all right?" She was talking quietly, but with a distinctly pleading tone of voice.

Phil finished his drink, pushed back, and stood up. He reached in his pocket for some money and said to the bartender, "How much?"

"Her drinks are fourteen dollars."

Phil put a twenty-dollar bill on the bar.

"Thanks for the drinks anyway, mister. You sure you want to go? If you don't want to stay here, we could go to my place. It's not far from here."

"You know, there's something about you that seems to be decent and good. So I'm going to ask you a question. May I?"

She nodded her head.

In a serious voice, he asked, "How much?"

"What do you mean, how much?" she answered, as if puzzled.

"Now, now, don't forget, I just called you an honest woman."

She looked at him with tired but still pretty blue-green eyes, now overshadowed by false eyelashes and too much mascara. She then hung her head and looked away. "Is fifty dollars too much?" she reluctantly whispered.

"You say that as if it were negotiable." She blinked her eyes, but before she could respond, he continued, "It isn't negotiable? The amount, I mean?"

"That doesn't sound like it would be too much for a man like you. Is it?"

"Of course not. I was just trying to see if anything has changed. It hasn't. Everybody in business will charge what the market will bear. Here, take this," he said, and he handed her a one-hundred-dollar bill. "That's to thank you for the simple pleasure of your company. I really have to go now."

"Thanks, mister," she quietly mumbled, glancing at the hundred-dollar bill in her right hand. In a firmer voice, as he began walking away, she said, "Will I see you again?"

"I doubt it, but we will see."

Phil wasn't sure, but he would later have a vague memory of her saying as he walked out, "Gee, what a nice man."

Phil stepped outside into the bright Florida sun and left for the Oyster House. Upon his arrival, the place brought back sweet memories, particularly from the last time he had been here with Vickie. What a night that had been. Though it had been only four years, those days with her now seemed long ago and far away—another lifetime, really. He shook his head to clear his mind; he needed to focus on what he could do to resolve his immediate problem.

He ate some oysters on the half shell and drank a beer. Then he left the Oyster House for the Ponte Vedra Inn and Club. He searched throughout the place, but he couldn't find her there.

Walking from the club to his Mercedes, Phil blanched, cursing himself, remembering that fateful day he and Hugh Benson had met the AG for lunch at the Florida Yacht Club.

CHAPTER 20

It was dusk now, and as he approached his Mercedes, Phil could feel the effects of an afternoon of drinking as he opened the driver's door of his car and slid in behind the wheel. Sitting there with nothing in particular on his mind, other than whether he would ride back with the windows down or with the air conditioner on, he noticed out of the corner of his eye a convertible Mercedes pulling into a parking space some distance from him. He looked closer, thinking, *that's just the kind of automobile Victoria would be driving.* Sure enough, she stepped out of the dark blue Mercedes cabriolet. He frowned, knowing she had bought it with his money. "That ostentatious bitch!" he mumbled.

He waited for a few minutes and then went directly to the restroom to wash his face and admire himself again. *I've still got to look my best,* he thought, and seeing his reflection in the mirror, he once again felt he was still a good-looking man, bald head and all.

He only glanced into the bar as he slowly walked directly to the patio. The place was crowded but not full. Phil moved to the small patio bar, where he remained standing so that he could look over the whole area, and ordered a scotch on the rocks. He finally spied Victoria sitting alone at a small table on the far side, closer to the beach. *Damn, she is a fetching woman,* he thought. Dressed in a khaki skirt and a short-sleeved white cotton shirt, and with the wind lightly rustling her shoulder-length soft dark hair, she would catch any man's eye. It was more than that, though. There was an added attraction. *She looks downright wholesome,* Phil thought, *and maybe even like she was to the manor born.* His thoughts trailed off, and he shook his head, mumbling,

"I'm thinking like a moron again." *She is a clever and devious woman*, he told himself. As Phil kept that in mind, every sip of his drink washed away any and all earlier nostalgic memories of her, as he became more and more concerned about his dire situation, a plight only she could help him out of. Yet he was still uncertain how he felt. Maybe like a child who truly hates his mother, the very person he loves the most? *Do I hate Victoria?* he wondered. *No, I don't think I hate her, but right now I would sure like to strangle her.*

Phil swallowed back a lot of vitriol, tried to look pleasant, and began to casually walk among the tables, as if he were looking for somebody or for someplace to sit. A couple leaving a table for two, some distance from Victoria, was his opportunity. He slid into one of the vacant chairs. Looking about casually, he looked twice at Victoria, as if to make certain it was she. She did not acknowledge his presence. He stood up, strolled to her table and took a seat across from her.

"Well, well, well, fancy meeting you here."

"I live here at the beach. Please don't linger, okay?"

"I've heard you are now living in a plush condo out here. No doubt you like it, or you wouldn't have bought it, right?"

"I guess you could say that."

"And you've had no surprises? What I mean is, life here on the beach has been what you expected?" he said with a creased forehead as he leaned closer to her. The delicate fragrance of her perfume reminded him of just how intoxicating she could be. He recognized it as one of her favorites. He mildly inhaled and then said, "You smell better than ever. I know it must be Chanel No. 5. But maybe a special kind, a Channel No. 69?" He arched his eyebrows in mock amusement.

She bit her lip and gave him a doubting look. "That's disgusting. Can you hear yourself? I can't believe you said that. You think you're so funny or maybe just entertaining. But you're not funny, and you're certainly not entertaining me. What I really can't believe is that you're even trying to talk to me."

"Why not?" he said in what he hoped was a seductive tone, as if his comment about the perfume had succeeded beyond all expectations. "You're as gorgeous as ever. Your new hairdo is particularly becoming. I do believe the salty air ..." He paused. "And maybe the salty life has been most beneficial for you. I see you have about finished your cocktail.

Let me buy you another." He signaled the waitress for another drink for her.

"No, Phil. I don't want you to buy me—"

"Now, now," he gently interjected. "Let's remember there was a time you actually looked forward to me buying you a drink, and I might add, I always looked forward to it too. So what have you been up to lately that you want to tell me about?"

As she sat in silence, the waitress arrived with her gin and tonic. When the waitress departed and was out of earshot, she quietly stated, "The last thing I want is a goddamn scene, Phil, so I'll have a stinking drink with you. Then you take your drunken ass, bald head and all, out of here. You have ruined the dinner I was planning on having."

His casual approach was not succeeding, at least not yet. *Just be patient*, Phil told himself. *This reaction is not unexpected. What I need is a strategic retreat or diversion, and then, when she is most vulnerable, I can attack.*

"Now that's more like the old Vickie I used to know. Not this wealthy, stylish lady from Ponte Vedra, although you wear the *new* extremely well."

"Phil, why are you doing this? You must know I don't want you around me, so go."

"Go where?" He laughed. "Just because you're going to put me behind bars isn't any reason we can't be friends," he quietly said, smiling. "Now is it?"

"I should think it would be a damn good reason, and ..."

"And what?"

"You know damn well you are not supposed to be talking to me like this. For god's sake, I'm a state witness against you."

"Now, Victoria, you will just have to learn how to be more sophisticated. Sophisticated people don't let little matters damage their friendships, particularly when the little matters can be taken care of."

"What in the devil are you trying to say?" Her forced neutral expression slipped. She was getting upset.

"Now, now, my dear, one mustn't cause a scene, certainly not here in the Ponte Vedra Club," he softly admonished with an exaggerated smile.

"I'm not causing a scene. If anyone does that, it will be you," she calmly replied while stabbing toward him with her right index finger.

"Me? Why, I've only sat here pleasantly chatting with an old friend and even bought her a drink. I shouldn't think anyone could call that a *scene*."

"Phil, seriously, what do you want?"

"So the lady is perceptive. Well, I could say I want what you and I used to have together, but I'll let that wait. No, what I want to do, Vickie, is make a deal … and we need to leave here so we can talk more freely."

"I can't believe I'm agreeing to talk to you, but exactly what do you have in mind?"

"Shouldn't we find someplace that's more private?"

"You can tell me something now or …"

"Money," he quickly but quietly said, while looking away from her to get the server's attention and request the bill.

"Hmm," Vickie said, looking down, obviously reflecting on the magic word. "Okay, Phil, I'm going to walk on out to the front. You take care of the check."

"Don't you want to finish your drink?" Phil said as she pushed her chair back and started to get up.

"No. I'm going to drop by the ladies' room. I'll meet you out front."

He stood up with her and quickly tossed several bills from his pocket on the table. He was not waiting to sign the check. "That should take care of it," he said just before gulping down her gin and tonic.

Once outside, Vickie successfully insisted they go to her condo in separate cars.

Phil smiled to himself at the simplicity of his plan. He didn't even consider that his plan could go awry now. No, he had gotten his foot in the door, so to speak, when she did not get up and leave him in the bar.

The Royal Palm Condominiums consisted of several two-story salmon-colored buildings with barrel-tile roofs. Each building faced the beach, and the entire complex was surrounded by a security fence. By the time he followed her through the coded gate, however, she had talked herself out of any deal. They were standing next to his car in an open parking area set aside for visitors when she said, "Phil, there is no point in going in together. There isn't going to be any deal."

"No deal? Well, what the … no deal," he repeated. "Well, I guess that's that," he sulked. "Then let me have just one more drink with you for old time's sake?"

She hesitated.

"Please?"

"Oh, okay, but you have to go after one drink." Neither she nor Phil said anything as they walked from the parking lot to the elevator and then up to the second floor.

She said, "You still want to come in?"

"Yes, Vickie, I do. I'll just have one drink; then I'll be on my way." He knew his pleading tone was worse than ever.

"Oh, what the hell," she mumbled and unlocked the door.

Phil entered the condo and immediately set off on a self-directed tour. He looked about as he strolled past a spacious, immaculate kitchen separated from the dining area by a ten- or twelve-foot breakfast bar. An expensive blond wood dining room table, set for four, blended well with the off-white plaster walls and a crystal chandelier that hung above it. He lingered at the bar for a moment before continuing through the large living room, tastefully furnished with faux bamboo furniture, to the balcony overlooking the beach. He then returned to the living room. "Very nice. Very nice, indeed. I love those Monet prints you have. What is that? Do I recognize a Picasso in his blue period? Yes, it is."

Vickie nodded.

"My dear, you have outdone yourself. Nothing garish, only style and taste." Glancing into an alcove that connected to the bedrooms, he exclaimed, "Ah, here I see the whiskey bar, and I bet you have … yes, you do." He picked up a bottle of Glenlivet. "You, my dear, are coming of age. Join me?" He held up the bottle.

"Sure. It's not my usual, but right now, I'm still in shock at your audacity."

"Now, now, don't be so, shall we say, astonished. I know you're not really in shock because nothing I could do would shock you—not you, Vickie." He began pouring her scotch. "Tell me when …"

"When. Well, since you're here, what is it that you have in mind?" she coolly asked, picking up her scotch on the rocks.

"Do we have to talk business right away? I think I'd prefer we took some time to renew our old acquaintance—get to know each other again." He stopped for a sip. "And you know what I had for lunch?" Before she could respond, he continued, "I had two dozen oysters on the half shell at the old Oyster House, and you know what they say about oysters …" He put out his arm to bring her close.

205

She blocked his arm as it descended behind her shoulder and backed away. "Phil, none of that. We had a good time, and I'll admit we probably could have had a sweet life together, at least for a while, if you hadn't treated me, well, like you did. No, Phil, it's all over. I shouldn't even be talking to you, much less anything else. Not only that, but you're getting drunk. You're holding it well, but ..."

"Not drunk, just amorous, Vickie. I don't have to be drunk to want to bed the prettiest woman I've ever met," he said and took a step toward her. She tried to retreat toward the kitchen, but he managed to cut her off, so she drifted toward the balcony. "Vickie, you shouldn't be so intractable with the man to whom you will soon be bound by holy matrimony."

"Holy matrimony? What in hell are you talking about? Phil, you've got to go. There is nothing else for us to discuss."

"Vickie," he pleaded, "just hear me out. Hear what I have to say before ordering me to vacate the premises. I promise not to try to hug or kiss you, okay? Anyway, let me get a good breath of that ocean air before leaving ..."

Vickie backed onto the balcony as Phil walked toward her. "Okay, you sniff the air. Say what you've got to say and leave."

"God, I had such hope that my plan would be imparted to you in your bedroom, in your bed ..."

"You wish. Here or nowhere."

"Okay, okay. Don't get all excited. But I did eat all those oysters just for you. I don't even really like them," he lied. "Uh, well, maybe for me too."

"Phil, I've never heard such putrid bullshit ... can you hear yourself? Now you get on out before I call security."

"Please, Vickie, let me finish. To start over, I've been thinking a lot about you for a long time now. Didn't want to admit it, but I'm in love with you and have been since the first day we met." He paused. Her incredulous expression let him know the old charm was no more. But he hoped it just momentarily wasn't working with her. "Surely you remember the passion of our more intimate moments?"

She said nothing.

"No? Well, some of us can't recall the best moments of our lives ..." He again paused. She was becoming more and more exasperated.

"Get on with it, Phil."

"Okay. I came here with the intention of proposing marriage. We could get married, and I would immediately transfer a lot of property to you, if you wanted it. Then I'd have a good argument, frankly, with the state attorney about dropping the case against me. Who would want to break up a happy home? But if necessary, if you would go along with it, I could bribe the state attorney down there. Forget Larry Singer. His boss will take a dive if the price is right. Never met a politician who wouldn't."

"I've never heard anything so absurd in my life. Here I am, trying to salvage what's left of my life, and you want me to crawl back into the gutter with you. I was a damn fool to leave the club with you. Frankly, I think I was so apprehensive about you causing a scene that I just gave into you. Do you understand what I'm saying? I left with you to get rid of you. Now you get out of here before I call the police."

"Does that mean you won't marry me?" He smiled just before he took a big drink of his scotch.

She didn't immediately answer, but just looked at him searchingly.

"I guess no answer is the same as no." He polished off the rest of his drink. "Just one more, Vickie. You know how the song goes—one more for the road." He walked inside from the balcony and started toward the bar.

Vickie started laughing as she followed him inside. "Just one more for the road? Pretty soon you won't be able to get out to the road. No, sir, Phil, you don't get another drink, not here." She stepped between him and the bar and held out her hand to take his empty glass.

"It used to be you understood you were never to stand in the way of me and my liquor."

"Forget all the used-to-be's. They are just that: used-to-be's. I'm serious. I want you to go. I'm not marrying you. And I know that's not an honest proposal. You're just up to your old tricks to get yourself out of a mess. But even if it were honest, you can forget it, and I'm not the least interested in going to bed with you. Can't you get that through your head?"

"Can't I just have a good-bye fuck?"

"For Christ's sake, no! Give me your glass and go!"

"How about a pity fuck, then?"

"No way! Now give me your glass, Phil."

Phil said nothing; he just held the glass and glared at her.

207

"I said give me the glass," she harshly demanded. "You're on your way out of here, or you're on your way to jail for trespassing and tampering with a state witness."

The words were barely out of her mouth when the underlying turmoil Phil had kept in check, just below his calm persona, broke through his veneer of self-control in a torrent of rage. He drew back the glass and shouted, "I'll give you back your goddamn glass!" Just before he could slam the glass into her face, she blocked the assault with her right arm. The glass exploded in a shower of blood from her arm and his hand. She staggered back, screaming, with blood spurting between the fingers of her left hand as she clasped tightly to her right arm.

"There, you bitch, is your glass back! And goddamn it, look what you made me do!" he shouted as he hurried to the kitchen area adjoining the living room. He wrapped his cut hand in a dishcloth.

When he turned back to the living room again, Vickie wasn't there. "Victoria!" he hollered over and over as he stomped through the condo. He found her in the bathroom, securing a hand towel around her arm. Standing in the doorway, he commanded, "Why in hell didn't you answer me?"

She reached for the curling iron sitting on the sink and quickly plugged it in. She did not answer him but instead stood her ground and waved the curling iron at him. He did not approach her. Instead, he took a step backward, extended his hands in a reassuring gesture, and nodding toward the curling iron, said, "There is no need for that; I'm leaving." He turned away and stomped toward the front door.

As Phil raced down the last flight of stairs, he encountered what looked like, to his astonishment, a big, burly police officer coming up the stairs toward him. Before he could consider how a cop had arrived so fast, the man raised his hands, signaling Phil to stop. Phil's first inclination was to push the cop out of his way. But upon instant reconsideration, he realized that was a bad idea. He did not know what he was going to do, but he slowed his fast pace. Almost at the same time, he recognized that the man was a big, burly *security guard*, not a policeman, who with some urgency in his voice asked, "Where're you going in such a big hurry?"

"I'm hurt and need to get to the hospital," Phil said quickly and condescendingly as he showed the guard his bloody right hand, still wrapped in the dish towel, and rushed past him.

"Do you need some help?" the guard asked.

"No, thanks. I cut my hand, but I can drive myself to the emergency room." Phil knew he could not get trapped into giving a detailed explanation to the guard. That could have all kinds of adverse repercussions, particularly later. Because of his guilty conscience, Phil was truly afraid the guard knew what he had done and would insist on assisting him anyway, just to get information. But the guard did not follow him.

As he continued down the stairs, he now felt his heart throbbing in his throat, and he could breathe only in short, shallow bursts. *God almighty, after all this, I'm having a goddamn heart attack*, he thought. The sweat beading heavily on his forehead dripped into his eyes, and a wave of nausea left him trembling. At the same time, his legs grew weaker and weaker. He was surer than ever he might die. *I've always wondered how I would die*, he thought, *and now I know—a heart attack*. Desperately afraid of fainting or falling, he pushed on through sheer willpower. He was so scared of what he had done that he irrationally rejected all thoughts of seeking help from the guard or anyone else.

Just as he felt he could go no farther, his hand touched the car door, and he was able to rest for a few seconds, leaning on the car. Opening the door, he collapsed under the wheel with a deep sigh of relief. After a needed moment to rest, calm down, and partially recuperate, he inserted the ignition key with a shaking, still-wrapped hand. Though he was exhausted mentally and emotionally, he was beginning to feel safer now that he was comfortably seated in the familiar surroundings of his automobile. Reflecting, with a brain saturated in booze, about what had just occurred, he strongly suspected Vickie had not called and would not call the police, and he slowly regained his usual composure, but not his usual invincibility. As his labored breathing eased up, thoughts of dying slipped away, and he concentrated on getting back to Jacksonville.

This little soiree had gone poorly. But not so poorly that he couldn't survive it, very possibly as if it had never happened. He slowly shook his head, thinking, *Am I lucky? Hell yes. Despite all this mess, I'm lucky as hell she was able to throw up her arm and keep me from smashing that glass into her face. What in hell was I thinking? I could have blinded her, maybe even have killed her. No one but a fool would lose control like that*. Reflecting on what could have happened and almost did happen made him shiver. Trembling all over, he shook his head to free his mind from those terrible mental images. Still haunted by the events, he wasn't quite ready to smile, but the sick feeling in his stomach subsided somewhat as he cranked the car and backed out, all the while repeatedly mumbling, "It could have been worse. I've got to get to Jacksonville." Like a hunted animal seeking refuge, Phil perceived Jacksonville as a personal sanctuary. It was his town, and he was still repeating that refrain when the Mercedes exited the Royal Palms Condominiums complex and began traveling north on A1A.

CHAPTER 21

P hil was thinking in his whiskey-soaked brain that he should take the deal the state attorney had offered. Mike was really not a fool, and after a year or so, this mess would just be a bad, albeit expensive, memory. It was dark now, and the ocean's salty mist had clouded his windshield. The windshield cleaning system failed to work, and the wipers just smeared the salty mist, along with something else. *Crap, it's some kind of grease*, he realized. *I must have parked too close to a kitchen exhaust fan at the Oyster House.* His effort to be ultra-careful driving had no meaning. It was time for him to pull off the road and stop, and he knew it. He had managed to stay well below the speed limit. Yet he didn't want to go so slow as to attract the attention of a cop. *Damn, I think I'm driving fine*, he thought, *but I'm drunk and might very well be weaving all over the road.* As he passed the Ponte Vedra Club, he was irrationally focused on getting past the Oyster House or maybe stopping there for a cup of coffee. Then he considered that he should have stopped at the club and tried to sober up, but that wouldn't do; he could not be seen in the Ponte Vedra Club with a dish towel wrapped around his hand. No, that would never do.

Squinting, to keep his eyes adjusted, through a clear slit in the windshield, he foolishly crept north, though he had to hang his head out of the driver's window a time or two, to make sure of what he was seeing through his windshield. The Oyster House loomed ahead. With welcome relief, Phil thanked god, for he could stop there. But the idea had barely materialized when he rejected it. Like the beach club, he could not go in there with a bloody dish towel wrapped around his hand. Damn, would this drive ever end? He knew it could end in tragedy. And that could be more likely than not if he didn't stop and clean the windshield. Instead of stopping, he tried one more time to get his windshield cleaning mechanism to work. "Crap, you pay seventy thousand dollars to have all this junk on a car, and when you need it the most, it doesn't work," he murmured to himself as he jiggled the switch one more time. He was going to have to stop and get a Coca-Cola to cut the grease and salt off the windshield. Still creeping north, he realized the closest place for him to get a Coke to clean the windshield with the wipers was the bar where he had met Sally. Going in there with a bloody dishrag around his hand would not be a problem.

He began to hang his head out of the driver's open window a little so that he would not miss the parking lot across the street from the bar. As the parking lot came into sight, the anxiety churning his stomach began to subside. He was going to make it. Mounting apprehension subsided as he relaxed and swung left into the parking lot. As soon as he pulled into a parking space, however, his heart skipped a beat at the sight of a patrol car pulling in behind him with its blue lights blinking. Then he heard over the patrol car's loudspeaker, "Sir, remain in your car."

Thinking he would at least be arrested for DUI, Phil took several deep breaths, sat back in his car seat, and expressed his feelings in one word—"Shit"—as he concentrated on trying to relax and look sober. He heard the cop's car door squeak open. Turning his head slightly, Phil could see the policeman was an older man, but he was stepping with authority toward him.

When the officer reached Phil's open window, he said with professional courtesy, "Good evening, sir. Are you lost?"

"Good evening to you too, officer, but no, I'm not lost."

"Well, you were driving a little like you were uncertain about where you were or where you wanted to go. Have you been drinking?"

With that question, Phil's feeling that things might go well sharply dwindled. *I'm caught, but I won't throw in the towel yet.* "Well, officer, I wouldn't say I have been drinking, but I had a couple of drinks some time ago. My windshield washer isn't working, and I was looking for a place where I could get a Coca-Cola to clean my windshield with. I intended to get a Coke in the bar across the street."

"Well, to some people that answer might not make a lot of sense, but I happen to know that old Coca-Cola remedy for cleaning grease off the windshield is a damn good one."

"I've known about it ever since I was a kid in Miami."

"Hmm, let me see your driver's license." While Phil was getting his driver's license, the cop looked at his windshield. Phil handed him the license. "Yeah, you got a little grease and salt. Probably would take more than your car washer to clean it, even if it worked. I'll be back in a minute. You stay in your car for now."

As the cop walked back to his patrol car, Phil's mind entertained one bad scenario after another. *Damn, things have gone from bad to worse in every sense of the word,* he thought. *This has been a really bad day.* Depressed and scared but not yet terrified, Phil thought for just a fraction of a second about cranking up and driving away. Just as quickly, he dismissed that notion as the ultimate in foolishness. He wasn't that drunk, and the policeman had his driver's license. No way could he escape. *I'll just have to take what comes,* he decided. *But I can't give up hope.* He concentrated more fervently than ever on trying to act sober. But the field sobriety test could really be a problem. And he couldn't even entertain the idea of a breath test. He sighed to himself, knowing he could not be proactive in this situation; he could only wait and respond. Trying to be important or take umbrage with the police officer would absolutely be the worst thing he could do. No, if he were ever going to be nice to anyone, this was the time to be nice. He and the officer had gotten along pretty well up to now, and that was somewhat reassuring.

Phil glanced up and saw that the patrolman was returning. He was holding Phil's license and glancing at it as he reached the driver's window. He paused for a moment, as if making a decision. Phil tried not to breathe in his direction. Finally, as he handed the license back to Phil, he said, "Well, I know you didn't steal this car. And Mr. Griffin, I don't want you to wreck it and kill or hurt yourself, or someone else. So be careful if you do drive after cleaning your windshield. Frankly, I would like to know that you have made arrangements not to drive anymore tonight, okay?"

Phil wondered whether he should say thank you. "Officer, I'm going to go in there"—he nodded to the bar—"but I know somebody I can call." With a revived feeling of invincibility, Phil rolled up his window, slid out of his car, and with deep concentration managed to walk more or less normally to the bar. As he crossed the road, he thought, *While this has not been the best day of my life, I have certainly not been deserted by lady luck,* and he imagined figuratively wiping the sweat from his brow. By the time he reached the weather-beaten door of what he perceived to be an emporium of sin and flesh, he had firmly decided to no longer tempt fate.

As he opened the door, he was strangely disappointed that Sally wasn't still sitting at the bar. But no, it was more than that—he felt cheated. For whatever reason, his libido or otherwise, that's the person he had expected to see. Still, this urge for Sally left him emotionally confused. Why had this day, perhaps his life, come to this sorry state? *It must be because I'm drunk, or maybe I'm just crazy.* Shaking his head in exasperation, he mumbled, "All I really need to do is call Mike, or someone else in the office, to come get me, or maybe call a taxi." As he took a seat at the bar, he scanned the booths and tables. Of the three seated at the bar, he immediately recognized one who had been there earlier in the day and who was still sitting on the same stool, looking, well, not exactly worthless—no, it was more like he was lonely, without a friend in the world. Phil instinctively considered himself better than that sad soul, yet at the same time, he could and did identify with him. *I don't like to admit it, but I really do feel alone,* he thought. *Alone and . . . what?* After a moment of total thoughtlessness, he jerked back and shook his head. *For Christ's sake, I'm slipping into a funk. Crap, I'm not alone. What the hell am I thinking? I've got plenty of friends, and a lot of people admire me, and not just for my professional acumen. I have simply got to get this mess I'm in down south behind me.* And Vickie? Phil shook his head, confident she was not hurt that bad and would just let it go rather than deal with the police. He slightly smiled, thinking that on balance, he had a lot to be thankful for. Now was not the time to chastise himself, although he deserved it. *Nothing I can do right now about anything anyway, so shouldn't I make the best of what remains of the day?*

Taking a seat at the bar, Phil continued scanning the room. Other than the men at the bar, all he saw was a young man and a girl sitting across from each other in one of the booths. He did a double take; they looked too decent to be in that place. The young man was neatly dressed in jeans and a polo shirt, was clean-shaven, and sported a crew cut. He definitely had that all-American look. The girl looked awfully young, and Phil wondered whether she was even old enough to be drinking. Dressed in a blue button-down oxford shirt, a rather short straight denim skirt, and loafers, and with her soft dark hair pulled back in a loose ponytail, she not only was attractive but also exuded an air of innocence. *And what the hell*, he thought, *she's old enough to be drinking or doing anything else she wants to do, whether she's twenty-one or not.* Looking at this pair triggered melancholy memories of his own younger days. These two were only concerned with each other. If they were not in love, they sure acted like they were. It was no more than just a touch of hands across the table, but for Phil, and he suspected for them, it was unmistakably a sweet, erotic caress. They smiled as they talked, and it seemed with the slightest movement or tilt of her head, her short ponytail jiggled and danced, sending the oldest signal in the world. "Oh, for the snows of yesteryear," murmured Phil as he swiveled the stool to fully address the bar.

By then the same bartender who had been there in the afternoon was standing opposite Phil on the other side of the bar. For no good reason Phil was massaging his chin, as if he were making a major decision. The scruffy-faced, greasy-headed man, however, saved him the trouble of pretending to make up his mind when he asked with raised eyebrows and a nod of his head, "One more of the same?"

"Yeah, I guess so."

"Yes, sir, one Glenlivet on the rocks." The bartender slipped away to prepare the drink, leaving Phil drumming his fingers on the bar, as if he could hardly wait to get the drink. He was still thinking about the couple in the booth. He felt like going over there and telling them they should leave this shithole. No, that was a bad idea. Anyway, who was he to be telling anybody what to do? Those two were experiencing the best life had to offer. The moment was theirs; he should let them have it.

The bartender asked, "You want to run a tab?" as he placed Phil's scotch on the rocks on the bar.

"Yeah, sure, why not," Phil said as he picked up the glass.

"Anything else I can do for you?" The bartender raised his brow and wrinkled his forehead, as if he expected Phil to ask for something else.

"Well, maybe there is something you can do for me."

The bartender flashed a questioning expression in the form of a friendly smirk.

"You know the girl that was in here this afternoon—you know, Sally?"

"Yeah, I know who you mean. She comes around once in a while. But to say I know her would not be quite accurate."

"You have any idea how to get in touch with her?"

"Hell no. What do you think I am, mister, a pimp?" His tone was rough, maybe even threatening, like Phil had insulted him.

Phil immediately became apologetically defensive. "No, no, please don't get the wrong idea. I just felt that she and I had a nice conversation this afternoon, and maybe she would be around tonight. Please accept my apologies if I have offended you. Rest assured that wasn't my intention. My name is Phil, Phil Griffin, and I'm not really having a good day."

"Phil Griffin, huh? My name is Burt Reynolds, but you may call me Burt. Things haven't been good for me either lately—tried to get a job as a mixologist in Tony Martin's Supper Club in Hollywood, California, when Hollywood dumped on me, but it didn't work out. So here I am in this esteemed establishment." As he spoke, he cast his eyes all about in an obvious effort to be funny, or perhaps he was just being facetious. "And no offense taken. Do you live around here, or where?" Burt's tone had truly softened, and Phil wondered whether he had really taken umbrage at the suggestion he might know how to get in touch with Sally.

With a polite laugh and thin smile, Phil relaxed. "Yeah, I guess you could say I live around here. I live in Jacksonville. And Burt, it's good to see you haven't lost your sense of humor, despite falling on hard times ..."

"Speaking of a sense of humor, what happened to your hand?"

"Oh, nothing much."

"What did you do, catch your hand in your car door or something?"

"Well, not exactly. Let's just say I put my hand in the wrong place at the wrong time."

"But now you would like to put your hand, or whatever, in the right place. And that could be why you are looking for Sally, or at least something like that?" Burt arched his eyebrows and wrinkled his forehead in a knowing expression.

"Well, not exactly, but something like that."

"Stick around awhile. She'll probably float by sometime tonight," Burt commented as he moved away to tend to another customer. About that time, Phil heard the door open, and he quickly turned to see if it was Sally. It wasn't. It was an older man and woman. Phil took little notice of them as they crossed the room to sit side by side in one of the booths. Disappointed, Phil somewhat reluctantly admitted to himself it was only Sally he wanted to see come through the door; for some strange, inexplicable reason, he felt comfortable with her. *But why do I have this almost longing to see her? Maybe because I'm all alone, and she's not a total stranger. But, she really is a stranger, not someone I should have any genuine interest in.* Confused about his true feelings about Sally, Phil wondered why he even cared. Hadn't he always said that people had to accept what life had to offer, good or bad, and not be judgmental—just deal with it? *If she's what I want, just like I want this single-malt scotch whiskey, then what the hell, I should go for it. What I need right now is a person like Sally—not specifically Sally, just someone I can comfortably talk to and who will show me a measure of sympathy. Sympathy, is that what I'm looking for? Of course it is; everybody's looking for sympathy. So what if it costs money. It doesn't matter whether you pay for it or not. It is all the same. Strokes are strokes, and I need to be stroked.*

With each sip of his scotch, the disturbing events of the day and his other problems receded farther into the foggy valleys of his brain. Even so, a spark of sanity filtered through, and he decided that if Sally did not show up within the next few minutes, he would call Mike or a taxi. The word "taxi" echoed in his mind. He could always call a cab to take him to a motel. *I'll have another drink before making a decision*, he ultimately decided. *Right now I'm safe and can peacefully drink as much as I want to.*

After he'd spent some time sipping his drink and thinking more or less of nothing, his mind drifted to the towel wrapped around his right hand. The thing was covered with blood. *Crap, I might have to go to the emergency room. I don't want to do that.* Somewhat concerned about the extent of his injury, he signaled the bartender that he would be right back and ambled toward the men's room. In sharp contrast to the rest of the place, the restroom was amazingly clean. The wall paint was old and in some places flaking, and the metal fixtures on the two urinals, the toilet, and the lavatory showed graphic effects of salt erosion, but the offensive smell so common to similar establishments was absent. Either that, or the stale smell of the barroom had deadened his olfactory senses. Taking note of a soap dispenser and a full rack of paper towels, Phil was further surprised—*we never know what's around the corner*, he concluded. He proceeded to remove the bloody dish towel and began to wash his hand under the warm faucet. The warm water felt good.

And he felt even better as he realized only his index finger was actually cut. The blood had been all over his hand, but only his finger was injured. "Hmm," he murmured, inspecting his finger as well as several superficial wounds. He surmised some of that blood had been Victoria's. The bleeding had practically stopped. Phil retrieved a handkerchief from his inside coat pocket, tore off a small strip, and fashioned a bandage around his finger. The injury was not nearly as serious as he had thought it would be, and in his whiskey-drenched brain, the diminished injury meant the terrible event with Victoria had not been so bad after all. He felt better about everything and took the time to primp and admire himself in the mirror before leaving the restroom. More than just satisfied with his personal appearance, he whispered, "It's show time," as he emerged from the restroom.

CHAPTER 22

His elated mood solidified when he saw Sally sitting next to his place at the bar. Was he having an adrenaline rush or what? To say he was really glad to see her would have been a gross understatement. But in a way, he was not surprised. After all, Burt had told him she would probably drop back in. As he walked across the concrete floor, he entertained the idea that Burt had indeed called her. He reached the bar and took his seat next to Sally. "What the hell? Fancy meeting you here again!" he said. Before she could respond to that inane comment, he continued. "No, I'll be honest. I actually thought we would meet again. Oh, I don't know, I just figured you would be here."

She said, "Well, it's just a coincidence, but I'm glad you're here."

Phil motioned to Burt, with a common hand signal, to bring her whatever she wanted to drink and to bring him another scotch on the rocks. "Damn, I feel good. I really do." His tone was soft, and he was sure his smile was Phil Griffin at his inebriated best. Maybe he was subconsciously fantasizing that all was well, that the woman sitting next to him was just a sweet woman he had met in a bar, and not a lady of the evening. The booze, and no doubt deeper psychological problems, morphed him into a modern-day Don Quixote. And like the man from La Mancha, he was playing a role in a story he composed from moment to moment. Not entirely aware of what he was doing, he was led on by his subconscious, and he expected the other characters in the bar to play their parts appropriately. So far, the only other character was Sally, not only a pretty girl but also a nice person who obviously found him attractive and interesting. She would be graciously flattered by his gentlemanly attentions.

"How you doing, handsome?" She smiled and placed her left hand on his right knee.

"Handsome?"

"Yes, handsome. I've got to call you something." She lightly squeezed his leg right before delivering a couple of pats and then removing her hand altogether. "You don't mind, do you?"

"Your innocent touch is most welcome. And though I know your reference to me as handsome is somewhat misguided, thank you. But why don't you call me Phil? That's my real name. And ..." He trailed off as the drinks were set before them.

"And?" she asked in a quizzically friendly tone while picking up her drink.

"And I see you are still drinking White Russians."

"But that's not what you were going to say."

"You're right. I was going to say, and I shall call you Sally if Sally is your real name."

"It's my real name. You can count on it," she mumbled just before taking a sip of her drink.

"But your last name is not Rand?"

"No," she laughed. "Sally Rand was well before my time. How old are you?"

"Before my time too. And I'm no older than you want me to be," he answered, trying to convey friendly mischief in his eyes and voice. After a short, meaningful pause, he continued with arched eyebrows and a thin smile. "Now that we have our names basically sorted out, I think we should have a toast. Another nice toast to celebrate what I know will be an unforgettable evening from here on out."

"Unforgettable?"

"Yes, my dear, unforgettable, and I mean that in the same sense Nat King Cole did in that wonderful old song. You remember, don't you? *"Unforgettable, that's what you are."* With a faraway look in his eyes, he started quietly humming the tune of the song and waved his hands about as if conducting an orchestra for a few seconds before turning his gaze back to Sally. He arched his eyebrows and turned his open palms slightly toward her in a gesture of expectation. "You do remember, don't you?" Phil was talking and acting as if he and Sally had long ago, and perhaps far away, been romantically involved.

"Remember? Sure, I remember. I'll never forget that sweet song. Let me have some money, honey, and I'll play us some good music."

"Splendid idea, my dear," Phil said with an exaggerated flourish, attempting to imitate one of the old-time matinee idols like James Mason, as he handed her a five-dollar bill. "Play us some Nat King Cole if there's any on the jukebox."

She took the money and sauntered over to the modern successor to the nickelodeon. In short order Phil heard something he hadn't heard in a long time, the soothing tenor of Bobby Vinton: *"Roses are red my love, violets are blue ..."* As the song played, Sally returned to her seat. "I like that," Phil said. "It's not Nat King Cole, but very good. And I might say nostalgic." He had dropped the exaggerated flourish. "I have a lot of nice memories associated with this song, or perhaps I should say with the era of the song. After all, I was a young man then. But you know that, don't you? And you, my dear, must have been only a child."

"I like it too. Nice music makes me feel ..." She paused, looked down for a short moment, and then softly, almost in a whisper, said, "Makes me feel *nice*."

Damn, I believe I really do like this woman, Phil thought. *What am I going to do?*

She continued in a woeful, perhaps melancholy tone. "You do remember me that way, don't you?"

He did not immediately respond.

"You, being such a nice person yourself, you must remember?"

"Yes, yes, I do remember. You are not only a nice person but also an honest woman. No guile whatsoever." Phil hesitated, with a pensive expression, like he was truly trying to remember, just before their eyes locked in a meaningful way. Then they both sipped from their drinks and visibly relaxed. Her blue-green eyes fluttered and sparkled, unmistakably sending the message she was interested. At least that was what Phil pretended in his fog-shrouded brain; he tried not to consider that she might just be playing along, following his cues as best she could. They continued to talk about things that never had been, but that sometimes intertwined with reality. He discovered she did not go to the movies much and read very little outside the supermarket's tabloids. Neither invited the other to discuss their line of work. He obviously knew what she did, and she knew not to inquire about what he did for a living, beyond a casual suggestion that whatever it was, he must be very successful.

Even though he was inebriated, the idea that he was acting like a moron (and anywhere else in the world, would be making a spectacle of himself) began to emerge from the backwash of his brain, where the scotch and god knows what else had conveniently buried it. *God almighty, I've lost my mind*, he thought. Of course, in a way he had. Too much scotch could do that. Yet he couldn't deny he was still enjoying himself, like a child playing a game, an adult game to be sure. He thought, *I can't remember when I've had such a satisfying experience, in a peculiar sort of way. Just one more drink and then—well, we'll see.* He caught the bartender's attention and signaled for two more drinks.

Sally quickly said, "No, not one for me right now." Shaking her head, she looked toward Burt and gestured not to bring her one.

"You sure you don't want another White Russian or something else?" he said with a tone that urged her to have another. "If you don't drink with me, I might think you don't like my company." He wondered whether he should read anything into her not having another drink, but he said nothing more.

"I like your company. Maybe more than I should. It's just that I haven't finished this one, see?" She lifted her drink and lightly shook it. "Anyway, I don't want to get drunk—just a good buzz—and I don't think you would want me drunk either, would you?"

"Having never seen you drunk, I just don't know whether I would like to see you drunk or not. I certainly hope you don't mind seeing me drunk—because I think I'm probably drunk right now." He smiled and blinked his eyes as if to say, "Please say it doesn't matter."

"Oh, you're not drunk. Not yet anyway. You have certainly been drinking. But drunk? No."

The bartender placed the scotch on the rocks for Phil on the bar and hesitated a minute to catch Sally's eye, to make sure she did not want another one. She shook her head no. Turning to Phil, she picked up her drink and said, "I've still got some left for our toast."

"Oh yes, we were going to have a toast. Should you do the honors or ..."

"Oh, I could, but why don't you do it this time? You're not really drunk like you think you are, and I bet you can come up with something nice. A good-looking man like you can certainly come up with a nice toast."

Even three sheets to the wind, Phil recognized her exaggerated compliments for what they were; Sally was selling something. He let it go but decided it was time to stop the nonsense. "Well, I'll try." As their glasses touched, he said, slightly slurring, "Whiskey is good, sex is better, but I like mine mixed together, don't you?" His flashing eyes and wrinkled forehead suggested her answer should be yes. Sally lightly smiled, and her eyes searched his face as she sipped to the toast. He took a small sip of his scotch on the rocks. "Was that a nice toast or what?"

"It's not exactly what I had in mind, but yes, it was a nice toast and, I might say, to the point. But you know, sometimes too much whiskey can cause a problem. You know what I mean?"

"No lesser authority than William Shakespeare said alcohol increases the desire but lessens the performance. But on that score you should have no fear. Phil Griffin has never missed a performance, drunk or sober."

"Would you like to have something that will really make you perform better?" she cautiously suggested.

"What are you talking about? Viagra or something like that? I can assure you I do not need anything like that. Just let me finish this drink, and you will find out."

"No, Phil, I'm not talking about anything like Viagra. I'm talking about something we both can use that will make the sex really something to remember. You know, you would like something to *remember* me by, wouldn't you?"

It occurred to him that she might indeed leave him with something to remember her by. But he quickly dismissed that inconvenient truth. "I think I'll remember you no matter what. But what the hell are you talking about?"

"You know."

"No, I don't know. Why can't you just tell me?"

"You know, the white powder magic, the stuff that changes the world for you. And when it comes to sex, well, you can't believe it unless you've tried it. I wouldn't even suggest this for just anybody, but you are special, at least special to me."

"Sounds to me like you are talking about cocaine."

She nodded her head and squeezed his leg.

"I can't say I've never tried it, but generally speaking, I don't indulge." He stopped to think. He knew he shouldn't, not because he had any moral compunction about snorting cocaine, but because it was against the law, and he was with someone he really didn't know. He heard this little voice deep within his inner being telling him not to do it, but it was drowned out by the booze. Any inhibitions he had left were washed away in a sea of alcohol. Ignoring his better instincts, and despite some trepidation, he announced with authority, "Why the hell not? Sounds like a capital idea. Do you have some with you, or somewhere else, somewhere where you can go get it?"

"I can get us an eight ball for two hundred dollars."

"An eight ball …that would be what, four grams?"

"That might seem a little high, but actually it isn't, not for the quality stuff I can get."

"And of course, I've got to take care of you too." Phil took another sip of his drink, and once again his eyes met Sally's. He was trying to determine whether or not it would be okay to deliver two hundred dollars to her. In a situation like this, it wasn't completely out of the question that the woman would take the money and never show up again.

Sally batted her eyelashes and took a small sip of her White Russian. "You have already taken care of me; don't you remember? If later you feel like giving me something, fine. If not, that's fine too. Anyway, you must know I really do like you." An honest, though pleading, quality to her voice convinced Phil.

He took several bills from his pocket, counted out two hundred, and handed the money to her. "How long do you think you'll be gone?"

"Not long. Maybe fifteen or twenty minutes," she said as she rose from her seat and slid the money into her small purse. "Don't leave, now; I'll be back. It might take a little longer than I think. But you will see me again, that's for sure." She was so anxious to reassure him of her return that it crossed Phil's mind that he had probably parted with two hundred bucks for nothing.

He continued to sip his scotch as his mind replayed the events of the day. The longer Sally was gone, the more regrets he had about even coming out to the beach. *Crap*, he thought, *I had no plan, unless you want to call driving out here just to see how things would go "a plan."* To get anything done and done right took preparation. The booze was no longer masking his true situation. Sitting there, with Bobby Vinton's rendition of "Blue Velvet" wafting through this extremely bad excuse for an assignation, left him shaking his head in self-denigration. Thirty minutes elapsed, and no Sally. For obvious reasons, his patience was wearing thin, even though he had suspected this would happen. Somewhat exasperated, but with a firm resolve, he told himself that as soon as he finished the drink on the bar before him, he was going to leave and go home or get a room somewhere.

After a few minutes of running one bad scenario after another—like catching a loathsome disease, maybe even AIDS, or getting arrested for something associated with the cocaine, or even getting rolled—all traces of impatience and disappointment melted away. He was actually relieved. This misbegotten day was spinning more and more out of control, and he was glad it was about over.

As he picked up his drink to finish what little was left, he thought through the haze in his brain that the two hundred dollars he'd given Sally might very well have been the best two hundred dollars he had ever spent. She was gone, and that was that. Then the door opened, and to his mild surprise, there she was. She didn't say anything immediately; she just took her seat and placed her cloth purse on the bar. "Gee," she said, "I was afraid you might have left. I am really glad you didn't. Aren't you glad you didn't?"

"It's debatable, but I think I probably am. Your apprehension that I might not be here was justified. I had about decided you weren't coming back. However, you have once again proved that you are an honest woman, and I like that. Would you like another drink before we, you know, go somewhere else? I assume my money was well spent." Like she had played his game, he was now playing her game, except her game was for real and not make-believe.

"Yeah, I could use one more drink. Just one more, and then we can go, okay?"

Phil caught the bartender's eye and gestured for another round. Sally reached over, lightly touched his leg, and said, "I've got some really good shit." She opened her purse and retrieved a small tinfoil packet. "Here," she said, showing the packet to Phil. "I've got to go to the ladies' room for a minute, so you keep this." All in one motion, while she was talking, she stood up and slid the packet into his coat's side pocket. "I want you to keep it so you won't have to worry about me tooting it up in the ladies room. I'll be back in a minute."

"Okay." Phil swiveled his stool to directly address the bar and wait for his drink to be served. He thought he knew how the night was going to play out now. As he glanced around, he noticed Sally pause briefly by a man sitting at the bar before she continued on toward the restroom. It was the same sad-looking man who had been there earlier that day.

Phil returned his attention to the bar, but a moment later, he heard someone behind him say, "Mr. Griffin." Phil turned around. It was the same man from down the bar. "Mr. Griffin, I'm a cop. Would you step outside please?"

"Bullshit. You're no cop," Phil snapped, immediately taking umbrage at what he thought was a barfly who obviously believed he was stupid enough or drunk enough to walk outside to be robbed and maybe beaten up. But when Phil slid off the stool to take a war stance, he realized the man was well over six feet, with bulging arm muscles, and despite a two or three day stubble, he appeared healthy and, to Phil's astonishment, sober. Sitting on the stool, he had appeared to be a rum-soaked derelict. *What the crap is going on here?* Phil suddenly wondered. Then he knew. But he didn't want to know. He suspected this was an undercover cop on some kind of stakeout, but to Phil, suspicion was not true knowledge. He refused to accept the obvious.

"Calm down, sir. I am the law. See?" He showed Phil his badge. "Now, come outside so we don't have to have a scene in here." As he spoke, he grabbed Phil's arm to walk him outside.

Phil shook his head and looked around, particularly for Sally, all the while thinking, *is this guy really a cop, and do I have to go outside with him? I don't think so.* "What the hell did I supposedly do?" Phil angrily said in an escalating voice as he tried to pull away from the cop's grip.

"Don't do that again," the cop commanded as he increased his grip on Phil's arm, "or …" He was probably going to say, "or I'll have to arrest you right here," but Phil interrupted his warning by once again trying to pull away. The cop stopped talking and in a flash stepped behind Phil and jerked his arm up behind his back, causing him to bend over and cry out in pain; at the same time, the cop brutally pushed Phil off his feet to the nasty concrete floor. "You are now under arrest for interfering with an officer in the performance of his duty. Do you understand?"

Phil was lying with his face pressed hard to the floor by the cop's ham like hands and with a knee in the pit of his back. The dusty smell of concrete filled his nostrils as his face was ground into the damp, rough floor. All he could manage was an unintelligible gurgle. Indignant, he was trying to say he was a lawyer, and he'd sue the city and everybody else if the cop didn't let him go. Out of the corner of the eye not pressed against the concrete floor, he could see Sally. He still couldn't say anything that could be understood, but he was trying to tell the cop to ask Sally, and she would confirm he had done nothing wrong. She would save him unless—and then it hit him, like he had just been told a giant tsunami was minutes away: he was being arrested for what had happened with Victoria. That had to be it. Then he heard Sally say in a flat, matter-of-fact way, "That's him, and I thought he was such a nice man."

Her words caused his heart to skip a beat. *What in hell have I gotten myself into, just when I felt my luck was on the rise?* The pressure holding his head down eased slightly, and he was able to understandably gurgle, "Let me up, and I can explain. For Christ's sake, I'm a lawyer, and I will sue the hell out of all of you."

"Keep your mouth shut. You are under arrest now for solicitation for the purpose of prostitution. Do you understand?" Phil felt the pain of handcuffs being tightened around each wrist. With that a dark cloud of doom engulfed his innermost being.

Phil managed to mumble, "Yes." He also understood that his luck had completely run out. *Goddamn, I can't believe this. I've been done in by two first-class bitches within a matter of hours.*

By the time Phil was handcuffed, two uniformed policemen had arrived, and they were now helping pat him down for weapons or contraband. One of them was the patrolman who had approached him in the parking lot. As the arresting officer retrieved the tinfoil packet, he looked at the others and smirked. "Well, well, what have we got here? If it's what I think it might be, what we have here is now a felony. Advise him of his rights and take him on to a patrol car. I'll field-test this, and if it's bad, we'll have to book him."

The patrolman from the parking lot addressed Phil with a distinct note of sympathy in his voice. "Now, Mr. Griffin, we are going to get you up. Please do not say anything." Once Phil was on his feet, the officer quickly advised him again that he didn't have to say anything, that he had a right to remain silent. "Mr. Griffin, I wish you had gone on home. I never expected something like this to happen," he said as he carefully walked Phil to the patrol car. "But it's too late now. Just take it easy. You can bond out tonight. Just don't cause any more trouble." Outside the bar, the officer locked him in the backseat cage of the patrol car. Phil just hoped the "good shit" was baby powder or some other legal substance.

From one shithole to another, he thought. The pungent odor in the patrol car, like someone had recently vomited in this stifling cage, was about to smother him. Though he was outwardly quiet, his mind was racing; he should have killed Victoria. And Sally, well, she was just a lost soul trying to get by in this tough world. But with Vickie, he never should have let his emotions take over. A grim smile crept over his face as he thought of the satisfaction he had momentarily felt in almost smashing that glass into her mouthy face. But that moment was gone, and he knew it would never return. Why hadn't she just gone along with his plan? The question echoed in his befuddled head. That's all she had to do, but no, she wouldn't. Instead, she'd made him do what he did, and now he was in all this extra trouble. "The whole thing was her fault," he mused to himself while looking around the stinking cage in which he was now trapped. Still, he wasn't totally helpless. All he needed was to bond out. He was entitled to a bond, to a reasonable bond, under the Constitution. With that realization, his distress diminished, and he tried to focus his muddled mind. An idea began to stir around in his head: he could claim that the assault on Vickie with the glass had been self-defense. *No, sir, all is not lost; I'm not convicted yet*, he thought. Then he remembered that committing another crime while free on a bond could be grounds to revoke the bond. Phil had not yet fully grasped the reality of his situation, but he was beginning to.

Lost in his own mixed, anxious thoughts, he was startled when the driver's side door of the patrol car suddenly opened. He heard the cop say to someone outside, "Yeah, yeah, I know the test was positive. Yeah, positive for cocaine. I'll take him on to the jail."

Phil shook his head, completely resigned to the worst. He'd thought he was already at the bottom, but his spirits sank even lower now. Overwrought and depressed, he slumped down in the backseat. *No one will ever believe someone slipped that cocaine into my pocket*, he thought. *For god's sake, I don't even believe it. Christ, what am I doing? I don't have to believe anything. But what possible defense can I have? It's my jacket, and it's definitely my pocket.* After the officer had started the car and begun accelerating, he casually said, "Mr. Griffin, I'm going to have to take you in and book you. Your bond should be one thousand dollars, and you will be allowed to make a phone call."

The words "phone call" echoed through Phil's head. That was something he should have done way before now. When the officer helped him out of the patrol car at the jail, Phil asked, "Officer, can I make my phone call now?"

"Yeah, that should be okay. You can call someone to come get you, and in the meantime, we can get you booked."

The officer took Phil to a telephone, where Phil dialed Mike's number. "Mike, don't ask for explanations right now, but I'm in jail out here at the beach."

"How much will it take to bond you out?"

"A thousand dollars."

"I'll be there as soon as I can. How in the hell did this happen?"

"Just lucky, I guess, but come on."

CHAPTER 23

P hil was in his office three days after being arrested for possession of cocaine and solicitation for prostitution in Jacksonville Beach, a city in Duval County. "Okay, Mike, you still think we need to take their offer?"

"Yes, we've got to put this mess to bed before it gets out of hand."

"You think Vickie is going to do something?"

"I know you can't believe she would, but if she got medical treatment, and she probably did, the doctor or hospital will report it to the cops and they could arrest you on probable cause or easily get a warrant. And if that happens, it may be impossible to keep you out of jail and negotiate a decent disposition of your cases."

"I know we've been over and over the case; you still don't think we have a defense if she charges me?"

"Not a credible one. Hopefully, it will never become an issue, but if you are charged with aggravated battery, we need to have that thing in East Bay involving Kevin Charles already put to bed."

"Okay, call Singer. We'll take the offer of probation."

"Good decision," Mike said as he left for his office to make the call. He was back in a few minutes. "Singer is out, but he'll call me. I just hope it's not too late."

"You think they might have already revoked my bond down there?"

"Let's hope not."

Phil's secretary interrupted them over the intercom. "Mr. Griffin, a deputy sheriff is out here to see you."

"What in hell now?" Phil said as he walked out.

"You're Phillip Griffin?"

"Yes, I'm Griffin."

"I have an arrest warrant for aggravated battery and tampering with a witness." He immediately turned Phil around and handcuffed him.

"Can I have a second to tell my associate something?"

"No, sir." Then he led Phil past the office Christmas tree and out into the hall.

By then Mike was on the scene. "I'll come to the jail once I find out what's going on."

During the booking process at the Duval County jail in Jacksonville, Phil learned his bond was two hundred thousand dollars, but even if he posted it, he would not be released because East Bay County had revoked his bond and put a hold on him so he could be transferred for the scheduled trial.

After he was booked, the jailers made him strip and gave him a full body search. They returned his underwear, kept his other clothes and personal property, and gave him an orange jumpsuit to wear. Phil was also given a thin pillow and mattress, a blanket, and a toothbrush. Then he was taken to a more permanent cell, with only two bunks, that already had two inmates, a black man and a Latino man. Both were in their early twenties with ample tattoos. This was a standard jail cell: double bunks on one wall and, between the bunk beds and the other wall, a sink and a toilet without a seat. Some kind of fetid stench, barely detectable but nevertheless smelly, penetrated the atmosphere of the whole cell, but it seemed to come and go.

"Where in hell am I supposed to sleep?" Phil said more to himself than to either of his cellmates.

"What de fuck, man? Dis is all ya got. De flo', right there in front of de throne," said the black man as he walked out into the cell block's common room.

Phil, still standing, holding the pillow, mattress, and blanket, turned to his Latino cellmate, seated on the bottom bunk. "My name is Phil Griffin, and I'm an attorney," he said as he approached and extended his hand. "What's the routine in here?"

The inmate ignored the gesture and said, "If dat be so, you musta really fucked up, and I don't want to hear anything 'bout it. You tend to yo' business and don't worry 'bout mine."

Phil shook his head and looked at his unshaken hand as if it was contaminated. After a moment reflecting on how bad it was going to be in jail, he looked at the man sitting on the bunk and said, "And a merry Christmas to you too."

The Latino looked startled as he said, "Huh?"

Phil ignored him and proceeded to stash his stuff on the floor at the end of the bottom bunk. Then he wandered into the common area, where most of the inmates stayed during the day, watching TV or playing cards. The smell of body odor and some kind of unpleasant cleansing agent hung in the air. No one bothered him, and since all the chairs were occupied, he sat on the floor. Phil's mind began spinning with one frustrating scenario after another. *So here I am in a jail without a bond. But what am I doing in jail? I'm not supposed to be here. Jail was never in the game plan.*

A man approaching caught Phil's attention. *Crap, here comes some derelict looking for a place to put his ass.* Phil desperately avoided making eye contact but to no avail. The guy sat within a foot of Phil, who couldn't avoid the putrid, urine-like stench of his body order. He was thankful the man didn't try to say anything to him.

He stood up to stretch as part of a plan to move a few more feet away from the man. He sat again on the floor at least two feet farther over, but there was no escape from the scent of men in the overheated cell block. *It's December. Why can't the weather be cooler,* he thought, *like it usually is this time of year? For shit's sake, even the weather's against me.*

He shook his head as he looked around upon these men, who were all guilty of serious crimes, whether adjudicated or not. *And here I am, just another inmate in my orange suit, just like them. There has to be some way out of this shithole. I wonder what my friends in Tallahassee would think about my situation. Maybe I can get Hugh Benson to pull some strings for me.* The more he dwelled on that, the less he thought of it as an option; a man who attacked a woman was definitely a pariah among his so-called friends. *Maybe I should have killed her.*

As soon as the thought emerged in his head, he squeezed his eyes shut in an effort to dispel the image. Then he was startled by the sound of a voice. "What be de matter wid you, old man?"

He opened his eyes to see a young inmate. "What's that?"

"I say, why you looking like that?"

"Oh, for Christ's sake, nothing's wrong with me. Just had a bad thought."

"I'm Hondo. Try to have good thoughts. You get used to it. Could be a whole lot worse. I'll get back to you, Mr. Lawyer." And he walked away.

So now I've met Hondo. So what! I've got to control what's going on in my head, or I'll go mad. And an asylum could be worse than this godforsaken place. By now sweating from anxiety and the temperature, he more calmly thought, *God, I'm grateful I didn't do more damage to her.* That thought somehow brought a slight respite from the all-encompassing depression that had descended upon him as soon as he was locked up.

He could really use a drink of single-malt scotch, he thought. Then his brief feeling of hope evaporated with the realization it would be days, maybe years, before he'd taste his favorite scotch again. Then it hit him that he might never again drink when he pleased or have a sex life, and a strange numbness washed over him like he was at the bottom of a black sea.

Why, oh, why did I even get involved with the tobacco thugs in the first place? he asked himself. *I was at the top of my game when they approached me with their plan to keep the legislature from interfering with the sale and use of tobacco by making it illegal or raising the taxes so high it might as well be illegal.* Phil shook his head in dismay. He didn't even believe tobacco should be a legal product. But at the time, it had seemed well worth the effort, even the kickbacks he'd paid them. They were making money. But he'd known that was what it was all about from the start. Why had he gone against his intuition that he should tell them thanks, but no thanks?

Suddenly, another young man approached him and said, "Someone said you're Phil, and you're a lawyer."

"That's true. And your name?"

"Tyrone. Maybe I could talk to you sometime?"

"Not right now."

"Okay, okay. Lighten up. We're gonna be getting supper pretty soon. I'll be seeing you tomorrow."

As Phil watched Tyrone go to one of the tables, he slipped back into reviewing his past. *I let them manipulate me into their nefarious business. I was simply blinded by the enormous amount of money to be made, but*

I'm stronger than that. Yet here I sit, a bought man. And Mike, he never should have let me wander off, looking for Vickie. He should have told me he couldn't find her. His mind churned on to the whiskey producers—they were the reason he was an alcoholic—and back to the tobacco industry as he thought about all the others who were somehow responsible for his downfall. He even blamed Vickie. She, he thought, was at fault for letting him into her condo.

As he thought of one example after another of ways his plight had been caused by others, it crossed his mind that Frank had never promoted or encouraged what they had done to Kevin. But why hadn't he put a stop to what they were doing? *Why,* he thought, *couldn't I have been content to just get Kevin in trouble with the bar? No, goddamn it, I had to get him charged with rape, when just a common, garden-variety fuck would have done the trick. And did I kill Frank? No, he killed himself. He never should have done the things I had him do. He's the reason I'm here.*

So now what? Phil wondered. *I need to listen to my lawyer.* For about an hour, Phil questioned himself and continued to run one version of absurdity after another through his mind. None of his thoughts crystallized the blame on anyone in particular, but the truth that he was responsible for his being in jail remained in the dark recesses of his mind. Finally, he was summoned to a conference room when Mike came around five o'clock.

"Phil, I assume you know about your bond situation."

"Yeah, they told me when I was booked."

"The hold on you will expire, though, if they don't come get you in three days."

"Has Singer called back?"

"Yes, he did. They've withdrawn the offer. There's nothing on the table now except getting prepared for the trial down there."

"Well, shit. That's all I have to say. Did he say anything about them transferring me?"

"No, but it's usually done on time."

"I guess all we can really do is wait till I'm down there. But keep trying, okay?"

Mike then tried to bring Phil up to date on the cases pending in the firm and said he would send an accounting that would show money they knew was coming in and sums that were expected or probably would come in. They were going to have to wait to see what was going to happen to Phil, before any real projections could be made.

Upon returning to his pod, Phil saw a stack of empty food trays to be picked up by a trusty—an inmate who had the privilege to do little jobs in the jail. When the trusty came to collect the empties, Phil asked, "Where's my dinner?"

"You were served."

"Yeah, but I wasn't here."

"If you're not here, it gets served anyway. Someone else must have ate it."

"What kind of fucking place is this that would let someone else eat my food?"

"This is a jail," the trusty said as he hauled away the trays.

Phil quickly decided it would be unwise to complain to the correction officer who checked on them periodically. And he certainly wasn't going to try to find the man who'd eaten his dinner. He wished he had something to read, but magazines were not allowed because these morons would stop up the toilets. So once again, he sat on the floor in the common room, but this time he tried to watch a basketball game on the TV.

At ten o'clock, all were locked back in their cells, and the lights were turned off. As soon as the lights were out, he began scraping the handle of his toothbrush on the floor. He hurried when he realized that his cellmates were busy with self-abuse. It took awhile, but eventually, he fashioned a sharp-pointed weapon, which he tightly held all night.

Around six o'clock, the lights came back on, and the cells were unlocked. The trusty and a guard were waking people up for breakfast. It wasn't long before he was in line to get his tray, after which he found a place to sit on the floor in the common room. He was hungry, but what he saw on his plate was a runny fried egg, the white not cooked enough, two pieces of stale bread that were supposed to be toast, and a slice of soft, flimsy bacon that was mostly undercooked fat. *God almighty*, he thought, *am I going to eat this?* He felt nauseous just looking at the bacon. He thought he would vomit if he tried to eat it. Maybe, he thought, the egg could be sopped up with the bread. He took the only eating utensil handed out, a spoon, and pushed around on the egg, but that stirred up the undercooked white of the egg and caused him to gag. *What's going to happen to me in here? Am I going to starve to death?* He shook his head, thinking, *I can't eat this.* Then he took a sip of his lukewarm but strong coffee.

He noticed that all the other men were busy spooning this mess like they were starving to death. *I'll eat the so-called toast and wash it down with the coffee,* he decided, *and hope for something at least edible for lunch.* Maybe he could get something out of the commissary. He would have to get some money in his account and check that out as soon as he could.

While he was sitting there eating the bread, an inmate approached him and said, "You don't want that?" as he pointed to the revolting food.

"No, I'm not hungry enough to eat it."

"I'll eat it." And he picked up the tray. Phil watched him walk away and wondered just how hungry a person had to be to get used to this slop.

Mike met him again that morning.

"I missed last night's meal. It was served while you were here, and one of my cellmates or somebody else ate it."

"We both know that kind of thing goes on in a jail. You be careful, and don't trust anybody, okay?"

"Yeah, that was a bummer. But if it wasn't any better than breakfast, I didn't miss a goddamn thing."

"How's that?"

"My fried egg wasn't well cooked. What I mean is it wasn't properly prepared. It was not done enough to hold together, the white part was disgustingly runny, the toast was really just stale bread, and the bacon wasn't cooked."

"Damn, Phil, I'm sorry."

"So that's life in the big house." He paused. "Mike … I need a favor."

"If I can do it, I will."

"I didn't have much money on me when I was arrested, and I need some personal shit. Can you put a hundred in my jail account?"

"Sure." Mike reached for his wallet.

"I can't have any cash. I can get stuff at the commissary, and they debit my account. Have you found out anything more?"

"Not much, but Singer says they'll get you back down there on time, probably tomorrow. Phil, don't be surprised if you're moved in the middle of the night. They'll just rouse you up at an ungodly hour, and you'll be on your way. They don't want anyone to know when an inmate is moved, for security reasons. But it isn't personal. The sheriff's people work around the clock. It's irrelevant when things are scheduled. How you doing other than the supper you missed and the slop for breakfast?"

"Robert Mitchum said it: it's just like Palm Springs but without the riffraff."

"Good to see you haven't lost your sense of humor," Mike said with a chuckle.

"So far, no one has bothered me. I stick with the guys in my cell and to myself. There's a kind of territorial instinct. The cell is yours and your cellmates'. It's not openly expressed; it's just a feeling that the cellmates look after each other to some extent. As for having a sense of humor, you have to have that, or you'll go crazy in here. You can't begin to imagine what it's like being penned up with a bunch of animals. Most don't really talk; they just sort of grunt at one another. I'm lucky to be as big as I am and in good shape. Even so, I was up all night scraping my toothbrush handle on the floor."

"So now you have a weapon. But for god's sake, Phil, don't let anyone push you into a fight. Just be careful."

"I hope I don't have to fight, but if I do, I intend to win. Don't worry about me. I'm no weak sister, you know."

Phil was transferred the second night of his arrest around two o'clock in the morning and had been in the East Bay County jail for one day when he met with Mike again.

"Okay, Mike, it's time to get me out of this shithole," he said. "This isn't constitutional, to keep me in here without a bond."

"As you know, we have a hearing to get a bond set within the next few days. I've been talking to Singer, and he doesn't think you should be walking the streets after what happened with Vickie. Of course, he thinks you'll be found guilty and get some time, and if you're out on bond, it will just be revoked, and you'll be back in jail. So his attitude is, why bother?"

"I've got some things I need to take care of," said Phil. "That's why. Doesn't presumed innocence mean anything anymore?" He squeezed his interlocking fingers.

"I presume you know the law allowing the court to revoke your bond in the first place."

"Mike, don't presume I know anything."

"Okay, no presumptions, but Phil, we need to negotiate something with your cases in Jacksonville and here to resolve the whole thing. If you go to trial and lose, you can kiss your ass good-bye. I don't think we have a chance in going to trial on either case. But if you have to plead to the court, the fact you've pled should buy you something."

"Hell, I know all that."

"You told me to not presume you know anything."

"So I did. But I didn't say throw in the towel."

"I'm doing the best I can."

Because the sheriff recorded all inmates' personal and telephone conversations (though prosecutors claimed they never used what was said between an attorney and his client), Phil slipped a piece of paper to Mike that read, "Can't we bribe someone?"

Mike took it, balled it up, and stuck it in his pocket. "Phil, don't get pissed, but maybe you need a new lawyer."

"No. Stick with me, Mike." After about thirty minutes of proposing one impossible thing after another, Phil finally said, "For Christ's sake, who are we trying to kid? I don't see much of a chance of self-defense in Jacksonville … but you can never tell what might happen in a trial. "Still, would a woman half my size actually attack me? Not likely. And I can just see the prosecutor in his final argument, pounding the podium as he tells the jury I attacked her because she was going to testify against me … So just fuck it. Get the best deal you can, and we'll see."

"Now you're facing reality."

"And it was my hand that was cut. Couldn't be any better evidence I was holding the glass." Phil stopped talking for a moment. "Do you have any good news at all?" he asked, rubbing his forehead.

"No, but I want to work a deal to plead to both cases and be guaranteed that the time in both would run concurrently."

"I guess the old offer of probation is still off the table."

"The old offer is gone, Phil," Mike said, putting his hands out, palms up.

"If I get the maximum in both cases, I'll be in prison for sixty-five years if they are consecutive. And 80 percent of that is a lot of time.

Damn, I won't live that long. It'll be a life sentence. Any way to get around that 80 percent?"

"No, the state wants you to spend at least 80 percent of your sentence in prison. It ought to be possible to negotiate something less than the maximum sentence, but any deal with the state is going to include time."

"You're just full of good news, aren't you?"

"Phil, I'm your lawyer. I can't just tell you what you want to hear. I've got to let you know my honest opinion."

"I know, I know." Phil's eyes rolled back in his head. "Well, first things first. We've got to get me out of this jail. Try to work out something that will let me plead in Jacksonville for a specific sentence, but be left free on bond to go to trial here."

Mike rubbed his chin and said, "Maybe, and I'll do my best. But as far as you going to trial here, I don't know, Phil."

"Why the hell not? It's simply a case of her word against mine."

"Christ, Phil, you're contradicting what you just said telling me to work out the best deal we can. We've been all through this before. The state's case goes far beyond simply her word against yours. They have all the e-mails and phone calls between the two of you before she ever went to see Kevin Charles. Aside from that, they can easily prove, through your own records or your secretary's testimony, that Victoria had been in your office well before she ever went to see Kevin Charles, and she was sent to you by Gary LaBlanc."

"God, I just don't know. Maybe it's being in this shithole," Phil said, again rubbing his forehead. "I can't remember or think straight. Like anybody else in a mess, I need a lawyer."

"You said it, and no one but a fool, Phil, would think the objective evidence doesn't support her testimony."

"Fool or no fool, see if we can get a continuance for my trial here, so we can work something out. I'll agree to go to Jacksonville and enter a plea of guilty to the charges there and be sentenced, if I can remain on bond. Then I can come back here and plead guilty, or whatever we have worked out at the time. I want to remain on bond because I've got things that need to be done."

"Well, you'll get credit for the time you're in jail."

"I know that. But I still want to get out, so don't lose sight of that, okay?"

"Oh, I'm going to try to get you out. I hope Singer will go along with concurrent sentences, and I know the assistant state attorney in Jacksonville, Jeff Horton, who's handling your case—not really well, but I do know him. I'll see Singer this afternoon, and then I'll call and see if I can get in to talk to Jeff in the morning. Don't worry, Phil. I'll get right on it. Before I go, do you need anything I can get for you?"

"No, not right now."

"Are things better in this jail?"

"Yes, here I have a bed, and the food so far is edible."

"Well, like you said, I've got a lot to do. I'll see you again when I know something."

Before Phil was back in his cell, his mind was again on getting bond. *If I can get out,* he thought, *I can buy my way to a foreign country that has no extradition treaty with us. That is the only chance I have. Otherwise, I'm going to be rotting away in prison for years, if not the rest of my life.* Suicide was also lurking deep in the shadows of his mind.

Mike went straight to Singer's office and told him what he had in mind for a deal.

"Well, the case will be called up during the next three-week trial period, and that begins in another week. So time could be a problem. I have no objection to a concurrent sentence if that will take care of both cases. The key to this is to have him sentenced first in Jacksonville because then it really makes no difference what the Jacksonville judge does, as long as the court here gives him a concurrent sentence. The hang-up will be getting the Jacksonville court to allow him to remain on bond until he is sentenced here. Not only that, I don't think Judge Williams is going to grant your man a bond here. But there is no way this office will agree with a specific term of years to coincide with what he gets in Jacksonville. Not now, after what he did up there. As you well know, under the guidelines, he can be sentenced up to the maximum, which in this case is forty years. I'll think about reducing the two fifteen-year perjury charges, depending on what you get in Jacksonville. The sentence will be strictly up to the court. Time is a problem. But if we have a deal, I'll work with you."

"Fair enough," Mike said. "I'll call you before I come back for the hearing next week and let you know what the Jacksonville people will agree to, so you can confirm it with them before the hearing, okay?"

Mike left, called the prosecutor's office in Jacksonville, and made an appointment to see Jeff the next morning at nine o'clock.

Mike took a seat across the desk from Jeff. He then outlined his conversation with Singer.

Jeff said, "I'll do what I can to let the sentences run concurrently. But to do it the way you want, we'll have to get the court on board."

"Well," Mike asked, "can we see the judge and make sure he will go along or whatever?"

"I'll call his judicial assistant right now and find out if he can squeeze us in sometime today," Jeff said as he picked up the phone. When the assistant answered, Jeff asked if they could see the judge for a few minutes sometime during the day. After nodding his head a couple of times, he offered a thank-you, ended the call, and looked back up at Mike. "We can see him for a few minutes at twelve o'clock in his chambers."

Judge Curtis said, "I understand what you're trying to work out. So you don't have to elaborate any more than you already have. But I'm not inclined to allow Phil Griffin to remain on bond after I've sentenced him. He can remain on bond for a month or so after he pleads guilty, until he's sentenced. Of course, he's down there in East Bay waiting to go to trial within a couple of weeks or so, and that trial will come and go unless he's brought up here for a plea before his scheduled trial date. And he hasn't yet even been put on a docket for trial here in Jacksonville. If he gets sentenced there first, I'm not agreeing to concurrent time. Doesn't mean he wouldn't get it, but he might not, okay?"

"Well, Your Honor, thanks for hearing us," said Mike as he got up to leave.

Jeff and Mike went back to the state attorney's office, and Mike called Singer.

"Hello, Larry. I'm calling to let you know we can't get anything done here in Jacksonville as far as a deal goes. So what do we do?"

"Without a deal in Jacksonville, the court is not going to grant you another continuance in the case here. So if you get busy, maybe Griffin can get scheduled to plead guilty in Jacksonville within a few days. Most judges will always make room for a guilty plea. You will have to cancel the bond hearing, which means nothing anyway because the judge isn't going to grant it. Use that date to have the court hear your motion to transfer Griffin. The best I can do here will be to not object to a concurrent sentence. But the way I see it, if he doesn't go ahead and plead in Jacksonville and then plead here, he has no chance of reducing the damage.

Another thing: if he pleads in Jacksonville, the judge might release him on bond on that case until he's sentenced. The required presentence investigation should take one to two months. But the hold on him we have in the case here in East Bay will keep him from being released from the Duval County jail. Phil Griffin isn't left with a whole lot of choices. And you need to move fast, or we are going to find ourselves in a trial here in about two weeks. I'm ready for it, as you well know. So I guess it's up to you and your client. Of course, I'll not get in the way of any motion you file to transfer him to Jacksonville for a plea."

After the phone call with Singer, Mike said, "Jeff, go ahead and get us a date next week to enter a plea in this case. I'm pretty sure the court down there will give him a concurrent sentence since the state will not object."

After some phone calls, Jeff said, "I've got it set up with the court and the sheriff. And the court is issuing an order for your client to appear next Friday morning at nine o'clock."

Mike called his secretary to prepare the motion for transfer. He had to make another two hour drive to East Bay to talk to his client and file his motion to transfer Phil.

At the jail, Mike told Phil everything that had transpired since he'd last seen him.

"Do what you think is right," Phil replied. "That's all I ask. However, there's one other matter I want taken care of. Victoria has sued me. Settle the case if you can do it for less than two million. It can help us, I think, particularly since it's a lot more than the state would order as restitution, and it won't wipe me out entirely." Phil then handed the complaint, signed by Jack Merchant, Kevin's associate, to Mike.

"Anything else Phil?"

"Well yes. See if the settlement can buy us anything?"

"If you mean what I believe you mean, any such effort would be a serious violation of the rules." Mike sat back with a sour expression and shook his head.

"No, no I didn't mean anything like that. I meant a big settlement should make the prosecutors a little less tough on me, that's all. Anyway I know Victoria isn't going to soften up on me, no matter how much I pay her."

"Uh-huh. I'll make sure everybody knows about the settlement."

Judge Curtis went through the standard colloquy with Phil to make sure his plea of guilty was free and voluntary and consistent with the plea paperwork. Phil pled guilty to the court on aggravated battery and tampering with a witness. On the cocaine charge and on solicitation for prostitution, he pled *nolo contendere*, or no contest, maintaining he was innocent of those charges. With this plea, the court could still sentence him as if he had pled guilty.

The judge then granted Mike's routine motion for bond until he was sentenced, but because the East Bay hold on him was still in effect, Phil was remanded to custody in the Jacksonville jail until the presentence investigation was completed.

When the day came for the sentencing, Judge Curtis looked down at Phil from the bench. "Mr. Griffin, I've known you for years, and I now have the benefit of the presentence investigation and the regretful duty to sentence you. At least financially, you have been successful. You have apparently taken care of all your children and your ex-wives without much acrimony, if any, and you've also done some good for the Florida bar from time to time on a voluntary basis. You have also made a reasonable settlement with Mrs. Roberts in her case against you. But what you did to Victoria Roberts, not only in the physical altercation but also in getting her involved in that Kevin Charles matter is simply beyond the pale. Your motivations are transparent, so I'm not going to get into all that right now. But you could've blinded or even killed her. It's just fortunate she was able to defend herself enough to reduce her injuries. What you did is simply beyond my comprehension. Do you have anything to say before sentence is passed?"

"May I speak, Your Honor?" asked Mike.

"Go ahead."

"As you have already stated, and as it is reflected in the PSI and the other letters we have submitted to assist the court in determining what would be an appropriate sentence in this case, let me say that this altercation and other crimes are totally out of character for my client, a distinguished attorney here in our community and way beyond." He continued to extol the virtues of Phil Griffin for about fifteen minutes. Then he stopped and said, "Phil, do you have a few words to say to the court?"

Phil nodded. "Judge Curtis, there's nothing I can say that would excuse what I did to Victoria Roberts. I have no excuse, but I joined AA while in jail and have adhered to the twelve-step course. I have settled a lawsuit with the victim. You have a copy of the settlement. The day this happened, by the victim's own testimony, I was drunk. There's no other way to put it. I was drunk. I know I'm going to get a prison sentence today. But I'm hoping that Your Honor will take into consideration the fact that this incident was not consistent with the rest of my life. Just like you said, most of my life I've been a good citizen, and I hope you see a way to give me something less than the maximum sentence of twenty-five years. The score sheet indicates a ten-year sentence would be appropriate. I deserve some time. But I hope you feel like the record does not justify the maximum. That's all I have to say, Your Honor."

"Any recommendations from the state?" asked the judge.

"Only that voluntary drunkenness is not a legal defense and is not an excuse as far as the state is concerned."

"Okay, count one, aggravated assault: I sentence you to fifteen years with the Department of Corrections and a $10,000 fine; on count two, tampering with a witness, the sentence is five years with the Department of Corrections and a $5,000 fine; and on the separate case of possession of cocaine, the defendant is sentenced to five years with the Department of Corrections and a $5,000 fine. Each to run consecutive to the others. However, all but ten years is suspended. Upon your release, you will be placed on probation for fifteen years. This means if you violate your probation, at a minimum you'll go back to prison to serve the time suspended. On the prostitution case, I hereby sentence you to time served." The court then added some incidental legal costs to be paid to the state once Phil was released from custody.

Mike and Phil shook hands before Phil was taken back to the jail.

Two weeks later, in March 1999, Kevin flew in from London to Orlando, only forty miles from East Bay, where Phil Griffin faced his second sentencing.

Singer had called Vickie and advised her a deal for a guilty plea had been worked out for a Tuesday afternoon during the trial week, and she didn't have to be there till one o'clock on that day. She drove down that morning, had lunch with Kevin and they were in the courtroom when Judge Williams went through the necessary colloquy with Phil so that the record would show his plea of guilty to the charges was free and voluntary. Phil pled guilty to each count. Singer had reduced counts one and two to lying under oath.

"Okay," said the judge, "I've read the PSI from the case in Duval County and the letters and other documents submitted by the defendant and see no reason why sentencing should be delayed. Mr. Griffin, the paperwork is all in order. Do you or your attorney have anything to say before I sentence you?"

"Your Honor, what I did in this case is totally inexcusable. I simply have nothing to say except that I am indeed guilty. But aside from my saying so, the PSI shows I have been a reasonably good man most of my life. Not to malign my parents—they did the best they could— but I had very little and made something out of myself. I worked hard, and I took care of my children as well as my ex-wives. The letters you have confirm that I treated the lawyers and others in my firm with respect and dignity and extended that respect to attorneys who represented the other side from me in numerous cases. I was always professionally courteous to any opponent. Judge Williams, I just don't know what else I can say. I have certainly had a drinking problem and am now a member of AA. Of course, I should have started that years ago. Maybe it would have made a difference. I just don't know." Phil went on and on for about thirty minutes, saying basically the same thing over and over. Finally, he said, "I just hope the sentence you give me will run concurrent with the time I've already been sentenced to."

Mike spoke next. "Your Honor, this is a bad day for all of us," he said. He then spent about ten minutes extolling his client's virtues in an effort to justify a concurrent sentence with the one Phil had been given in Jacksonville.

When Mike was done, Singer said, "The state, Your Honor, doesn't have much to say except we agree that this is a sad day. But lawyers are just like everybody else. And though we have a high regard for our profession, some of us fall, and there is never an excuse for such wayward or, in this case, criminal behavior. On the other hand, we have no objection to a concurrent sentence. That's all."

"No one else has anything to say?" asked Judge Williams. "Okay, let me say, Mr. Griffin, you still haven't told me why you committed the offenses. But as far as the court's concerned, that opportunity has come and gone. But I know there's more involved here than you just wanting Mr. Charles out of the get-rich group. You're a man with astonishing abilities as an attorney; except for your problems here and in Duval County, you've been a real credit to your profession. And I'm impressed with what you have done for Mrs. Roberts in her wrongful death suit and in settling her lawsuit against you, in an effort to compensate her for what you did to her. On the other hand, what you did, scheming to ruin a perfectly innocent man and basically blackmailing a naive woman into helping you in your criminal endeavor, is impossible to explain or understand; you even threatened to kill Mr. Charles if Mrs. Roberts didn't go along with your scheme. Crime merits punishment in every case, but maybe even more importantly, the person who commits the crime deserves punishment. What you did here to Kevin Charles and Mrs. Roberts and what you did to her in Duval County paints a mighty black portrait of you. You're a disbarred lawyer, so I know you understand this is not a case for leniency. However, I'm going along with the state's reduction of the first two counts.

"On count one, lying under oath, the sentence is five years with the Department of Corrections and a $5,000 fine; on count two, lying under oath, the sentence is five years DOC and a $5,000 fine; on count three, conspiracy to perjury, the sentence is five years DOC and a $5,000 fine; and on count four, for conspiracy to perjury, the sentence is five years DOC and a $5,000 fine. All these sentences are to run consecutive to each other." Then he added incidental costs to be paid to the state.

"Your Honor, may I address the court?" asked Phil.

"Go ahead."

"Does this run concurrent with my sentence in Jacksonville?"

"No, it's consecutive."

Phil hung his head as he followed the bailiff to be fingerprinted. During the fingerprinting, he turned to Mike. "I'm hiring someone else for the appeal, or better still, I'll do it myself."

"Phil, that's probably best, but you and I both know we were behind the eight ball. If I can help in any way, let me know, and good luck." Without shaking hands, Mike returned to his table, put his file in his briefcase, and walked out.

After they said good-by to Singer, Vickie, dressed in a conservative light blue suit and Kevin in his usual grey suit and repp tie, walked out together.

"Did you hear what Phil said to his attorney?" Vickie asked.

"Afraid I did. Let's go downstairs and get a cup of coffee?"

"Good idea."

Once they were seated at a table, Vickie asked as she stirred her coffee, "Did you have anything to do with reducing the charges?"

"Late yesterday Singer asked if I had any objection. He felt if he reduced the charges Phil wouldn't change his mind about pleading. And Singer didn't want to put you through a trial, so I told him no."

"Mr. Singer is really a nice man. But I'm puzzled, Kevin. What's left to appeal after a guilty plea?"

"As silly as it sounds, he's entitled to one. Usually, it's a claim the court didn't properly advise him, or his lawyer was ineffective in some way. The attack on his lawyer usually comes in a postconviction motion. There's a lot more to it. Let's just say Phil will be spending a lot of time filing motions to set aside his plea and get a new trial. Most postconviction motions fail. And even if it's granted, he'll just be put back on the docket for trial. A successful appeal would only set aside the plea and put him back on the trial calendar."

"An appeal is not likely to get him out then?"

"No. But the sentences might be excessive when compared with the sentences given to other defendants for similar crimes. If an appellate court finds his sentences to be too far out of line, too harsh, the case could be sent back for a new sentence but not a new trial."

"You don't do criminal defense stuff, do you?"

"No."

"Well, can you explain exactly what he's facing?"

"Sure. He can't serve probation while incarcerated. So he'll have to spend at least 80 percent of the thirty years with DOC before he's released. Then his fifteen years of probation will start."

"Well, that's clear enough." After a long pause, she flipped her hair back, sat up, and said, "Oh, I don't know, but with Phil now in prison, I have a strange, I don't want to say elated feeling, it's more like a really bad part of my life has come to an end, you know what I mean?"

"I know what you mean—the end of some kind of era. It's hard to explain. It's like a dark cloud over your head has drifted away." He took a sip of his coffee.

"Kevin, we all know he had something to hide."

"That's for sure."

"He was up to no good and suspected you would find out about it."

"That's true. And I've finally decided the tobacco companies might have been behind the whole damn thing."

"How do you figure that?"

"They benefit, that's why."

"How?"

"They sell poison and believe their product will sooner or later be declared illegal, so maybe the whole thing was a scheme by them so they could remain in business long enough to diversify. By agreeing to a thirteen-billion-dollar or so settlement to be paid over twenty-five years, they've created a situation where the legislature has to keep them in business so it can be paid."

"Could be, I guess. And by saving the companies, they save the shareholders, particularly their own shares. I don't know, Kevin. The idea that they could be legislated out of business sounds a little —"

"Far-fetched? Maybe, but don't be so sure it couldn't happen. This country has made it a crime to possess a *weed*."

"Maybe you're right, but this settlement only affects this state."

"So they will do the same in every state or if necessary figure out some other way to buy time. This whole thing was based on a specific amendment to the Medicaid Reimbursement Act for a specific purpose, and it's already been repealed. It was a one-time thing."

"And Phil, no doubt, bribed the right people to get the statute amended."

"That's true." He paused for a moment, thinking. "Or maybe it was all just a clever plan by a bright attorney, who legitimately sold it to the right people, to make a lot of money." Kevin stopped talking and stroked his chin. "Oh, what the hell, who knows what the tobacco companies believe or were up to? Maybe we'll all know if Phil tries to reduce his time by ratting on the politicians and tobacco executives—if any were really involved—but that's another story". Kevin sat back. "I tried once to get Hugh Benson to tell me exactly what was going on, but he never did. Of course, maybe he didn't know. On the other hand, it's bothered me that he never said, 'I don't know.' I believe he didn't want to lie to me, so he just sort of didn't answer."

"Whether the tobacco companies were in on it or not, Phil had to have promised the right people something to get the Reimbursement Statute amended. Of course, he couldn't tell you and the other attorneys what he was doing. But he thought you suspected something illegal, payoffs or bribes or something, and he worried you might do something about it."

"You're right. And the tobacco companies' settling in a case that was, to say the least, so shaky constitutionally certainly tells us something."

"Oh, Kevin, we could talk about Phil forever. Maybe one more cup before I go. It's nearly two thirty, and I want to get home by five and make reservations for dinner at the club. Is seven thirty okay?"

"Make it eight, okay?"

"Eight's fine," she said with a knowing smile. He went to the counter and brought back two more cups of coffee. "When you called yesterday, you said you were going to visit Kathy; and for me to come down today. Did it go okay?"

"It did. I took her out to dinner and a movie, *Message in a Bottle.*"

"I've read it's really a contrived tearjerker."

"Yeah, it is, but because the actors are so good in unbelievable situations, it's mildly entertaining. Kathy liked it though."

"And Sherrie and her husband?"

"They seem to be doing okay."

"What are your immediate plans?" She took a sip of coffee.

"I'm not certain. Jack, the lawyer I left in charge here, has held things together pretty well—"

"So you're ready to pick up where you left off?" she said, sitting forward and putting her hand on his.

"Maybe. Or I might go up your way and open an office in the city or the beach."

"Now *I* think that's a really good idea."

"Or I might try something other than the law."

"Like what?" she said, putting her cup down.

"I don't know yet."

"Why do you even want to go back to work? You could just keep wandering about, searching for artwork, here or in Europe."

"You can afford not to work, so why are you still slaving away to get a graduate degree in economics?" he asked, raising his eyebrows.

"Good question. Sometimes it sort of gets to me, but I like what I'm doing. If I can get in, I'm even thinking about getting a PhD at the University of Florida."

"Damn, Vickie, I'm really proud of you. Then what?"

"Oh, I don't know. I'll just see what comes my way. Are you really serious about moving to Jacksonville or the beach?"

"Yes."

She slightly squeezed his hand. "Oh, Kevin, I hope you do. And you aren't going away anytime soon?"

"No immediate plans," he said as he made an open-hands gesture. "You know, before I left, I told you I felt we should spend some time apart."

"Yes, I remember you saying something like that." And she nodded.

"Well I've had enough of *apart,* and if I travel around in the future, and I will, you'll be with me, okay?" He leaned forward and took a sip of coffee.

"If that's the way it has to be, it's okay with me." An endearing smile crossed her face, and her brown eyes sparkled as she put her cup on the table."

"I've really missed you." And he placed his hand on hers.

"Oh, Kevin, you just don't know how happy I am you're back." She took a sip of coffee. Then glancing at her watch, she added, "It's getting late. I need to get started. Still going by your office?"

"Afraid so, told Jack I'd be by. And if I do it now, it's done and I won't have to think about it. Otherwise, I'd just follow you. Drive carefully. There's no rush. What I've got to do in the office won't take long."

"So I'll see you around six thirty?"

"I'll try to get there between six and six thirty, maybe even sooner." Then they left the courthouse.

AUTHOR'S NOTE

I finished the first manuscript for this book in February or March 2003. In the April 27, 2004, edition of the Orlando Sentinel, I happened upon an article that indicates excise taxes on cigarettes should be imposed to raise money to reimburse Medicaid for medical expenses paid by Medicaid for the treatment of diseases caused by the use of tobacco.

"TALLAHASSEE—Cigarettes made by companies that were not part of the multibillion settlement with the state over the cost of treating sick smokers would be taxed an additional 40 cents a pack under a bill the Senate passed Monday. . . . All cigarette companies now pay a state excise tax of 34 cents a pack. The tax would be on companies not included in the settlement that the four largest cigarette makers— Philip Morris, R. J. Reynolds, Brown & Williamson and Lorillard— are paying to help Florida cover Medicaid costs incurred in treating smoking-related illnesses."

The Senate approved the cigarette tax, but the House didn't.

Printed in the United States
By Bookmasters